WRITERS JOURNEY EDITION

# THE FIFTH MAN

AN OXYGEN NOVEL

JOHN B. OLSON
RANDY INGERMANSON

THE FIFTH MAN - WRITERS JOURNEY EDITION by John B. Olson and Randy Ingermanson
Published by Marcher Lord Press
8345 Pepperridge Drive
Colorado Springs, CO 80920
www.marcherlordpress.com



Cover Designer: Kirk DouPonce
Creative Team: Jeff Gerke, Dawn Shelton



Originally Published (without bonus content) by Bethany House Publishers, 2002
E-book version available through DitDat, Inc., www.ditdat.com

Library of Congress Cataloging-in-Publication Data
An application to register this book for cataloging has been filed with the Library of Congress.
International Standard Book Number: 978-1-935929-53-6

Printed in the United States of America

# Books by the Authors

**Fiction by John and Randy**

*Oxygen*
*The Fifth Man*

**Fiction by John B. Olson**

*Adrenaline*
*Fossil Hunter*
*Shade*
*Powers*

**Fiction by Randy Ingermanson**

*Transgression*
*Premonition*
*Retribution*
*Double Vision*

**Nonfiction by Randy Ingermanson**

*Writing Fiction for Dummies*

# Technical Note

The Martian day—known as a *sol*—is 24 hours, 39 minutes, 35.244 seconds. Approximately. Clocks on on the Ares 10 mission are set to run slightly slower than on Earth, so that they tick off twenty-four Martian hours in each sol.

This causes times on Earth and Mars to be continuously getting out of sync with each other in a very annoying way. Each sol, astronauts on Mars will lose about thirty-nine Earth minutes relative to Mission Control, and so about once every thirty-seven days, they will have to drop a sol from their calendar in order to stay roughly even with the Earth calendar.

In this book, dates and days of the week refer to the Earth calendar, whereas clock times are local—either Houston time or Martian local time as observed at base camp. We have sited the Ares mission base camp at 30° south latitude, 95° east longitude—within easy rover distance of at least six geologically distinct and interesting regions, but more than 1100 miles from the massive underground ice ocean near the Martian south pole.

We apologize for being compulsively nerdy about the subject of timekeeping. And much else. Undoubtedly, we are two sick gentlemen with too much time on our hands.

Who is the third who walks always beside you?
When I count, there are only you and I together
But when I look ahead up the white road
There is always another one walking beside you
Gliding wrapt in a brown mantle, hooded
I do not know whether a man or a woman
—But who is that on the other side of you?

T. S. Eliot, *The Wasteland*

# *Part I: The Fifth Day*

"Sometimes I fancied it must be the devil, and reason joined in with me upon this supposition, for how should any other thing in human shape come into the place? Where was the vessel that brought them? What marks were there of any other footstep? And how was it possible a man should come there?"

Daniel Defoe, *Robinson Crusoe*

# CHAPTER 1

Monday, March 16, 2015, 3:45 p.m., Mars Local Time

Valkerie

Water. Valkerie Jansen forced one foot in front of the other, a weary survivor on a death march across a dry and barren planet. *Water.* Valkerie's soul cried out for it. A patch of frost. A dark stain in the dust. Subterranean ice . . .

Dry dust coated her visor—red streaks across a blur of powder-white scuffs. The grit was everywhere. Valkerie could taste it, acrid and dry in the filtered air she breathed. She could feel it grinding in the joints of her EVA suit, eating deeper and deeper into the fragile seals that stood between her and death.

She plodded to the edge of a deep canyon and scanned the rocky walls below.

Heavily shadowed grooves started at a point a hundred meters below her and snaked their way down the rocky walls, dividing into smaller and smaller subbranches.

Weeping fissures. They looked so promising, so much like erosion gullies back on Earth. But where was the water? She and Lex had searched hundreds of fissures, but they were all dry. Dry as . . . the rest of Mars.

"Okay, Lex. Here's another one." Valkerie bit into the butterfly valve of her water bag and took a reluctant swallow of sweat-sock-flavored water.

"How's it look?" Geologist Alexis Ohta's voice crackled over the comm speakers.

"Good enough. Pull the rover all the way up." Valkerie pointed to a line two meters back from the four-hundred-meter drop-off.

The six-ton rover inched forward, climbing over rocks and small boulders like a monster truck at a redneck fair. Only in this case the rover was more of a monster minivan—with a laboratory, airlock, and bunks to sleep four.

"Okay, that's good." Valkerie waved at the rover's gold-tinted windshield.

The rover shuddered to a halt and sank down on its hydraulic suspension. "I've got this one." Lex's voice sounded in Valkerie's helmet, followed by bumpings and thumpings as she made her way to the back of the rover. "Out in a second."

Valkerie flipped open an external storage hatch and pulled out a tool bag.

The puttering of the compressor motors faded to nothing as Lex evacuated the airlock.

Nine months on Mars and already the pump valves were wheezing. She'd have to mention that to Bob—

*No.* Valkerie took a deep breath. She could look at them herself. Bob had enough to worry about right now. The last thing he needed was more whining from her. She'd caused him enough pain already.

A gloved hand clasped Valkerie's shoulder. "You okay?"

Valkerie rocked back and forth in a slow nod. "Want the MoleBot?"

Lex shrugged. "Let's get it out, just in case."

The two women hoisted the badgerlike digging robot from its bin and eased it to the ground. On Earth, it weighed almost sixty pounds. Here on Mars, barely twenty. Lex strapped the winch controller to her wrist while Valkerie attached the cable to Lex's rappelling harness.

"Okay, go." Lex backed toward the drop-off, pulling the line from the rover's winch taut.

Valkerie flipped a switch and watched Lex disappear backward over the edge. She stayed by the winch controls, not bothering to watch Lex's progress. She would call if she needed anything.

Valkerie shifted her weight from one leg to the other and, using the mirror on her wrist, checked the gauge on her chest. One more hour and they'd call it a day. Then home for an obligatory evening of awkwardness. Then tomorrow the whole thing would start over again. Two hundred and ninety-six days to go. How was she ever going to make it? Bob was so . . .

She stomped her foot to shake out a cramp. Didn't he know what he was doing to her? They were astronauts. They had a job to do. The whole world was watching. NASA hadn't paid fifty billion dollars so she could . . . so she could let her guard down. What a—

"Val!" Lex's frantic voice blared in Valkerie's helmet.

Startled, Valkerie peered over the edge. "What's wrong? Hit another patch of—"

"Send down the mole! And a bigger pick!"

"What? Did you find something?" Valkerie squinted at her friend. "What is it? More sedimentary rock?"

"Salt deposits. I can't believe it! In a depression. This is . . . I mean, it's a ledge, really. Not very big, but it's . . . Val, I need the brush set and—"

"A depression?" Valkerie's heart slammed into overdrive. "At the top of the fissure?"

"It only goes back a couple of feet, but it's crusted with salt deposits and—Val, we don't have much time. Send down the tools."

Valkerie scrambled to the side of the rover and pulled out the remote control for the mole. She strapped it to her arm with trembling fingers and worked the miniature joysticks to guide the small robot to the edge of the canyon. A torch, a brush set, more sample bags . . . She buckled them to her tool belt and attached lines to her harness ring and the mole. Guiding the robot over the edge, she hit the remote winch controls and followed it down.

"Val, what are you doing? You're supposed to stay with the rover. If Bob finds out—"

"Bob's not here." Valkerie maneuvered the mole alongside Lex and toggled off its winch control. She let herself continue down a few feet farther and stopped her descent. Lex moved aside to let Valkerie see. A small basaltic overhang overshadowed a scree-filled depression in the canyon wall. Thick, powdery deposits caked the rocks that filled the shallow groove. Layer upon layer of tan-and-rust-smeared white.

"Did you touch it?" Valkerie searched the deposits for evidence that they had been disturbed.

"I don't think so. Does it matter?"

"Probably not." Valkerie pulled the torch off her belt and heated a platinum scoop in its flame until its edges glowed a dull red. She waved it in the thin Martian atmosphere, waiting impatiently for it to cool.

Valkerie extended her arm to Lex. "Get the mole ready. We're running out of time."

"What channel is it on?" Lex unfastened the robot controller from Valkerie's arm and transferred it to her own.

"Three." Valkerie scooped up a sample of crust and slid it into a collection bottle, then snapped the pen cap off the back of the scoop handle and labeled the bottle. There wouldn't be anything alive out in the open, exposed to all the peroxide dust and UV radiation, but maybe back behind the loose rubble . . . She worked her way back under the overhanging rock, collecting and labeling samples as she went.

"Ready to start digging?" Lex's voice sounded tense, eager.

"How much time?" Valkerie took the offered pick and started digging back into the loose gravel.

"Thirty-five minutes . . . to zero . . ."

*And thirty minutes of reserve beyond that.* Valkerie completed Lex's thought and swung the pick harder, pulling out the loose debris with her left hand. She scooped a sample into a vial and kept on digging. If there was anything interesting it would be deeper inside.

"We'll have to wait until tomorrow. There's not enough time." Lex's voice hung with an unspoken question.

Valkerie dug furiously through the rubble with her shovel. "We'll use the mole. We've got to get behind this regolith." She swung around on her tether and pulled the dangling robot toward the ledge. "More line."

Lex lowered the robot and helped Valkerie detach the winch line and position it on the edge. "Okay, stand clear." Lex flipped a switch on the remote control panel, and the robot churned forward, biting into the mound of loose gravel, pushing the debris backward between its heavy metal treads. Valkerie inched along after the robot, scooping out the rocks that mounded in its wake.

"It's going to take forever to—"

The robot surged forward and disappeared. Lex whooped in triumph

"Turn it off! Turn it off!" Valkerie yelled into her mike. It was a cavity! The MoleBot had broken through to some kind of cave. She aimed her light into the gloom. The walls and floor of the small tunnel were crusted with glittering white. She couldn't even see the back. "We've got to go in now while it's fresh. Help me dig out the opening. I've got to sterilize." Valkerie backed out and torched her pick and scoop.

Lex dug furiously to enlarge the opening.

Valkerie looked at her watch. Eighteen minutes to zero. Forty-eight with their reserves. They didn't have much time. "That's enough. I've got to go in."

Lex raked aside two more scoops of scree and moved aside. "Val . . . ?"

"Okay, give me some line." Valkerie stretched out and wormed her way into the constricting tunnel, holding her flashlight and collection kit out in front of her. She took two quick scrapings and wriggled on her belly, working her life support backpack through the narrow passage.

When she came to the mole, she pushed it aside and pointed her flashlight down the dark vent.

Something moved at the end of the tunnel. Something big.

Valkerie sucked in her breath.

"Val, what's wrong?"

Valkerie probed the darkness, training the trembling beam of light on the point where the passage curved out of view.

Nothing.

She held her breath, afraid to blink. What had she seen? A rolling rock? She raised the flashlight.

A dark shadow leaped down from a protruding rock.

"Val, are you okay? What's happening?"

"Sorry, I'm okay. Got spooked by a shadow, that's all." Valkerie forced a laugh.

"Well, you'd better hurry. We're running out of time. Fifteen minutes to reserves."

"Okay. Copy." Valkerie pushed the mole ahead of her and wormed her way forward. The best samples would be deeper. She swept the walls with her light, but her eyes kept darting back to the end of the vent. Then she saw it—milky pink striations on an outcropping of white, just beyond the overhanging rock. She tried to duck beneath the jagged protrusion, but her helmet was too big.

"Thirteen minutes, Val!"

"I found something. Just a little bit farther." Valkerie reached out, stretching out as far as she could reach with her pick. Too far. She tried to back up.

Stuck!

A surge of electric panic shot down her spine. She pushed harder. Harder. "Lex!"

"What's wrong?"

The alarm in Lex's voice shamed Valkerie to stillness. She squeezed her eyes tight and forced herself to take a deep breath. Then, undulating gently from side to side, she inched her way backward. Just enough to let her get a good shot at the stony spike that barred her way.

"Talk to me, Val. I want to hear you talking right now."

"It's okay now. I'm fine." Valkerie swung at the protrusion. Her pick only struck a glancing blow, but the rock seemed to move. Maybe it was loose. She swung again, this time higher up, where it disappeared into the ceiling. The pick embedded itself into soft dirt. She pried her fingers into the scar and pulled on the rock with all her might. It swung down reluctantly with a drizzle of dirt and sand.

Then, with a shudder, a shower of gravel pelted her body, pinning her to the ground.

She was trapped.

## Monday, March 16, 2015, 4:15 p.m., Mars Local Time

### Bob

Heavy breathing—at first faint and irregular, then swelling to fill his helmet—sounded in Bob Kaganovski's earphones, washing away the sound of his own breathing with its insistent roar.

Bob ran his fingers along a row of long, irregular scratches in one of the struts at the base of the Mars Ascent Vehicle. Where had those marks come from?

He caught movement out of the corner of his eye—a white flash against the rust-colored backdrop of low hills.

"Kennedy?" Bob spun around and searched the Martian terrain, squinting through his dust-streaked visor.

Nothing.

*Great, I'm going nuts. Seeing things.*

"Commander?" Bob shook his head. Where could Kennedy Hampton have gone? He had been standing next to Bob just a second ago—or had it been more like half an hour? Repairs to the ISRU fuel factory had taken longer than expected. He tried to think back, but couldn't say for sure when he'd seen Kennedy last. Could he have gone back to the Hab? Icy fingers crawled up Bob's spine.

Something was watching him.

Bob whirled to look behind him.

Nothing.

His pulse began notching upward. *Relax, Kaggo. You can't afford another panic attack.* He began pacing around the Mars Ascent Vehicle, desperate to ward off the nameless fear that was settling around him like thick fog.

It didn't work. The tension ratcheted up second by second. Raw fear raced through Bob's veins—like he was a hobbit facing all nine Nazgul. His heart hammered at his ribs, and the sound of his breathing roared in his helmet.

Bob started to run, tripped, and fell in the dust. He lay there, clutching the cold regolith, gasping.

The fear peaked in one awful *Psycho*-shower-scene burst and then receded.

Slowly, the adrenaline rush ebbed. Bob lay on the ground until his heart had slowed to a decent *clackety-clack*. It was his third panic attack this month. There was no reason for it. None at all. If he told anyone . . .

But what if he didn't tell anyone? What if it got worse? What if he did something crazy? What if he went stark-barking mad and walked off a cliff?

The chill of the Martian surface penetrated to his marrow.

Bob pushed himself to all fours, then staggered to his feet.

He had to tell someone.

He didn't dare tell anyone.

"Hey, Kennedy, where are you?" Bob's voice sounded weak inside his helmet. *Get a grip, Kaggo.*

"I'm up in the MAV doing a systems check. I told you that."

*You did not.* Bob bit his tongue. The last thing he wanted to do was to get in an argument with the Hampster.

"So what seems to be the problem down there?" Kennedy's Southern-gentleman voice. If that was supposed to be reassuring, it wasn't working.

"I, uh . . . I need you to look at something down here." Bob forced the tension from his voice. "It's kind of important."

"All right. All right. You'd think I could leave you alone for five minutes without the world coming to an end."

Bob clenched his teeth to keep from screaming at Kennedy and checked his watch. 4:30. Only two more hours of oxygen left in his backpack. Pacing back and forth, he tried to stamp some warmth into his toes. The heat in his EVA suit was turned up to max, but his feet were freezing. He glanced up at the sky. A too small, too yellow sun pierced the peach-colored haze. It was almost minus twenty degrees Celsius outside—balmy by Mars standards. Why was he still so cold?

"See? That wasn't so bad." Kennedy's voice blared in Bob's ears.

Bob turned to look up at the MAV. Kennedy was standing at the top of the stairs, just outside the small capsule, spinning the wheel that locked down the hatch. Come January, they'd all climb in there and blast off into Mars orbit, where they'd link up with the Earth Return Vehicle for their long trip home. It couldn't happen soon enough.

Kennedy clomped down the metal stairs. "Okay. What's wrong now?"

Bob led Kennedy around to the scratched strut at the base of the MAV. "Listen, it's not a big deal, but I was wondering if you might have brushed up against the base unit here when you drove the rover in to refuel yesterday."

"You said it was important." Kennedy had switched to his innocent, injured tone.

"It is important."

"Kaggo, basic logic lesson. You said it was important. Then you said it's not a big deal. It can't be both. Now, which is it?"

"It's . . ." Bob took a deep breath. "Listen, Kennedy. You decide. The MAV is our bus ticket home—our only bus ticket, since the backup crashed and burned eight months ago. We've only got twenty-two tonnes of fuel left and we need eighteen to get us off the planet. So you tell me—is it important that we all try to drive the rover carefully when we're refueling?" He pointed at the fresh scratches on the steel frame.

Kennedy inspected them for a moment. "Why, sure it's important," he drawled. "But it doesn't make a lot of sense to blame me. What did you do, Kaggo? Hit it with the MuleBot?" He pointed at the half-ton cargo robot that Bob had left near the fuel factory. Bob's tool chest lay open on the mule's broad, flat back.

"Hampster, don't be ridiculous. The scratches are too high up. You—"

"So maybe you did it with the rover. But it's kind of silly to be quizzing me about it. I didn't have nothing to do with it." Kennedy took a step toward Bob, his eyes puffy and bloodshot behind the gold-tinted visor of his helmet.

Bob stepped back. "Uh, Kennedy? You filled up the rover's tank yesterday, remember? It's even on our schedule back at the Hab."

"Of course I did." Kennedy spoke in calm and slow tones, as if Bob were some kind of moron. "And you filled the rover before me. But I didn't hit the MAV with it. I'm the pilot, remember? You're the one who drives a Texas block to avoid having to parallel park."

"Look, just because I'm cautious doesn't mean I can't drive. I'd know if I hit the MAV. I never even got close."

"And you don't think I'd know? I lost an eye—not a brain."

A hiss of static broke through on the CommSat emergency channel. "Bob! This is Lex. Valkerie's in trouble!"

Bob spun around, fumbling with his channel switch.

"Bob, are you there? Come in."

Bob's pulse hammered in his ears. He cranked the gain all the way up. "Loud and clear, Lex. What's wrong with Valkerie?"

"She was exploring a cave. The whole thing collapsed. I need you to get—" A burst of static cut through the signal.

Bob spun around and bolted for the Hab. "Lex! You're breaking up! Please repeat!" He ran faster, ignoring the rocks that tipped and turned beneath his feet. *Faster.* He leaped over a boulder and switched gait to the peculiar bounding skip that was the fastest way to hoof around on Mars. The Hab was a quarter mile away. If they'd lost the signal cone from the CommSat . . .

"Lex—please repeat." He adjusted his comm controls, focusing on the static through the rush of his gulping breath. "Lex—can you—hear me?" The static seemed to fluctuate in a regular rhythm. Three beats per second. One for each beat of his pounding heart.

The Hab loomed nearer.

"—Valkerie, are you—" Lex's voice cut through the static.

Bob tripped and sprawled on his face in the dusty regolith. An instant later, he was up and running again. Fifty meters to go.

Twenty.

Five.

Bob reached the hatch of the airlock, yanked it open, and leaped inside. In one fluid motion, he pulled it shut again and hit the buttons to pressurize.

The pressure gauge needle swung to the right.

Bob began spinning the wheel to the inner door. He threw open the hatch and raced inside, up the stairs three at a time.

Tearing off his helmet and gloves, he raced to the CommConsole and flipped to the CommSat channel. "Lex, this is Bob! I'm in the Hab, now talk to me! What's wrong with Valkerie?" The Hab's comm system was way more powerful than EVA comm. It had to work.

Static.

Three-beats-per-second static.

Could it be interference from Kennedy's radio? Bob hammered the keyboard with a flurry of commands. *Valkerie.* His gut turned to ice. He should have gone with her. If only he'd made more of an effort to work things out . . . He brought up the comm diagnostics and checked the gain and antenna bearing. CommSat 1 sat a million kilometers above the Martian surface at the day-side Lagrange point, the stable position where the gravitational tug from Mars and the sun balanced. If the antenna wasn't locked on—

Bob slumped onto a stool and stared at the controls. The antenna bearing was perfect, but he still couldn't hear Lex. All he could hear was that weird, pulsing static that sounded like . . . like . . .

But that was impossible. Kennedy's radio didn't have a strong enough transmitter. And there was nobody else on Mars who could be jamming his radio signals. Nobody.

# 2

Monday, March 16, 2015, 4:40 p.m., Mars Local Time

Valkerie

"Lex! Can you hear me?" Valkerie struggled in her suit, desperate to move—her shoulders, legs, toes—anything. "Lex?" She groped forward in the darkness. At least her hands were still free. She tried to push herself backward, but she might as well have tried to move Olympus Mons.

"Stay cool, Val. I'm right here behind you."

"I can't move!" Valkerie knew she was shouting, but she couldn't help it. "You'll have to dig me out."

"Working on that right now. Give me a few minutes."

Valkerie felt clacking vibrations behind her feet. "How are we doing on oxygen, Lex? I can't see my gauge."

"Don't worry. We've got plenty of time . . . almost forty minutes." Valkerie felt a weight lift off her boot. "I've got you. Hang on. I'm almost there."

Valkerie lay silent, trying to still her breathing. Minute by minute, rock by rock, she felt the weight lifted from her legs.

"How about now? Can you get out?"

Valkerie pushed backward with all her might. "Pull my feet. Use the winch."

Valkerie felt her feet lifted and a cable being attached.

"Okay, I'm going to put it on superslow speed and see what happens. We don't want to rip you apart."

The tension built up slowly in Valkerie's knees. Harder. Harder. Too hard.

"Stop!"

The force released instantly.

"Okay, Val, we need a Plan B. Any ideas?"

"It feels like there's loose gravel wedged between my backpack and the top of the tunnel. Think you can clean it out?"

Quick, strong hands burrowed along Valkerie's hips and lower back. "The tunnel's too narrow. I can't get all the way up." Lex's voice sounded edgy with the first traces of fear.

"Okay, can you push me farther in? The tunnel opens up enough ahead that I should be able to shake some of the rocks off."

"I'll brace your feet so you'll have something to push against. Are your hands free? Can you pull yourself forward?"

"There's nothing to grab on to." Valkerie pushed off against Lex and felt the rocks slip, but strain as she might, she couldn't push herself through. "Bad news, Lex. I'm stuck." Her breath was coming faster now. How much more time? She didn't dare ask. "If I just had something to grab on to, I think I could pull . . . The MoleBot! Move the mole backward. About two feet."

There was a long pause. "I . . . can't. I unstrapped the remote so I could dig, and while I was digging I must have stepped . . . It's crushed. Val, I'm so sorry."

"Lex, it's okay. Listen. Call Bob and tell him to tele-operate the mole from the Hab. Tell him straight backward on slow for about a second."

"I've been trying to get through to him, but there's some kind of interference—"

"Then contact Houston. They can tele-operate it from there just as well. Just make sure they move the mole and not the rover."

"But the time delay. We've already switched to reserves—"

"Lex, please . . ."

Minutes passed. Suddenly the mole's motor began vibrating. It pushed its way backward—right into Valkerie's hands.

"Val, did it work? I finally got through to Bob."

Valkerie grabbed the linking ring with both hands and held on tight. "Thanks, Lex. I'll do it manually from here." She hit the control to activate the coring tool. The machine vibrated in her hands as a powerful drill began boring straight down into the hard floor. When it had bored in several inches, Valkerie stopped the drill and tugged on it. Good—well anchored. "Wedge my feet again, Lex. I'm gonna push and pull at the same time."

"Okay . . ."

"On my mark. Three, two, one, mark!" Valkerie pulled as hard as she could; Lex's powerful legs shoved on Valkerie's feet.

Nothing.

"Try again." Lex's fighter-pilot drawl. "Three, two, one, mark!"

This time, Valkerie felt something above her slip. "I'm moving! Let's do it again."

She edged forward, inch by precious inch.

And then she was free. "Got it, Lex! Go back to the rover! I'll be out in a minute." Valkerie squirmed forward, reversed the mole's drill, and backed the auger up out of the hole it had made.

"Val, are you okay?"

Valkerie shined her flashlight into the narrow chamber. The pink striated rock was inches from her faceplate. She examined it carefully—filmy pink layers in a salt white slag. Her heart pounded in her throat. It was absolutely certain. She had seen it a million times on Earth, but never on Mars.

Until now.

"Val, get out of there!" Lex's voice snapped her back to reality. "I've dug the tunnel clear."

"Go back to the rover. I'll be right behind you." Valkerie dug a frantic hand through her kit. She had to have a clean sample bag somewhere!

"I'm not leaving until you're out. Hurry! We've only got fourteen minutes of reserve!"

"But I've found it!"

"Found *what*?"

"What we've been looking for since we got here. Life!" Even as she spoke the word, awe skittered across her overloaded nerves. "Life, Lex! It looks like some sort of halobacteria."

"I don't care! Get out of there *now*!"

The rock shimmered hypnotically in the trembling light. *Life!* She'd always hoped, of course, but never dreamed it would really happen.

"Val, are you listening? *Move!* "

But here it was. Right in front of her. Was it alive or dead? It might not matter. For this kind of bug, there wasn't a whole lot of difference.

• • •

## Monday, March 16, 2015, 4:55 p.m., Mars Local Time

### Bob

"Lex . . . Valkerie . . . was that enough? Should I move the MoleBot any more?"

Bob pounded his fist on the table. This didn't make sense. The CommSat was sitting right in the middle of the acquisition cone. Signal strength was high, and he couldn't hear a thing but the *hiss-hiss-hiss* of static. Downstairs, the airlock door slammed. An instant later, the sound of Kennedy's cursing echoed through the cylindrical metal stairwell at the center of the Hab. Kennedy wasn't bothering to wash down his suit—he was coming upstairs, bellowing like a wounded bull.

Bob stood.

The stairwell hatch blasted open.

Kennedy stormed in, waving his helmet. "What'd you do that for? You could have killed me! I ought to have you court-martialed! Look at this!" He shoved the helmet into Bob's solar plexus.

Bob staggered back. What was Kennedy yammering about? "Didn't you hear Lex's message? Valkerie may be in trouble."

Kennedy flipped the helmet over and jabbed a finger at a long, wicked scratch streaking up the faceplate of the helmet. "I'll have your head for this!"

Bob stared at it, wondering what in the world he could have done. "How did that happen?"

Kennedy blasted him with a raging stream of curses.

Bob stepped back, raising his free hand. "Whoa! Whoa! I can't understand a word you're saying. Now slow down and start over—and this time try English. How did that scratch get there?"

"You pushed me!" Kennedy spat out the words. "Knocked me onto my face from behind. You could have killed me!"

Bob narrowed his eyes and studied the Hampster. *Pushed?* He'd been over five feet away from Kennedy when Lex's call came in. "Hey, buddy, I don't know what you're talking about. I didn't push you."

Kennedy's eyes flared. "Well, *somebody* pushed me. And since Uncle Martin's back on Earth—"

Bob flinched at Kennedy's spitting sarcasm.

"—I want to know why you did it. Trying to get rid of me so you'll be the last man on the planet? Is that the only way you can get a woman, you pathetic—"

Bob slammed the helmet onto the floor. "Shut up, Kennedy."

"—such a loser, you—"

Bob felt the heat rise in his neck and face. "I said shut up."

"—no wonder she dumped you—"

Bob grabbed the DCM unit of Kennedy's suit and yanked it forward. Hard. He glowered down at Kennedy, rage pounding in his veins.

Veins bulged at Kennedy's temples. The skin around his eyes turned beet red.

Bob relaxed his grip. *Easy, big guy. Don't let him push your buttons. Don't play his game—whatever it is. Valkerie needs you. Focus . . .*

Without a word, Bob released Kennedy and turned back to the comm diagnostics. He had to find out if Valkerie was okay. Kennedy wasn't, that was for sure, but he'd had a few loose wires ever since launch. When they reached Mars, it had looked for a while like he was doing better. But lately . . .

Lately something rotten had hit the fan. *Is it him who's losing it, or me?*

Bob shook his head, desperate to focus on the problem. A jumble of meaningless graphs and numbers joggled on the display. *Focus, Kaggo.*

Kennedy's labored breathing sounded close behind him, jittering up and down his gridlocked nerves. The floor creaked.

Bob wheeled around. "Would you mind?"

Kennedy jumped backward like he'd been shot and stood rigid, both hands clasped across his chest.

Bob forced himself to speak calmly. "Valkerie's in trouble, and I can't get comm working." He pushed past Kennedy and headed for the stairwell. "Stay on comm. I'm going after them."

"What, on foot? That's insane."

"I've got to do something. Just stay on comm!" He ducked through the lower-level hatch.

"Request denied. You're staying right here. That's an order!" Kennedy's voice pursued him to the suit room.

Bob pulled a fresh oxygen bottle out of his locker and swapped it with the one on the back of his suit. He checked the charges on the battery packs lined up by the wall.

"That's a direct order, Kaggo. Take one step out of this Hab, and I won't be held responsible for the consequences."

Bob turned in the direction of Kennedy's voice.

The Hampster was nowhere to be seen.

"Kennedy, listen," Bob shouted back toward the stairwell. "Lex told me to move the MoleBot. Maybe it got wedged under the rover, I don't know. Maybe they had a breakdown on their way back to the Hab. If I can't find them in two hours, I'll head back. But you need to stay by the radio in case they call. Okay?"

Silence.

"Kennedy?" *Great. Not again.* Bob stormed up the stairs with clenched fists. Okay, so they'd all been a little irritable lately, but Kennedy was really starting to lose his glue.

*You knocked me onto my face from behind.*

Right. Bob checked the command center. No sign of Kennedy. Then circled back to Kennedy's room. The Hampster must have tripped and whacked his helmet on a rock. Sure. That would explain the scratched helmet . . . and the odd behavior.

Bob frowned. *But why blame me? Why would Kennedy say I pushed him?* For that matter, why the big outrage act? He tripped and scratched his helmet, but it hadn't cracked. That Plexiglas was practically unbreakable. Why make a mountain out of a molecule?

Frustration escaped Bob in a long, exasperated breath. *I don't have time for this.* He threw open the door to Kennedy's room, ready to slap some reason into him. "Kennedy, didn't I ask you to stay—"

The room was empty.

Monday, March 16, 2015, 5:10 p.m., Mars Local Time

Valkerie

"Get out of there! Right now!" Lex's voice screeched over Valkerie's earphones. The tether attached to Valkerie's harness spun her around in the underground chamber, drawing her through the narrowing tunnel.

"Lex, stop! Turn off the winch. I'm coming out." Valkerie chipped the halobacteria fossil from the wall with her pick and wormed her way back into the narrow vent, pushing the loose gravel and grit ahead of her.

"Ten minutes, thirty seconds. This isn't funny, Val."

"I'm on my way." She wriggled forward. "Turn on the winch . . . on my . . . mark!"

The rover's powerful winch jerked her the last few feet through the tunnel and swept her out into the dizzying void.

"I've got—" Valkerie's words were lost as she slammed into the face of the cliff. She clung to the fossil with both hands, twisting around, trying to get her feet against the moving wall. "Can't you slow this thing down?"

"No time!" Lex's voice was tight and controlled—too controlled.

Valkerie caught sight of her twenty feet up, bounding up the face of the cliff with staccato skips and jumps. If Lex could do it, so could she. She swung her legs around in an attempt to push off the face of the cliff, but her feet slipped out from under her, and her chest pack smashed into the rock wall. A protruding shelf slammed into her shoulder and spun her around, dissolving her world into a blur.

She gritted her teeth, waiting for the rush of vacuum—the first and last sign she'd get of a torn suit. Her left side thudded against a rock and spun her around onto her back. A chilling, metallic scrape ran down her spine as her backpack slid across biting stone. She hugged the fossil to her chest, clinging to it with aching, trembling hands. For a long minute she slid, wondering if the lumps rolling across her back were rocks or torn pieces of her pack. And then . . .

Silence.

The canyon that stretched out below her had rattled to a sudden stop, throbbing and swaying to the rhythm of her wildly beating heart.

"Valkerie, come *on*!"

A tug on her shoulder. Valkerie sucked in her breath as she started to tip sideways.

"Help me get you turned around. I can't get you around the bend with the winch."

"Bend?" Valkerie's mind snapped into focus. Oh right, she was already at the top. Valkerie threw her weight to the side and kicked herself around to face the cliff. Slowly, still cupping the fossil in both hands, she clambered over the edge of the ledge as the winch drew her slowly toward the rover.

"Go!" Lex unhitched Valkerie from the cable, yanked her to her feet, and pulled her into the airlock at the rear of the rover. The hatch swung shut and the airlock light glowed halogen orange.

"Lex, I've found it!" Valkerie opened her hands a crack. Still there. All of it. It hadn't even broken. "Life, Lex. Mars had life!" Valkerie looked up.

Lex was slumped against the wall of the airlock, checking her DCM panel with her wrist mirror.

"Two minutes. I only had two minutes left. You had five." Lex pulled off her helmet and shook her head to dislodge the glistening tendrils of black silk that clung to her olive skin. She spun open the hatch that led into the rover.

"Lex!" Valkerie took off her helmet and followed Lex through the hatch. "Don't you even want to see it?"

Lex whirled and turned smoldering eyes on Valkerie. "Don't you even *care* you almost got us killed?"

Valkerie took a backward step. "Lex, we found it. You and me. The two of us together."

"Two minutes. We were home free, but you had to stay inside dinking around. Do you have any idea how long you were in there?"

"I told you to get back to the rover."

The look on Lex's face told her what a monomaniacal idiot she'd been.

Valkerie winced.

"You could have been . . . killed." Lex's voice broke. "I was so afraid you . . . weren't going to get out."

Valkerie set the fossil on the lab bench and took a step toward her friend. *Me. She was worried about me, and I was worried about a stupid fossil. She's not the same Lex who started this trip.* "I'm sorry. I was wrong." She pulled Lex into an awkward embrace—the best they could do in their bulky suits.

"I . . . When I saw the fossil . . . I just didn't think. Can you forgive me?"

"We could have come back for it tomorrow."

"I can't believe I was so stupid. As it is, I just ended up contaminating it."

Lex hesitated, and some of the old fighter-pilot intensity flared in her eyes. Then it flickered out and she grinned. "So much for the history books. I guess we both mucked things up pretty bad."

"We?"

"I stepped on the MoleBot remote. I couldn't even get comm to work. If anything had happened to you . . . Bob!" Lex broke away and clambered to the front of the rover. "Bob still thinks you're trapped. Our comm went haywire." She flipped a switch on the dash, and a strange rhythmic static filled the rover.

Valkerie climbed forward and watched Lex work the controls. "What is it? Sunspots?"

Lex shook her head. "Too regular. Probably a transmitter malfunction at the Hab. Buckle in. We've got to get back before Bob has an aneurysm."

Valkerie hurried to the back and eased the fossil into a sample bag. So much for her sterile technique. She sank back into one of the oversized bench seats and buckled her harness.

Some friend she was. She hadn't even considered that Bob might be worried. And Lex. She'd actually endangered Lex's life. And for what? A pink rock. A simple halobacteria fossil. Lex had really been upset, and she'd tossed her concerns aside like a chunk of common regolith.

The rover's engines whirred to life, and Lex set off at top speed for the Hab.

Valkerie stared out the window, watching a dead, barren planet transform itself before her eyes. Mars. It had once been a home. The rocks and dust . . . Could they be just a blanket—Mars's way of tucking her children in at night?

*Could some of those children still be alive?*

The static in the rover suddenly went quiet.

Valkerie leaned forward. "Hey, Lex, what's up?" She unbelted herself and walked forward, bracing herself against the lurch and sway of the rover.

"The static's gone. Bob must have fixed something." Lex flipped the transmitter switch. "Bob, this is Lex calling from the rover. Val and I are on our way home."

Bob's voice burst from the speakers. "Thank God! What happened? Is Valkerie okay?"

The relief in his voice raised a lump in Valkerie's throat. Bob was such a—

"Hang on. She can tell you herself. In fact, I'm patching Houston in on this too. Val has an announcement to make, and I think they might be interested."

Lex stopped the rover and held out the microphone. Valkerie just stared at it. All this time she'd been searching . . . she'd never even considered what to say if she actually *found* something. Whatever she said, it needed to be big. Significant. Poetic. *What hath God wrought? A giant leap for mankind?* How many generations would remember her words?

Lex pushed the mike into her hand. "Val, go."

"Um . . . Houston, this is Valkerie Jansen and Alexis Ohta calling from the rover. We have just discovered the fossilized remains of some halobacteria. The sample is approximately ten by five by three centimeters, milky white with pink striations. It was located in what appears to be an old thermal vent at the top of weeping fissure 342 of canyon 13. Um . . . we are now heading back to the Hab, where we'll do a complete analysis and send you our results. Over."

Valkerie lowered the microphone and shrugged. Cold, hard science. It didn't capture the grandeur of the universe, but it was always an easy fallback when you didn't have time to think.

## Monday, March 16, 2015, 4:05 p.m., CST

### Josh

Flight Director Josh Bennett felt like an army of ants had invaded his central nervous system. *Life on Mars!*

"We are now heading back to the Hab, where we'll do a complete analysis and send you our results. Over."

The Flight Control Room, which had been an oasis of quiet sixty seconds ago, erupted into cheers. Shouting. Dancing. Handshaking all around. The doors flung open and a stream of engineers and managers flooded into the room. EECOM bustled up the aisle and wrapped Josh in a hug.

Josh planted a big kiss on her forehead and let loose with a whoop. Life! After nine months of labor they had finally found it! The big payoff. Mars was back on the map.

And the crowd kept growing. Where had all the people come from? Nate Harrington, the Mars Mission Director, strode into the FCR, grinning like he'd just bought a van Gogh at a garage sale.

Josh pushed his way through the reveling throng. A slap on the back from the Capcom, Jake Hunter. A high five from CATO. Josh turned and almost collided with Cathe Willison, the up-and-coming young engineer who had saved the crew's lives barely a year earlier on the outbound journey. Josh raised his hand for another high five.

She stepped back to let one of the flight docs pass between them.

"You okay?" He had to raise his voice to be heard.

"Better than okay. I just can't wrap my mind around it all." She scanned the crowd, an amused grin lighting up her eyes. "It's amazing the difference a single fossil can make."

"Not just a fossil. It's another mission. And another, and another . . . As long as we keep finding reasons to go back."

"And you want to be on one of those missions, don't you?" Her rosebud lips were pressed together in a childish pout.

"Absolutely! But that's not for me to—"

Cathe turned with a shrug and pushed her way down the aisle, swaying like a slender reed in a gentle breeze.

He stared after her, wondering what that was about. She seemed almost sad, like she—

"Okay, everybody, ice your jets! This ain't Mardi Gras!" Nate Harrington was bellowing in Josh's face. "Josh, I hope you haven't forgotten you're the Flight Director right now. Anyone who doesn't belong in FCR needs to be out of here five minutes ago, or I start bowling heads. We've got a mission to run here, and God just upped the ante. Who's Capcom?"

"Jake Hunter." Josh reached over and whacked Jake on the shoulder. "Jake, we need you!"

Nate was swabbing his glistening forehead with a tissue. "Okay, Jake, you need to get on the horn to our boys and girls right now and *remind* them that there are some procedures to follow. Valkerie needs to keep that fossil in a glove box and follow sterile interface protocols to the semicolon."

Hunter nodded and pushed his way to the Capcom station.

Josh put two fingers in his mouth and whistled a long, piercing shriek that got everyone's attention. "Okay, people, we're all excited. We just made the science breakthrough of the century. Anyone who wants to party, I'm buying drinks tonight at The Outpost. But right now, we've got a mission to run, and Nate's promising to tickle anyone who doesn't belong in here with a red-hot poker. So take the party outside."

The room cleared almost as fast as it had filled up.

Josh looked back at the big, soundproof glass wall that separated the tourist section from the Flight Control Room.

Forty-odd people in Bermuda shorts and sunglasses were giving them a standing ovation.

Nate grabbed Josh's arm. "The Outpost is gonna have to wait for another day. Tonight, we're doing the biggest press conference since Orson Welles did his *War of the Worlds* shtick. And tomorrow, we're going to Congress to get back all that money they took out of our hide. We *will* fly the Ares 14. And it's not going to take another twenty years either."

Josh nodded and reached for his phone. "I'm calling the networks now."

Monday, March 16, 2015, 5:45 p.m., Mars Local Time

Bob

Bob paced the length of the suit room floor. What was taking the girls so long? They should have been back five minutes ago. He started to turn around, but his foot shot out from under him on the wet floor.

Bob picked himself up and turned to the door. "Kennedy, you left a mess in here!"

A metallic rattle sounded from the supply room they'd converted into a greenhouse.

That was where Bob had found Kennedy hiding after Lex's call. He'd claimed to be watering the flowers, but Bob had checked. The soil was dry in every pot but one. Watering the flowers—oh sure. When Valkerie and Lex were in trouble. Right after Bob had supposedly tried to kill him.

Made perfect sense.

Bob shook his head and pulled a towel from the lockers to swab up the water. It gritted across the floor like semi-fine sandpaper. So far the Martian dust was the biggest problem they had faced on the mission. Micron sized, laced with peroxides, the stuff worked its way into every nook and cranny of the human body, every seal on an EVA suit. They'd all developed painful rashes and had gone through their first set of suits in a month before they realized what was chewing everything up. Now every EVA had to end with a wet scrub.

Another metallic clang rang through the Hab—the sound of the rover hot-docking.

Bob jumped to his feet and tossed the wet towel into a bin. He wiped his hands on his coveralls and hurried out to the airlock. He spun open the hatch wheel and pulled open the inner hatch.

The exterior hatch swung open, and Valkerie stepped into the airlock. Her dark blond hair was matted to her head in a profusion of damp curls. Her shoulders sagged with fatigue, but her eyes looked radiant. Bob had never seen her so excited.

"Valkerie." He took a step toward her, then stopped. "I was so worried."

Valkerie's grin put the flutters in Bob's chest. "Thanks for sending back the Mole. You saved my life." She took a tentative step toward him, then stopped. "Wet scrub! We need to get cleaned up first. Then we'll talk."

Bob dropped his outstretched arms to his sides and awkwardly wiped his hands on his coveralls. *Then we'll talk . . .* These days *we'll talk* was never good. When was he going to learn? He had to listen to the words coming out of her mouth—not her mouth or her lips or her mesmerizing eyes . . .

"Valkerie!" Kennedy squeezed past Bob and wrapped Valkerie in a big hug. "You had us worried sick. Don't ever do that to me again."

Bob felt the heat rise in his face. "Don't do that to *you*? I was the one who wanted to go out after them. You were watering flowers in the supply room." He reached over Kennedy to put a hand on Valkerie's shoulder.

Anger flared in her eyes. "What part of 'wet scrub' are you two unclear on? There's a reason for the protocols, so both of you just back off."

Lex poked her head into the airlock. "She's not kidding, guys. This is serious. Quit clogging up the works."

Bob leaned toward Valkerie. "We need to talk. Soon."

Her eyes lasered into his. "For the last time, can you give me some space to clean off this wretched suit?"

Kennedy spun around and pushed Bob out of the airlock. "She's right, Kaggo. I'll take care of it." He swung the hatch shut.

"Wait a minute!" Bob stood outside the hatch and peered in through the small window.

Kennedy was spraying Valkerie's suit, the water flying out at full pressure. A streak of mud blasted the window.

Bob jumped back. "Hey! Turn down the pressure a little, will you?" He banged on the hatch. Kennedy was going to make a swamp in there if he didn't take it easy. What was it with Kennedy and water? What was it with Kennedy, period? Bob cracked open the hatch. "Turn down the—"

The flow of water stopped.

"Do you have any idea how much water you just wasted?" Bob tried to sound reasonable, but it wasn't easy.

"Had to." Kennedy stepped out of the airlock and headed for the corridor. "You saw how dirty Valkerie was. I couldn't ignore the risk of contamination."

"Oh, right." Bob hands tightened into fists. The only thing contaminating Mars was Kennedy.

"Bob, what's gotten into you?" Lex stepped out of the airlock and started shucking off her wet EVA suit. "Every time Valkerie and I leave you and Kennedy alone, the two of you fight like gamecocks."

"It's not me. It's him." Bob checked the corridor to make sure Kennedy wasn't skulking about. "He disappeared on me while I was working on the fuel factory. Didn't say anything. Didn't even answer comm. Just that awful breathing thing he does."

"So where was he?" Valkerie's muffled voice filtered out from the middle of her EVA suit as she wriggled her way out of it.

"In the ascent vehicle. He said he was doing *maintenance* on it. Whatever that means. Oh yeah, and then I found scratches on one of the MAV's support struts—like somebody ran into it with the rover. And guess who tried to blame it on me, even though he was the last one to refuel?" Bob helped Lex hoist her suit back into her locker. "And then he claims I pushed him from behind and tried to kill him." Bob held up Kennedy's helmet for the women to inspect.

"So did you?" Lex took the helmet from Bob and ran her finger down the scratched Plexiglas. "Push him, I mean?"

"No!" He turned to Valkerie for support.

She was looking back toward the airlock, her expression a million miles away.

Bob felt uneasy. "Valkerie, I think we need to talk. Alone." He looked to Lex with what he hoped was an apologetic expression.

She gave him an encouraging nod. "I'll be upstairs changing for the press conference." Lex stood and made for the door.

"Press conference?" Bob said. "Oh, right. For the bacteria thing. Where is it? Can I see it?"

Valkerie just sat there. Staring.

"Valkerie?"

"Yes?" She stood suddenly and started to move about the suit room.

"Uh . . . I was so worried about you today. It scared me to death." *Careful, Kaggo. Don't crowd her.* "I thought I was going to lose you and . . . I couldn't bear it if—"

"Bob, I wish I could talk. I really do, but I *have* to figure out what to say for the press conference. I have so much work to do, I don't even know where to start." She ducked into the airlock hatch and disappeared into the rover.

Bob turned to follow her but stopped and sank back against the wall, tracing the long scratch in Kennedy's visor with cold, wet fingertips.

• • •

## Monday, March 16, 2015, 11:30 p.m., CST

## Nate

Nate Harrington rubbed his sweaty palms on his pant legs. Two more minutes till the media feeding frenzy.

It was 11:30 at night. Normally the Johnson Space Center would be quiet at this hour. The parking lots would be mostly empty—just the night crews for the Space Station and the Ares Mission and a few engineers who never seemed to sleep. Nate would be getting some actual work done in his office.

But not tonight. Not after Valkerie's discovery. The rock that rocked the world. He'd never seen such a PR piranhafest. *NASA Discovers Life on Mars.* The six-o'clock news hour had lasted four hours. A live video feed with voice-over from Valkerie. A question-and-answer session with the whole crew—carefully choreographed to work around the forty-minute radio time delay. By 10:00, there were photomicrographs of the new halobacteria on the JSC Web site and on every TV set in the world. At 11:00, they'd put together a full media show here in Teague Auditorium, and the place was swimming with news-droids. Nate hadn't seen anything like it. The crew hadn't created this much excitement since they'd died.

The half-hour science briefing was over now. Time for a few questions.

Steven Perez stepped carefully to the podium. Watching him, Nate winced. Perez had looked run-down all last summer. They all had, of course. Way too many sixteen-hour days. But once the mission on the Martian surface began, they all started getting some rest and feeling better. All but Perez. By late fall, Perez finally took some time off to see his doctor.

The news was bad. Real bad.

Perez had Parkinson's disease. He wasn't going to die anytime soon, but he wasn't going to get better either. And so NASA, in its infinite wisdom, was looking for a replacement for the Director of Johnson Space Center. Crazy. If Perez was careful, he would be good for another five or ten years. But somebody up high wanted Perez out within twenty-four months. And Nate didn't want the job. He wanted to retire as soon as this sorry mission was over so he could go fly ultralights in Colorado, where he belonged. That didn't stop the water-fountain experts around JSC from speculating, though. Everyone thought Nate was just playing hard to get. Bunch of morons. What did they know, anyway?

"Good evening." Perez's voice rasped over the PA system. "This is an extraordinary day in the history of the National Aeronautics and Space Administration. We'll now move into the press conference. I'm sure many of you know Nate Harrington, the Mars Mission Director. Mr. Harrington will take questions from the floor."

Applause. Perez stepped back to his chair. The spotlight zoomed over to Nate.

Nate smiled and leaned toward his mike on the table in front of him. "Good evening. It's nice to see a few new faces around here this late at night." He peered into the sea of frantically waving hands and pointed to a clean-cut young guy in the front row. He looked safe enough.

The guy stood, and one of the sound techs hurried over to him with a cordless mike on the end of a four-foot boom. "Ron

Sanders, religion editor of the *Houston Chronicle*." He waited while the TV cameras zoomed in on him.

Nate swallowed hard. *Religion* editor?

"Mr. Harrington, how does today's discovery impact the question of creation versus evolution?"

*Oh good. A nuclear bomb in my face on the first question.* Nate cleared his throat while he tried to figure out what to say. There were still people in America who thought that question hadn't been resolved. As far as Nate could see, it was answered a hundred years ago. "Thanks for that insightful question, Mr. . . . um, Sanders. As you know, I'm not a biologist, but I do have a pretty good handle on the science mission we're trying to accomplish here. While today's discovery is a remarkable one that opens up a large number of new questions, it really doesn't change anything in that particular arena you just mentioned." A nice ambiguous answer. Sanders would probably read it one way, while people who had a clue would read it the exact opposite.

Sanders raised his eyebrows, and his jaw dropped open. He reached for the mike, but Nate pointed at a graying woman in the third row. "Next question."

The tech took the mike around to her. "Michelle Owens, *New York Times* science editor." Short pause for the cameras again.

Nate wondered if she'd hopped the first plane to Houston or if she'd somehow been in town already.

"Mr. Harrington, I'm sure you're aware that a sample of halophilic bacteria here on Earth was brought back to life after being encased in a salt crystal for two hundred and fifty million years. Will there be any efforts to revive the halobacteria Dr. Jansen discovered today?"

Nate felt his gut relaxing. Nice to get a pro. "That's an excellent question, Ms. Owens. We're not sure at this time that the fossil contains DNA, but even if it did, it's very likely that the DNA would be damaged beyond repair. The issue is pretty simple. The sample you mentioned was found deep underground, where it was well shielded from cosmic rays. Those spores were able to last hundreds of millions of years with minimal damage to their DNA, which is the genetic information that encodes life processes. That's not likely to be the case on Mars. Today's sample was found underground, but not all that deep. And as you know, the Martian atmosphere is less than one percent the density of ours, so it provides little protection from ionizing radiation. We don't have a firm age yet for Valkerie's discovery. It was partially protected by its underground location, but if it's more than a few thousand years old, I'd be doubtful it can be revived. You can be sure we'll be looking at that question very closely in the coming weeks."

Nate leaned back a little. As long as they kept to science, this wasn't going to be too bad. "Next question." He pointed toward a sea of hands in the fifth row. Let the fittest of them grab the mike.

"Liz Proust, author of the Nebula Award-winning novel *Bactamination*."

Nate's pulse quickened a notch. He'd never met this Proust woman, but she was supposed to be a regular Ms. Loose Cannon on the *Titanic*. "Yes, Ms. Proust. Go ahead."

"Mr. Harrington, there are some serious issues that need to be addressed here. As you know, back-contamination of Earth by Martian microbes is a question that has long been feared."

Nate cleared his throat. *Right, ever since your stupid book came out.*

"Mr. Harrington, what are the odds that this bacterium you've discovered might be dangerous to humans?"

Somebody at the back of the auditorium laughed out loud, which was exactly the right response.

Nate leaned toward his mike. The answer, of course, was zero. "That's—"

"Along those same lines, what procedures have you put in place for a quarantine, in case this Martian bacterium turns out to be toxic?"

The room had gone completely quiet, except for a low buzz in the journalist section. Which wasn't surprising, because most journalists were morons when it came to science.

Nate's knuckles were white, he was clenching the mike so hard. This was ridiculous. "As I was say—"

"And finally, if there turns out to be a problem in your procedures, have you considered the knotty ethical question of whether it would be right to bring the crew back to planet Earth? In short, have you considered the very dangerous possibility of bactamination?"

*Idiot.* Nate yanked his mike directly up to his mouth. "Ms. Proust, it's pretty clear your strength is writing fantasy. If you ever chance to read a book on evolutionary biology, you might ask yourself how any bacterium, evolving on another planet, probably using different DNA base pairs, different codons, different proteins, and different cellular structures, could possibly adapt itself, sheerly by chance, in just such a way as to infect a species on a different planet. Life is extraordinarily complex, and disease-causing bacteria are adapted to their hosts. Humans don't get the same diseases hamsters do, and—"

"Mr. Harrington, you haven't answered any of my questions."

"Ms. Proust, you haven't understood any of my answers. Now, if there are any other questions from *intelligent* life-forms . . ." Nate glared around the room, daring anyone to ask something.

No takers. "Thank you all, and good night." Nate turned and walked away toward the center of the stage to join Perez. He looked at the enormous video screen behind the podium. The TV camera had zoomed in on Liz Proust's face.

She was talking to a dozen reporters and holding aloft a copy of *Bactamination*. And smiling.

# CHAPTER

Wednesday, March 18, 2015, 12:15 p.m., Mars Local Time

Bob

Bob closed his eyes and tried to pretend he wasn't getting scalped.

"Don't keep moving like that," Kennedy growled. "I'm going to cut off one of your ears if you keep twitching."

Bob tweaked one eyelid open just a notch and stared again at the worst haircut in the history of mankind. It was even worse than the one Sister Marianne gave him back in seventh grade.

Kennedy snicked the scissors again and swore through clenched teeth. "This is on your head, Kaggo. I told you I don't cut hair."

Bob heaved a sigh. So much for his great idea. All he'd wanted to do was spend a little male-bonding time with Kennedy to try to figure out what was going on in the guy's head. Maybe find out what had really happened two days ago with Kennedy's helmet. But he'd forgotten rule number one: Never give a grounded pilot a pair of scissors and a razor.

*Here, Hampster. You seem to have a lot of pent-up frustration. Why don't you take it out on my head?*

"Will you sit still! What's wrong with you? I'm doing this with one eye, you know."

Bob tightened his grip on the arms of the chair. What *was* wrong with him? He should have waited for Lex to do the honors. But Lex would have just found an excuse to pawn off the job on Valkerie. And at this point that would be way too . . . awkward. Valkerie hadn't spoken three words to him since bringing home that little chunk of rock. Not that they'd had a lot of time for conversation. Valkerie and Lex were spending about twenty hours a day studying the halobacteria from canyon 13. Even so, it felt an awful lot like she was freezing him out of her life. Even more than before.

"So . . ." Bob tried to think of a neutral topic. "How's the garden going?"

A loud snip snicked in Bob's ear. "You really like the fact that I got stuck with the poop-scooping detail. Think it's funny, don't you?"

Actually, it *was* pretty funny. "No, I . . . Valkerie told me you got a pansy to bloom. First flower on Mars. That's pretty cool."

Kennedy moved around to stare hard into Bob's eyes. "*Valkerie* and I did. She's been helping me a lot the past month. Seems to really like working with me. Why do you suppose that is?" His upper lip curled in a lopsided smile.

"She misses Earth a lot more than the rest of us. I think she just likes being near the plants."

"She and I both miss Earth. We talk about it a lot. I miss flying, and she misses walking. I never realized how much we have in common." Kennedy shuffled back behind Bob and took another snip.

Bob clenched his fists. *Just make it through the haircut. This is no time for another argument.*

"You and Lex seem to be spending a lot of time together too. Anything going on that I should know about?" The scissors clipped across Bob's forehead, and Kennedy stepped back, frowning for a long minute. "Sorry about that." He didn't look sorry. "Tell you what—don't look in the mirror yet. Papa Kennedy is gonna fix that before you ever—"

Bob fumbled for the sheet tied at his neck. This was crazy. Lex could spare ten minutes to finish the job.

Kennedy pushed Bob's hands back down. "Stop moving, I'm almost done." He made a few more snips in front and then stepped to the side. "Now, tell me I didn't do a great patch."

Bob winced. It was too horrible for words.

"Stop moving." Kennedy picked up an electric razor. "Okay, I'm going to cut your neck, big guy." He flicked it on. The whine for the next few minutes gave Bob an excuse not to talk. Finally the massacre ended.

"And there we go. Good enough for government work." Kennedy grabbed a small whisk broom and began brushing loose hair off Bob's neck and shoulders. "I know you had your heart set on Valkerie for a while, but there are other fish in the ocean, ya know, Kaggo. And we're swimming in a pretty small pond here."

Bob didn't say anything. The Hampster was the kind of guy who thought of women as fish. Interchangeable commodities. Fine, let him think that.

Kennedy untied the sheet draped over Bob's shoulders and shook the contents onto the floor. He grabbed a broom and began sweeping. "And once we get back to Earth, you'll be swimming in fish. Know what I mean?"

"Kennedy, I don't—"

"Sure you do. Chicks go for famous guys." Kennedy knelt down and scooped the loose, sandy hair into a dustpan. "Even guys like you."

"What's that supposed to—"

The hatch of the central stairwell burst open. Lex came in, followed by Valkerie.

Bob turned to look at them.

Valkerie's face blanched.

Lex spun furiously on Kennedy. "Hampster, you ought to be ashamed of yourself. Hey, Kaggo, next time let me do it, okay?"

"It looks . . . fine." Valkerie passed through to the galley.

Kennedy disappeared after her.

"It does *not* look fine." Lex planted her hands on her hips. "Bob, what in the world were you thinking? Kennedy's got the artistic sense of a rhino."

Valkerie reappeared with an armful of food packets. "Let's get back to work, Lex."

"Valkerie, wait!" Kennedy came out of the galley. "I've been keeping this in my room just for you—a little celebration for your discovery." He pinned a small pansy to her jumpsuit collar. "The first flower grown on Mars."

Valkerie smiled at him. "Thanks, Hampster. That's really sweet of you."

Kennedy gave her that *aw-shucks* look he'd probably practiced in the mirror a hundred times.

Lex grabbed some of the food packets from Valkerie's arms and pulled open the hatch. Valkerie went through into the stairwell, Kennedy puppy-dogging right behind her. Lex gave

Bob a look that told him he was an idiot, then followed them down.

Bob shoved the hatch shut. He wanted to strangle Kennedy. It was crazy, but that's what he wanted to do. Wouldn't that make a nice little male-bonding exercise? *Hold still, Hampster, while I squeeze your neck.*

"Ares 7, this is Houston, come in," Josh Bennett's voice crackled over the radio. "Ares 7, this is Houston. Just a little update. You guys are still the big story down here on planet Earth. That Proust woman got herself on TV this morning with Karla Faust from Stanford. Karla annihilated her, so don't worry about a thing."

Bob had a lot bigger things to worry about than some idiot novelist with delusions of adequacy. He pulled up a stool to the CommConsole and adjusted the gain on the signal. The radio had been on-again-off-again ever since Valkerie and Lex had come back with the fossil. No one at NASA seemed to know what the problem was, but they all agreed on one thing: The interference wasn't coming from Earth.

"Anyway," Josh continued, "if Bob is around, I wanted to check in with him to see how things are going with . . . the MAV and everything. Bob, if you want to talk things over, I'll be in a private room on an encrypted link. Standing by for your response."

Bob grabbed the mike. "Josh, this is Bob. And, boy, do I need to talk. Everyone else is busy right now, but I'm gonna switch this channel with full crypto to my room and pick it up again in fifteen seconds. Stand by."

He walked through the galley and into the circular hallway that ran around the stairwell. He passed Kennedy's room, checked to make sure it was unoccupied, and jerked open the door to his own quarters. It was a tiny wedge of a room—like a piece of pie with the point bitten off, maybe seven feet long, and five feet at its widest point. Home sweet shoebox.

Bob slammed the door shut, threw on a headset, plopped down on his bed, and punched in the password to pick up the encrypted comm session he'd started at the console.

"Hey, Josh, this is Bob again. I'm in my room, and the others are all downstairs—for the moment. I'll get to the point and I hope you don't take this the wrong way, but I'm real worried about . . . all of us. Kennedy's acting weird. Valkerie and Lex are off in la-la land with that fossil. And I'm . . . Josh, I think I'm cracking up."

Bob took a deep breath. Okay, he was committed. Better get it all out. "Josh, remember the flight docs talking about hypervigilance? About how, when monkeys leave the rain forest and head out on the plains, they just amp out because of all the pressure? Anyway, I think I'm starting to go into that mode. Maybe Kennedy too, but me for sure. I had another panic attack a couple days ago, the worst one yet—really lost it for a few minutes. Then, just now, Kennedy gave me a horrible haircut, and I got so mad I wanted to . . . kill him. Literally, for a second I wanted to strangle him. Scared myself to death. Josh, you know me. I'm not like that—not even with Kennedy. But he's really starting to get to me. Everything is. I think I need help. Maybe a neuro exam or something. If the Hampster pulls one of his . . . you know—one of his stunts again, I'm scared I'm gonna murder him." Which was an exaggeration. He hoped and begged and prayed it was just an exaggeration. But what if he *was* cracking? Under the pressure they all lived under, who wouldn't crack?

Bob sat back to wait out the radio delay. He hated talking like this—sending a long message, then waiting for a long response—but there wasn't any choice until somebody figured out faster-than-light communications. It was better than nothing, but not by much. So he talked to Josh at least twice a week, despite the agonizing delays. With Lex giving him Miss Manners tips twice a month, Valkerie playing the role of the sleeping princess, and Kennedy doing the Dr. Strangelove bit, Bob needed Josh more than ever.

A few months ago, Josh had been promoted to Flight Director. Good for him. As long as nobody spilled Josh's secret, his job was safe. No way was Bob planning to rat on him. Josh hadn't meant to endanger the crew on the way to Mars. It just kind of happened. Bad luck. And anyway, all he'd been trying to do was make sure that a week like this one would come along.

*Life on Mars. It feels a little anticlimactic, but we found it, buddy, and we didn't even need your insurance policy.*

## Wednesday, March 18, 2015, 12:30 p.m., CST

### Josh

"Hey, Kaggo, this is Josh." Josh hesitated. The shrinks thought the rest of the crew should be kept in the dark about Kennedy, but if Bob thought the problem was him and not Kennedy . . . What if he started questioning his judgment in other areas? "Listen, there's nothing wrong with you. If you want to kill Kennedy, it's because you're normal. Everybody here wants to kill him too. He's a snake. The lowest kind of snake. Don't trust him as far as you can throw him—back here on Earth I mean."

Josh closed his eyes and concentrated on the four people all alone on a rust-bucket of a planet two hundred million miles away.

"I'm not supposed to tell you this, and you have to promise not to tell anyone else— especially not anyone here. But . . . we have proof that Kennedy was the guy who knocked me off the mission. And he did it intentionally. He laid some doubts about me in the shrinks' minds. I read the transcripts of an interview with him, and he was pushing their buttons without them even knowing it."

Josh stopped again, trying to regroup. "I know what you're thinking, Kaggo. You think it was that interview you had with the shrinks that did me in. Well, you're wrong. Kennedy set them up, too, just like he set you up. The guy's a master at manipulating people. He leaked some plans of the Hab to a Japanese terrorist group—from *my* e-mail account. He framed me, Kaggo!

"Maybe you're wondering how we know all this. You remember that FBI woman Nate's been hanging around with? Agent Yamaguchi? Anyway, before you guys reached Mars last summer, she got us a warrant to search Kennedy's apartment. You would not *believe* how much stuff he had on psychology. He had every paper our shrink team has written on crew selection, teamwork indices, that kind of thing. More psych books than Sigmund Freud. The guy is a genius at manipulation. That's what you're dealing with, Bob. If there was a degree in manipulation, Kennedy would have a Ph.D. So my point is real simple: I don't think you're the problem. I think Kennedy's punching your buttons. Why, I don't know, but he's doing it.

So you just hang tough, okay, dude? I . . . we . . . love you guys. Give Valkerie and Lex a hug for me, will you? Over."

Josh leaned back in his chair, letting the emotions flood through. Rage. Fear. Guilt. Love. The usual suspects. Now he had forty minutes before Bob's message came back. No wonder they were all getting claustrophobic up there, penned in together in a tuna can the size of a few dorm rooms.

Josh shook his head. What was Kennedy up to? All those years, Josh had thought he knew the Hampster, and then it turned out the little weasel stabbed him in the back.

And now he was going after Bob . . . But why? What was he after? Was it just a coincidence that Kennedy was going flaky at exactly the same time the communications were going haywire?

Comm was mission critical — especially now with tension levels set to deep fat fry. It was time to take another hard look at the evidence room. Somebody had to figure out what the Hampster was up to. The shrinks could only see what Kennedy wanted them to see.

Josh pulled out his cell phone and walked out of the crypto room. Cell phones weren't allowed in Mission Control, but if he stepped outside it would be okay. He walked down the hall and pushed his way outside.

The phone answered on the first ring. "Harrington."

"Nate, this is Josh. I need to talk to Agent Yamaguchi. Have you got her number?"

• • •

## Wednesday, March 18, 2015, 1:30 p.m., Mars Local Time

### Bob

Finally Josh's voice came in over Bob's headset. "Hey, Kaggo, this is Josh. Listen, There's nothing wrong—"

*Skkkkkkkkrrrrrrrrrrr.* Josh's voice dissolved into static. Bob leaped to the console and flicked switches. "Don't do this to me, Josh. *Please.* I need you, buddy."

Nothing. Three beats per second. This was not atmospherics. Not a loose wire. Not an accident.

*There's nothing wrong . . .*

Right. The interference was man-made, or he was an amoeba.

Somebody was jamming the Deep Space Network.

*Bad idea, whoever you are. You better watch your back, because you've now officially got a Mad Kaggo on your tail.*

## Wednesday, March 18, 2015, 2:00 p.m., Mars Local Time

### Valkerie

Valkerie's head rocked back and forth against the rover headrest. Her body tingled with exhaustion, but her mind raced ahead, flitting from one unfinished task to the next. The last two days had been brutal. Five press conferences. Mission Control to-do lists a mile long. She and Lex had spent every waking minute in the lab—and the nonwaking minutes dreaming about the lab. It felt so good to sit down. To be surrounded by the relative quiet of the rover's engine, whining and creaking over the rocky Martian terrain. To be away from Bob and his haunted eyes.

At first, when Lex suggested this trip back to the thermal vent, Valkerie had objected. She was too tired. They didn't have enough time. But she eventually gave in when Lex threatened to go without her. Perhaps it was just as well. The excuse for a few minutes' rest was worth it. She wished the drive out could last forever.

The engines rumbled to a stop.

"Okay," Lex called from the front of the rover. "We're here."

Valkerie shut her eyes and tried to summon the energy to stand.

The rover swayed from side to side as Lex made her way back to the main cabin. Air whooshed from the bench cushion opposite Valkerie.

"One more minute. Let me sit just one more minute."

"Take all the time you want. I'm taking a nap."

"What?" Valkerie opened her eyes.

Lex was lying on her back with her hands clasped beneath her head. "I turned the radio off. We're not going back until you get some rest."

Valkerie sat up. "But what about the thermal vent? The new samples? I've still got a ton of sequencing to do . . ."

"Absolutely not. Not until you rest. Have you still got a headache?"

"Yeah, but—"

"So rest." Lex rolled onto her side and faced the wall. End of discussion.

Valkerie slid onto her back and closed her eyes. Her pulse pounded against her temples. She couldn't rest. She had DNA to sequence. She and Lex had isolated DNA from spores that had been trapped in the salt crystals. It was too astonishing for words. Some of the fragments were thousands of base pairs long. Martian DNA. The 16S-oligo-binding study results looked pretty firm. The best explanation seemed to be that the halobacterium originated on Earth rather than on Mars. Which was quite a surprise.

Everyone had known for a long time that, in principle, a meteorite could smash into Earth so hard it tossed up chunks of rock that floated around the sun and eventually wound up on Mars—seeding it with bacteria. Intra-system panspermia. But the usual scenario went the other way—Mars to Earth. Gilbert Flood was going to get a good chuckle over this. Scientists had been laughing at his theory for years. If only she could be present when he read her paper . . .

Her paper. The image of sweaty, picket-carrying protesters leaped to mind. Valkerie labored to her feet and staggered to the back of the rover. How many people would read her paper? How many people would be talking about it? It could be millions. Billions. The newspapers. Television. Her family and friends. Everybody would be talking about the implications. Not just biological. Philosophical. Theological. Was she going to be another Galileo? Branded as a heretic for reporting what she saw?

She paced to the front of the rover and stared out the window.

Rock walls rose up on all sides.

What was going on? Lex hadn't taken them to the canyon after all. She had driven them to the site they called Stonehenge, a ring of eerie, butte-like formations standing tall and proud in the middle of a shallow, mile-wide bowl. The crew had spent most of their first three months digging in and around Stonehenge. The geology was so unique—the place was full of gray hematite. And it was beautiful—disquietingly so. She stared out the window at the crisscross of blue-gray stones. Lex had parked in the area Bob called the Garden. It was Valkerie's favorite part of Stonehenge. If only she had the leisure time to sit back and enjoy it. To enjoy anything.

But she had work to do. Science. Analysis. The scientific method. She stared out at a band of crisscrossing shadows, a purple frieze against the impossibly clear amber horizon. It didn't make sense. She'd traveled three hundred million miles for what? To be locked in the bowels of a lousy laboratory? To run a sequence analysis on a simple halobacterium? Not a Barsoomian artifact, not the skull of a Thark. No buried space-ship to transport them across the galaxy to meet an ancient alien race.

Maybe she'd been all wrong. Maybe nobody would even care. Who was going to get excited about a bacterium? Especially if it turned out to be of Earth origin. People weren't hungry for more analysis. For more theories . . . The world was already too cold, too scientific. Where was the life? The purpose? The magic? It was all so unsatisfying, so meaningless.

What had she been expecting anyway? An image flitted across her mind, followed by a memory—the faint prickle of stale adrenaline. Had she been hoping to find a real live Martian? Is that why she thought she had seen movement at the end of the tunnel? It didn't make sense. Why did humans, with all their powers of reason and finely honed senses, find reality so unsatisfying? What was the point of having a thirst that couldn't be quenched?

And what was the point of doing science when people weren't going to like the results? There was just no way to make everybody happy.

She moved to the back and collapsed onto her bench. "Lex, are you awake?"

"Hmmmph?" Lex rolled onto her back.

"I know you're tired, but I really have to talk."

Lex peered out from under droopy eyelids. "Okay, shoot."

"Remember those protesters? The ones outside the main gate in Houston?"

"Which ones? Right wing or left?"

"The Christians. What do you think they'll say about the halobacteria? Think they'll read our paper?"

"Doubt it. Either way, I don't really care." Lex rolled back onto her side.

"You realize that we're using an evolutionary argument—of sorts, anyway. We're saying the halobacterium probably came from Earth because it's on Earth's philogenetic tree. And you know the panspermia weirdos are going to grab that and blow it way out of proportion—the whole aliens-seeding-the-universe-with-life thing. And then the fundamentalists are going to—"

"So?"

Valkerie leaned forward. "So doesn't it bother you what people are going to think? Doesn't it bother you that a whole lot of people are going to be mad at us?"

Lex's shoulder twitched with what could have been a shrug. "Val, you think too much about what other people think."

"And *you* don't? What if they picketed our homes? I don't want to be monkey-trialed. I don't want to be . . . shunned." Valkerie slid onto her back and stared up at the ceiling of the rover. "Know what's really scary? I'm not even sure what my pastor will think. Or my old Sunday school teachers back home. I don't want to be the enemy. I'm just doing my job, trying to learn new things. I can't help it if God is a little more creative than some people want Him to be."

Silence.

"Lex?"

No answer.

Valkerie felt the warm trickle of tears running down the sides of her face. She swiped at her ears. Nine more months of hard labor. No shore leave. No vacations. No punching the clock and going home at the end of the day. And nobody to listen. Nobody to understand what it was like to be a sheep in wolf's clothing. It was too much. She couldn't do it. Didn't have the strength.

If she were at home she could give two weeks notice and find something easier. Something that would allow her to have a life. Even as a graduate student she had had time for friends. She'd dated—a little. But this . . . And now that they'd discovered life, Houston had been tripling their work schedules. She felt so hollow—so trapped. But what could she do? NASA hadn't sent her to Mars to round out her social calendar. Certainly not to fall in love.

She had a job to do.

But what if that job alienated her from everyone who cared about her? It was already alienating her from Bob. He didn't understand why she couldn't balance work with a relationship. She'd already tried it and failed. Miserably. She'd almost flunked out of school. Wouldn't *that* have made her father proud? And she hadn't felt for Sidney nearly what she felt for Bob.

She hadn't had seven billion people watching her every move either. Hanging on every press conference.

"Lex?"

No reply.

Valkerie raised her voice. "Lex, I don't think I can do it."

Silence.

A muffled creak sounded from the back of the rover. Thermal pings. The temperature was dropping.

Valkerie nodded her head and took a deep breath. There was no way around it. She'd accepted this work, and she had to do it. Even if the whole world was going to read her paper, dissect it with a dull-edged scalpel, and parade the bits they didn't like on pikes held high above their heads.

She could already hear their outraged tones. The whispers behind her back. The accusations to her face, people telling her what she did and did not believe. Griping that her faith got in the way of her science. That her science got in the way of her faith.

She squeezed her eyes shut, but she could already see the looks of condescension. The silent assumptions that would never be voiced.

But none of that mattered. She couldn't back out now. The next plane didn't leave Mars for nine more months. And anyway, she had given NASA her word. She had to at least try. Even if it meant being crucified.

Wednesday, March 18, 2015, 4:00 p.m., CST

Nate

Fresh back from the airport, Nate grabbed a mug of coffee and barged into the Flight Control Room. During actual flight operations, the FCR usually held twenty or thirty engineers. Today, barely a dozen were in, hunched over a few consoles, peering at data. Everybody was smiling. Happy, happy, happy.

"I hate to interrupt the love fest here, but I need Josh right now."

A young blond woman in a T-shirt and shorts pushed back from her console. "He's talking to EECOM in conference room two."

Nate spun around and charged out. Thirty seconds later, he found the room and burst through the door.

Josh sat at a table with EECOM, a short, older woman with red hair and rounded shoulders. As far as Nate knew, she didn't have a real name—just *EECOM*. Josh had drawn something on a tablet, and EECOM was looking across the table at him with that adoring look Josh got from every woman in the universe who had a pulse. Josh Bennett, rock star.

Nate wanted to heave.

Josh turned to look at him. "Hey, Nate, how was D.C.?"

"Hot and cold. Freezing rain, steaming president. She didn't like how we manhandled the righties on the whole *religious implications* thing and the lefties on the back-contamination thing." *I should have sent you—maybe that would have cooled her jets.*

Josh shrugged. "Even the nutcakes vote, but that's her problem not ours, right?"

"Right." Nate took a sip of coffee. "The good news is we might get more funding. NIH is going ape over Valkerie's find, and they're talking us up to the morons on the Senate budget committee. We're going to need you to be the face for the PR push."

Josh made a note on a pad of paper. "I'm on it, as soon as we get our comm issues fixed."

Nate narrowed his eyes. "Comm issues?"

"On the Deep Space Network. We're getting some intermittent static. Too regular to be an accident, not regular enough to track yet. Looks almost like somebody's jamming us."

Nate scowled. "Maybe it's our old friend, the saboteur."

"After all this time?" Josh reached for his coffee cup and almost knocked it over. "No way."

Nate studied EECOM. She had worked on the DSN years ago, and she was the acknowledged Unix wizard on Gold Team. "So track it down and fix it."

"That's a problem, sir." EECOM pursed her lips and frowned. "You can't fix a problem until you diagnose it. CommSat 1 and CommSat 2 are working perfectly most of the time."

"Most of the time ain't all of the time." Nate stood and began pacing, then turned to Josh. "When did that Russian ship reach Mars? Maybe they're jamming us."

Josh shook his head. "We don't know if it ever made it far enough to do a Mars Orbital Insertion. We've been eavesdropping on transmissions from their high-gain antenna since they launched. Those stopped about three weeks ago, and we haven't detected any signal since then."

Nate stopped pacing and leaned against the wall, drumming his fingers on the plasterboard. "We don't even know what mission the Russians are running. What kind of data were they sending back?"

Josh shook his head. "It was all encrypted, same as our data. All we know is they sent a lot of it. We're just trying to think of ways to do traffic analysis on it."

"Any way to decrypt it?"

Josh played with his coffee cup. "Decryption is a black art, sir. Right now we're using the DEADHEAD cipher for our own data, and nobody can break that. I gather theirs is similar."

"We don't know whether the National Security Agency could break it," EECOM said. "The NSA's capabilities are classified. It's possible they could provide us some assistance—"

"Get it." Nate sat down again. "I betcha the Russians are up to something."

"You can't talk to somebody over in RSA?" Josh said.

Nate sighed. After the fiasco on the International Space Station, the Russian Space Agency was in crisis. Again. "Who do I talk to? Yablonsky resigned. Petrov doesn't return my calls. Lifshutz is drunk all the time." He rested his chin in his hands. "What do we know about that mission anyway?"

"Nothing official," Josh said. "One of their engineers let slip to one of ours at a conference that it's a robotic orbiter mission. Of course, he had half a liter of vodka in him, and our guy had more, so it's anybody's guess. Officially, RSA never even acknowledged a launch."

"That's ridiculous," EECOM said. "One of our satellites photographed it on the pad. It was an Energia launch vehicle—"

Nate held up his hands. "I know, I know. Heard all about it."

"—and the burn signature when they left orbit showed a payload mass of eighteen tonnes."

Now, *that* was news to Nate. He gawked at EECOM. "Eighteen? But . . . that's almost as big as our Hab. Where'd you hear that?"

"Cathe Willison," EECOM said. "She's been in till midnight for the last eight months doing image analysis on the video clips. She developed a new method for calculating flame temperature and mass flux from images, and it proved that our first estimates were off by a factor of 2.4."

"Eighteen tonnes for one orbiter?" Nate shook his head. "Maybe it's a multiple deployment?"

"Nope," Josh said. "It's a single package, at least as of three weeks ago. We'd have detected multiple transmission sources otherwise."

Nate digested that. "What about landing capability? Maybe they're running a scoop-and-fly mission, trying to trump us."

Josh didn't say anything. EECOM just shrugged.

Nate pushed back, slamming his open palm on the table. "What you're telling me, bottom line, is that we don't know *diddly* about their mission!"

EECOM's face flushed. "Sir, that's not—"

"I betcha dollars to dimes they lost comm and now they're piggybacking through our CommSats." Nate pointed at

EECOM. "I need *you* to get to work decoding the transmissions they sent before their antenna bought the farm."

She shook her head, looking befuddled. "Sir, I deal with environmental systems. Cryptanalysis is not part of my job description and—"

Nate slammed both of his hands on the table. "What do you mean, not part of your *job* description? You're the best engineer I've got. Do you think putting out fires in D.C. is part of my *job* description? I kind of expect that you people are gonna step up to the plate and throw some blocks, whether it's your *job* or not."

Josh raised a hand. "Nate—"

"Don't sweet-talk me," Nate said. "Just get it done. That's all I'm asking."

EECOM leaned forward. "I don't think you understand the situation, Mr. Harrington. I don't have any training in cryptanalysis and I'm working fourteen-hour shifts trying to keep the Hab from poisoning our crew. If you have a problem with that—"

"I have a problem with the job not getting done. If you don't have what it takes—"

EECOM snapped to her feet. "This is the last straw, Mr. Harrington." She threw her security badge on the table and stalked to the door.

Nate stared at her. *Oops.* "Okay, let's be reasonable. Josh, talk to her. Make her sit down."

Josh stood up. "Margaret, please."

EECOM opened the door and stepped out. "I'm so very sorry, Mr. Bennett. You might inform Mr. Harrington that he can't *make* people do anything." The door clicked shut behind her.

Nate sighed and looked at Josh. "Go back and get her." Women liked Josh. He was young. Good-looking. Dark hair, rugged jaw—the works. All the female engineers were gaga over him, even the older ones, like EECOM, who ought to know better.

Josh picked up the security badge and studied it in silence. Two of those coveted little Silver Snoopy awards were clipped to the badge below the picture ID. He pocketed it. "I'll talk to her."

"Crazy woman."

"Nate—"

He stood up and began pacing again. Wasn't it enough that he had congress-critters to deal with? Now he had to handle overly sensitive female engineers? "Listen, Josh, I need somebody to take charge of this issue, and I'm appointing you. I'd do it myself, but I'm filling in for Perez half the time now. And it's only gonna get worse."

"Hope you get your promotion."

Nate spun around and glared at Josh. "What's that supposed to mean?"

Josh studied his hands.

"Okay, this is strictly between you and me, right?" *So don't tell a soul except your twelve best friends.* "I don't want Perez's job. I don't even want mine. I've given Perez written notice that I'm retiring when our boys and girls land on planet Earth. That gives me about . . . seventeen months of eating fire and then I get to bail. But when I walk out of here, I want this place to be in one piece, and I want NASA to still have a mission. And I want somebody good in charge."

Nate stopped pacing right behind Josh and clapped a hand on his shoulder. That was the carrot. Now for the stick. "I want you to solve this comm problem fast. Our kids are going to be doing more exploration, and comm is mission-critical. Fix it. Because if anything happens to them, you're out of here, just as far and as fast as I can kick you. Clear?"

"Clear."

"Okay, go do it." Nate walked out without waiting for a reply.

### Wednesday, March 18, 2015, 4:15 p.m., CST

### Josh

Josh caught up to EECOM at the north duck pond, just outside Building 30. As far as he knew, no ducks ever swam there, and he was probably the only person at JSC who called them duck ponds, but he liked to think that ducks *would* swim there if they had the chance. "Margaret, wait up!"

She jerked to a stop as though she'd been shot. Her shoulders rose and fell, accompanied by a hoarse sigh.

"Margaret, don't worry about Nate. He's not worth it."

EECOM spun to face him. "Mr. Bennett, I work very hard. I have taken on more responsibility than—"

"I know. You're the best of the best. This mission would have died a million deaths without you. Nate knows that."

"But he just said—"

"He's just being Nate, and we're the only ones he can manipulate without having to act nice. He knows good and well it's not our job to decode Russian transmissions. If he thought he could bully the NSA into doing it, he'd be in Washington right now."

"But cryptology is a very specialized field. And I don't have time to—"

"Nate doesn't expect you to do it. That little tantrum back there was for my benefit, not yours. He threatened to fire me if I don't fix it, but he didn't mean that either. He's just lashing out. Something's bothering him, and it probably doesn't have anything to do with the Russian transmissions." Josh held out Margaret's badge.

She reached out a reluctant hand to take it. "So what are you going to do? He said he would fire you . . ." EECOM straightened the Silver Snoopy pins on her badge and clipped it to her collar.

Josh laughed. "How many times have I heard that one? Don't worry. I'll think of something." They fell into step together as they headed back to Mission Control Center. "This place is crawling with whiz kids and wanna-be hackers who'd love to take a shot at the problem. In fact"—he gave her a wide grin—"I think I know just the person."

Josh paced back and forth in the empty conference room. 5:09. Where was she? She wasn't in er office. He had asked Cathe Willison to meet him at 5:00. Could she have gone to the wrong building?

Josh plopped down in the chair at the head of the table and drained his coffee. He should have gone with his first instinct and asked her out to dinner. She wouldn't have stood him up then. He leaned heavily on his elbows and pressed his palms into his eyes. But then he would have been using her. Manipulating. Just like he'd done with—

Josh jumped up from his chair and spun around to face the wall. Even now—twelve full months after the explosion—it still ripped through his mind, burning into his soul like a hot branding iron. Over and over. He couldn't escape it. Sure, he did it because he wanted to save NASA. But even with that excuse, would the pain ever go away? He'd almost killed them. His best friends in the solar system.

*"Hugs to you, Josh Bennett. We know how desperately you wanted this mission to succeed, and the extraordinary steps you took to make it so. Please don't blame yourself if . . . something happens to us. We know you did everything you could, and we love you."*

The words seared into his brain. Valkerie and the others had forgiven him. She'd even said she loved him. How could he ever make it up to her—to them? Nothing he could do would make it go away. He had betrayed them all. And if—no, *when*—they got back home . . . What then? How would he live with himself? The only thing holding him together now was the need to get them back. Now this thing with the static. Nate was barking up the wrong tree if he wanted to reopen the question about the saboteur. Josh had to fix this. Fast.

The door burst open. "Sorry I'm late." Cathe Willison's low, sultry voice spun Josh around. "The ISS damage-control meeting ran late, and my boss was there, so I couldn't very well—" Her eyes met Josh's and then went wide. "What's wrong? The Ares 7 . . . They didn't . . ."

"Nothing's wrong." Josh forced a smile. "I just had an assignment you might be interested in. Please, have a seat." He motioned to the chair across from his and pushed a covered Styrofoam cup in front of her. "Sorry about the coffee—it used to be hot."

Cathe lifted the cover and took a cautious sip. "It's fine." She studied him over her cup, her eyes large and liquid.

Josh stared back. Was she flirting with him? No, that wasn't it. Just . . . curious. Or maybe her eyes looked that way all the time.

"Well." Josh looked down at the table and tried to focus. "In the last few days, communication over the CommSats has been intermittently disrupted by static. Real regular static. Nate and I think it's a coded transmission from Mars . . . from Russia's new orbiter."

Her eyebrows went up. "The one that dark-launched?"

"Right. Margaret says you've spent a lot of overtime studying the burn profile when they did Trans-Mars Injection."

"Who's Margaret?" Cathe's voice sounded tight.

"EECOM."

Cathe nodded. Smiled. She seemed relieved. "Are you sure the payload even reached Mars? I thought transmissions cut out on it weeks ago. From what I heard, it was DOA at Mars."

"We don't know for sure, but we suspect." Josh leaned over the table. "They were transmitting direct to Earth until three weeks ago, but the signal was definitely getting weak near the end—like their high-gain antenna was having problems. Bob's been picking up a lot of static on radio traffic through the CommSats. Encrypted transmissions would sound just like static—by definition. It looks like maybe the Russians lost their high-gain antenna and decided to piggyback their telemetry through our comm satellites at Mars. If the Russians pick the wrong channel at the wrong time, their signal could drown out our crew. With disastrous results. Anyway, we *think* that's what's been happening, but we don't have any proof, and RSA is not likely to give us an explanation."

"So you want me to crack the code for you." Cathe's expression intensified, but Josh couldn't tell whether she was excited or displeased.

"If you're interested. I asked around, and all the managers tell me you're one of the best analysts we've got."

Cathe gave an eager nod. "I'd love to take a shot at it, but I'm not making any promises. Just send me the data. All of it." She reached a hand across the table.

Josh stared at it for a long second. Why the big rush? He'd been hoping to ask her to dinner, but if she had another appointment . . ."Thank you." He folded her hand in his. "So . . . how much do you know about cryptography?"

"Nothing yet." Cathe shook his hand, stood, and glided to the door. "But come tomorrow morning, I'll know enough to talk to the people who do. That much I *can* promise." She cracked open the door and slipped through it.

Josh followed her out and watched her walk down the hallway. No, the meeting hadn't gone at all as he'd expected, but she *had* taken the assignment. Wasn't that what he had been hoping for?

He shut the door and sank back down into the conference room chair. Cathe Willison. She wasn't nearly as cold as he remembered. A year ago, her suggestion that two of the Ares crew members had to die to save the others had thrown him for a loop. But hadn't everyone else said pretty much the same thing? For some reason, it had just been more shocking coming from a woman. Weren't guys supposed to be the ones who made the hard, dispassionate decisions? The steely-eyed missile men?

But Cathe was the one who could talk about the calculus of suffering as if it really were an arithmetic problem. And in the end, she was the one who solved their problem.

Josh closed his eyes and smiled. A lovely little paradox. A logical mind with a delicious voice. A brilliant engineer with dazzling blue eyes.

Wednesday, March 18, 2015, 10:15 p.m., Mars Local Time

Bob

Bob stood in the galley looking into the commons. A sickly chill tingled across the damp skin of his arms. Josh had sent him an e-mail after their session was interrupted, and it was now official. Someone was jamming their communications system.

Most of the message focused on the theory that it was the Russians—which all sounded reasonable enough—but if Josh was so convinced it was the Russions, then why all the questions about Kennedy at the end of the message? Did Josh think Kennedy was jamming them? It didn't make sense. Even if he was half the psycho Josh said he was, what would he have to gain? And how would he raise the issue with the others without sounding even more paranoid than he already was?

Valkerie and Lex were still talking about that stupid pink rock. You'd think they had discovered a real live Martian, not just a bit of petrified snot.

"Look at this." Valkerie's voice practically vibrated with excitement. "Alan Crane from Stanford is telling reporters, and I quote: 'We've known for years that Mars once had bacterial life—ever since the findings from the Allen Hills Mars meteorite.'" She stared at Lex. "How do you like that?"

Laughter from Lex. "Remember his article on inorganic mechanisms for magnetite crystal formation? Next thing you know, the pope will be taking credit for discovering that the Earth isn't the center of the universe."

"And I was worried nobody would believe us."

"I wasn't," Lex said. "I knew, once we had solid proof, they'd fall in line."

Bob stepped into the room and cleared his throat.

"Hi, Bob." Valkerie slipped out of her hammock mesh chair and unhooked it from the ceiling.

"Don't get up. Please." He moved to head Valkerie off before she could escape. "I heard you girls taking a break and thought I'd join you."

"Actually, I've got to get back to the lab. I—"

"But it's after 10:00 p.m. You've been working all day." Bob threw an imploring look at Lex.

Lex responded with her commander voice. "Bob's right. We're at a good stopping point. We can finish the test tomorrow."

Valkerie turned slowly and perched on the edge of one of the computer tables lining the wall. She looked ready to bolt any second.

"I . . . uh . . . wanted to talk to you about . . ." Bob swallowed back the lump that was forming in his throat.

"Well, I've got an early day tomorrow." Lex jumped up and made for the hallway that circled the central stairwell. "You two stay up and chat, but I've got to get some sleep."

Valkerie stood to follow. "I should probably—"

"Please, guys, both of you." Bob met Lex's questioning gaze and gave a slight nod. "It's about the Hampster. I'm worried about him."

Valkerie stopped in mid-stride. "About Kennedy? What now?" She leaned against the table and fixed him with a decidedly worried gaze.

Bob turned to her, surprised at the concern in her voice. "Well, um . . ." He felt the color creeping into his face. What could he say? He had promised Josh he wouldn't tell.

Lex took a step closer. "Bob, what's wrong?"

Safe ground. He needed to stay on safe ground. "Haven't you noticed how much time he spends in his room? And he's been so edgy. Exploding at every little thing."

"This is Kennedy we're talking about, right?" Lex shrugged. "I'd be worried if he wasn't edgy. He's not exactly a social butterfly." She turned toward the hallway.

"Well, I think he did this"—Bob indicated what was left of his hair—"to me on purpose."

Lex laughed. "Is that what this is all about? Your haircut? Don't worry. Lexie will make it all better in the morning. Night-night, widdle Bobby." She pinched Bob's cheek and disappeared around the bend in the hallway.

Valkerie started to follow.

"Valkerie, I'm serious. I think something's really wrong. Something psychological. Like maybe Kennedy's motherboard needs to be reseated. Couldn't you run some tests?"

Her eyes narrowed. "Kennedy seems fine to me. I mean, he's been through a lot, especially losing an eye. We all have, for that matter. If I were to pull out my syringes every time someone gets a bad haircut . . ."

Bob wished he could just tell her everything Josh had told him. But he'd promised. "It's not that, it's just . . ."

"What?" Valkerie's voice rang with impatience.

"Well, like this morning. He told me he actually liked gardening."

Valkerie sighed and turned to leave.

"He said *you* liked gardening with him. A lot. He practically implied that you two . . . that you were an . . ."

Valkerie pulled her shoulders back and took a step toward her room.

"Valkerie, wait." Bob placed a hand on her shoulder. "He acts totally different when you're around. You don't see the real Kennedy. It's like Jekyll and Hyde."

Valkerie spun to face him. "Is that what this is all about? What do you want me to do? Stop being nice to Kennedy? Stop talking to him? Bob, we live in a twenty-five-foot tuna can."

*I'm blowing this big time.* "All I'm asking is for you to check him out. Make sure he's okay. What's so wrong with that?"

Valkerie searched Bob's expression for what seemed like an eternity, then shook her head. "I'm not giving him an unscheduled physical. He'd want to know why. And what could I tell him? That you're . . . jealous?"

Bob looked at the floor. He'd brought this on himself. He should never have brought it up. "Well, at least be careful."

"About *what*?"

Bob winced at the frustration in Valkerie's voice. "The Hampster. You don't know him like I do."

"I don't know him? I've practically lived with him for the last two years. What's gotten into you? You used to be so . . ." Tears formed in Valkerie's eyes. "Bob, I'm sorry. I just can't . . ."

Bob swallowed hard. "Can't what?" It was all he could do to force out a whisper.

Valkerie looked at the floor and shook her head. Bob watched her turn and plod down the corridor. He took a step after her, arms outstretched, then let them fall to his sides. The firm click of her door as she closed it between them spoke clearly to his aching heart.

He'd lost her.

## Wednesday, March 18, 2015, 10:30 p.m., Mars Local Time

### Valkerie

Valkerie belly flopped onto her cot and buried her face in her pillow. Why did Bob always manage to ruin everything? Two days ago, she had made the biggest discovery of her life—maybe the biggest of the twenty-first century. She was supposed to be deliriously happy. Supposed to be celebrating, dancing the night away . . . not suffocating herself in a tear-soaked pillow.

Why couldn't he just forget his toolbox of petty jealousies and be happy for her? Why couldn't he celebrate with her? Dance with her. Sweep her off her feet. Crush her in his arms . . .

Valkerie pounded the pillow with her fist. She would *not* go there. It wasn't professional. It wasn't even moral. NASA hadn't spent fifty billion dollars to send her on a Love Boat luxury cruise. She had a job to do. Thousands of scientists were counting on her. Billions of people were watching her every move. Every day the newspapers were running stories.

A guilty pang stabbed through her. What was wrong with her? Hadn't she learned *anything* from her freshman year? She should never have put Bob off. Why hadn't she told him the second he asked? She only caused him—and herself—pain by putting off the inevitable. They weren't going to get to know each other any better. Not on Mars. The daily work schedule. Press conferences. The ever-present eye of the camera . . .

It all made a personal relationship impossible.

The longer she waited to say that, the harder it would be—for everybody. She knew what her answer had to be to Bob's marriage proposal. Whether the press liked it or not, she had to do the right thing. It was her moral duty.

Valkerie rolled out of the cot and dabbed at her puffy eyes in the mirror. She looked terrible. Good. Maybe that would make things easier.

She pushed open her door and tiptoed through the corridor to Bob's door. Knocking softly, she put her ear to the door for an answer. Nothing. She knocked a little louder. No way could she wake Kennedy with a few raps, but Lex was a light sleeper. "Bob, can I come in?"

Silence. She breathed a sigh of relief. He was probably asleep. Either that or he was too mad to talk to her. She shuffled off through the galley and into the commons. She could hardly blame Bob for being angry. Not after she'd acted like such a child. It was just that he put so much pressure on her. Every look he shot at her hung with an unspoken question.

A noise in the darkened commons made Valkerie jump. She waited for her eyes to adjust to the darkness. Bob stood staring out the porthole into the night sky. A heavy weight settled in her stomach.

Now was her chance. But how could she tell him? What could she say?

He turned slowly and fixed his expressionless gaze on her. Valkerie's heart stopped dead. His eyes were moist. A trail of spent tears glistened on his cheek. He was miserable. It was her fault. She had to do something. He was too nice, too heart-rendingly endearing, too good. Bob didn't deserve this. He deserved better than her.

She took a deep breath. "Bob, I don't know what to say. I'm so, so sorry."

He nodded in resignation. "It's okay. It's my fault. I shouldn't have asked you when I did. I put you on the spot. It was way too soon. All it did was make things awkward between us."

She took a step closer. "No, you were fine. I was the one . . . Don't you see, I'm the one who's . . . not right."

Bob shook his head slowly. His expression held so much sadness. So much pain. It made her want to cry out for forgiveness.

"Bob, I told you about how I almost flunked out of school my freshman year? Because I partied too much. Because of this guy."

Bob nodded. "Sidney Nichols. You were . . . in love with him, weren't you?"

Valkerie jerked her head up to meet his eyes. "No, I . . . Of course not. I was just infatuated. In love with the idea of being in love."

"Then . . ." Bob lifted his hands. "I guess I don't understand. If you're not in love with the memory—"

"Bob, don't you see? I . . . I *care* for you. Much more than I ever cared for Sidney. I almost let what I felt for Sidney ruin my life, and it was nothing compared to . . . If I . . . Don't you see how many people are counting on me? This mission cost taxpayers fifty billion dollars! Don't tell me you don't feel the pressure!"

He shrugged and his face contorted into a goofy grin. For some reason, his eyes seemed brighter.

Valkerie felt herself breathing easier, like the weight of his misery had just lifted off her chest. "So you don't hate me?"

Bob brightened even more. "Do you want an honest answer?"

"Bob, I'm serious. Don't you understand what I'm trying to tell you?"

"What?"

"I'm trying to tell you . . ." She searched the room, looking at everything but Bob's eyes. Why was saying *no* so hard? "Bob, I'm trying to tell you that I . . . can't say yes. Not now. Not . . . ever."

Bob stiffened. Like he'd just been stabbed. "But why? You just said you cared for me."

"I do, but . . . How can I be sure with all this?" She swept the room with a broad gesture. "We've been through so much together. How long have we been in danger? We almost didn't make it. Of *course* we have strong feelings for each other. It's only natural."

He took a step toward her.

She felt her heart constrict. *Don't. Please, don't . . .*

"So why can't you just trust those feelings? They're right. I know they are."

"How do you know it's not just psychology? Biology? Stimulus-response?"

"Because I'm not an amoeba."

"Bob, weren't you paying attention in training? Remember what the shrinks told us about the apes leaving the rain forest and crossing the open plains? They're so stressed and hyper-vigilant that if nothing attacks them, they end up turning on themselves and killing each other. How is being on Mars any different? No atmosphere. Cramped quarters. To-do lists a mile long. If we're ruled by our feelings, we could end up killing each other."

Bob took another step. "I'm not an ape either. I know what I know."

Valkerie stamped her foot. "I'm the only single female within a hundred million miles. Of *course* you're going to be attracted to me. Of course I'm attracted to you. It's only natural, but that's not a good enough reason to make a decision that could affect the rest of our lives, is it?" She drew a steadying breath. "I appreciate you asking me to . . . I really do. But it was wrong for me to ask for more time. I'm sorry. That only made things bad between us. I should have said no right away. I want to go back to being friends."

Bob sighed. "Once we're back on Earth . . . think you'll be able to trust yourself then?"

Valkerie shook her head. He wasn't getting it.

"No, not now." Bob held up a hand. "Later. Until then, I promise not to bring up the subject of marriage—or anything more than friendship. Not until after we're home and in a normal environment. And until then . . . Suppose we could just start over?"

Valkerie hesitated. Was it possible? Could they start over? *I hope so.* She gave a slow nod. "If you can forgive me."

Bob laughed, a ringing sound that broke like beams of sunshine through the storm clouds choking her mind.

Valkerie couldn't help it. She stepped forward and walked into his open arms, burying her face in his chest. She breathed out a long sigh, letting him enclose her in his strong arms and rock her gently from side to side, like a mother rocking her child. Wonderful. They should have had this conversation months ago. She pulled back to look up into Bob's face—and screamed.

Right outside the Hab, illuminated by the exterior lights, something large and alien had moved across the porthole.

### Wednesday, March 18, 2015, 10:45 p.m., Mars Local Time

### Bob

Bob's heart climbed into his throat. Valkerie's scream still echoed in his ears.

She pointed over his shoulder. "Out there! I . . . I saw something."

"What?" Bob turned to look out the porthole. "I don't see anything."

Footsteps thumped in the hallway. A second later, Lex came tearing into the commons. She threw on all the lights. "Val! What's going on?" She gave Bob an accusing look. "What did you do to her?"

"There's something out there!" Valkerie pointed again. "Turn the lights off. I can't see anything now."

Bob went to turn off the banks of LED lights. When he returned, Lex and Valkerie stood huddled around the dark porthole. "Do you see anything?" He peered over their shoulders into the night. Phobos and Deimos, the twin moons of Mars, weren't up in the sky. In another hour or so, one of them would probably come speeding low across the horizon. But at the moment—

Kennedy's uneven footsteps thudded into the commons. "What's going on out here?"

Bob heard the crack of a shinbone against the CamBot. *Oops.* Bob had left the short robot parked by the CommConsole after wasting all afternoon trying to fix its drive system.

Kennedy spent the next twenty seconds swearing and thumping around on one foot.

"Valkerie, what exactly did you see out there?" Bob asked.

"It was . . . something dark," she said. "And big."

"How could you see anything at all out there?" Lex asked.

Valkerie pointed to the Ares 10 Hab, the ship they had come to Mars in. Bob had tried to tow it closer to the Ares 7, but it had gotten stuck when the suspension system broke down. Right now it was about two hundred yards away, its outline invisible except where a few LEDs shone on its exterior. "I was looking up at Bob, and then I saw something behind him on the other side of the window. It was just . . . weird. But I know it was real—and close enough that I could see it from the lights on our Hab."

"But what was it?" Bob studied her features. "How big?"

"It was . . . pretty big," Valkerie's eyes went wide at the remembrance. "And it had an uneven surface. But other than that . . ."

"Are we talking dog sized, moose sized, elephant sized?" Bob's heart was thumping away. This was ridiculous. Absurd. There wasn't anything out there.

"I just don't know." Valkerie shook her head. "It could have been any of those. But . . . that's impossible. There aren't any animals on Mars."

"Probably a dust devil," Kennedy said. "The wind scooped up some dust and made a little mini-tornado. That's all it was. It's late, and your eyes are playing tricks on you. I say we should all go back to bed."

"There aren't any dust devils at night," Bob said. "No sun, no thermals."

Kennedy scowled at him. "How do you know? What else could it have been?"

Lex put a hand on Valkerie's shoulder. "It's been a long day. You're tired. Is it possible that—"

"Possible that what?" Valkerie's tone hardened. "That I'm seeing ghosts? I don't think so. You saw it too, didn't you, Bob?" She turned to look up into his face, her eyes begging him to back her up.

Bob hesitated. He hadn't seen anything. But then, he hadn't been looking.

Valkerie's eyes widened at his hesitation. "You had to have seen it! I pointed it out and you looked. Come on, Bob, tell them what you saw."

He cleared his throat, his heart sinking. He couldn't believe he was going to disappoint her again. "Uh . . . I must not have been looking in the right place. I'm sorry, Valkerie."

Anger flickered in her eyes. "So you don't believe me either. Nobody—"

"It doesn't matter," Lex said. "It's been a long day, and you're tired, Val. We all are. Let's go out and look for tracks in the morning. Hundred to one we don't find any."

"Second that motion," Kennedy said. "Let's get to bed, people. There's nothing out there, and that's an order."

"You can't just order there to be nothing out there," Valkerie said. "Bob, are you sure—"

"Yeah, I'm sure I didn't see anything." Bob shook his head. "My night vision isn't that good." He turned to Kennedy. "But I believe Valkerie. She doesn't make things up, and she knows what she saw. Tomorrow morning, as soon as it gets light, I'm going out to do an EVA."

"It's a poltergeist," Kennedy muttered.

The four of them headed toward the hallway in the darkness. A small hand brushed against Bob's, brushed again, then seized it. Bob turned to look at Valkerie.

"Thank you," she whispered into the darkness, just loud enough for him to hear. The squeeze she gave his hand sent shivers up his arm and straight into his heart.

# Part II: Bactamination

"Expecting a probe to return with possibly life-packed Mars rocks within a generation, a scientific advisory board is urging the U.S. government to begin work on a quarantine facility. The chance that martian samples would contain dangerous organisms is extremely low, most space scientists agree . . . . In the meantime, a facility that protects Mars rocks from terrestrial contamination and safeguards Earth organisms from possible extraterrestrial microbes will take seven years or longer to design, construct and test, the National Research Council scientists said in a report released Tuesday."

www.CNN.com, May 29, 2001

" . . . it has been estimated that these Martian rocks continue to rain down upon the Earth at a rate of about 500 kilograms per year. So, if you're scared of Martian germs, your best bet is to leave Earth fast, because when it comes to Martian biological warfare projectiles, this planet is smack in the middle of torpedo alley."

Robert Zubrin, *The Case for Mars*

# CHAPTER 7

Thursday, March 19, 2015, 7:00 a.m., CST

Josh

Josh waited impatiently while the FBI woman punched in a six-digit combination. What was he doing here? The whole thing was crazy. Kennedy wasn't jamming comm. It was the Russians. It had to be.

But what if EECOM was right? There was a good chance the signals were originating from Mars. If that was the case, then Kennedy was the only rational explanation — because crazy people didn't need rational explanations for what they did. And Kennedy was as crazy as they came.

"All the materials we confiscated are cataloged." Agent Yamaguchi pushed open the door and led the way in. "There's a photocopy machine in the corner. You'll be expected to copy anything you want to take with you. We need to keep the originals here. Chain of evidence, you know."

"Chain of evidence?" A lump rose up in Josh's throat. "For what investigation?"

"I'm guessing the same thing you're working on—the Hab explosion. If you have anything new on Kennedy . . ."

Josh shook his head. "Nothing yet. Just a hunch." *A hunch with a capital K.*

For a tension-filled second Yamaguchi pierced him with a penetrating look. Then she shrugged and held out a logbook. "Okay, sign right here." She pointed to the end of a long list of handwritten names. "And make sure that anyone who comes in here signs in and out."

Josh scanned down the list of names. Ed Sha . . . something, Jennifer Williams, Tom . . . squiggle. There must have been fifteen different FBI agents working on the case. They weren't kidding about still trying to find the saboteur. A cold sweat tingled down his spine. He'd hoped that they'd forgotten all about it. Apparently not. Josh signed his name, suddenly self-conscious. He'd heard that experts could tell a lot about a person just by their handwriting.

"If you need me, you've got my cell number." Yamaguchi shook her head. "Our people have been over this pretty carefully. If you want to see their analysis—"

"Um . . . better that I come at it with fresh eyes." Josh gave her what he hoped was a casual smile. "But I'd really appreciate reading your team's analysis after I've formed some impressions of my own. Thanks for offering."

Yamaguchi nodded and looked up at him with an unreadable expression.

Josh shifted and glanced around the small room. A filing cabinet. Government-issue desk. And one of those horrible old gray metal chairs—a Mercury-era original, from the looks of it.

Josh turned back.

Yamaguchi was still watching him. She didn't look suspicious or angry. Just the opposite. It was almost like . . .

"My niece Brittany is a major fan of the Mars mission." Yamaguchi broke into an embarrassed smile. "I was, um, wondering if you could autograph this *Scientific American* article?" She pulled a magazine from her big, floppy handbag. "She's eleven years old."

The ice in Josh's gut turned to water. He grinned. "Sure, I'd love to. I was crazy about space when I was her age." He flipped to the article and signed across the full-page picture of himself and the other team members—the team as it had been two months before he was dumped from the mission. He took the time to write a personal note. *Dear Brittany: Dream big and study hard and maybe you can go to Mars someday! Josh Bennett.*

He handed the magazine back to Yamaguchi. "By the way, I'm glad you've been a part of Nate's life these last couple of years. Life hasn't been easy since his wife left him. Thanks for helping bring back some of the old Nate."

Yamaguchi beamed at Josh, then looked at her watch. "Well, I'd better let you get to work. Let me know if you need anything."

Josh smiled her out the door, then turned to look at the stash. A gray filing cabinet sat in the corner, four drawers deep. He opened the top drawer. Everything was neatly filed by topic. *"Abrams Journal Articles." "Hartmann Journal Articles." "Internal Reports." "Interviews With Crew."*

The second drawer was nearly full too. The third and fourth contained textbooks on psychology, alphabetized by author. Josh pushed them closed without looking at them. How in the world was he going to make sense of all this? Somewhere in this file was the secret to Kennedy's weird behavior. Should he be systematic or try the shotgun approach?

He decided to riffle through each file and just get a feel for what was there. Look for patterns. Find the common thread.

No, better—find the one that stood out, the bright red thread running through the pastel tapestry that was Kennedy's life.

Two hours later, he came to the interview transcripts and straightened in his chair. All the scientific articles Kennedy had squirreled away had big sections highlighted in yellow. Josh smiled. *Thanks for the help, buddy.* Kennedy must have used a ruler—the yellow highlighter lines were straight as an arrow, and each exactly the same length, to the millimeter. That was Navy precision for you.

Josh scanned the information. Bottom line, Kennedy had picked out precisely those passages dealing with selection of the crew commander. Until about a dozen years ago, NASA had never really done much thinking about psychological aspects of crew selection. They basically used the shrinks to screen out the weirdos, and that was it. Then, right around 2003 or so, when Congress made the commitment to go to Mars, NASA decided to get serious. They brought in a bunch of high-priced shrinks from the military and academia.

And those guys had a theory. There was a particular kind of profile they were looking for in a crew commander. Kennedy had worked that profile into a precise, ten-point list noted in the margins of their papers. He had a nice, neat way of printing.

Josh read the cover of the interview: "An Interview with Mr. Kennedy Hampton, August 8, 2012." It had been almost a year since he'd first read this thing, and it still burned. He flipped it open and began reading.

Three pages in, a question caught his eye.

Q: How do you relate to the commander, Mr. Joshua Bennett?

A: Josh is an excellent commander. He's quick and decisive and doesn't hesitate to move rapidly in a crisis. He doesn't dillydally around trying to get a consensus when there's an emergency. He just gives the order, and we follow it. I was trained to do that in the Navy, to follow the orders. We all were. We love the guy—we'd do anything Josh asks.

Josh leaned back in his chair. Point four on Kennedy's list of what the shrinks were looking for was "Commander should not dominate the crew." The Hampster had really punched that button. And made it sound like a compliment. Josh kept reading.

Q: Please rate the diversity of the group.

A: We were pretty diverse coming into this thing. I was raised in the South in a fairly well-to-do family. Lex is half-Japanese and comes from Santa Barbara, where she was raised by a single mom. Bob comes from a middle-class Polish family in Chicago, and I think he grew up Catholic. But Josh has really pulled us together into a great team. He grew up in Houston, and his dad worked for NASA, and he's got us all thinking as one. I know what Lex is thinking before she says it, or Kaggo, or Josh. It's like one brain and eight hands. You wouldn't believe how efficient we are now. And that's all Josh's doing. He's great at welding us together into a team.

Josh slammed the sheaf of paper down on the desk. *What a load of lies!* Kennedy was doing a major number on the shrinks—and on Josh. Point six on the shrinks' list was "The crew must represent a diversity of viewpoints—the more the better."

Kennedy had nailed Josh to the wall, but he'd been careful to make it sound like high praise. Josh rubbed his eyes. The Hampster had set him up—he'd known that for a full year. But he still needed an answer to the real question. What was Kennedy up to now? A guy like Kennedy needed a mission like he needed air. He needed to be the center of attention, the hero. How could a one-eyed pilot grab the spotlight while he was still on the ground?

A loud rapping interrupted his thoughts.

Josh went to the door and opened it.

Cathe Willison stood there in jeans and a Bay-To-Breakers T-shirt. "Hi, Josh! Did you forget our appointment at 8:30? I've been looking all over for you. Your secretary said—"

"Sorry." Josh looked at his watch. 9:15. "I got . . . sidetracked. How are you doing on that decryption problem? Any evidence it's coming from Mars?"

She shrugged. "Nothing so far. I've made some progress on the decryption, but it's slow. Can I come in? Or should we go somewhere else?"

"Please. Come on in." Josh stood aside.

She brushed past him with the faint scent of spring flowers.

He pointed to the logbook. "You'll . . . uh, need to sign in. Sorry, there's only one chair. Have a seat and fill me in."

Cathe signed the register and slipped into the chair, crossing her legs and leaning back with her hands behind her head. "Okay, here's the story. I talked to the Gold Team CATO and a couple of our guys who've trained in Star City and really know the Russians. And I called a guy at the National Security Agency. The Russians have traditionally used a straightforward 128-bit encryption scheme for their data transmission. They don't know it, but we can crack it really fast, thanks to a black box NSA gave us a few years ago."

Josh began pacing. "And now they've changed the code, is that it?"

"It's a 512-bit code now, and the NSA box doesn't work."

"So that means . . ." Josh did the arithmetic. "That means it's going to be four times harder to crack now, right?"

Cathe shook her head. "Not hardly. Every extra bit makes it twice as hard. The complexity is exponential. It's two raised to the 384th power times harder than it was before."

Josh felt his eyes bulging. "That's a big number."

"It's huge. You know how many protons there are in the universe? Ten raised to the 90th power. It's way bigger than that."

He stopped in his tracks. "So you're telling me there's no hope of cracking this encryption scheme."

"I didn't say that." Cathe leaned forward in her chair. "My ex-boyfriend Gary was doing quantum computing at Caltech before he moved to Houston. And you would not believe what those guys are doing now. The NSA took that whole project black a few years ago, and that's when Gary decided to get out of it. Now he's working for ExxonMobil."

Josh nodded, his mind buzzing. "Apparently, you don't mind working with NSA."

"My father worked for them until he died. This guy I talked to is good, really good. He can't tell me much, but NSA is working on a box that can break 512-bit encryption. He's willing to let us test a prototype."

"Great." Josh forced his eyes away from her face. "So . . . if that works, I guess our mystery will be solved."

Cathe leaned forward as if she was about to stand.

Josh scrambled for something to say.

"Um . . . I'm sorry to hear about your father. Mine died a few years ago—heart attack."

"It was pneumonia with my dad." Cathe looked up at the filing cabinet. "So what brings you to this dinky little room?"

Josh returned the file he had been studying and closed the cabinet drawer.

Cathe's wide eyes studied him. "Sorry. Did I say something wrong?"

Josh licked his lips. Why not? She had a Secret clearance. Another perspective might be just what he needed. And if Kennedy was behind the comm problems, then she had a need to know. "Listen . . . I need your word that you won't talk to anyone about it."

Cathe raised her right hand. "Scout's honor."

Josh filled her in on what he knew.

Cathe leaned back in her chair and closed her eyes. She looked so different with her eyes closed. Like her face was somehow softer—warmer.

"Here's an idea." Cathe opened her eyes. "Let me toss a what-if at you and see what you think. What if we take Kennedy's comments at face value? Why don't you read through his interview again and pretend Kennedy is telling the absolute truth about what he thinks is important? What does he value?"

"He values order, for one thing." Josh looked down at the stack of papers scattered about the floor. "Neatness. Precision."

"That's his Navy training. What else?"

"I'd have to read the transcript again." Josh picked it up. "If you want, you can have a look through those files there." He began flipping through the transcript.

Fifteen minutes later, Cathe hissed quietly.

Josh looked up. She was carefully peeling a label off the front cover of one of Kennedy's notebooks. "You really shouldn't be—"

A line of handwritten text appeared behind the sticker. Josh leaned in closer but couldn't make out any words. "What—"

"It looks like some sort of coded message. Think it's Kennedy's handwriting?" Cathe pulled a phone out of her pocket and photographed the four lines of text.

"It's definitely Kennedy's writing, but what do you suppose it means?"

"He referred to it more than once." Cathe held out the sticker. The sticky side of the label had picked up multiple, overlapping prints of the text.

Josh nodded. *Clue number one.* "So . . . what's your best guess?"

"Isn't it obvious?" Cathe made typing motions with her fingers in the air. "This is his password list." She narrowed her eyes and studied Josh. "Any chance you could get me five minutes on the computer in his office?"

Thursday, March 19, 2015, 10:30 a.m., Mars Local Time

Valkerie

Valkerie flung her phone at her pillow. Of all the stupid orders! She had a million experiments to run on the most important find of the century, and Houston wanted her to waste time examining a crew member who was perfectly fine.

"Bob!" Valkerie stalked through the galley and into the commons.

He wasn't upstairs.

"Bob!" She plunged down the central staircase and circled to the workshop.

Bob sat on a stool, taping an EVA suit. He smiled at her when she came in. "Hey, Valkerie, want to see what I—"

"How could you do this to me? You *know* how much work I need to do on the stromatolite."

Bob seemed genuinely puzzled. "How could I do what?"

"How could you—" Valkerie lowered her voice to a whisper. "How could you nark on Kennedy? Now the shrinks want me to do a complete neurological exam on him. Do you know how much time that's going to waste? I don't—"

"It wasn't me. I never even talked to Flight Med."

"Right, and I suppose they were just eavesdropping last night when you asked me to examine him."

"I promise. It wasn't me." Bob looked perplexed. "Maybe Lex said something. She talked to Houston this morning."

"Lex? Oh *right*." Valkerie turned and stormed out of the workshop. That comment didn't even deserve a response. Lex would never nark on Kennedy—not to Flight Med. She knew how many experiments they had to do. Valkerie swung through the stairwell hatch and almost ran into Lex on her way down the stairs.

"Hey, Val, ready to get back to work on the sequencing?"

"I can't," Valkerie spat out the words. "I've got to do a med exam on the Hampster."

"You're kidding. What's wrong?"

"Terminal jealousy."

Lex raised an eyebrow.

"I know the answer to this already, but you didn't say anything to the flight docs about Kennedy, did you?"

"Me? Talk to Flight Med?" Lex let out a haughty laugh, then frowned. "You don't think it was Bob? He wouldn't—"

"Right. Kennedy narked on himself." Valkerie ran up the stairs three at a time and headed for the med center. She threw open the instrument bin. Stethoscope, sphygmomanometer . . . Where was the electroencephalograph? She pulled out the lower bin and riffled through the contents, tossing everything she needed into a plastic washing pan. Okay, now for the ticklish part. Valkerie went up to Kennedy's room and knocked on the door. "Kennedy, it's me, Valkerie. I need to talk to you."

A confusion of bumps and muffled scrapes sounded through the door.

Valkerie waited . . . and waited. What could be taking so long? Should she knock again? She raised a hand.

Kennedy's voice sounded. "Okay, come on in."

She opened the door slowly and peeked into the dimly lit room.

"Hey, Valkerie, sorry about the mess." Kennedy sat on his cot, leaning against the wall. "The maid service here is terrible. I've a mind to complain to the management."

Valkerie picked her way among the debris that littered the floor. *What a pigsty.* It smelled horrible.

Kennedy looked from Valkerie to the pan she carried—and stiffened. Smiling, he leaned forward in a formal bow. "So what can I do you for? Got any new results on the *Halophilis valkilexus*?"

She didn't even try to hide her frustration. "Like they're even giving me a chance to work on it. Unfortunately, I've got to give you a med exam. Flight docs' orders."

Kennedy shook his head. "You don't have time for this kind of nonsense. Don't those idiots know you've got real work to do?"

"Apparently not." Valkerie set the pan down on Kennedy's desk.

"Tell you what. Just leave that stuff here. I'll take my temperature, shine a flashlight in my eyes, and whack myself a couple of times with a hammer. They'll never know the difference."

"Thanks for the offer," Valkerie pulled the blood-pressure cuff out of the pan and wrapped it around Kennedy's arm, "but if I know them, they'll want to look at all the data themselves." Valkerie pumped up the cuff and released the pressure. 140 over 90—a bit on the high side, but she'd released the air pretty fast. Close enough. She tossed the cuff into the pan and brought out the EEG.

Kennedy eyed it—then her. "So why the sudden interest in my health?"

She bit her lip and started untangling the electrode leads. What would Kennedy do if he found out Bob had narked on him?

Kennedy leaned close and whispered, "It was Bob, wasn't it? I've been really worried about him."

Valkerie looked up from the electrodes. "What do you mean?"

"Don't tell me you haven't noticed. He's been downright paranoid. Even more than usual. And all the accusations about my driving. I don't know what to make of that."

"He's just being Bob. Now relax. The gel's a pain, but at least it's painless." Valkerie roughed up his scalp with grit and dabbed twenty-seven blobs of electrophoretic gel in a grid pattern on Kennedy's head. Then, working the gel down to his scalp, she pressed the filamentous electrodes into the greasy patches.

"And what about all that talk about the Russian satellite jamming our communications?" Kennedy rolled his eyes. "After all we've been through . . . almost seems like some kind of bizarre delusional disorder—maybe a jealousy thing."

"Delusional disorder? Bob?" Valkerie flipped on the EEG. Five traces squiggled across the instrument's LCD panel. The alpha trace was almost flat, but the lower-frequency theta fluctuated wildly, pegging at the upper and lower amplitude bounds. Either Kennedy was more stressed out than he looked, or she had the gain way too high. She flipped the instrument over to check. Out of the corner of her eye, a rapid motion distracted her.

Kennedy was rocking back and forth on the cot, holding his right hand in front of him. A trickle of blood ran down his wrist.

"Kennedy, what happened?" Valkerie reached for his hand and tried to hold it still.

"Cut myself on the cot."

"Let me look at it." Valkerie forced open his fingers.

An inch-long slice ran down the tip of his index finger. Painful, but not bad enough for stitches.

Valkerie retrieved a first-aid kit from the med center and bandaged the cut. "So what happened?" She got down on her hands and knees to examine the cot's frame. There wasn't anything that could have caught on Kennedy's finger.

"Probably just an aluminum splinter. Don't worry. I'll find it," Kennedy said. "Just don't tell Bob."

Valkerie looked up at Kennedy. "Why not?"

"You know how he is." Kennedy dropped his voice. "Treats every little splinter like it's an international incident. And, well . . . right now I think it would be best to give him some space."

She pushed up onto her knees. "What do you mean? Because of the haircut?"

Kennedy laughed. "That was just an excuse. I told him I couldn't cut hair, but he made me do it anyway. I didn't understand then, but I do now."

"Understand what?"

"I don't know why, but he's been looking for a fight for weeks."

Valkerie frowned. Bob? Looking for a fight? "No way. I don't for a second believe Bob would ever—"

"Bob would ever what?"

Valkerie started and spun to look.

Bob stepped into Kennedy's room and fixed an icy stare on Kennedy. The air in the room crackled with tension.

Valkerie scooted back, taking in Bob's fists, which were clenched at his sides. He looked agitated. Angry.

Kennedy gave her a knowing look and then turned to Bob. "Nothing, I was just about to ask Valkerie to help me in the outdoor greenhouse tomorrow when she's through with the last of the sequencing. What do you think, Valkerie? Mind giving me a hand?" He gave her an almost imperceptible nod and a wink.

*What in the world is this about?* "Sure, I guess." She looked up at Bob.

His eyes went wide, then he fixed Kennedy with a glare. No doubt about it. What she saw on Bob's face was anger. Raw and undisguised. Veins bulged at his neck. His whole frame seemed to shake. Just when Valkerie thought he was about to strike out at Kennedy, Bob turned and hurried from the room.

She sighed and began scooping equipment back into the plastic pan. This whole med exam thing was a charade, and she didn't see the point of playing it any longer. So Kennedy's glue was a little soft. Big deal. She'd been telling Flight Med that for months. The one who really worried her wasn't Kennedy—it was Bob.

# CHAPTER 8

Thursday, March 19, 2015, 11:45 a.m., Mars Local Time

Bob

"Okay, Bob, this is going to be kind of short, but I can fix it." Lex stood behind Bob, but he could hear the frown in her voice. "Sort of fix it. Next time, don't let Kennedy near your hair."

"I thought—" Bob stopped. Lex wouldn't understand.

"Thought what?" Lex sprayed water on Bob's hair and worked it in with her fingers.

"Oh, nothing. Just wanted to talk guy-talk with him. You know."

"Meaning you wanted to talk about women."

*Of course not.* Kennedy had wanted to talk about women. About Valkerie. Bob had wanted to talk sports. The weather. Whatever. Guy-talk. *And, oh yeah, are you the jerk who's jamming the Deep Space Network?*

Lex grabbed the scissors. "Now be good. This is going to hurt you more than it hurts me." She began snipping hair.

Bob closed his eyes so he couldn't see his reflection in the small mirror set at a crazy angle on the workbench. A sound brought his eyes open, and he saw Lex close the door to the workshop. *What . . . ?*

Lex lowered her voice. "Kaggo, can I ask you something personal?"

He didn't say anything. She was going to ask no matter what he said.

"What's going on with you and Valkerie?"

Bob took a deep breath and held it. He didn't want to talk about that.

"Let it out, Bob. Something's bugging you bad, and it'll help to unload it. My lips are sealed, I promise."

"Have you noticed how much time Kennedy spends with Valkerie?" The words were out before he could stop himself. Oh well, in for a penny . . ."He's always hauling her to one of the greenhouses, or wanting to help her when she's on kitchen duty. I mean, it's not like Kennedy to be so eager to work, right? And then that stunt with the flower yesterday. First flower on Mars. Big deal, right? But he made it a big deal. He makes me sick, just watching him." Bob closed his eyes. There. He'd said it.

"Hey, Kaggo, I'll ask the question again, and this time maybe you'll answer it. What's going on with you and Valkerie?"

*Huh?* Bob turned his head to look at her. "Didn't I just—"

"Bob! I can't cut your hair when you squirm like that! I almost cut off your ear!"

"Great, that's just what Kennedy said. What is this, a conspiracy?"

Lex stopped snipping and hit him with a chunk of silence.

"Hey, Lex, that was a joke. Right?"

"You say so." Lex spent several minutes just trimming.

Finally Bob couldn't stand it any longer. "Valkerie doesn't even like Kennedy, right?"

Lex slammed down the scissors and walked around in front of Bob. "Mars to Kaggo, come in! I'm talking about you and her. Why are you talking about him and her?" She mussed up Bob's hair with both hands, grinning. "Now spill. You and Valkerie were out in the commons last night doing *something.* And then she shrieks like she's trying to raise the dead. I come running, and what do I find? You with your arms around her, and she's freaking out. And if you think that cock-and-baloney story she made up about something scary outside . . . Well, come on! There weren't any tracks out there this morning. What did you do to her?"

Bob just stared at Lex. "I . . . care for her. I really admire who she is and what she is. I wouldn't do anything to hurt her."

"She didn't sound like she was being admired. She sounded upset. Really upset." Lex folded her arms across her chest and glared at him. "Listen up, Kaggo. Valkerie's my friend—maybe the first honest-to-God woman friend I've ever had. So don't give me this nonsense about how you *care* for her, like she's a car or something. Women don't just want to be cared for. They don't want to be admired from afar. And that old song about how girls just wanna have fun—you heard that one? That's a lie. A girl wants to be *loved,* Kaggo. So you just listen to mean old Lex. You either start acting like you love her or you back off, 'cause you're making her crazy. You keep messing with her head, and I'm gonna kick you right into orbit. You got that?"

Bob swallowed hard. "Sure, Lex. I got it." *Except I promised last night to back off. All the way off, until we get back to Earth. And I'm going to keep that promise.*

Lex smiled and pinched his cheek. "She likes you, big guy, but I think she wants to be chased some first. So you just pursue and pursue and pursue, all right?"

"Um . . . right." Bob stood up and grabbed the mirror. "Are we done here?"

"You're done for the next six months." Lex whacked him with a comb. "Now get out there and give chase."

Bob just sat there. *Right. Give chase. Fat chance.*

"Kaggo, here's a thought." Lex backed up to the door to cut off his escape until the lecture was over. "We're starting to get low on food in the pantry, and I just saw on the sat-pix that there's a dust storm picking up down at the South Pole. Somebody needs to go get a bunch more food from our stash in the other Hab. How about you and Valkerie do that tomorrow morning? Take the rover, go over there, and . . . don't rush. Just talk. Be natural. Okay?"

"Sure, Lex." Bob grinned at her. "Thanks."

She stepped aside. "Good luck, big guy."

Bob opened the door and went out. The sound of water running upstairs in the galley meant Valkerie was on kitchen duty for lunch. Maybe he could go help her. Yeah, that would be the ticket. Just kind of talk while they worked together. That'd be natural. He could just be friendly. That wouldn't break his promise. It would be a nice, fresh start.

Bob started up the stairs, then jerked to a halt at a different sound drifting from the kitchen. Kennedy's voice. Laughter. Kennedy and Valkerie laughing together.

A surge of anger pumped through Bob's veins. Clenching his fists, he ran up the stairs two at a time. What did Kennedy think he was doing? Bob stopped at the top of the stairs. No.

Valkerie was talking now. He couldn't just barge in on them. What would she think? It wasn't a crime to talk. Was it?

Bob slipped through the hatch and circled back through the corridor to his room. He shut the door and collapsed onto his cot. What was wrong with him? *Hypervigilance. That has to be it.* But was that all? Or was he losing his mind the old-fashioned way? One brick at a time. He lay on his back and tried to breathe deeply. In through his nose, out through his mouth. Big breaths. From the diaphragm.

A hoarse sigh shivered down his spine. Bob sucked in his breath and held it. A rasping hiss sounded in his ears. The sound of breathing. *Kennedy's* breathing. Bob jumped up and looked in his closet, but nobody was there. Of course not. Kennedy was in the galley.

He slumped back down on his cot, listening. The breathing intensified to a pant. Louder and louder until it echoed off the walls and merged with the sound of Bob's own panicked breath.

*We've all been running on too many volts for way too long. We're all going bonkers at once. Every one of us.*

Thursday, March 19, 2015, 1:00 p.m., CST

Josh

Josh punched the elevator button. He was going to get to the bottom of this, no matter what.

Cathe Willison puckered up her nose. "I can't believe all those files were so . . ." She threw her hands in the air.

"Immaculate?" Josh looked at her as they reached the fifth floor and the chrome doors *ching*ed open.

"Obsessive."

"He's a Navy pilot. They stay alive by being obsessive." Josh turned right and led the way to the double doors separating the world at large from the astronauts' offices. "Ever been in the inner sanctum?" He punched in the combination on the metal buttons and pushed open the door. He stole a glance to see if she was one of those astro-groupies who thought this was Mecca.

She seemed oblivious to it all. "I had a weird aunt who was obsessive like that," Cathe said. "You know, every pencil lined up just so. Every shoe, every blouse, every towel. I bet even the cockroaches marched in formation."

Josh walked down the aisle and turned right to the offices of the Ares 10 Prime Crew. Nothing had changed in over a year. The first door had a little name tag beside it in Bakelite letters: *Kennedy Hampton*. Josh pushed the door open.

Cathe gasped.

The place was a mess. A ramshackle mound of papers a foot deep perched on the desk. A paperback novel lay on the chair, half its pages coming loose from the cracked binding. Stacks of manuals littered the floor. Josh opened a filing cabinet. Twinkie wrappers covered the front half of the drawer. Loose papers were jammed into the back part.

Cathe reached in and pulled a sheet out. It was an article about flight-crew selection. The abstract was clumsily underlined in red ink. Comments scrawled their way down the margin.

Josh stared at the chaos around them. What was going on here? "This is really weird."

Cathe dropped the article on Kennedy's chair. "Show me the other offices."

He opened Valkerie's office next. A neat, feminine room. Pictures of an older man—Valkerie's dad. Josh had met him once. Nice guy. There was one picture of a young couple in wedding clothes. The styles and hair told Josh the photo had to be about forty years old. The young man smiling out was a younger version of Valkerie's father. The woman was stunning—a twentyish version of Valkerie, but not quite Valkerie. That would be her mother. If Josh remembered correctly, she died when Valkerie was off at school.

"Let's try the other offices." Cathe set down the Ares 10 flight team photo she'd been examining. "There's nothing much here."

Lex's office was next. It looked very Air Force fighter jock. Posters of planes. Pictures of Lex in a red uniform playing volleyball. A photo of an older Japanese woman. A couple of triathlon trophies.

When they got to Bob's office, Josh hesitated. "What exactly are we looking for?"

Cathe shrugged. "It's a fishing expedition. We're looking for fish."

Josh pushed open the door. As he expected, it was neat. Not compulsive, just neat. Bob liked things orderly. He had posters of old cars on the walls. A photo of a candy-apple red Mustang on the desk. A family portrait of a man and woman with Bob and a guy that had to be his brother. The brother looked—different. Like he was there but not really there. Bob wore his trademark goofy grin.

"See any sharks?" Josh glanced at Cathe.

She shook her head. "No surprises. Okay, I'm calibrated now. I know what normal is. Let's look at Kennedy's office again. I'm ready to try out his computer."

"Hang on. We can't log on without administrator privileges." Josh pulled out his cell phone and led the way back to the Hampster's office. He punched in a number. It answered on the second ring.

"Bruce Dickey here."

"Hey, buddy. Josh Bennett. I need a password for a machine over here in the astronaut offices. Kennedy Hampton's old clunker."

Two minutes later, Josh typed in the administrator password, then held the chair out for Cathe. "Care to drive?"

She plunked into the chair and adjusted its height. "First thing to do is to sort all files on his hard drive by date, going backward. That'll tell us what he was up to just before launch."

She pulled up a search window and started typing.

Josh cleared some papers off a chair and sat down to watch her work. Even if she didn't find anything, it was a pretty good show. Lightning fast, efficient—and very easy on the eyes.

Finally Cathe leaned back in her chair and licked her lips. "Okay, I see a ton of files—incredibly well organized. Are you sure this is the same guy who did the Twinkie-wrapper decor for this office?"

Josh nodded. "What about his applications? Do you want to check his e-mail?"

Cathe opened the e-mail program and scanned it. "Wow. A separate folder for each person, organized hierarchically. He kept it all clean, but it'll take a while to go through them all. But my hunch is that those passwords are for web sites. People either use the same on on everything or they use a different one for every site and have to write them down. I'm guessing he was using one-offs."

Josh nodded.

She opened up Kennedy's Web browser and opened the history folder. "Interesting!"

Josh leaned forward, scanning. He gave Cathe a sideways glance. *Interesting* wasn't the word. *Suspicious* was more like it. "He must have scrubbed it clean just before he left."

Cathe pulled down the Favorites menu. "Let's see where he hangs out."

The Favorites menu looked innocuous enough. All the submenus were the defaults, except one. Cathe clicked on it. The submenu showed four entries, each just a number: 1. 2. 3. 4.

Cathe selected *1.* A window opened up to the EZMail Web site.

Josh drummed his fingers on the desk. "What's he up to? EZMail is pretty harmless. Why call it 1? Why not just label it EZMail?"

"1, 2, 3, 4. Cute." Cathe yanked out her phone and flicked it open. She typed in one of the numbers she had photographed from Kennedy's notebook into the *Username* field. She tried the second number in the *Password* field.

The screen changed. *Your EZMail account is currently inactive, because you have not accessed it in 15 months. Would you like to reactivate it?*

Cathe clicked the Yes button.

The screen changed again. There was nothing in the In Box or the Out Box. Cathe clicked on the Addresses button. Half a dozen entries popped up.

Josh read the names out loud. "Kenji Hirota. Mitsuru Yamamoto."

"All Japanese," Cathe said. "That's odd. Does Kennedy have friends in the Japanese Space Agency?"

"Not that I know of," Josh said. "I've got friends there, but I don't recognize any of these names."

Cathe expanded one of the nicknames. "This guy goes to Unpronounceable Technical University."

"Or he did a couple years ago." Josh thought a moment. "Do a search for this guy. Let's see where he is now."

Cathe typed in the first name, then pasted in the name of the university.

The browser window filled with the first twenty entries. The first was titled "Résumé of Kenji Hirota." Cathe clicked on it.

Josh pulled his chair closer. Together, he and Cathe scanned down the résumé. The guy had recently graduated from his university and taken a job at Motorola in Tokyo. He was an electrical engineer, honors student. Interested in signal processing, wavelets, noise reduction—

Josh stopped. Read again. Then he leaned back in his chair. *Satellites.*

Cathe put her finger on the word and gave Josh a startled look. "Josh . . ."

"Bookmark this page, and let's see what else this guy has on his Web site." Josh grabbed a pad of paper and began taking notes.

Cathe clicked on the guy's Main Page. Josh began scribbling furiously on his paper. When he looked up, Cathe was leaning in close to the screen, her mouth hanging open. "Josh, what was the internal code name for the CommSats?"

"Hermes," Josh said.

"No, that's what AresCorp called it. What did we call it in-house before we took delivery on it?"

"Gabriel."

"Well, I think we've just found Lucifer." Cathe pointed at an indistinct blob in the upper-left corner of the onscreen schematic. "Because unless I've gone completely blind, the fine print there says GABRIEL."

# CHAPTER 9

Friday, March 20, 2015, 6:30 a.m., Mars Local Time

Valkerie

Valkerie lay perfectly still. The tapping sounds had stopped, but whatever was making the noise was still there. Just outside the Hab wall. Waiting. Listening to her while she listened to it.

Cold sweat ran down her face and soaked into her damp pillow. An involuntary shudder ran through her body.

The tinkling sounds started again as if in response. As if the whole Hab was covered with tiny metallic spiders. Listening for her. Boring through the hull.

"Bob!" Valkerie threw off the covers and stumbled from her cot.

The night air hit her sweat-drenched body like an arctic blast.

"Bob!" Her voice was lost in the violence of the shivering fit that seized her. They had gotten through. They were inside the Hab. Valkerie flung open her door and staggered into the corridor. The tiny feet of a million spiders prickled across her skin. She could feel them boring into her stomach, injecting her with a fiery venom.

She fell writhing to the floor, rolling over and over, screaming out the terror that welled up inside her.

Hands grabbed her from every direction. Voices. Panicked screams.

Valkerie fought to her hands and knees before a spasm of nausea convulsed her frame. She vomited again and again until, finally, weak and trembling, she let herself collapse into the hands that held her suspended above the floor.

The voices receded to a distant whisper—a whisper that buoyed her up into the music of her name. She was Valkerie, and she would be just fine.

### Saturday, March 21, 2015, 10:00 a.m., CST

### Josh

Josh pushed open the door to Kennedy's apartment and handed the key back to Agent Yamaguchi.

She led the way. "I doubt you'll find anything here. Our team was pretty thorough."

Cathe followed her in. "They missed the passwords and Kennedy's EZMail account."

Yamaguchi gave a brusque nod. "Congratulations, Miss Willison. That was a lucky catch. If you find anything else, which isn't likely, I'll need to log it right away."

Josh followed the pair into the living room and gasped. The place was immaculate.

"Do your agents do windows too?" Cathe circled the room.

Yamaguchi sat down primly on the couch. "I assure you, everything is exactly as we first found it. And you will keep it that way. Am I making myself clear?"

"Crystal." Josh grinned at Yamaguchi and then turned to exchange glances with Cathe.

Her look said it all. Kennedy's apartment couldn't have been any more different from his office. It was eerie.

Josh wandered through the two-bedroom apartment. The kitchen, living room, both bedrooms, office, two baths—every room was neat. Meticulously so.

Compulsively.

Josh looked at Cathe. "Where do we start?"

"You go through the living room. I'll play with his computer. Keep your eyes open for anything weird."

"Right."

An hour later, after he had finished going through every book on the shelves, Josh turned to Kennedy's TV and the shelves of carefully labeled DVDs on either side of it.

It turned out Kennedy liked shoot-'em-and-kick-'em flicks. Schwarzenegger. Bruce Lee. Jake Lloyd. Josh flipped through the stack of DVDs, wondering what qualified as weird enough. At the bottom of the shelf was a handful of DVD recordables in jewel cases. All of them were labeled. "Katy's Birthday Party." "Rusty's Little League." "Family Christmas, 2012."

Cathe walked out into the living room. "Find anything?"

Josh held up the stack.

"I found some of those in the office too. Who are Katy and Rusty?"

Josh tried to place the names. "Niece and nephew, maybe?"

"You don't know?"

Josh shrugged. "I've never met them."

"We've already checked those." Yamaguchi moved to stand in front of the TV and looked pointedly at her watch. "They're all what they say they are: birthday parties, Little League, kids unwrapping presents . . ."

"You watched all of them?" Cathe popped open the jewel case and inserted the DVD into Kennedy's player. "All the way through?"

"Enough to verify the contents . . ."

Cathe fast-forwarded through a half dozen hyperfrenetic kids wearing party hats.

Josh shifted under the weight of Yamaguchi's impatient look. "Cathe, I appreaciate your thoroughness, but maybe our time would be better spent—"

The television went black and the party scene was replaced by a black and white image of an office.

*His* office.

It was a little skewed, but there was no doubt about it. He could even see the screensaver on his computer—a bunch of animated penguins playing baseball in fast motion.

"I don't *believe* this." Yamaguchi's voice was tight and controlled.

He just stared at the screen.

His TV image entered his office and sat down at the computer. Cathe aimed the remote at the player, and the scene slowed to normal speed. The Josh on the screen typed in something. A little box popped up and he entered his password and then started up his e-mail program.

"Did you see that?" Yamaguchi turned to him, eyes narrowed. "The camera had a perfect view of your right hand. I couldn't see the left hand, but if it just had a little bit better angle, he could have run it in slow motion and picked off your entire password."

"That's how he did it!" Josh grabbed the remote from Cathe and replayed the scene from the beginning. "He set me up!"

He sank into the couch as Cathe and Yamaguchi fast-forwarded through one DVD after another, but he didn't need to see more footage of his office or the password-protected schematic of the Hab to know that Kennedy had been trying to frame him. If he hadn't been replaced by Valkerie when he was, Kennedy would have seen to it that he was kicked off the mission. Kennedy wasn't just crazy. He was a psychopath. He wanted what he wanted and was willing to bury anybody who stood in his way.

A buzz vibrated into his leg, pulling him reluctantly back to the present. He let the call go to voicemail, but it rang again a few seconds later. Whoever it was wasn't taking no for an answer. He yanked the phone out of his pocket and held it to his ear. "Okay already! What's the big emergency?"

"I need you here right now." Nate's tight voice. "Valkerie's unconscious, and they're saying she might be sick."

"What?" Josh was already on his feet and heading for the door.

"Not a word to anybody until we understand the situation. Got it? If word gets out now, those bactamination fearmongers might not allow our boys and girls to come home."

Saturday, March 21, 2015, 5:00 p.m., Mars Local Time

Valkerie

Valkerie woke to a soft touch on her cheek. She opened her eyes and squinted up into dark eyes and a white surgical mask. "Bob?" She winced. Her throat felt like it had been scraped raw. Her head throbbed with the echoes of her voice.

A cool hand soothed back the hair from her forehead.

Her face was on fire. She reached a trembling hand to Bob's. His skin felt sticky. Rubbery. She turned her head and blinked the hand into focus. He was wearing latex gloves.

"Bob, what's wrong?"

"It's okay." His voice sounded remote. "You were sick, but you're going to be just fine."

Valkerie closed her eyes and tried to make sense of it all. Why was Bob wearing gloves? And a mask? She was obviously sick—with something that was either very contagious or . . . Valkerie opened her eyes and tried to sit up, but gloved hands held her down.

"Easy, now. Don't try to move. Think you can drink some water?"

She shook her head. "Flight Med made you wear a mask, didn't they?"

He nodded. Worry flashed across his eyes.

"They can't think I caught something here. That's ridiculous." She watched his eyes, searching for the answer. But where else could she have caught it? No one had been sick since leaving Earth.

"It's just a precaution. You know how the flight docs are." Bob's voice sounded hollow.

"There's something you're not telling me, and I want to know what it is." Valkerie tried to sound angry, but she didn't have the strength. She met his eyes again. "Bob, please."

He hesitated, then nodded. "Flight Med's worried it might be the bacteria from the micrometeorite. We tried to tell them—"

"That's ridiculous. Josh said he used a permafrost bacterium from Antarctica. It's not infectious. He injected himself just to be sure."

"But they don't know that."

Valkerie shut her eyes and tried to put herself in Flight Med's place. Did they really believe a micrometeorite could carry living spores? Well . . . why not? It was looking like the halobacteria might have come from Earth. Its morphology looked surprisingly similar to that of Earth archaebacteria. Could life have been carried between the two planets on impact meteorites? How else could it be explained? Convergent evolution? That just didn't make sense. The halobacterium was—

"Wait a minute." Valkerie opened her eyes. "Why are you still wearing a mask? You know it's not Josh's bacterium. You don't think . . ."

Bob shook his head. "I don't know what to think."

"But it can't be Martian. That's ludicrous. There's nothing out there. If there was life, I would have found it by now."

"It took you nine months to find the petrified snot . . ."

"Bob, that's—"

"What else could have caused it? One minute you're fine and the next you're puking all over the hallway. Valkerie, you've been out for thirty-six hours. And you've got a fever of 101. For a while it was 104. We were afraid you wouldn't make it."

"A hundred and four?" Valkerie swallowed and grimaced at the ragged pain in her throat. "How long?"

"Lex put you in your LCG and cooled you down pretty fast. But still . . ."

"What about strep? Or maybe a staph infection? I could have carried it from Earth—and my throat feels like it's gone through a shredder."

"Lex did a throat culture. Definitely not strep—or staph. Plus she's done all kinds of other tests. Must've taken a gallon of blood."

"Food poisoning?" Valkerie stared up into Bob's eyes. It had to be food poisoning. There was no other explanation.

Bob shook his head slowly. "We checked all the empty food packets. Went back over two weeks."

"But that's . . . impossible. You made a mistake. You had to."

"You're probably right." Bob turned his face to the open doorway. "I, uh . . . I should go tell Lex you're awake. I'll be right back. Okay?"

"Sure."

He rose to leave, holding his hands out in front of him like a surgeon in preop. If he really thought she had food poisoning, why was he still wearing a mask?

He was just being paranoid. They all were. Jumping at shadows. Screaming at reflections. There was no life on Mars. There couldn't be. It didn't make sense.

### Sunday, March 22, 2015, 8:53 a.m., CST

### Nate

Nate scrubbed the whiteboard clean. When he turned, he saw that, for the first time in the history of NASA, everybody had arrived early for a meeting. Seven minutes early, to be exact. It was a fairly large group. Six doctors from Flight Med; Dr. Frazier, the NASA epidemiologist; some expert on infectious diseases from the Centers for Disease Control in Atlanta; Steven Perez; Josh Bennett; and all the engineers who'd been in the Flight Control Room for the last forty-eight hours. That was when Bob called in with news that Valkerie had an unknown infection. The kids looked haggard, but not one of them wanted to go home.

"Okay, that's everybody. Sit down and circle the wagons." Nate shut the door, then stepped to the whiteboard. "As most of you know, Valkerie is not out of the woods yet, but she's on the rebound. None of the others have come down with it yet, so we're hoping it isn't infectious. Dr. Frazier, have you got an assessment on what this thing is yet?"

Frazier was a short guy with a white goatee, white mustache, white eyebrows, and no hair. He pushed up his black plastic glasses. "My first thought on Friday morning was that it sounded like a virulent form of Legionnaires' disease."

"Any signs of mental incapacitation?" The man from the CDC put his elbows on the table and rested his jowls on his fleshy hands. "Any hallucinations? Dizziness? Forgetfulness?"

"No," Nate said. "Not that I know—"

"Actually . . ."

Everybody turned to look at Josh.

Josh took a sip of coffee. "I had a chat with Bob the other day. You know, just talking. Anyway, he mentioned in passing that they did an EVA Thursday morning just outside the Hab. He was kinda embarrassed about it, but they were looking for . . . footprints."

"Footprints?" Frazier said. "The astronauts walk outside all the time, don't they?"

"Apparently, Valkerie saw . . . *something* Wednesday night. Just outside the porthole in the commons on the second floor." Josh looked around at the others. "Looking in at her."

Nate leaned back in his chair. "What kind of a something are we talking about? Some kind of peeping Martian Bigfoot? That porthole's got to be fifteen feet off the ground."

Josh shrugged. "Valkerie wasn't quite sure what she saw. Not a dust devil—not at midnight. But it could have been just the wind blowing dust around. There's a dust storm kicking up at the South Pole. Or maybe she was just tired. But she saw something—a couple of nights before she came down sick."

Nobody said anything.

Nate twiddled a whiteboard marker in his hands. *I love it when they tell me these things right away.* "Okay, getting back to the tangent, Dr. Frazier, what's the consensus on Valkerie's disease?"

The doctor consulted a sheet of paper. "Like I said, it sounds like Legionnaires' disease. It doesn't seem to be a virus. Therefore, it's got to be some sort of bacterial infection—but not one of the usual ones. We've ruled out strep, staph, E. coli, and a dozen others. The problem with this theory is that it should have manifested itself on the crew long ago if they brought it with them from Earth. And it is implausible in the extreme that they picked it up on Mars."

"How implausible?" Nate crossed his arms. "Are we talking one in a hundred, one in a million, what?"

"Not even one in a billion," Frazier said. "It is most certainly not possible. Any bacterium that had adapted to survive on a cold, dry planet with almost no atmosphere could not be adapted to a human host."

That was pretty much what Nate had always believed, but it was good to hear it from an expert. "But you're saying it's got to be some kind of bacteria."

"Or some unknown life-form," the man from the CDC said. "It is impossible to speculate—"

"Then don't." Nate glowered around the room. "Listen, people. Time is short and we need to keep things simple here. I'm looking for facts—"

"Well, then, why don't you listen?"

Everyone turned to Cathe Willison in shocked silence.

"You keep interrupting everybody." She jutted her jaw at Nate. "Why don't you listen to what we've got to say?"

Who did she think she was, anyway? He would have thrown her out, but he couldn't afford to break security.

Perez tapped his pen on the table. "Nate? I think the young lady has a point. Less haste, more speed. Okay?"

Nate could see by the averted eyes and unsmiling expressions around the circle that the majority agreed with Perez. "Okay, fine, less haste. But, folks, we don't have a lot of time, so let's keep on subject. Now, here's the real problem, which is why I called this meeting: There's a small possibility that this bacteria might not be of Earth—"

"You're barking up the wrong tree, Mr. Harrington." The man from the CDC shook his head. "Even if that fossil could be resuscitated, halobacteria are harmless. I understand your crew has already done the sequencing to show that your fossil is an archaebacteria from Earth's own Tree of Life. We don't know of a single species of archaebacteria that has ever—"

"If you wouldn't mind"—Nate all but growled the words—"I'd like to finish *my* sentence. Most of you don't know this, but on the trip to Mars, the ship briefly got itself infested with some kind of bacteria that Valkerie didn't recognize. She suspected it came from a micrometeorite that embedded in the exterior foam shielding of the Hab. Kennedy stuck his finger in the impact hole and didn't decontaminate his glove afterward. Valkerie eventually traced the microbe back to the glove."

"And you didn't notify *us* about this?" The man from the CDC looked like he'd just swallowed a frog.

"I had a few other things to worry about," Nate said. "Like keeping my astronauts alive."

"We don't know that the infection came from space." Josh leaned forward. "It could have come from Earth."

"Valkerie didn't recognize it under the microscope," Nate said. "She didn't have time to characterize it then—she was kind of busy trying to breathe."

"So it *could* be from Earth." Josh had that look in his eye that said he wasn't gonna let go of this one.

"Or it could be from space," Cathe said. "Panspermia. Life seeding the galaxy from another star system."

Frazier glowered at her over the rims of his glasses. "Who are you, young lady?"

She stood up and walked over to stand in his face, turning up her ID badge so he could see her Silver Snoopy pin. "If it weren't for me and a whole bunch of other *kindergartners* who worked our tails off last year, those four astronauts would be dead right now."

Josh came up behind her and took her elbow. "Dr. Frazier, Cathe's one of our best engineers. Cathe, how about you have a seat?"

She stalked back to her chair.

Nate returned to the whiteboard. "We've got a few different possibilities, so let's make a decision tree. First off, either the infectious agent is from Earth, or it's from Mars, or it's from somewhere else." He wrote those three possibilities on the board and circled them.

Josh cleared his throat. "Well, if it's from Earth, then it's not a big deal, right?"

"Right." Nate wrote *No Big Deal* beside the Earth circle.

"And the probability for that is fairly large," Josh said. "Like maybe 99 percent?"

"If I didn't know about the micrometeorite, I'd agree. But I do, so I don't." Nate wrote *90%* beside the Earth circle. "Obviously, it's not headline news if Valkerie has come down with food poisoning. So the real question is what to do if Valkerie's caught some kind of space flu or Martian bug. Dr. Frazier, what's the probability that this halobacteria is causing the problem?"

"I told you already," Frazier said. "Zero. It can't happen."

Nate wrote *.1%* beside the Mars circle. "And there's only one possibility left, which is the micrometeorite bacteria." He wrote *9.9%* next to that circle. "There aren't any other options."

The man from the CDC took off his glasses and polished them on his tie. "So they were exposed to this micrometeorite bacteria a year ago? That's an awfully long incubation time. It doesn't make sense. Why aren't the other astronauts infected?"

"If it made sense," Nate said, "we wouldn't have flown you out here to get your opinion."

Josh had a visible sheen of sweat on his forehead. "So you're saying it's at least 90 percent that this is of Earth origin."

"And 10 percent that we've got a major disaster on our hands." Nate felt horror rising in his gut. This was not how the mission was supposed to go. They were supposed to zoom in to Mars, do their research, and zoom home.

Steven Perez held up a copy of the latest *New York Times*. "Major disaster is right. That *Bactamination* woman has gone from the *Enquirer* to a serious editorial in the *Times* in less than a week. And that's just on the strength of a halobacteria that's been dead for millions of years. The president has called me three times this week to make sure I'm sure that we're sure that we have things under control. It sounds like . . . we don't."

Dr. Frazier shook his head. "If they're sick with an alien bug, we can't bring them back."

"What?" Josh jumped to his feet and took a step toward Frazier.

Nate waved him back to his seat. "Is that a scientific opinion or a political one?"

The man from the CDC stood up. "From where I sit—both. The press would crucify you if you told them what you just told me. And scientifically, I would have to agree. If Dr. Jansen's fever is due to a bacterium of non-Earth origin, then it would be irresponsible to bring your crew back. Pending more information on the nature of the infection, of course."

"That's a big *if*," Josh said. "We don't know—"

"Josh." Cathe put a hand on Josh's arm. "It's a 10-percent sized *if*. We need to think about what to do—"

Josh flung her hand away. "That's my crew up there! Four people. My *friends*. What is it you people are planning to do if you don't bring them home?"

Nate put his marker down on the tray. *Oh good, a family squabble. Just what I was hoping for.* "Listen, Josh, they're my friends too. Let's hope that what Valkerie's got is just some bug they took with them. A good old Earth bacteria. Food poisoning. Or something that hid out in the soles of their shoes for fifteen months. But if it isn't . . . we need to plan for that contingency."

Perez cleared his throat. "Nate. Dr. Frazier. What about a quarantine when we bring them back?"

Nate sighed. "That's gonna be really hard. Really expensive. You're talking total quarantine, possibly for the lifetime of the crew, maintaining a sterile interface. It's never been done. The National Research Council recommended years ago that we build one. It even got funded. Then it got de-funded, like the second rover we were gonna send. And the backup nuclear reactor. And the—"

"We lost those battles, Nate." Perez sounded tired—really tired. "Let's focus on winning the war. Can we get a quarantine facility built before the crew returns?" He turned to his left. "You're the expert, Cathe—when exactly are they getting back?"

"August 5, 2016," she said. "Plus or minus a few weeks, depending—"

"Sixteen months from now," Frazier said. "The NRC's proposal was for seven years."

"We need a crash program," Nate said. "Need to get a lot of people working on it."

"You can get nine women pregnant if you want," Frazier said, "but you won't get a baby in a month."

Josh shook his head. "Don't give me that Wernher von Braun claptrap. We're not talking about a baby, we're talking about a quarantine facility! And we agree we have a ninety-percent chance that we won't even need it."

"What about—" Cathe Willison stopped.

Everybody turned to look at her.

"What about a resupply mission? If they just stay on Mars, the energetics would be favorable for a rocket to reach them in July of next year. They've got supplies to last that long at base camp. Mars is the second safest place in the universe for them."

Nobody said anything for a full minute.

Finally Nate grabbed his coffee cup. "That's not a bad idea." In fact, it was a really good idea. That was the one thing he really liked about Cathe—she had a lot of great ideas. "We need two Tiger Teams to evaluate those two options. Dr. Frazier, you're in charge of the quarantine team. Josh, you look at the resupply question. Keep your teams small, and give them whatever resources they need."

"And keep them secure," Perez said. "We don't need the press running articles on this."

"We'll also need a support team to help our crew on Mars characterize that halobacteria," Nate said. "Just so we can rule it out. Valkerie's sick, so she can't work on it. That means we'll need to hold the hands of the other three, walk them through the procedures. Hunter, you coordinate that."

The man from the CDC stood up. "My understanding is that Dr. Jansen has responded favorably to antibiotics, and so far we have no evidence the disease in question is infectious. That, coupled with the relatively low probability that the disease is extraterrestrial, means that there may not be an immediate cause for alarm. But"—his gaze hardened and he pinned Nate with a warning look—"if any of the others get sick, or if they show any signs of Legionnaires'-style hallucination or dementia, I'm going to have to take this to the president. Bringing back a Mars fever is one thing—we might be able to live with that. Bringing back Martian mad cow disease is an entirely different one."

Nate nodded. "You heard the man. You've all got your tasks. Dismissed."

The group quickly left the room, chattering tech-speak. Nate slouched into a chair and covered his head with his hands.

*No. Not back-contamination. Not on this mission.*

*Please.*

Sunday, March 22, 2015, 9:30 a.m., Mars Local Time

Bob

Bob reached out a gloved hand. Valkerie's head lay on her pillow, afloat in a sea of wild curls. He ached to take off his gloves, to run his fingers through the tumble of amber waves. She was resting comfortably now, her face placid, serene, as though she were frozen in time like some enchanted sleeping beauty. If only he were a prince . . .

*No.*

He pulled back his hand and hugged it to his chest. He had promised to back off—all the way off—and that meant even when she was asleep.

Valkerie shifted in her sleep and turned toward him, her lips parted in a half smile. They tugged at his heart like a siren's song. His thoughts plunged and surged, tossed to and fro on the storm of battling emotions.

He lifted the surgical mask from his face. So what if he got sick? He leaned in closer . . . closer . . .

*No.*

He stopped. Closed his eyes. Something was wrong. He didn't understand it, but somehow, deep inside he knew that he'd be breaking her trust. Shattering her one moment of peace.

Valkerie's eyes fluttered open. Her face melted into a placid smile, and Bob waited breathlessly. He could kiss her if he wanted. Her eyes were warm and open, an unspoken invitation. Except he had promised.

"Have you been with me all night?" Her voice fluttered soft and weak. The voice of a little girl.

Bob nodded slowly. "All morning too. It's 9:30 a.m." He placed the mask back over his face and drew away.

"Thank you." She smiled again, a tired smile, but it lit up the room like a floodlight. "I knew you were here. I could feel it in my sleep."

"You seemed to be troubled. Like you were having a bad dream."

Valkerie's face clouded. "I keep hearing things. Noises on the outside of the Hab. And . . . Have you ever felt like you were being watched?"

Bob lowered his eyes. "You mean like while you were asleep?"

"No, when I'm awake too. Ever since I caught a glimpse of . . . of something looking in at the porthole. Sometimes it's a sound. Sometimes just a feeling. Like I'm being watched. Like we're all being watched."

"Well, you've been very sick. Maybe that's why—"

She shook her head. "No, I felt it before I got sick. I know it doesn't make sense, but something's not right. You do believe me, don't you?"

How could he say no? Especially when she looked up at him with those large, pleading eyes. "Of course I do. I mean, I . . ." Bob hesitated. Did he really believe her? Sure, he believed *she* believed what she was saying was true. She wasn't making it up. You could believe someone was honest without necessarily believing they were right. Right?

"You don't believe me."

"Of course I do. I know you'd never deceive me, but you've been sick. You were hallucinating when your fever was higher. How do you know you haven't been hallucinating all along?"

"I know it doesn't make any sense. I mean, it's impossible, but . . ." She took a deep breath and let it out slowly. "Maybe you're right. I can't know for sure." She turned her head to look away, but Bob could see the disappointment in her eyes.

"I can't know for sure either. I tell you what, though. How about I do another EVA to check things out? Now that I think about it, I never did inspect the Hab walls outside this cabin. If you're hearing noises, maybe a loose cable is tapping against the Hab when the wind blows."

Her face brightened. "Thanks."

"You'll be okay without me?"

She nodded.

Bob turned and hurried for the door, glad that he could do something concrete to ease Valkerie's mind. But why hadn't he just told her that he believed her? What kind of an unfeeling beast was he? One nod and she would have been fine.

And he would have been a liar. Nice to know this integrity thing was so easy.

Bob pounded on the door to Kennedy's quarters. "Hey, Hampster. Come on out."

No answer.

"Rise and shine. We've got an EVA to do." Bob tried the door latch. It was locked. "Hey, Lex. Do you know what time the Hampster turned in?"

Silence. Lex wasn't answering either.

"Kennedy!" Bob went to the computer in the commons and activated the emergency door release. "Kennedy?" He swung the door open. A foul stench slugged him in the gut. Bob flipped on the lights. Kennedy lay huddled on the floor just inside the door, encrusted in his own vomit.

"Lex! Get in here!" Bob rolled Kennedy onto his back and felt for his pulse.

Kennedy's skin was hot to the touch—even through the latex gloves. His pulse throbbed shallow and weak.

"Lex!" Bob lifted Kennedy onto his cot and ripped open his favorite shirt. "Sorry about that, Hampster. I'll sew it back. I promise."

Bob raced from the room and flung open Lex's door. Good, she wasn't there. The last thing he needed was another patient. "Lex!" Bob ran into the kitchen and pulled Valkerie's ice bag from the freezer. He ran back and packed Kennedy in the ice and wet him down with a bag of cold water.

Okay, what was next? The IV? The antibiotics? He was terrible with needles. Lex had done Valkerie while he averted his eyes and prayed like a church mouse. Bob ran down the spiral staircase and circled the lower level. Laboratory. Shop. Suit room. Airlock. Greenhouse. He couldn't find her anywhere. "Lex!"

A sinking feeling hit Bob in the gut. What if Lex was sick too? They'd all be counting on him. And if he got sick? Valkerie wasn't even strong enough to get out of bed. They'd all die. Nobody back home would even know what happened.

Bob changed his gloves and threw the old ones in the biohazard waste. A chill washed over him. He'd been *that* close to kissing her. Three more seconds and he might have killed them all. What had stopped him?

Bob walked carefully up the stairs. They were all counting on him. One stumble, one false move, and the mission could be over. He strode to the radio and flipped it on. "Houston, this is Ares 7. We have an emergency. Repeat. We have an emergency. Kennedy Hampton is sick and in critical condition. He seems to have the same bug as Valkerie. I'm still trying to find Lex. I need complete instructions for administering the IV and antibiotics and everything else you can think of. Over." Bob shut off the transmitter, and the receiver crackled with high-pitched thrumming static. *Great.*

"Lex!" Bob screamed at the top of his lungs, letting his frustration fly.

A dull clank sounded behind him. A soft flutter—like the rustling of dry leaves.

"Lex, where—" Bob spun around but the commons was empty. The noise sounded like it had come from . . .

His eyes widened. It sounded like it had come from the outside wall.

### Sunday, March 22, 2015, 1:00 p.m., CST

### Josh

Josh paused while the waitress placed a banana cheesecake in front of him. "Sure you don't want any?" he asked Cathe.

She shook her head. "I'm running a 10K next Sunday, and cheesecake makes me sluggish." She sipped her iced tea, which was, like the cheesecake, an Enzo's specialty.

"So what did you want to be when you were a kid?" Josh was still trying to figure Cathe out. She was . . . different from most NASA women. If she was going to be working for him, he needed to understand how she thought.

Cathe grinned. "Let's see, when I was four, I wanted to be a bus driver. Then when I got to be six, it was a pole vaulter. Then in fifth grade, I wanted to be Hillary Clinton."

"First Lady?"

"New York senator."

"I thought you were from Texas?"

Cathe shrugged. "Hillary's not from New York either. I'm adaptable. Then in high school, I wanted to be Jenny Mitford."

Josh gave her a blank look.

"The marathoner." Cathe smiled. "Turned out I'm talented, but not in Jenny's league. But running paid the bills through university."

Which explained her legs.

"And what did you want to be?" Cathe's eyes—big and blue and liquid—hadn't left Josh the entire meal.

"You'll laugh." Josh attacked his cheesecake.

"So? Make me laugh. We could all use a good laugh about now."

"You remember Gene Kranz in Apollo 13?" Josh angled a look at her. "The flight director—the guy with the vest?"

"Mr.Failure-Is-Not-An-Option?Mr.I-Am-Flight-and-Flight-Is-God? Who could forget?"

"Gene was the failure-is-not-an-option guy. Chris Kraft put that flight-is-God shtick in his book, but you do know he was poking fun at himself, don't you? My dad knew both of 'em, and they were the real McCoy. Righteous dudes. I wanted so bad to be just like them." Josh blinked rapidly several times. "And now . . ." He turned his head so she wouldn't see his eyes.

"And now you are."

*Wrong. I'm the guy who blew it up. They wouldn't even be talking about quarantines if it weren't for me. They'd be focusing all their attention on good old-fashioned food poisoning and leaving the science fiction to Isaac Asimov.*

Cathe put a hand on Josh's. "I understand. It's hard."

He gripped her hand. "It's different than in the movies."

"Apollo 13 wasn't just a movie. It was real life. I'll bet Gene felt a lot like you do now."

*Except that Gene Kranz was the good guy.* "Gene brought them back alive. I might not get that option. You heard the news. Kennedy's sick too. If we decide to run that resupply mission, they'll be stuck on Mars until the 2018 launch opportunity. And maybe forever."

"It depends on the nature of the disease they've got. If they get over it, if we can knock this thing, then they can come home. Otherwise . . . the moral thing—the *right* thing—is to protect Earth."

"Moral? What's moral about leaving them on Mars to die and rot? If we bring them back here, we could help them. We don't even know for sure that it's really a Martian disease. What if they took some weird bacteria with them somehow?"

"We'll figure that out, I guess. But it *is* moral," Cathe said. "Renormalized morality."

"Renormal—what?" Josh stared at her.

"Renormalized." Cathe finished off her tea. "My uncle is a physicist. Used to talk all the time about renormalization. For elementary particles—their charge and mass and stuff like that. Yeah, sure, I want to bring back the crew as much as anyone else does. But the big picture is what's right for the seven billion people on planet Earth. If it's wrong for them, then you can't do it."

"Just like that?" Josh put down his fork. "Four human lives on Mars don't count? You cut them off just for getting sick?"

"First you do everything you can," Cathe said. "But sometimes you don't have a choice. It's only then that you renormalize your morality."

Josh picked up his napkin and looped it around his finger. *The greatest good for the greatest number. Sorry about the ones we had to sacrifice, but life's a bummer sometimes.*

There had to be a better way. There *was* a better way.

"I have an idea that might tell us where the static is coming from ."

Good, she was changing the subject. Josh didn't want to get into an argument. He'd been round and round on this with Nate and the epidemiologists all morning. All of them were reasoning without one critical fact: They didn't know that Josh had sent hitchhiker bacteria to Mars. A harmless strain—the one Valkerie had found on the flight out. There wasn't any micrometeorite bacteria. But since Nate didn't know that, he was actually considering sentencing the crew—his friends—to a permanent quarantine on Mars.

"Spock to Josh, come in."

*Spock. Good analogy.* Josh met Cathe's curious look. "Let's hear your idea."

"We may never be able to decrypt that signal coming through the relay satellites," she said. "The NSA box isn't working. But maybe we can figure out where the originating transmitter is. We can at least rule out a few possibilities."

"Such as?"

"What if it's coming from our own Earth Return Vehicle?"

"You think Kennedy is transmitting from the ERV?"

"Maybe . . . Or maybe it's one of the other crew members. We can't rule out any possibilities until we know for sure. Remember, we never did figure out who the bomber was on the outbound flight."

*Because it was me.* "Uh . . . right."

"So maybe it was one of the crew, and he or she still has some plan to disrupt things."

Josh shook his head. "Kennedy, I can believe. But not the others. But if we can't decrypt the messages, how are we going to prove it?"

"All we need to do is put some detection software on the ERV. If it's coming from there, we should be able to figure out who's sending it."

"And if it's not?"

"Then we can eliminate it as a possibility and focus on ruling out the other options. I could reconfigure the relay satellites to detect whether the signal is originating from Mars or Earth or somewhere in between. I tried to explain it to CATO yesterday, but he didn't get it." She sighed. "It's frustrating. I'd really like to solve this problem, but if nobody is willing to step out of their ignorance zone . . ."

Josh leaned forward. "How long would it take you?"

"A couple days or so to do the programming. After that, a few minutes a day to watch and see what develops. See, the Russian orbiter and anyone on Mars all pretty much look the same to the CommSats. The CommSats are both sitting out about a million klicks from Mars, so everything on the planet or in low orbit looks like a single point source."

"So how do you tell the difference between a fixed source on the planet and an orbiter?"

"You can do a differential analysis of data rates coming in and get a time-dependent estimate of relative velocity between the source and the CommSat. The Doppler effect, you know. Remember, anything on the surface looks like it's first coming toward the CommSat, then moving away from it, as the planet rotates."

"Okay, I get the picture. You're gonna put in a speed trap kind of thing."

"Exactly. The CommSats don't have real Doppler measurements. If they did, this would be trivial. We'll have to measure data rates over long periods of time. The signal is going to be horribly noisy, but it should have a sine-wave pattern with the rotational period of the source. That's different for a source on the ground and one in orbit. So we collect data for long enough and run a fast Fourier transform, and boom! Out comes the answer."

"Oh right, I bet you do fast whatever-they-are in your head."

"No, but MATLAB does. Faster than you can think it."

Josh grinned. *This just might work!* "Okay, you've sold me. What do you need to get it done?"

"CATO could do it. He's got the access code to the CommSats. Once I finish the software, all he has to do is blip up my new program, and then we let it analyze. Every couple hours, we blip down the running results and run it through MATLAB to see if there's an answer yet."

"You said CATO doesn't understand the method."

"He gets the main idea, but he doesn't think it'll work." Cathe shrugged. "I don't think he likes me."

"How about if I just promote you to be a backup CATO and get you the access codes yourself?"

Cathe hesitated. "That would work, but . . . I'm awfully young to be a Communications and Tracking Officer. Are you sure you want to do that?"

"You don't seem too eager."

"I just don't like horning in if I'm not wanted."

"*I* want you. I'll talk to CATO and get you the access codes. How long to get your software written?"

"I started prototyping it last night—worked on it till 2:00 a.m. It should be ready in a day or two. Then I'll be testing it in a Monte Carlo simulation to characterize the signal-to-noise ratio of the technique. That'll give us a back-of-the-envelope estimate of how long we'll need to get an answer."

"Just one more question," Josh said.

Those big blue eyes opened a little wider. "Shoot."

"Is there any magic you can't do?"

"On a computer? No."

"What about in real life?"

Cathe blushed. "Well . . . I still can't break thirty-six minutes for a 10K."

# CHAPTER 11

11
Sunday, March 22, 2015, 10:00 a.m., Mars Local Time

Valkerie

Valkerie squinted at Bob, trying to bring him into focus.

His words tumbled out in a jumble of exclamations and incoherent shouts.

"Bob . . . slow down. Tell me what you saw." She had to force her thick, unresponsive tongue to form the words. "Was it something outside?"

Bob looked down at her. Was he angry? "Kennedy . . . is . . . sick." He emphasized each word as if he thought she was too dull to take them in. "Lex . . . is . . . missing. Valkerie, I need your help. Do you understand? I can't get in touch with Houston. I need to know what antibiotics to give Kennedy."

The meaning of the words sank in slowly. Kennedy was sick and Bob needed her. She nodded and tried to sit up.

Bob put out a hand to stop her.

She shook her head. "He'll need fluids. I have to start him on an IV."

"Just tell me what you need me to do."

"I need to see him."

The room tilted around her and she felt herself lifted off the bed.

A wave of dizziness made Valkerie gasp. "Wait. Slow down." She closed her eyes and waited as the nausea gradually subsided. Slowly, she relaxed into Bob's arms, laying her head against his chest. She slid a hand to his neck and tried to hold on. His heart beat madly beneath her ear. Strong and rapid, it pounded out the urgency of their situation. Kennedy was sick. What if Lex and Bob got sick too? Or was Lex already sick? What had Bob said about Lex? "I'm okay now. You can take me to Kennedy."

Valkerie felt herself lifted in his arms, and she nestled against him as he carried her to Kennedy's room. He set her down on the floor, her back against the wall. She felt a flash of loss and almost reached for him, drew him close again, but she . . . couldn't. Now was not the time.

She turned to touch Kennedy's face. His skin was hot and dry. His breath came in quick, shallow pants.

"Okay. I'll need a . . ." Valkerie stared at the wall, trying desperately to bring her thoughts into focus. "I'll need an IV kit. And antibiotics. Bring me the whole antibiotics tray. Second bin from the floor—in the med bay."

The sound of footsteps faded into distant rattles and muffled *whumps*. The room grew darker. A warm, comfortable silence washed gently over her . . . .

"Valkerie, wake up! Please. I need your help!"

She opened her eyes and stared at Bob. He wanted her to do something, but what? Why didn't he ever tell her what he wanted her to do?

"What's going on?" Lex's face appeared over Bob's shoulder. A pair of earbuds hung around her neck. She was wearing her red exercise sweats.

Valkerie blinked her eyes and tried to focus. Lex looked so good in red. It wasn't fair.

Bob and Lex were arguing now. Something about going to the bathroom. They stopped arguing, and Lex bent low over Valkerie.

"It's okay, Val. I'll take care of Kennedy. You go back to bed."

Bob reached down and scooped her into his arms. Valkerie shut her eyes and snuggled into his chest, wondering if she shouldn't pretend to be asleep.

No, wait. Bob wasn't her daddy. He'd carry her whether she was asleep or not. She smiled, wrapping her arms around his neck as he maneuvered into her bedroom. Bracing herself for the chill of her pillow and cold sheets, she clung tighter. She felt herself rocking gently back and forth. She sighed and relaxed into Bob's arms. Ever so gradually, she drifted off to sleep.

Valkerie woke with a start. Her ears echoed with the ring of false silence. She lay motionless in her bed—trying to hear above the din of her pounding heart. Something was wrong. The darkness pressed down on her, black and foreboding. Something had awakened her. Had she heard the scratching sounds in her sleep?

A gentle voice murmured through her open doorway. Lex talking to someone—down the hall in Kennedy's room. Another sound. The faint rush of a welding torch. She'd heard it a hundred times. Bob was working in the shop right below her. He'd probably knocked something over. Accidentally rapped the ceiling.

Valkerie shut her eyes and relaxed back into her pillow. She felt better. Her fever must have broken sometime during the night. Maybe later she'd be able to—

A metallic clang broke the silence. It sounded like it had come from the commons.

Kennedy? Wasn't he supposed to be sick? Hadn't Bob woken her up to help tend Kennedy—or had she just dreamed it? She slid out of bed and stood, bracing herself against the wall. Not too bad. She felt a little dizzy, but at least she could stand.

She felt her way out into the corridor and pushed herself along the wall.

A faint *chirrup*ing noise sounded in front of her. She could just make it out above the whir of the air handlers.

"Kennedy?"

Movement in the darkness. Something low and close to the floor.

Panic crawled up Valkerie's spine. She swatted at the wall, her fingers fumbling for the light switch.

A dark shadow darted across the room.

Valkerie stumbled backward. Her shoulder slammed into the wall and spun her reeling onto the floor.

"Bob!" Her scream pierced the blackness. She rolled onto to her hands and knees and tottered forward.

A metal chair clattered to the floor behind her. A low, rumbling moan. It was getting closer.

She scrambled to her feet and started to run, feeling her way with outstretched hands.

The moan rose in pitch to an angry growl.

"Valkerie?" Bob's voice rang out from the stairwell.

A powerful blow cut her legs out from under her.

For a heart-wrenching second she flailed through the air in a dizzying arc. Pain exploded in her skull, followed by halos of red-and-white light that faded slowly to darkness.

### Monday, March 23, 2015, 8:15 a.m., CST

### Nate

Nate looked around the war room at two dozen tense faces. "Okay, I guess you all know Kennedy is sick now with the same thing Valkerie had. High fever. Chucking up."

"What about hallucinations?" Dr. Frazier turned to look at Josh. "That seems to be the key issue. A fever, we can live with."

"I haven't heard anything. Anybody know otherwise?" Nate scanned the circle. "This is critical, people. If you know something, speak now or forever hold your breath."

Silence.

Josh coughed.

Nate looked at him. "You know something I don't know?"

"Um . . ." Josh looked stricken. "Something was told to me in confidence."

*Meaning Kaggo told you.* Nate drummed his fingers on the table. "Okay, you don't need to give the name of your source, but if there's something life-threatening going on here, we need to know about it. That's the moral and right thing to do."

Josh didn't say anything.

Dr. Perez leaned forward. "Josh? We really need to know."

Josh closed his eyes. Folded his arms across his chest. Sighed deeply. "Bob and Kennedy were out on an EVA last week—the day Lex and Valkerie found the halobacteria. Lex called them in a panic. Remember, Valkerie got herself in a jam, and Lex needed help? So Bob went running back to the Hab. He assumed Kennedy was going to follow. Maybe ten, fifteen minutes later, Kennedy showed up at the Hab and his faceplate was scratched pretty bad. And he said . . . Bob pushed him from behind and then ran off. He was really angry. Almost started a fight, and you all know who'd win if Bob got mad."

"So *did* Bob push him?" Dr. Frazier asked.

"Of course not!" Josh glared at Frazier. "I *know* Kaggo. He wouldn't do that. Anyway, he was in a hurry. This is Valkerie we're talking about here. No way in the world would Bob waste five milliseconds to push Kennedy."

"So what are you saying?" Nate did not want to hear this. He had to hear this. "That Kennedy imagined it?"

"I don't know."

Nate frowned at the tortured look on Josh's face. What was going on?

"But he never said anything about Valkerie seeing things."

Nate stared into Josh's eyes. He knew something. Something he wasn't telling.

EECOM had been doodling on a pad with a green pen. She raised her head. "If Kennedy was hallucinating last Monday, *before* the girls brought back the halobacteria, then it follows that the halobacteria isn't causing his hallucinations."

"We knew that anyway." Dr. Frazier tugged on his white goatee. "It's absurd to think the halobacteria could cause any kind of symptoms at all in a human host—even if it were alive. Which, I should remind you, it isn't."

"Well, it is nice to have a bit of logic to back up your theory." EECOM's smile was cool.

Roger Abrams, the mousy chief shrink, raised his hand.

Nate jabbed a finger at him. "Go, Dr. Abrams."

"We have no evidence at all that would indicate that either Kennedy or Valkerie is, in fact, experiencing hallucinations. Neither of them have been examined by competent, trained psychology professionals—"

"Yeah, well, the timing seems kind of suspicious, wouldn't you agree?" Abrams, with his prissy, overeducated mumbo jumbo, had always given Nate the creeps.

"It could all be coincidence," Abrams said. "My point is that we lack sufficient data to reach a conclusion. But should we begin to see a whole pattern of hallucinatory phenomena, we would rapidly reach the stage where we could with confidence reject the null hypothesis that—"

"All right, all *right*!" Nate clenched his hand into a fist. "I get your drift. We'll wait and see if they keep hallucinating. But we're getting off track here, people. Tiger Teams, I need reports. Tiger 1, what have you got?"

Dr. Frazier tugged on his white beard and shoved his black plastic glasses up on his nose. "We have investigated the possibility of a long-term-to-permanent quarantine here on Earth. There are two problems to be faced, both probably insurmountable."

"If it's only two impossibilities, that's not so bad." Nate played with a roll of antacid tablets.

"First is the issue of microbial contamination of the Earth Return Vehicle."

"They're going to abandon that before they capture into Earth orbit," Josh said. "Not a problem."

"I misspoke." Frazier consulted his report. "Not the ERV, the Earth Landing Capsule. The mission plan calls for the crew to transfer to the ELC about twelve hours before Earth Orbit Insertion and aerobrake in and deploy a steerable parafoil to a dry-land touchdown. Assuming they are still infected at that time, they will contaminate the ELC."

"But only the inside," Josh said.

"No, the outside cannot be presumed to be sterile. We know for a fact that the Pathfinder mission in 1997 had spores attached to the exterior of the ship that landed on Mars. If we can't even *send* a sterile ship, which we packed ourselves in a clean room, then we most certainly can't bring one *back* sterile. The ELC *will* be contaminated. The second problem is the long-term quarantine of the crew. There is just no way to guarantee zero transfer of pathogens from the crew's environment. We can make the probability small, but not zero."

"That's an acceptable risk," Josh said.

"Not if it endangers the lives of seven billion people!" Cathe Willison said.

Josh scowled at her. "You can never eliminate all risk—"

Nate held up his hand. "We do have another option that would do exactly that. Tiger 2, your turn."

Josh played for a moment with the sheaf of papers on the table in front of him. "It's not difficult to resupply the crew every two years or so with a cargo vehicle. They've got about a fifteen-year supply of energy in their nuclear reactor, so that won't be a problem for a while. All they need is food and other supplies. We can't land an unmanned cargo vessel on a dime like we did with the crew, but we can bring it in to a landing ellipse of about fifty by a hundred kilometers, almost every time. That's well within the rover range. But if we do one of those feet-meter bungles, they all die."

Cathe Willison rolled her sheaf of papers into a tube and tapped the table. "It's not a big risk, and it's only four people—"

"Four people we committed to bring home!" Josh's voice had that mama-bear-protecting-her-cubs ferocity to it. Which was what Nate liked about him.

Dr. Frazier inspected his fingernails. "It's a calculated risk."

"Right. We calculate. They risk." Josh pushed back from the table and stood. "What *is* it with you people? These are our *friends* we're talking about here, not some . . . lab rats in an experiment. They're human beings. Kennedy Hampton. Lex Ohta. Valkerie Jansen. Bob Kaganovski. They have names. Brothers and sisters. Moms and dads. Not too long ago, we cried our eyes out because we thought they were dead. Now you're telling me we're thinking of letting them rot on Mars? You can't be serious. If the odds of a cargo mission failure are 10 percent, then after ten missions, they're dead."

"No, their odds of survival at that point are roughly one over *e*," EECOM said. "Thirty-seven percent. That's basic calculus—"

"Oh, sorry I did the numbers wrong!" Josh was shouting now. "Well, let me clue you in, people, those are *not* numbers up there on Mars, they're our crew, and we're obligated—"

Nate had heard enough. He stood. "Josh, calm down. We haven't decided anything yet. We're going to watch Valkerie and Kennedy, see how they respond to antibiotics. And we're going to make sure they're not having any hallucinations. That's our big concern. If we see a problem, then we're just suggesting that we leave them there for another two years so we can reevaluate."

Josh glared at him. "Right, then another two, and another. When does it end? Do we just wait for them to die? Who thinks we ought to bring them home on the next launch opportunity, no questions asked? I want a show of hands."

Three hands went up around the table, including Josh's. Even Dr. Perez kept his hands in his lap.

"This ain't a democracy, but just for curiosity, who agrees that we need to wait and see before we decide?" Nate counted the hands, then turned to Josh. "With me, that makes twenty-three votes. Listen, Josh, if there were any other way—"

"You'd still do it your way, wouldn't you? You could show a little conscience on behalf of your crew, but you won't, because you couldn't stand the heat, could you? It gets a little too hot in this kitchen, doesn't it?"

That stung. Nate took a lot of heat that nobody in this room knew about, and he just plain did not *need* a backseat movie critic right now. "Josh—"

"Forget it!" Josh stormed to the door. "Talk to me when you grow yourself a backbone."

The door slammed behind him.

A second later, Nate was at the door, yanking it open. "Josh, I'd like to remind you of a certain executive order which you *will* respect this time—unless you want to go to jail."

Josh kept walking.

Nate shut the door and plumped into his seat. "Dr. Perez? This could get out of control if he—"

"He's not going to tell the press. He didn't last time, either, remember? That's what he said. And you said you believed him."

*Right. So he lied and I lied. Prosecute me.* Nate put his head in his hands.

"And Josh won't tell this time, because the press would be against him," Cathe said.

Nate looked at her sharply.

She shrugged. "Everybody in their right mind is afraid of back-contamination."

Heads nodded around the table.

"We'll have to notify the press anyway." Perez sighed heavily. "A resupply mission is going to cost billions, and we'll need to get that from Congress. And we need it now if we're going to run that mission."

Nate felt his stomach do a barrel roll. "The Senate subcommittee is going to have a cow and a half."

"Will they like the alternative any better?" Perez's question hung heavy in the silence for a long moment.

Cathe was the first to speak. "Maybe, in a very weird, renormalized sense, this will all turn out for the best."

Nate glared at her. "You want to explain why that isn't the most Pollyanna-stupid thing you've said all year?"

"It's simple." Cathe didn't even blink. "Congress cancelled the Ares 14 mission, so if our crew comes back, we lose our presence on Mars—maybe for a very long time."

"Oh, I get it." Nate hadn't thought his gut could turn more sour. He'd been wrong. "This way we get to stay as long as we want. And did it ever occur to you to ask what happens if Congress cancels the resupply mission at some point? They don't care two cents about four kids lost in space."

Dr. Frazier took off his glasses and held them up to the light. "None of us do, if we're honest. Not as much as we care about saving our own hides. And that"—he finished his inspection and jammed his glasses back on—"is just as it should be.

If *Homo sapiens* didn't have a survival instinct, we wouldn't be here now. It's good that we're selfish."

Nate wanted to tell him he was a liar. But he couldn't.

"Fine, then." Nate yanked out his phone and made a note. "I'm heading to Washington to shake down our happy little gang of thieves in Congress for all the money they saved on the Ares 10 and Ares 14 missions. Josh!" He looked around the room, then remembered.

"I'll go find him," said Dr. Perez.

"Tell him we've got a resupply mission to get started down the pipeline—at least until we decide different—and it needs to launch in . . ." He flipped through the pages of the Tiger Team 2 report.

"Three hundred and thirty days."

Nate looked at Cathe Willison. The kid just had every duck lined up in neat little rows, didn't she?

She pointed at one of the bullet points in the report. "But we're going to have to move fast before they scrap the launch vehicle that was being built for the Ares 14 mission."

"Make it so." Nate flinched. Picard would never have sentenced four people he loved to life imprisonment on Mars.

# CHAPTER 12

Monday, March 23, 2015, 5:45 a.m., Mars Local Time

Bob

Bob knelt on the floor beside Valkerie and slid a towel under her head. "Valkerie, can you hear me?"

Her nod was slow and weak. Finally her eyes flickered open.

"Are you okay? Can I get you anything?" Bob's voice trembled. He felt so helpless.

"I'm fine. I just—" Her eyes went suddenly wide. She rolled her head back and forth, looking around the room.

"It's okay. Try not to move." Bob eased her back to the floor as she struggled to rise. "You fainted and hit your head."

Lex's footsteps sounded behind him. "Is she awake?"

"I'm fine." Valkerie shrugged off his hands and pushed herself up onto her elbows.

Bob helped turn her so she could lean against the wall. She was so weak. So vulnerable . . . His heart felt like it was going to explode.

Lex held an ice bag to the side of Valkerie's head. "What were you doing out of bed? You're supposed to call me or Bob if you need something."

"I didn't faint." Valkerie looked from Bob to Lex. "Something . . ."

Bob watched as the determination on Valkerie's face melted into . . . what? Confusion? Fear?

"Something pushed me," Valkerie said weakly. "Something ran across the floor and knocked me off my feet."

Bob exchanged glances with Lex.

"I know what it sounds like, but you've got to believe me. It hit me hard. I can still feel the bruises across the back of my thighs."

"So what were you doing in here to begin with?" Lex asked the question Bob was afraid to ask. *Spiders*. Valkerie had screamed that she was covered with spiders when she was sick.

"I . . . heard something in the galley. Bob was downstairs, and you were—"

"You knew I was downstairs?" Bob lifted the ice bag and gently slid his hand across the bulge on the side of Valkerie's head.

"I heard you welding down in the shop before all this happened."

"Sorry." Bob replaced the bag. "I woke up at four this morning and couldn't get back to sleep. My sleep cycle's still out of whack from . . ."

"From when you were taking care of me." Valkerie's weak smile charged the air between them with crackling awareness.

"So what else do you remember?" Lex blurted out.

Valkerie looked at Lex, and the connection was broken. "I . . . um, there was some kind of a clang out here in the commons . . . or maybe the galley. That's why I came out—I wanted to see what was making all the racket. And I remember I heard you talking in Kennedy's room."

Bob turned to Lex. "Kennedy was awake?"

She shook her head. "No, he's been out the whole time."

Bob felt his uneasiness returning. "Valkerie, are you sure you heard Lex talking? Maybe humming?"

"Sure, I'm sure." She jutted her chin at him. "Look, my fever's broken. I wasn't hallucinating. Lex was talking."

Bob sighed. "Valkerie, it's not that I'm doubting you, but you have been sick and maybe—"

"Kaggo." Lex stood up and began pacing. "I didn't say I wasn't talking. I said Kennedy was out."

He raised his eyebrows.

For the first time he could ever remember, Lex blushed. "I was just . . . talking. It's no big deal, okay?"

"To anybody we know?" Bob didn't know what else to say.

"No." Lex sat down, her face turned away from them.

"Right." *Great. Now Lex is seeing ghosts. Or at least talking to them.* Bob turned back to Valkerie. "So then what happened? You came out here and . . . Why didn't you turn on the lights?"

"I was trying to, but I couldn't find the switch." Valkerie shuddered. "Then I heard something. Kind of this groaning noise. And . . ." She hesitated. "I know it sounds crazy, but something attacked me. Ran straight at me from over there." She pointed across the commons, where it opened into the galley.

Lex shook her head. "This is just too weird." She got up and padded toward the galley.

Bob put his hand on Valkerie's shoulder. "Is there anything else—"

"Bob!" Lex's shout echoed in the galley. She backed out of the room, pointing at the floor.

He jumped up and bounded toward her.

"Lex, what is it?" Valkerie called out behind him.

Bob skidded up to Lex and followed her gaze.

The pantry door was flung open. Food packets lay scattered all over the floor.

"I don't *believe* this." Bob turned to Valkerie. "Did you come into the galley? At all?"

She shook her head. "What's wrong?"

"Food. All over the place. Our food."

Valkerie stood shakily to her feet. She was halfway across the room before Bob could get an arm around her for support.

He led her slowly to the galley.

She gasped. "Somebody's been eating our porridge."

"Impossible." But how could he deny what he was seeing? Bob put his arm around Valkerie's shoulder and guided her back to a hanging chair. "Impossible."

She held on to his hand. "Bob, listen. I know everything sounds impossible, but we've got to ask what's the *least* impossible?"

Lex came back to join them, her face drawn, tense.

"Look, there are four of us, right?" Valkerie held up four fingers. "We agree that Kennedy didn't make that mess, right?"

Bob nodded. "The galley was fine a couple hours ago. I got a tube of Jell-O and ate it in the shop."

"And I've been with Kennedy the whole time since then," Lex said. "He's the last person who could have done it."

"Okay, then that leaves one of us three." Valkerie folded down her first finger. "And I promise you guys I didn't do it." She folded down her second finger.

"I sure didn't," Lex said. "I was with Kennedy the whole time." When Valkerie folded down the third finger, the two women turned to Bob.

He shook his head. "I didn't do it either. Swear on a stack of Bibles."

The three of them looked at one another uneasily.

"One of us is fibbing," Lex said.

Bob nodded. That was the only possibility. But it was wrong. It had to be.

Valkerie shook her head. "Guys, that's impossible. After what we've been through, I know you two. I'd know if you were lying. And you're not. I *know* it. Neither of you made that mess."

Lex stared at her. "Valkerie, that's pretty much the same as admitting you did it. You know that, don't you?"

Bob spun on her. "Come on, Lex. Valkerie saved our lives to get out here. I would trust her with my life—have trusted her with my life a couple of times. She wouldn't tell us she wasn't hallucinating unless she was sure."

"Then who did it?" Lex stared back at Bob with an unflinching gaze. "In case you haven't noticed, there are only four people on this planet."

Valkerie took a deep breath. "I know it sounds weird, but . . . we're out of choices. It wasn't Kennedy, and it wasn't one of us. So it has to be something else. Or somebody else. Is it possible we brought a guest with us to Mars? A fifth member of the crew?"

"You mean like rats?" Lex sounded incredulous.

Valkerie rubbed the back of her thigh and shook her head. "It was way bigger than a rat."

Bob felt his insides lurch. A stowaway? That was ridiculous. Absurd. How could anything have hidden inside the ship all the way from Earth? It didn't make sense. Nothing made any sense. "This Hab was sent without passengers, remember? It didn't even have an atmosphere until a few months before we got here."

Lex's face was impassive. "Valkerie, tell us again about that thing you saw Wednesday night outside the Hab. What did it look like?"

"I don't know," Valkerie said. "That's just what made it so scary. I saw something move and . . . that's all."

"How big? Did it have a face? Arms? What are we up against here?" Lex crossed her arms and looked up at the porthole.

"One thing's for sure," Bob said. "We should do a thorough search of the ship."

"Bob?" Valkerie grabbed Bob's arm. "Is there any way we could . . . lock the door?"

He shivered. The airlock didn't have a physical lock of any kind. It didn't need one. There were just the four of them—the only living beings on the entire planet. No bogeymen, no burglars, no bad guys. No mysterious fifth man. "I guess I could jury-rig something."

Lex turned to look at him, her eyes wide, her jaw set. "First we search."

"Houston is going to think we've gone off the deep end," Valkerie said.

"No, they're not." Bob shot a glance at Lex. "Because we're not going to tell them. Right?"

"Then what are we going to do?" Valkerie looked frustrated, tense.

"That's simple." Lex squared her shoulders. "We're going to use our heads and work this thing out like rational human beings."

"So we've got a mystery on our hands," Valkerie said. "But one thing I know for sure. Something's out there. Likely as not, it's in here. And I'm not going to rest until I find it."

Lex turned toward the stairwell, but not quick enough to hide the look of skepticism that washed across her features.

Bob knew exactly what she was thinking. Valkerie had been sick. What if she'd been dreaming? Sleepwalking? He didn't want to believe it. Truth was he felt terrible for even thinking it, but there was no fifth man. There couldn't be. End of discussion.

But the way Valkerie had looked at him. Her eyes . . . she had said she wasn't dreaming. Said it really happened. She'd know the difference between a nightmare and reality, wouldn't she? She wasn't the type to say she was sure if she had any doubts. She wouldn't lie . . .

Bob jumped up and followed after Lex. "Just stay here and rest, Valkerie. Lex and I are gonna search the Hab from top to bottom. If there's so much as a pregnant cockroach onboard, we'll find it."

Bob snapped the last plastic wall panel back in place and stretched his aching back, letting his breath out with a sigh.

Lex shot him a troubled look from across the room. "Now what?"

Bob stepped toward the airlock and started examining the wheel. "I don't know. We tell her we didn't find anything. What else can we do?"

"What if she's still sick? Don't you think we owe it to her to let the flight docs know? They've been asking about hallucinations."

"That was back when they were thinking Legionnaires' disease. You checked the water system yourself. They've already ruled that out."

"Still, I think they should know. It might be important in diagnosing this thing."

Bob turned his head to look at the stairwell. "Lex, it's going to be kind of awkward if we go back up there. She's sitting right next to the CommConsole."

"Which is one reason we're having this discussion down here." Lex led the way out of the EVA-suit room and around the corridor to the workshop. "We can call from here."

Bob sat on a stool. He hated to admit it, but Lex was right. They had to report it. Even so, he couldn't help feeling that somehow, in some way, he was betraying Valkerie.

He sighed deeply, wishing he knew what was right. You *had* to tell the truth, didn't you? Even when the truth was the worst thing in the world. Better an ugly truth than a beautiful lie. Bob picked up the mike and handed it to Lex. "You do it," he said, his voice thick.

Lex keyed the mike. "Houston, this is the Ares 7 calling with an update on Valkerie's condition—"

A floor panel creaked.

Bob turned.

Valkerie stood framed in the stairwell hatch, her eyes brimming with tears.

"Valkerie, I—"

She turned and fled up the stairs.

### Monday, March 23, 2015, 9:45 a.m., CST

### Josh

Josh slammed the Tiger Team reports onto his desk and crash-landed into his chair. He pressed his face into his hands and leaned against the wall. It was all his fault. If he hadn't planted the charge . . . If it hadn't gone off on their ship . . .

He took a step toward the door. They'd probably fire him, but he had to tell them the truth. Once they knew that the bacteria came from Earth and not the micrometeorite . . . Once they knew the bacteria was safe, they'd forget all their back-contamination paranoia.

Josh paused at the door. But this wasn't going to work. It wasn't his bacteria making the crew sick. His little bug wasn't toxic. So what *was* infecting them? And who would stand up for them if Nate fired him? He was the only friend they had right now.

Josh spun on his heel and stalked back to his desk. Bob and Lex *had* to find the source of the contamination. They'd gone through every empty food packet in the waste system, but they'd already dumped the trash from their space flight. If they could just prove that one of the food packets had been contaminated. If they could just find a trace in the bioreactor, the greenhouse materials—anything.

A knock sounded at the door. Josh ignored it. If Nate wanted to kiss and make up, he could go cozy up to one of the reptiles he'd brought in to swing the vote his way.

Another knock. "Josh, it's me, Cathe."

Speak of the devil. Josh picked up his phone and started flipping through his calendar.

"Josh, please. I need to apologize."

Josh walked over to the door. "Apologize for what?" He waited with his hand on the doorknob.

No answer.

"Apologize for what?"

Silence.

*Oh great.* He swung the door open.

Cathe slumped against the doorframe, looking at the floor.

"Cathe, what's wrong?" He stooped his head to look into her face.

Her eyes were moist.

A lump formed in his throat. "I'm sorry if I got personal back there. I didn't mean anything by it. I was just . . . mad. Come in. Sit down." He guided her to the chair in front of his desk and crouched on the floor beside her.

Cathe blinked several times and looked him in the eye. "I just wanted to say I'm sorry. I know how bad it feels to be ganged up on."

"It's okay. You didn't—"

"Please, I need to explain. Here you've been so nice to me, promoting me to the CATO console—and then I side against you the first chance I get. If I were you, I'd fire me."

"No, you're fine. Everybody's entitled to their own opinion."

"But I should at least explain mine." Cathe paused, staring past him at the wall. "Remember I said my father died of pneumonia?"

Josh nodded. "You're going to tell me that's caused by bacteria, right?"

"In this case it was caused by a virus—the AIDS virus." Cathe's voice sounded dead. "They traced it back to his dentist. The jerk knew he was infected, but he didn't even bother to wear gloves."

"I'm . . . really sorry." Josh almost placed a hand on her arm, but didn't. She seemed like the kind of woman who didn't like to be comforted.

Cathe stared past Josh, at the pictures on his wall. He wondered which one she was looking at. The one of him and his father on their first camping trip? That was his favorite.

"Ever think what the world would be like if AIDS had never happened? I keep asking myself that. What if I could have stopped the epidemic before it ever began? What price would I have paid?"

Josh remained silent. You didn't have to be a genius to know where this was headed.

"I keep thinking. What if I had been my father's dentist? To know that I was responsible for—" She buried her face in her hands and took a deep breath. When she looked up, there was fire in her eyes. "I'm sure Drs. Jansen and Ohta would rather die than know they were responsible for a new worldwide epidemic. Fevers of one hundred and four. Do you have any idea how many people the fever alone would kill? And who knows what the long-term effects will be? Maybe the micrometeorite was carrying a virus too. Maybe something entirely new. People can carry the AIDS virus for years without even knowing it. Who knows what's in the crew's systems right now?"

Josh shook his head. "The so-called micrometeorite wasn't carrying anything. The bacteria in the Ares 10 came from Earth."

"You don't know that. We have to consider the possibility that—"

"Cathe, I know." Josh met her startled gaze head on. "For sure." He wanted more than anything to tell somebody. No, he had to be honest with himself. He wanted to tell *her*. It was more than just needing to off-load his burden. He needed her to know him for what he really was.

"What's wrong?" Cathe leaned forward, intoxicatingly close. The freshness of her hair surrounded him.

"If I tell you something, will you promise not to . . ." *No.* Josh shook his head. If he was going to trust her, well then he'd just have to trust her. But where to begin? He looked at her.

She was watching him. Waiting.

"When I was Ares 10 commander I did everything I could to make the mission succeed. Television interviews. Radio. Conferences. It was a full-time job, but I could tell it wasn't going to be enough. Don't get me wrong. I love Americans, but they have the attention span of a gnat with ADD. And when the people lost interest, so did Congress. They cut our funding four times. It was clear they were going to snatch Mars away from us after the first mission—unless we found something spectacular."

He looked at her face for a long time. It might be the last time he could look at her without seeing reproach in her eyes. "About that time a friend doing research in Antarctica discovered a new type of bacteria that could survive almost anything. Extreme temperatures, freeze-drying, radiation . . . We tested everything—including its toxicity to humans. I injected a solution of it into myself—just to be sure. I thought I was doing the right thing . . ."

"It—it was you?" Cathe's eyes went wide. "*You* planted the bomb?"

It was several seconds before Josh could find his voice. "I know it was wrong—stupid. But I was obsessed with making the mission work. I thought I had to do something. We'd worked so hard. When I got bumped off the mission, I made a capsule of bacteria and attached it to one of the parachute lines. The pyro was for spreading the bacteria in the Martian atmosphere. It wasn't supposed to go off until the chutes were released. You've got to believe me. I never dreamed it would go off in the solar-panel bay. How could I have known that Bob would find the leads on a spacewalk?"

"No wonder you were so upset," Cathe said. "I've never seen anyone so determined in my life. I thought you were going to work yourself to death."

"It was my fault. I would have given my life to save them." Josh lowered his eyes. "I'd *still* give my life to save them. I have to. Don't you see? Nate and Frazier and the rest of them all think the ship is contaminated with some bugaboo from outer space. I have to turn myself in. If I don't, they're going to let the crew rot on Mars."

"But you could be fired. You might even go to jail."

Josh bowed his head. "I *will* be fired. And as for jail . . . I deserve it. That and a whole lot more. I'd rather die than become your dad's dentist, but how could I live with myself if I were the reason my friends were trapped on Mars?"

Cathe slid off her chair and knelt in front of him. A hesitant hand slid around his neck, sending bolts of electricity up and down his spine. She pulled him forward slowly.

He felt his eyes drifting shut . . . .

"Wait a minute!" Her outburst brought him back to reality.

She pulled away from him, but held his gaze. "You said the bacteria isn't toxic. Are you sure?"

Josh nodded.

"Well, if it isn't the bacteria that's making the crew sick, then what is it?"

"I wish I knew. But it had to come from Earth. I was hoping it would turn out to be food poisoning, but so far all the tests of the food containers have come up negative."

Cathe stared into space for several seconds. "Don't tell them. Don't you see? It's not going to make any difference. If it's not your bacteria making them sick, then they'll have to assume it's something else. Something from Mars."

"It's not from Mars. It can't be. The doctors are right about one thing. That halobacteria couldn't have made them sick. So if it isn't that, and it isn't from the micrometeorite, then they must have picked up some kind of Earth bug. Maybe it's Legionnaires' disease after all. It's something pretty bad, but it's not going to back-contaminate Earth, because it came from Earth in the first place. It's all my fault that Nate thinks otherwise."

"You've got to get it through your head that you're *not* responsible for this. It's not your fault they're sick. You've got to let go of this guilt-trip thing you've got going. It isn't logical."

"But I *am* guilty. I almost killed four people."

"Almost. But you never meant to hurt them, so how can you be guilty? What you did was meant to save NASA. You meant to save their lives. If it weren't for you, they'd all be dead. They needed you. They still need you. If you want to help them, you've got to forgive yourself and move on. Okay?"

Josh looked down at the floor.

"Turning yourself in isn't going to make any difference. Whatever they've caught doesn't seem to be any of the usual bugs we already know about. If your bacteria isn't causing the infection, it has to be something else—and that something else is looking more and more like it's not of Earth origin. As far as bringing the crew back to Earth is concerned, there's no difference between an infection from a micrometeorite and one from the planet Mars. So no talk of turning yourself in. Okay?"

Josh nodded slowly, but not for the reason Cathe probably thought. He knew what he had to do. He would confess to the whole thing—the capsule, the bacteria, the pyro charge—everything. Everything except the fact that the bacteria wasn't toxic. He would lose his job, but if he could convince Flight Med that the sickness was caused by bacteria from Earth, his friends would be able to come home. After twelve months of agony, he'd finally be able to live with himself. Even if it was life all alone and in prison.

Josh's phone rang. He grabbed it and put on a smile. "Good morning! This is Josh Bennett."

"Josh, it's Nate. Lex just called in."

Josh sat up very straight in his chair. "And . . . ?"

"Valkerie's had another hallucination and probably some sort of amnesia. I'm sorry, Josh. It doesn't look good."

Josh stared at the wall for a long second.

"Josh, you there?"

"Nate." Josh swallowed hard and closed his eyes against the silent plea in Cathe's eyes. "Something's come up and we need to talk. Right away if we can. You, me, . . . and Perez."

# CHAPTER 13

Monday, March 23, 2015, 8:00 a.m., Mars Local Time

Bob

Bob waited in the airlock, watching the pressure gauge rise from eight millibars. Another pointless EVA. He'd just searched every square inch of the ground around the Ares 7. He'd even searched the Ares 10. The Hab they had made the trip to Mars in was stale and musty, but of course he hadn't found anything. Most of their food was cached in the Ares 10, because they needed the work space in the Ares 7. If something had gotten into their food supplies . . . But, no. No tracks, no tunnels, no discarded food packets, no sign of any life at all.

Of course there wasn't. How could there be?

The pressure hit 1,006 millibars. Bob pulled the water-spray hoses from the wall and started spraying off his suit. The sick feeling that had been sitting like a brick in his stomach all morning pushed its way up to his throat. Valkerie was much better now. Did it make sense to think she had hallucinated the whole thing? The noises, maybe. But she'd shown him the bruises on her legs. She couldn't have gotten them from falling. And what about the scattered food packets? Something or some*one* did that, and it just wasn't rational to think she had faked it all. Valkerie was a trustworthy person. Could it have been Kennedy? He sure as the devil wasn't trustworthy, and his condition had been improving a lot lately. Maybe he'd snuck out of his room to . . . to what? To scare them all out of their minds? And how could he have gotten out without Lex seeing him? Lex had been taking care of Kennedy all night.

*And how do you know that, Kaggo?*

He knew it because . . . Lex said so.

*Is Lex trustworthy?*

Up till today, Bob would have said yes without hesitation. What possible motivation could she have for freaking out Valkerie, messing up the food, and scaring them all to death—especially now when Kennedy was sick?

*When* Mission Commander *Kennedy was sick.*

Lex was second in command on this mission.

Bob shook his head. Nothing made any sense. Valkerie was the one who started the whole business. Her monster-in-the-window stunt had put them all on edge for almost a week now. Maybe it was hypervigilance, as he'd feared. A natural enough reaction to stress and lack of sleep. If so, it made sense that they were all hallucinating. Maybe they were crossing a wide savannah and needed somebody to beat up on.

A dark thought cast its shadow over Bob's mind. Was he sure that he hadn't scattered the food packets himself? Maybe when he was getting the Jell-O? What if he was the one cracking up?

Bob spun open the spoked wheel used to clamp shut the airlock door and stepped into the Hab. Lex stood rigid in the doorway of the EVA-suit room, watching him—a length of steel pipe grasped tightly in her hands.

Unclamping the clasps of his helmet, Bob twisted it to the side and lifted it off his head. "Peace, Earthling. I am Kaggo of Mars. I mean you no harm."

Lex's face twisted into a half smile. "I, uh . . . I just got off the radio with Josh. He sounded really weird. Something fishy is going down in Houston. They're not telling us everything. I think Nate's trying to pull a fast one on us again, but I can't figure out what it is."

Bob nodded. *And it's always the untrustworthy person who doesn't trust others.*

"So . . . I was just wondering. Did you find anything?"

"Of course not." Bob took off his gloves, unsnapped the top half of his EVA suit from the pants, and sat down on the bench. "What'd you expect?"

Lex shrugged. "You're the one who went out to investigate. I told you there isn't anything out there."

"Because Valkerie asked me to. Maybe the problem's inside the Hab after all."

"So you suspect Kennedy? Believe me, I was watching him the whole time. He was asleep all night. There's no way he could have gone out there."

Bob didn't say anything.

"I think Valkerie's cracking up." Lex looked over her shoulder. "If the same thing happens to Kennedy . . ."

*You'd like that, wouldn't you?* Bob was surprised at the thought. He leaned forward, letting gravity assist him in getting off the top half of his EVA suit. *What's with me lately? Am I turning paranoid? If I can't trust Lex—*

Lex's voice startled him from his thoughts. "Kennedy was getting pretty weird last night. Talking in his sleep, having some dream involving a woman. I gathered she wasn't enjoying the experience, but it didn't sound like she had much choice."

Bob narrowed his eyes. "You know, last week when I tried to say something about the Hampster, you got all over my case."

Lex shook her head. "That was just your jealousy talking, pal. And it was before our two friends got the Mars Madness."

*Mars Madness.* The words sent a chill down his spine. He lay down on the floor and wiggled his legs up and out of the pants of his suit. Lex stood in the doorway, idly hefting the steel pipe in her hands. Bob hastily stood up and sat on the bench again. "Uh . . . what's the pipe for, Lex?"

She flushed and started fidgeting with it, spinning it in her hands. Finally she shrugged. "You remember we promised Valkerie we were gonna try to find a way to lock the outside door."

"I'll get that latch made. I just need to find a way to anchor it to the wall."

Lex shook her head. "While you were outside I went looking for a different solution. A simpler one. A stronger one." Lex stepped to the airlock and wedged one end of the bar through the spokes of the wheel so that the other end jammed in the corner between the floor and the wall.

Bob stepped toward the hatch and tried to turn the wheel. It wouldn't budge. "So what are you so worried about? You're the one who's been saying we're not exactly in a bad neighborhood."

"Just wanted to make sure we had a really solid way to lock the door—just in case we need it." Lex shrugged and headed for the stairwell.

Bob watched her until she was out of sight, then he turned back to the wheel and pushed against it with all his might. It wouldn't turn. The hatch was locked up tighter than Fort Knox.

He turned back toward the stairwell. Lex had been approaching the hatch when he opened it. If she had locked it while he was outside on the EVA . . .

*What is wrong with me? I'm noiding out. Maybe I've got the Mars Madness too.*

Monday, March 23, 2015, 11:00 a.m., CST

Nate

Nate leaned back in his chair, studying Steven Perez. "Are you doing all right, sir? Can I get you some coffee or anything?"

Perez shook his head. "Nate, calm down. I'm not dead yet." He fidgeted, then leaned forward. "Josh didn't say what he wanted to talk about?"

"Just that it was very important and we both—" Nate's phone rang. He scooped it up. "Yeah, Carol?"

"Josh Bennett to see you, Mr. Harrington."

"He's late."

"No, sir, he's exactly on—"

Nate dumped the phone on the cradle and stood up. Before he reached the door, it opened. Josh looked even worse than he had at the meeting. He had shaved badly this morning, and his eyes looked sunken—like he'd missed a few months of sleep. "Josh, you look, um . . . great. Have a seat."

Josh shut the door, started to sit, then tugged on the door again. He slumped down on the chair next to Perez.

Dead silence. Josh's eyes were glued to his hands.

Nate felt a rush of fear. No. Josh could *not* resign from this mission. If somebody in industry was trying to lure him away with a pot of gold—

"Josh, what's up?" Perez said.

Josh swallowed hard. "I . . . have something to say, and you're not going to like it. You're going to be very angry with me, and I deserve it. And I just want you to know before I say it, that I'm really sorry. Really, really sorry. I never expected it to turn out like it did, and—"

"Josh." Perez put an unsteady hand on Josh's shoulder. "Everybody has to make their own decisions. Just tell us."

Nate's fist clenched. No way was he going to let Josh leave NASA. The guy was just too good in too many ways. "Josh, listen, we're not going to let you quit. I don't care what they're offering you—we'll find a way to keep you happy, all right? We're kind of limited in what we can pay, but—"

Josh shook his head. "It isn't about money. I . . ."

Nate leaned forward. If it wasn't money, then he had a chance. Maybe not a good chance, but a fighting—

"I really wanted the Ares mission to be a success." Josh's voice was hoarse, and he swallowed again.

"It is a success," Nate said. *Sort of.*

"Just . . . let me finish." Josh leaned forward with his elbows on his knees and covered his face with his hands. "We all knew what it was going to take to make the mission really work. We had to find something big on Mars. Something so big it would light a fire here on Earth."

Nate crossed his arms. *Right. Like the fire we've got right now with this back-contamination nonsense.*

Josh hesitated. "Anyway . . . I . . . wanted to make sure we couldn't fail . . . so I got some insurance."

Nate's heart lurched in a funny way. Josh snuffled heavily.

"Go on." Perez's voice quivered.

"There's an archaebacteria that grows in Antarctica," Josh said. "It's an extremophile—thrives in the cold, resistant to drying. It's anaerobic, but oxygen doesn't kill it. Soil peroxides don't kill it. Radiation doesn't kill it. A hardy little guy."

Long silence.

Nate leaned forward. "I'm not getting this. What are you trying to say?"

"I stole a couple of pyros and made a package. I meant for it to go off just before they landed—when they blew off the chutes."

"And something went wrong," Perez said.

"Way wrong." Josh's tear-streaked voice came through his hands, the words muffled and broken.

Nate stood up, fury flooding his veins. "You're telling me that *you're* the guy who practically got our crew killed out there?"

Perez looked up sharply. "Nate—"

"*You're* the bomber we spent three months chasing down?"

"Nate, he didn't mean to—"

"I'm supposed to worry about whether his *intentions* were good?" Nate stared at Perez. "That's not the way we do business—"

"Nate, it's over. It was a mistake. Now just calm down."

All of a sudden, Josh was crying. Bawling his eyes out.

Nate looked out the window, embarrassed. He could not *believe* this was happening. Josh . . . the bomber? That didn't make sense. Josh would do anything to make the mission work. *Anything.*

Nate hesitated, playing with the implications of that realization for a full minute. Josh wouldn't do anything he thought would endanger the crew. Not that kind of *anything.* The kind of *anything* Josh would do was browbeating NASA into an impossible lifeboat operation. And breaking a gag order to save somebody's life. Yeah, Josh had to have done that. Josh would do anything to save the lives of his crew. But he would never, *never* do something that he thought could kill them.

Josh was guilty as sin.

Josh was innocent as Mother Teresa.

Both at the same time.

Slowly, the acid fury in Nate's veins neutralized itself. Maybe Perez was right. What was the point in getting angry now? The damage was done. And fixed. Josh had fixed it himself. Nate breathed deeply, letting the strain of the last year drain out of him. There was no saboteur. Never had been. It was all just a mistake. A blunder—like the one Nate himself had made when he lied to the crew. Like the five or six Nate had made. Josh was human. He'd made a mistake and would have to—

A dagger of realization stabbed through Nate's thoughts. Crystal was still searching for the saboteur. The FBI was still working the case. There was no way he could obstruct a federal investigation. He'd have to come clean. Had to. There was no way around it.

Nate turned on Josh. "Do you have any idea what you've done? Do you know what you've just thrown away?"

"I—"

"Director of JSC—that's where you were headed. Director. Commander in chief. You were supposed to be NASA's future."

"Nate, I'm sorry, I—"

"You're *sorry*? Do you realize you could go to jail? Probably *will* go to jail . . ."

"That's enough," Perez said. "If you ask me, Josh has been through more than enough. He will have to answer for what he did—eventually. But right now we need him at Flight Director. We can worry about punishment *after* the mission is over." Perez glared at Nate.

Nate shrugged his shoulders. He could probably convince the Fibbies to hold off the prosecution until this latest avalanche blew itself out.

"So . . . Josh. What about the toxicity of this bacteria?" Perez asked. "Is it possible it's the pathogen infecting the crew now?"

Nate felt a surge of hope.

"It's . . . possible." Josh smeared his face with his hands. "I didn't think it could hurt anybody. It's an archaebacteria. But it's of Earth origin. It's on our Tree of Life. It's at least possible it is pathogenic to humans." He looked up at Nate. "There wasn't any alien bacteria on that micrometeorite. What Valkerie found on the outbound voyage was my little bug. And there is no way a fossilized Martian halobacteria could be infecting the crew. You know that, don't you, Nate? It's impossible."

"Do you have some more of that bacteria?" Nate stepped toward Josh. "We could run some studies on it. Prove it's the vector."

Josh shook his head. "I destroyed everything I didn't send on the mission."

Nate began pacing. "Where'd you get it in the first place?"

"I told you. Antarctica. I went down there to do some field studies for the 2011-2012 season. Our winter, their summer. Karla Faust invited me down."

"Remind me—she's that bacteriologist you were dating?" Nate said.

"Microbial ecologist. We were just friends—for a while. Until I got what I needed."

"So she still has a sample?" Perez sounded hopeful.

Josh shook his head. "She never knew it existed. I found it on my own. Cultured it myself. She would have killed me if she'd known."

Nate picked up the phone and pressed a button. "Carol, get Dr. Frazier over here right now." He hung up.

"What are you going to do?" Josh watched him, eyes wary.

"I'm going to have you tell Dr. Frazier exactly what you told me. Word for word—tell him the whole story. I want to get his opinion on this. Because if this idea holds water . . ." Nate sat down in his chair. "This gets us all off the hook. Bactamination, quacktamination. We're not looking at a Martian flu. We're looking at a good old Earth bug. Nobody's going to keep our boys and girls quarantined on Mars over that." Nate took a sip of his tepid coffee. "And that means we're home free. Josh, you just made my day." *And ruined your life.*

Perez gave a deep sigh. "Josh, it took a great deal of courage to come and confess like you did. A lesser man would have stood pat."

Josh stared at the floor. "Thanks . . . uh, Dr. Perez. I'd . . . do anything to save my friends."

Which was what Nate liked about Josh. "Okay, so back to business. Let's assume Dr. Frazier is going to buy into your idea on this Antarctica bug."

"He will," Perez said. "It's the only rational possibility."

"So once he does that," Nate said, "we need to think about the science mission. Bob and Lex are wanting to do another EVA to check out the source of that halobacteria, right?"

"Right." Josh sat straighter in his chair. "So they can go now?"

"Not just *can* go." Nate felt his energy returning like a flood. "If Dr. Frazier signs off on it, make that an order. I want them checking out that place ASAP. This little scare has got everyone's attention. Now let's go do some science, while our kids are in the limelight. This could turn out to be the best thing that ever happened to NASA."

# *Part III: Hypervigilance*

"All the conditions necessary for murder are met if you shut two men in a cabin and leave them together for two months."

Russian cosmonaut Valery Ryumin

"The ultimate challenge NASA faces may be building a tiny computer that can psychoanalyze astronauts and keep them from going nuts."

William Speed Weed, "Can We Go to Mars Without Going Crazy?"—*Discover*, May 2001

# CHAPTER

Wednesday, March 25, 2015, 11:00 a.m., Mars Local Time

Valkerie

"If there is intelligent life out there, I don't think it's like us. Intelligence doesn't make something human." Valkerie warmed her hands on her teacup and watched Lex through the ghostly whorls of steam that rose from her tea.

"What do you mean, *human*?" Lex leaned forward in her seat. "If you mean a bipedal primate with twenty-three pairs of chromosomes, I agree."

Valkerie took a sip of tea. "By *human*, I mean that extra something that biology and chemistry just can't seem to account for. That creative spark. Love. The sense of justice. Right and wrong."

"Is this you talking, or your faith?"

Valkerie frowned. "Who says there has to be any difference?"

"What I mean is . . . do you really believe it, or are you just saying it because, well . . . because you know you're supposed to? Because of your faith?"

"Lex, I don't believe things because of my faith. I have faith because of all the things I believe. Because of all the evidence I've—"

"But what about the life question? Doesn't your faith have a little problem with that? You already admitted that the sequencing data from the halobacteria indicates that it could be of Earth origin—that it could have been carried here billions of years ago by a meteorite. But why couldn't it have been the other way around? How do you know life on Earth didn't come from Mars? Or from . . . somewhere else?" Lex's voice faltered. She was looking over Valkerie's shoulder.

Valkerie turned to follow her gaze.

Bob stood in the doorway, his face tight and expressionless.

"I, uh . . ." Lex got up from the table. "I should probably go . . . see how Kennedy's doing."

Valkerie stood to follow.

"No, stay right there." Lex guided Valkerie back to her chair. "Sit down. Finish your tea. I'll be back in a few minutes."

Lex slipped out of the galley and into Kennedy's room next door, leaving Bob standing uneasily in the doorway.

Valkerie turned on Bob. "What was that all about? We were in the middle of a conversation."

Bob shrugged. "She's been monopolizing you all morning. I just wanted to tell you—"

"Monopolizing? So I'm a commodity now?" She fixed Bob with what she hoped was a disapproving glare.

"It's just that you've been spending so much time with Kennedy. I don't even think he's sick anymore. He's just pretending so you'll keep babying him."

She stood and pushed her way to the door. "Bob, it's a free planet. I can spend time with whomever I want. You don't get to choose."

She stalked through the corridor and into Kennedy's room. "Lex?" She poked her head through the open door. "Lex?"

The room was empty. Piles of clothes and trash littered the floor. The blankets on the cot were swept aside to reveal a dirty, stained mattress. The room reeked of stale vomit.

The angry knot in Valkerie's stomach melted into a sudden wash of sympathy. Poor Kennedy. Bob and Lex had left him to live like an animal. She'd been too focused on analyzing the infection. Even animals deserved better.

She bent down to pick up the latex gloves that littered the floor. He had never once complained, even through all the pain. Valkerie pulled the trash bag from Kennedy's waste-disposal bin and started picking up the trash. Sterile gauze. Syringe wrappers. Empty food packets.

A flash of silver beneath the cot caught her eye.

She spread out the half-empty trash bag on the filthy floor and got down on her hands and knees.

Food packets.

She reached out and rummaged through the pile. They were all unopened.

The door clicked shut behind her.

Valkerie spun around with a gasp.

Kennedy stood in front of the door with a self-satisfied smirk spread across his face.

"Kennedy? What are you . . . I was just cleaning up." She stood and held up the trash bag as proof.

He took a step toward her. His hair was dripping wet, his jump suit crisp and clean.

"You took a shower?"

Kennedy nodded slightly. His good eye bored into her like a laser.

"That's great! How do you feel?"

"A lot better, thanks to you." He stepped forward with open, outstretched arms. "Valkerie, you've been so much kinder than the others. So loving." He pulled her into a tight hug. "I really appreciate all you've done."

She squirmed in Kennedy's embrace. She couldn't believe how much strength he had recovered. It had taken her days to feel stronger than a newborn kitten, and she was still far from one hundred percent. "You're welcome. I'm just glad you're feeling better." She pried herself away and stood back to size him up.

He stared back with an intensity that made her almost uncomfortable. It was amazing. In one day he had gone from ghostly white to almost human.

"Do you still have a fever?" She stepped forward and reached a hand to Kennedy's forehead.

The door burst open. "Hampster, have you seen—" Bob's face appeared in the doorway, frozen in an expression of stunned bewilderment. "I, uh . . . Valkerie, we need you in the commons."

Valkerie didn't know what to say. "Bob, you can't just order me to—"

"Jake Hunter just contacted us. Josh is coming on the air in two minutes with an important message for all hands." Bob nodded to Kennedy. "Even you, if you feel well enough."

Valkerie started to follow Bob.

Kennedy stumbled behind her.

She turned to see him leaning heavily against the wall. "Need a hand?"

"I'll get there eventually."

Valkerie went back and ducked under his arm, pulling his weight onto her shoulder. She guided him through the galley toward the commons.

The farther they walked, the less support Kennedy seemed to need.

Bob met them at the CommConsole with a cold stare.

Valkerie ignored him, helping Kennedy into his seat before taking her own.

Lex cleared her throat. "Josh should be—"

"Ares 7, this is Josh Bennett with an important message. With me are Nate Harrington and Steven Perez. Please hold confirmation until after the entire message has been delivered." A nervous pause. "Ares 7, we are happy to report that all our concerns about a saboteur are unfounded. Nate, Steven, and I now know the truth. There is no saboteur and there never was one. We are convinced that the bacteria that contaminated the Ares 10 Hab is of Earth origin. It did not come from contact with the micrometeorite. Repeat, the bacteria is of Earth origin. All concerns about bringing you back home are unfounded. Now that Valkerie and Kennedy are well on the road to recovery, your new orders are to continue with the scientific exploration of Mars. Lex, you and Bob are now cleared to return to the site where you found the halophilic bacteria. Go out and bring us back more data on that fossil. Over."

Valkerie looked around the table. The confusion on the other faces mirrored her own feelings exactly.

"Could someone please explain to me what just happened?" Lex shook her head. "It doesn't make sense. Josh already told us last July that he caused the explosion, right?"

Bob nodded. "Apparently he didn't want Perez to know he'd already told us, but why not? And did Nate and Perez find out on their own or did Josh tell them?"

"And why did Josh wait until now to tell them?" Valkerie's voice trailed off as the answer to her question suddenly clicked into place. She looked up at Bob.

It was clear from his eyes that he was thinking the same thing she was. "Josh said that the bacterium was an extremophile. He assured me it was safe."

Valkerie nodded. "And did you catch that bit about how their concerns about bringing us back home were unfounded?"

Lex gasped. "You mean they were planning to . . ."

Valkerie couldn't believe it. Houston was up to its same old tricks. "When they thought we were sick with an extraterrestrial bug, they had doubts about bringing us back home."

"So Josh is letting them think we're infected with his bacteria," Bob said.

"Even though he knows we aren't." Valkerie crossed her arms. Josh was putting the crew in a tight spot, expecting them all to go along with a bald-faced lie.

"So what do we do?" Bob looked miserable. "They're going to wonder why we're taking so long to reply."

"We're going back to explore that hole." Lex's tone was determined. "That's what we should have been doing all along."

"No way!" Bob pounded the CommConsole. "I'm not leaving Valkerie here all alone with the Hampster."

"Why not?" Valkerie shot Bob a hard look. "I feel fine, and Kennedy is much better. You don't have to worry about us."

"Because I don't . . ." Bob looked down and brushed at something invisible on the table. "What if you have a relapse?"

"Both of us at the same time?"

"With all the stuff that's been happening? I just wouldn't feel right."

"It's not your decision. It's mine." Kennedy pushed himself forward, jutting his jaw at Bob. "And I say you and Lex are doing that EVA." He reached for the transmitter. "Houston, this is Kennedy Hampton, confirming receipt of your message. With me are Lex Ohta . . ."

"Roger that, Josh. This is Lex, confirming."

"Valkerie Jansen . . ."

"Hi, Josh. We understand your message completely."

"And Bob Kaganovski . . ."

Bob sat silent, glaring back at Kennedy.

"Well . . . We copy your message," Kennedy said. "There is no saboteur. The infection is caused by Earth bacteria. And Bob and Lex are doing an EVA to the halophilic-bacteria site. Immediately."

### Wednesday, March 25, 2015, 2:45 p.m., CST

### Josh

Josh sat back down behind the Flight Director console, ignoring Nate's scowl. Nate had obviously caught that little bit about their concerns about bringing the astronauts back home. Hopefully the crew caught it, too, and knew enough to play along.

Nate appeared at Josh's elbow. "Just what did you think you were doing?"

He put on his blankest expression. "Excuse me?"

Nate glowered at him. "There was no reason to say anything that might upset the crew. We need to be able to have frank and full discussions here without every word getting reported to the crew."

They spent forty-five minutes arguing in whispers about the rights of the crew to know what was going on. Then Kennedy's response came back through.

Josh shrugged at Nate. "See? Did they sound worried? They're going on an EVA."

"Kaggo didn't check off," Nate growled.

"He's fine. I know Bob. If something was bothering him, he'd speak up."

Perez walked into the FCR. "Nate? Ms. Yamaguchi just arrived in your office. You and I need to discuss something with her."

Nate stalked out.

Josh felt his whole body turn cold. Great, in Nate's current mood, he was probably going to tell Yamaguchi to throw him in the clink.

"Josh, could I talk to you for a second?" Cathe's low voice.

Josh turned to face her. Her smile looked calm, but Josh could tell she was upset—something about the way she couldn't stop fidgeting with her hands. "Sure. What's up?"

"In private?" she whispered, glancing to one of the FCR doors.

"I really need to hang right here until the shift ends." Josh checked his watch. 3:30. "Can it wait till five?"

She hesitated and then nodded. "Right after the next crew comes in, okay?"

• • •

Josh's heart pounded wildly as he followed Cathe outside. As soon as they were clear of the building, he reached a hand to her shoulder. "What's wrong?"

She turned slowly toward him and his heart sank. A stream of tears ran down her cheek.

"Cathe . . ." He started to reach for her, but his arms froze in sudden indecision. "What's wrong?"

"You told them, didn't you?"

"About the bacteria? Yes. I had to."

"And?" She bit her lip, looking up at him with more feeling than he had ever dared to imagine.

"I, uh . . . It's okay. Everything's going to be okay. They're leaving me as Flight Director until we get the crew back."

"But what if they don't come back?"

"They will. I told Nate and Perez it was my bacteria that was making them sick."

"But you know it's not—" Her voice broke.

"It's okay." Josh stepped forward and wrapped her in his arms. "It's okay. They're going to prosecute me after the mission, but I'm okay with that. I deserve it. Besides. It was either me or Kennedy and, well . . . Kennedy may be a schmuck, but he didn't sabotage the mission."

"Kennedy would have let you hang." Cathe's muffled voice sounded under Josh's chin. "He'd even volunteer to hold the rope. He's a raving psychopath."

"He is not—" Josh pulled back from Cathe and stared. *No.*

"I'm serious. What kind of a guy would frame his best friend for terrorism?"

*No, no, no, no.* Josh spun around to orient himself.

"Josh, what? What's going on?"

Josh whipped out his cell phone and selected Nate's number.

"Harrington." Nate's voice sounded strained.

"Nate, is Ms. Yamaguchi with you?"

"This isn't a good time, Josh."

"Nate, I need to talk with her right now. I need her to open that room with all the stuff they took from Kennedy's apartment."

"Josh, it's a really bad—"

"I don't have time! She can arrest me tonight. I don't care. But I want her over at that room in ten minutes. I've got a hunch and I need to check it out." Josh hung up. "Come on, Cathe. If I'm right, and I hope I'm wrong—"

"Would you please tell me what's going on?" She tugged at his arm as he led the way.

"I just had a bad thought. Real bad." Josh wouldn't say any more until they arrived at the room. This was crazy. He didn't even dare *think* it, much less say it.

When Nate and Yamaguchi arrived, Josh and Cathe were leaning against the door.

It took all of Josh's self-control to not yell at them for taking so long.

Yamaguchi wore a look of righteous fury. She wouldn't even look at Josh as she unlocked the door, but she didn't pull out any handcuffs, and that was way more than he deserved.

Josh signed in and went to the file cabinets. He yanked open the third drawer and began tossing books onto the desk. "Help me put them in order. Alphabetical by title. Try to group them by subject matter."

As he finished pulling out all the books, he heard Cathe gasp. He looked at the stack and started to read the titles. *"Abnormal and Clinical Psychology. Abnormal Behavior. Abnormal Behavior: Perspectives in Conflict. Abnormal—"*

"Starting to see a pattern?" Josh opened one of the books and searched through the table of contents—a laundry list of psychological aberrations.

Cathe picked up another book and started thumbing through its pages. "You've read the transcripts. Did he ever try to make the shrinks think you were crazy?"

"Nope. That's what's worrying me." Josh flipped through the pages. Searching for scribbled notes. Highlights. Anything.

"Uh-oh." Cathe breathed close to his ear. She pointed to a section on delusional disorders. The part on paranoia was highlighted with razor-sharp fluorescent yellow.

"Great. And all this time I thought Bob was just being jealous." Josh threw open his book and ran a finger down the index. Delusional disorders. Page 378. He flipped through the pages and stopped at a bright yellow patch. As far as he could tell it was the only highlighted section in the book.

Agent Yamaguchi stood at the door, her lips pursed in white fury. "Mr. Bennett, would you care to enlighten us on what you think you've discovered?"

Nate put his hand on her shoulder. "Crystal, as I told you—"

"Nate, please tell me Bob and Lex haven't started their EVA yet."

Nate looked at Josh, frowning. "Too late. They've been out almost an hour now."

Josh jumped to his feet. "Call them back. You've got to call them back!"

"What?"

"And get Dr. Abrams and his shrink squad to the FCR as quick as possible."

Nate crossed his arms. "Josh, could you explain things for us mere mortals? Because if you can't, I think Crystal wants to take you into custody right now."

"While you guys are playing cops and robbers," Cathe said, "maybe you could think about what might happen if you mixed together hypervigilance, Mars Madness, and"—she looked at Josh, and he nodded—"paranoid delusional disorder."

Nate stared from Cathe to Josh. "You two are nuts."

"No, we aren't. But Kennedy is." Josh pulled the phone out of Nate's shirt pocket. "Make the call, Nate. Then bake me into a fruitcake or whatever you have to do. I don't care. But don't leave Valkerie alone in that Hab with Kennedy."

# CHAPTER 15

Wednesday, March 25, 2015, 1:00 p.m., Mars Local Time

Bob

The rover tipped forward and jounced down a steep incline. Bob blinked his eyes. “Oops!” He gripped the wheel hard and took his foot off the accelerator.

“Easy there, Kaggo!” Lex’s voice sounded white-knuckle tense.

They reached the bottom of the grade, and the rover slowed to normal speed.

“Sorry,” Bob said. “Kind of lost focus there for a minute.”

“You’ve been spacing out since we left. What is with you today?”

“Just . . . daydreaming.”

Lex pointed to a spot about a kilometer away. “That’s the edge of the bluff. Approach it slowly, okay?”

“Gotcha.” Bob slowed the rover to a few kilometers per hour and concentrated on his driving. Focus. Stay on task. Don’t think about . . . anything else.

Which was hard, because there was a lot to worry about. Valkerie was better now. Kennedy too, more or less. They were over the worst of it. But what if they had a relapse? What if

Lex got it? Bob shivered. What if he did? Then there was the question of those . . . things Valkerie had been hearing and seeing. There hadn't been another episode, but Bob was scared. If something happened to Valkerie's mind . . .

And Kennedy. What if something *didn't* happen to his mind? Bob had been hoping that the enforced vacation would have knocked some sense into him. Pulled him out of the little pit he'd been digging himself into. But if anything, it had made him worse. More morose. More paranoid. More distant. More distant with everyone but Valkerie, that is. It was so obvious. Why couldn't Valkerie see—

"Bob!"

He jerked back to awareness, then hit the brakes. The edge of the canyon shuddered to a stop five meters in front of the rover.

"You're not getting a fever, are you?" Lex put a hand on his forehead, then shook her head.

"I'm fine."

"Well . . . focus!"

"Right." Bob set the parking brake and cut the engine. He fumbled around for his helmet, found it, popped it on his head, then tried to latch it down.

Lex reached over and rotated it thirty degrees, sealed it, then flicked on his UHF comm link. "Lex, comm check."

"Loud and clear," Bob said. "Comm check."

"Loud and clear." Lex stood up. "Okay, let's get out there and do some science, big guy. And if you would be so good as to keep your brains on this planet, in this location, on this task, I would be much obliged."

"Gotcha. Ready to roll." He stood and followed her to the airlock. They were running the rover at 5 PSI pure oxygen, so there was no need for prebreathing. Two minutes later, they stepped out onto the regolith.

"You're the boss," Bob said. "What's first?"

Lex led the way to the edge of the canyon. "Right down there is where we found the halobacteria. You can see where we dug out, right there."

"I . . . think I see it," Bob said. "I see what you mean by salt deposits."

"I'm going to rappel down and dig out the entrance to that cave some more, then check around inside for water," Lex said. "And a thermal vent. That halobacteria is geologically recent, and it couldn't have thrived here without an energy source." She went around to the side of the rover and hefted out the MoleBot.

"What do you want me to do?" Bob said.

She pinched his helmet with her gloved hands. "Sit here and look pretty."

"No, really."

"You stay up here and ride shotgun on the winch and be ready to send me down stuff when I need it."

Lex pulled out the water-detector system and checked the battery. "All right, I've got enough juice to scan for at least a couple hours. And I've got oxygen for nominally six and a half hours, which probably means three if I have to do any heavy digging. Grab me another $O_2$ bottle and a battery, will you?"

Bob went into the rover and came back with an extra oxygen tank and a battery pack. He bundled it all together with the MoleBot in a padded bag. Lex had strapped on the power supply for her water detector and tested the system, which looked a lot like one of those weed-whacker things people with lawns used back on Earth.

"Okay, let's get moving. We've got a good five hours before sundown." Lex hitched a winch line to the ring at her belt and backed up to the edge of the canyon, pulling her line tight. "See ya in a while, Kaggo. Stay on this planet, okay?" She pressed a button on her winch controller and stepped back over the edge as the line began paying out.

Bob attached a second winch line to the bag of goodies and lugged it to the canyon edge. Lex was already halfway down, bounding off the rocky wall every twenty feet or so.

He hit the winch controller button and watched the padded bag descend the wall.

When it reached the bottom, Lex waved up at him. "Thanks, Kaggo. I'll keep you posted when I get this cave dug out some."

"Roger that." He backed away from the edge and began pacing beside the rover. When Lex got going on something, she usually reported in once an hour. If that. They were going to be out here for five hours? He was gonna go stark-raving, flipped-out bonkers worrying about Valkerie.

## Wednesday, March 25, 2015, 1:30 p.m., Mars Local Time

### Valkerie

Valkerie sat across the table from Kennedy, pretending to read an e-book on her phone under the scrutiny of his unblinking gaze.

Kennedy stood suddenly and began pacing the floor. Every few minutes he stopped and glanced down the stairwell. He looked flushed.

Was he was running another fever? "Why don't you get some rest?" Valkerie studied him carefully. "They won't be back for hours."

He looked long and hard at his watch, then resumed his pacing.

She put down her phone. Where had his sudden burst of energy come from? It was driving her crazy. "Kennedy, are you okay? Do you feel feverish?"

He looked at his watch again and shrugged. Before she could probe, he turned around and disappeared into the corridor. His footsteps stopped somewhere near the door to his room.

Valkerie picked up her phone and went back to the novel she'd been trying to read all week. Ann Radcliffe's *The Italian*. Talk about creepy.

A door slammed.

Valkerie jumped out of her seat.

Another door opened and slammed. Another.

What was going on now? She edged to the corridor.

Kennedy stared back at her from the dark hallway, looking her up and down like a wolf sizing up its prey. He put a finger to his lips and stepped toward her.

Valkerie backed slowly away into the commons.

"Shhhh. Not yet!"

She started at his sharp whisper.

Without taking his eyes off her, he sidled across the room and disappeared into the stairwell. The Hab shuddered with a series of crashes on the steps.

Had he fallen? Valkerie crept to the stairwell. "Kennedy?" She peeked her head inside the hatch. "Kennedy?"

Slams and clatters echoed up the stairwell.

Valkerie tiptoed down the stairs and peered cautiously through the hatch.

Kennedy was in the suit room, searching through the lockers. A jumble of EVA suits lay on the floor. The airlock beyond was braced shut with a steel pipe.

"Kennedy, what are you *doing*?" She hurried to the airlock door and wrestled the pipe free of the hatch wheel.

Kennedy wheeled around and stared at her with a sickly smile. "It's okay. I've checked both decks. They're gone."

The pipe slipped from her hands and clattered to the floor. "*Who's* gone? Bob and Lex? Of course they're gone."

"If they really went to the bacteria site, they should be gone for at least another five hours."

"What do you mean, *if* they really went? Where else would they go?"

He shrugged, a low laugh rumbling in his chest. "I don't know. That's the problem, isn't it?"

A shiver of fear danced up Valkerie's spine. There was something about his voice. Something about the way he looked at her. "Kennedy"—she tried to control her voice—"why don't we go upstairs and talk about this? Okay?"

Kennedy flashed her his signature cocky smile. "Don't worry, I'll protect you. I won't let them get you."

"Let *who* get me?"

"That's just it, isn't it?" Kennedy took a step toward her. He leaned forward, speaking in a conspiratorial whisper. "Which one do you think? No more codes. Nobody's here but you and me." His breath smelled like rotting flesh.

Valkerie shrank back from him.

"Bob may be a good mechanic, but he's dumber than a pithed possum when it comes to codes." Kennedy advanced another step. “I almost laughed myself silly last time you were doing it. He didn’t have a clue what you were really saying.”

“And what was I really saying?” Valkerie backed against the airlock door. Her body went rigid. She looked along the floor. Where was the pipe she had dropped just a minute ago?

“What you’re saying right now.” Kennedy put out his arms and braced them on either side, penning her in. “Look at you. You want me so bad, you’re shaking like a leaf. I’m shaking too.” He leaned his face closer to hers.

She could feel the heat radiating from his fevered brow. “Kennedy, you’re sick. You have a fever. You don’t know what you’re doing.”

“I know what I’m doing, all right.” He brought his face closer to hers and then lunged.

Valkerie ducked and tried to dodge under his arms.

He grabbed her shoulders and slammed her into the airlock door. The hatch wheel caught her below the shoulder blades, and her head snapped back into the wall with a sickening crack. Kennedy’s face receded into a dark tunnel.

“Want to play rough?” A sharp slap across her left cheek exploded the room into focus. “Don’t think I was fooled. I knew all along it was you.” Kennedy’s left fist jabbed forward and connected with her right eye, spinning Valkerie into the wall.

She slid down the polished surface and crumpled into a heap on the floor.

“Know how I knew?” His voice sounded remote, like the memory of a long-forgotten dream. “You gave yourself away, that’s how. Pretending you wanted Bob. But I could tell.”

Valkerie rolled onto her back and looked up. Kennedy’s distorted face filled her vision. Her groping hand closed around something metallic and cylindrical.

"I knew it was me you wanted. Not Bob." Kennedy leaned in closer.

She jabbed the bar up as hard as she could into his solar plexus.

Kennedy made a retching noise and staggered back, clutching his belly.

She rolled onto her hands and knees and crawled for the door.

Behind her, Kennedy crashed to the floor, screaming obscenities.

Valkerie pushed up onto her feet and slammed into a wall. Grasping the pipe, she staggered toward the suit-room door.

A keening moan filled her ears. Heavy breathing.

She'd hurt him badly, but probably not badly enough. She launched herself through the doorway and collapsed back onto the floor. Crawling through the corridor, she turned into the stairwell and scrambled up the stairs using her hands as well as her feet.

The moans filled her ears, crescendoing with each breath she took.

*Gotta be quieter.*

Valkerie pressed her hand to her mouth. She had to be quiet. Had to get away . . . to where? She reached the top, ran into the commons, grabbed the transmitter, and flipped it on. "Bob?" Hugging the microphone to her chest, she held the pipe in front of her like a talisman while she fought to control her breathing. "Bob, it's Valkerie. Kennedy's gone crazy. He tried to . . ." Her voice was washed away by a wave of uncontrollable sobs. "Bob, he tried, he tried . . . to kill me." She held her breath and strained her ears to listen.

A jumble of raging obscenities echoed up the stairwell. Footsteps. The clank of metal on metal.

Valkerie dropped the microphone and ran for her room, clutching the pipe.

Footsteps rang out in the commons behind her.

She slammed her door and turned the lock. Then, backing slowly away from the door, she held her breath and listened.

Silence. Nothing but the pounding of her heart.

She sank slowly onto her cot. Had she imagined the footsteps? The swearing in the stairwell?

Valkerie lifted a hand to her face. It was warm and sticky, but not feverish. She looked at her hand, and a rush of shocked disbelief jolted through her. So much blood! The room tilted and swayed beneath her. If Kennedy had been hallucinating, how did she know she wasn't hallucinating too? They'd both had the same fever. That had to be it. Kennedy wouldn't attack her. It didn't make any sense. Could she have fallen and hit her head? Everything was such a jumble. Like a dream.

She rose unsteadily to her feet and took a step toward the door. Bob. She had to find Bob.

The lock rattled lightly. A moment of breathless silence.

Something smashed into the plastic door. Out in the corridor, Kennedy swore. Another crash. Another.

The door held.

Footsteps clomped down the hall toward the kitchen.

She reached for the radio at her desk and flicked it on. "Bob? Help me. Kennedy's trying to—"

Something heavy thudded against the door.

The mike slipped from Valkerie's grip. She felt for the pipe and tried to force her nerveless hands to grasp it like a baseball bat.

Another thud at the door. Another. A knife blade, long and impossibly bright, burst through the plastic.

"Kennedy. No!"

Her only answer was the sound of the knife sawing back and forth, back and forth, ripping a slow path through the thin plastic door.

Wednesday, March 25, 2015, 1:40 p.m., Mars Local Time

Bob

"Hey, Bob, I've got the entrance to the cave dug out good and wide with the MoleBot. I'm detaching from my winch line and going in to scout around."

"Sounds good, Lex. Don't go in far, okay?"

"Roger that. I bet there's a steam vent near the entrance."

Bob watched Lex's feet disappear into the side of the cliff. "Watch out for little green men."

"Ditto. I've bagged up some specimens from the ledge here for the lab. Go ahead and haul them up and stick 'em in the rover."

Bob peered over the edge. Lex had attached two bags to the winch lines. He punched the button and winched them up on the slow setting, watching to ensure the bags didn't snag on the way up. When they arrived, he detached them and lugged them to a storage bin on the right side of the rover.

Then there was nothing to do but wait for Lex to come out. He hunched down and scanned the horizon, watching for the telltale distortions caused by rising water vapor. Somewhere around here, steam had to be coming out. Water plus energy equals life. Mars had supported life once. If there was any liquid water left, it was a good bet that the critters would still be hanging around. Bob switched his comm frequency to the CommSat band. "Ares 7, this is Bob, come in." He repeated this message three times and waited. Because of the distance to the CommSats, there was a six-second delay for the message to go up to the satellite and bounce back down to the Ares 7.

Fifteen seconds passed. Nothing.

Bob felt his pulse jump a notch. *Chill, Kaggo.* Kennedy was probably sleeping—the lout. Maybe Valkerie was down in the greenhouse, or in the head, or whatever. Yeah, in the greenhouse. He'd try again in a few minutes.

Five minutes later, Bob felt the thin blade of worry slipping down his back. "Ares 7, this is Bob, come in!"

Still nothing. Bob began pacing back and forth next to the rover. What was going on? He drummed his fingers on the top step of the rover. "Come on, Valkerie. Get your act—"

"Bob?" Valkerie's voice, breathless and hasty.

*Thank God.* He took a deep breath. "Yeah, Valkerie, this is—"

"Bob, it's Valkerie. Kennedy's gone crazy. He tried to—" Her voice broke off. She was crying!

Bob leaped up the steps into the airlock of the rover. A roaring sound pounded in his ears, filling his head, vibrating his body. Valkerie was in trouble. He'd seen the signs and he had let himself get talked out of protecting her.

He slammed shut the airlock door and punched the button to pressurize. Valkerie's sobs echoed in his ears. "Bob, he tried . . . he tried . . . to kill me."

Then silence.

About three centuries later, Bob opened the inner door of the airlock and raced to the cockpit. He punched the starter button. "Valkerie! Talk to me! What's going on? Kennedy? Can you hear me? If you so much as lay a finger on her . . ."

He threw the transmission into reverse and punched the gas pedal. The rover jolted backward, tires spinning up clouds of reddish brown Martian dust.

"I'm coming!" Bob spun the steering wheel, jammed on the brakes, and punched the gearshift into forward drive. "Hold tight, Valkerie. I'm coming!"

The rover bounded forward, leaping over rocks. "Valkerie, what's going on?"

Silence.

"Valkerie!" Bob pressed the gas pedal down as far as it would go. Why, why, why were NASA engineers so conservative? This stupid moose maxed out at fifteen kilometers per hour. He unlatched his helmet and yanked it off. Sweat ran down his face. He roared up a slope and crested the first ridge. Another three kilometers to base camp and he'd . . . he'd wring Kennedy's neck.

The terrain crawled by.

"Come on, come on!" Bob shouted at nothing. "Valkerie, can you hear me? Kennedy, keep your hands off her or you're dead meat! You hear me?"

He waited out the twelve-second delay.

Nothing. The Ares 7 was silent.

Bob swore out loud, then caught himself. Bile rose in his throat. *Please.*

Finally he backed up to the airlock of the Ares 7 and punched the hot-dock button. Then he was up and standing in the rover airlock, waiting for pressure in the connecting tunnel to rise. Half a second early, he unlatched the hatch, and the pressure differential jerked the door from his hands. He raced through the tube and punched the button to pressurize the Hab's airlock. "Valkerie, hang on!"

Finally the needle quit moving.

He ripped open the door and forced his way through. An instant later, he was fumbling at the inner door.

Locked!

Bob peered through the window.

The legs of a metal folding chair were wedged in the wheel on the inside of the door.

"Valkerie! Let me in! I'm locked out!"

No answer.

Bob threw his shoulder against the door.

It shuddered but held.

He looked inside again. Where was Valkerie? Bob backed up and rushed the door again.

The chair slipped—just a hair.

Bob slammed into the door again. And again. And again.

Each time, the chair dropped a few more millimeters.

He grabbed the door and shook it. "Come on, open!" He shoved again.

The chair slipped out and the door flew inward.

Bob staggered forward, then tripped and fell flat on his face.

Spots of blood splattered the suit-room wall. A scream rang out. Upstairs.

"Kennedy!" Bob lurched to his feet, dashed through the corridor and into the central stairway. He raced up the stairs three at a time, flew out into the commons, and swerved into the corridor—then jerked to a halt.

Kennedy was kneeling in front of the door to Valkerie's room, a thin, broken knife in his hands. He spun to look at Bob, then jumped up.

Bob rushed him. "Valkerie! I'm here!"

Kennedy raised the knife, pointing it at Bob's heart.

Bob barreled into him.

The blade snapped on the DCM on Bob's chest.

He lunged for Kennedy's throat, let his weight slam into Kennedy's body. His momentum carried them both against the wall. They collapsed onto the floor. Bob twisted as he fell, and his left knee buckled beneath him. Pain shot up through his leg.

Kennedy lay crushed beneath him, gasping. From inside the bedroom came the sound of Valkerie weeping.

"What did you *do* to her?" Bob hissed. "If you touched her—"

Fear lit up Kennedy's eyes. His left arm snaked out, a jutting finger stabbing at Bob's right eye.

Bob twisted his head.

Kennedy's finger jammed into his temple, shooting fireworks into his skull.

Bob batted at Kennedy's arm. He couldn't fight in close like this. Not in a clunky turtle shell of an EVA suit.

Bob rolled onto Kennedy's arm and took a swing at his face. Too awkward. He had to get up or he was dead. And Valkerie with him. He kept rolling over onto his backpack, forcing it into Kennedy's face. He pitched his feet up and then rolled forward into a crouch. Now just stand up and—

Something leaped onto his back, grappling for his face.

Bob staggered, then let himself fall backward onto Kennedy.

Kennedy lost his grip and stopped struggling.

Bob heard him wheezing for air and flung both elbows back. They connected with some part of Kennedy's body. Pain shot through both funny bones. Great—he'd disabled both his arms. Bob lunged forward and made it to his feet this time. His damaged knee buckled beneath him. He grabbed a doorframe to support himself, then turned, hopping on his good leg.

Kennedy lay on the floor, gasping and clutching his abdomen.

"Bob?" Valkerie's voice floated through the door. "Bob, is that you?"

"Valkerie, I'm here! Stay inside." Bob limped forward, looking for his chance.

"What are you doing out there?" The door cracked open.

"No! Stay inside until I finish him off. How bad are you hurt, Valkerie?"

The door slid all the way open. "I'm okay." She stepped out into the hall. Blood smeared the left side of her face.

Bob felt his chest constrict. A cyclone of fury gripped his mind. Kennedy had hurt her. That piece of trash had hurt—

Kennedy's hand shot out and grabbed Valkerie's ankle. He rolled toward her, his other hand reaching for the broken knife. Valkerie screamed.

"No!" Bob dove onto Kennedy, letting his full weight hammer him. Before Kennedy could react, Bob was on top of him, pounding his face, his chest, his arms. He was going to smash the life out of Kennedy or die—

"Bob, stop it!" Valkerie threw her arms around Bob's neck. "He can't defend himself."

"That's the way I want him." Bob felt a trickle of liquid down his left temple.

"Bob, stop it right now!"

"And let him attack you again? Forget it." Bob pinned Kennedy's arms and stared into his battered face.

"Bob, I'll . . . get something to tie him up. Just wait. Don't hurt him any more. He's . . . sick."

"Sick in the head." Bob glared down at the motionless man. "He's crazy!"

"That's my point. Please. Just give me five seconds."

Bob looked up and met Valkerie's pleading gaze. He looked back down at Kennedy. *Okay. But if he moves . . .* He gave Valkerie a nod.

Her footsteps pattered away down the hallway. Bob heard her rummaging through something. Kennedy lay still, his eyes puffed closed.

"Found it!" Valkerie said. "Bob, don't move, just wait."

"I'm waiting." He felt his heart pounding, the acid rage in his stomach threatening to boil over.

"Okay, just bring both of his hands together." A ripping noise sounded in Bob's ear. "I've got some duct tape. I'm going to tape his hands."

"Do his feet first." First rule of street fighting—an immobile fighter is an ineffective fighter.

"Scootch up a little."

Bob moved forward. "Kennedy, if you're conscious, just listen to me. You're going to keep your feet still or I'm going to start fighting *really* dirty."

"Bob, please." Valkerie's voice trembled. "You're not helping."

He shook his head. "I just saved your life and *I'm* not helping?"

She didn't say anything. He felt her leaning against his back, heard the sound of tape hissing around Kennedy's feet. "Okay, got it," she said. "He's not going anywhere like this."

Bob moved back a little, yanking Kennedy's hands together hard.

"Bob, go easy on him!"

"I am." He gritted the words out. "He's still alive."

Valkerie ripped off another long strip of duct tape and wrapped it around Kennedy's wrists. Once. Twice. Three times.

Bob released Kennedy's arms.

They fell limp.

"Help me up." Bob put out his hands.

Valkerie's warm hands closed over them and she pulled him up.

He winced and clutched his knee, then looked into her face. "What did he do to you?" He reached out to touch her temple. "You're bleeding."

"So are you."

"I'm fine." He looked down. The Hampster lay motionless, his puffy face bruised and bloody.

Pitiful.

Valkerie leaned into Bob's side and pressed her face against his shoulder. He could feel her shaking.

Heat flushed through his cheeks. "I'm sorry I took so long. I came as quick as I could, but . . . that rover . . ."

"You were . . . wonderful."

He swallowed hard, then dared to look at her shining eyes. "You've got a bump on your head. What did he do to you?"

"He tried to . . ." She dropped her gaze.

Rage seared Bob again. That scum tried to . . . to . . . *Stay calm or you'll kill him.* On the heels of his anger came a wave of guilt. He never should have left Valkerie alone with Kennedy. *I'm sorry. I'm so sorry. I never should have . . .*

Valkerie glanced down at Kennedy's immobile form. "I got away from him and locked myself in my room. He tried to cut through the door, but I broke his knife with a pipe. That slowed him down some, but he kept trying. He was a maniac. He kept shouting that he knew I was in love with him, that I should come out and . . . Bob, I've been such an idiot." She buried her face in his shoulder.

He stroked her soft curls, smoothing them back into place. "It's okay. He won't touch you again. Never, ever, ever."

"Ares 7, this is Houston, come in!"

The two of them turned to stare at the CommConsole. Bob closed his eyes—he didn't think he could face talking to Houston right now.

Valkerie slumped against him. "Have Lex answer that, okay?"

*Lex!* Bob's whole body jolted.

Valkerie started back. "What's wrong? Where's Lex?"

"B-b-back . . ." *What have I done?* "Back at the canyon. I . . . just forgot all about her when I heard your call."

"Ares 7, this is Houston. We got part of your message, but were cut off. Please report."

"You've got to go get her." Valkerie pushed Bob toward the stairway. "I'll talk to Houston. If anything happens to her . . ." She looked down at Kennedy.

Bob shook his head. "What if he's playacting? I can't leave you alone here with that . . . *thing*."

"Well, you can't leave Lex where she is."

Bob met her gaze. She was right, but he was too. And he wasn't going to give in this time. "I'm not leaving him here."

"Well, then take him with you."

"That's crazy."

"Want *me* to get Lex?"

Bob shook his head. He had to get Lex. Right away. He had seriously violated mission protocol by leaving her alone out there. "Help me carry the Hampster downstairs."

Together, they trundled Kennedy down the stairwell. In Martian gravity, he only weighed about fifty pounds, so lifting was easy. Carrying wasn't, because he still had his normal inertial mass. It took five minutes to lug him into the rover and dump him on the floor.

Bob wiped his brow and looked at Valkerie. "You'd better go talk to Houston. And tell them we're all fine."

She looked up into his face, her eyes glistening. Suddenly she rose on her tiptoes and planted a kiss on his cheek. "See you in a few minutes, okay?" Before he could reply, she turned and hurried down the steps and back into the Hab's airlock.

Bob closed the rover's airlock doors and hit the button to reverse the hot-dock. He stumbled forward to the driver's seat. Smiling.

The rover roared to life, and Bob drove forward. Behind him, he heard a moan, then the sound of struggling. He looked back.

Kennedy had raised his wrists to his face and was gnawing at the duct tape.

Panic bolted through Bob's chest. There was no way he was going to drive four klicks out, pick up Lex, and drive all the way back with that maniac biting through his handcuffs.

He veered to the right and punched the gas. A minute later, he skidded to a halt in front of the Ares 10 Hab.

The mission plan had called for them to link this Hab to the Ares 7 and use it as lab space and extra living quarters. The only problem was that its suspension system had broken down, and they'd been forced to park it two hundred meters from the Ares 7. The place had electrical power, but they didn't use it much because it was just too inconvenient to get to. What a waste.

Bob hot-docked the rover to the Ares 10 and strode back to where Kennedy lay.

Kennedy stopped biting at the tape and glowered up at him. "You're under arrest, Bob Kaganovski. I'm on to you."

Bob shook his head and went through the airlock and into the Ares 10. He found a towel and came back. Kennedy was still gnawing at his duct tape.

"Taste good?" Bob grabbed Kennedy's hands and wrapped them a couple of times in the towel. Pulling on the huge knot, he jerked Kennedy out of the rover and bumped through the tunnel and out into the airlock of the Ares 10. "You're going to jail, Hampster. Go directly to jail. Do not pass Go. Do not collect two hundred dollars."

"You can't leave me here!" Kennedy's voice came out in a high-pitched whine. "I order you to release me."

Bob searched through the EVA-suit lockers. He found three working suits, one for Kennedy, one for Lex, and one for himself. He made several trips and lugged them all into the rover. He checked the life-support systems, the comm, the food supply. Everything was working, so Kennedy would be fine. He just wouldn't be able to leave. Not without an EVA suit or the rover.

Bob strode to the airlock, then looked back.

Kennedy spat a sliver of duct tape and glared at him, hatred burning in his eyes. "It's me she wants. Not you. Me. If you're not smart enough to get that, I'm going to have to explain it in language you'll understand."

For a moment—just a moment—Bob considered taking Kennedy out. Completely. Totally. For all time. *I could do it. I really could.* Then sanity whispered through him, and Bob let go the breath he hadn't even realized he'd been holding.

He closed the inner airlock door and spun the wheel, then walked back into the rover and undocked. Kennedy had wigged. Bad.

Or had he always been nuts and just hit a point where he forgot how to cover up?

Bob shrugged and returned to the cockpit. Next stop, Lexville.

"You're telling me you just up and *left* me out there while you went riding back in your shining armor to rescue the princess?" Lex glowered at him from the passenger seat. "What if I'd run into trouble? Have you gone out of your *mind*?"

"No, but Kennedy has." Bob met her skeptical look. "I'm telling you, he's gone nuts. Totally freaked."

"Bob, listen." Lex shook her head. "You're not going to win by doing weird stuff like this. I told you to pursue her, not abandon me. What did Valkerie say when you came prancing back? I bet that made a big impression."

Bob reached over and switched Lex's comm link to the CommSat band. "Why don't you call her and find out?"

She glared at him. "You are not being rational. Listen, this is not the way to impress a girl, okay? Trust me on this. Valkerie is just going to think you're a big jerk—"

"Lex, is that you?" Valkerie's voice overflowed with relief. "Bob, did you find Lex? Are you guys there? And how's Kennedy?"

Lex's brows arched.

Bob just smiled. "I left Kennedy in the Ares 10. It's kind of like jail. I took all the EVA suits, so he's stuck there. Lex is fine. I picked her up just a few minutes ago. She's got some questions for you."

Lex looked from him to the comm, her frown deepening. "Val, what happened? Are you okay?"

They waited out the twelve-second radio delay. "I'm fine," Valkerie said. "A little concussion, I think. I didn't tell Houston anything about Kennedy yet. They heard my distress call—I guess I sent that out on all channels when I called you and Bob. Anyway, they wanted to find out what was going on. I told them Kennedy was sleeping, which is sort of the truth. We'll need to figure out what to tell them, but I said we could talk more when you return from EVA."

Bob crested the last ridge. "Okay, we're in line of sight, Valkerie. ETA is about four minutes."

"Hurry. I'm . . . I miss you."

Bob grinned over at Lex.

The anger melted from her face. She flicked off her comm link and did the same on Bob's suit. "Uh . . . I think apologies are in order here. I guess I overreacted back there."

"It's okay." Bob coasted to a stop in front of the Ares 7. "And congratulations."

Lex looked at him blankly. "Huh?"

"As of now, you are the commander of the Ares 7 crew."

Wednesday, March 25, 2015, 3:00 p.m., Mars Local Time

Valkerie

Valkerie limped down the stairs, grasping the rail with both hands. Every step sent waves of nausea through her body. Her head felt like the kettledrum in the "1812 Overture." The Vicodin wasn't helping at all. She needed something stronger, but she couldn't risk a blackout until Bob and Lex got back. Bob would freak if she was unconscious when he returned. She could last another four minutes.

The radio upstairs buzzed in a steady monotone. Houston hadn't stopped hailing her since she'd called them. Apparently they weren't buying her explanation. She needed to figure out what she was going to say. Fast.

She stepped into the EVA-suit room.

A spray of dark blood covered the walls.

She gasped, and her stomach tightened spasmodically, throwing her to her knees. She moaned out her agony. It was her fault. Bob had warned her about Kennedy, but she hadn't listened. It was all her fault. Kennedy was sick. He didn't know what he was doing. How could she even blame him? She was the one who should have been thinking. She should have seen the signs.

Valkerie pushed herself up onto her knees. What a horrendous mess. She raised a hand to her face. Her left temple was goopy and hot, but was it her blood on the wall or Kennedy's? Either way, it didn't matter. The damage had been done.

Houston was going to quarantine them for sure. Unless . . . No, she had to tell Houston about Kennedy's fever. If she didn't, he would be held responsible. He could go to jail. But what would Houston do if they thought the fever caused Kennedy to become violent? They'd never let the crew go home. Not if they thought the infection originated from Mars. Not if it was shown to be contagious.

*Oh no.* Valkerie rose to her feet and wobbled to the lab. Gloves, biohazard bags, Chemwipes, bleach—she grabbed the items off the bench and hurried back to the suit room. Ignoring the fumes, she sprayed the walls with concentrated bleach and wiped them down. Bob and Lex could not get sick. They couldn't.

A clank sounded at the airlock. They were already back.

Valkerie threw all the used wipes into the biohazard bag and carried it back to the lab. Had she missed something? She hurried back to the suit room and stooped to pick up one of the EVA suits that Kennedy had thrown on the floor. The suit felt cold and gritty. She checked the label. It was hers.

"Val!"

She turned to see Lex framed in the hatch, eyes wide and horrified.

Lex pressed her hands to her mouth and sucked in her breath.

"It's okay, Lex. I'm okay."

"What did he do to you?" She stumbled forward, reaching for the suit Valkerie was carrying.

"No! Stop!" Valkerie cried.

Lex froze.

"Don't touch the suit. It's still gritty from our last EVA. It might be contaminated."

"I don't care. Let me help you."

"No, you've *got* to care. If all of us get sick, Houston will have even more reasons to quarantine us here forever."

"But . . ." Lex took a step forward.

"Valkerie's right." Bob appeared from behind Lex and put a restraining hand on her shoulder. "Have you told Houston anything yet?"

"Not much." Valkerie drank in the sight of him. "I was waiting for you to get back."

"Good."

Lex looked back and forth between Bob and Valkerie. "Would somebody please tell me why I'm the only one who cares that Val's just had her face bashed by a sleazo—"

"I'm fine, Lex. Really."

"We've got to figure out what we're going to tell Houston." Bob stepped around Lex and started shucking off his suit. "The longer we wait, the worse it will be."

"The worse it will be?" Lex crossed her arms. "Why?"

"Put yourself in Houston's place. They know Kennedy's sick with an unknown bug, and all of a sudden they get a message from Valkerie saying Kennedy is trying to kill her. What would you think?"

"But Josh told them we're sick with an Antarctica bug."

"He lied to them. It's bought us some time, but with these symptoms, NASA's going to have to order tests eventually. Wouldn't you?"

Lex nodded thoughtfully. Suddenly her eyes went wide.

Valkerie followed Lex's gaze to the back of the EVA suit. A brown smudge filled a small crease at the back of one of the knees. It almost looked . . . like clay! Wet clay—at least it used to be wet. She glanced up at Lex. The excitement in Lex's eyes told her everything she needed to know.

"Come on!" Valkerie headed for the lab, with Lex right behind her. She carefully set the suit down on the bench. Her head pounded with the beat of her racing heart.

"What's going on? We've got to decide what to say." Bob clomped into the lab. He had already gotten out of the upper half of the suit, but he still held his pants up at waist level.

"Make something up." Valkerie turned on the laminar flow hood and spritzed the filter down with ethanol. "Lex, get me petri dishes with all six types of media. They're in that bin—over there." Valkerie motioned with her free hand.

"But we've got to talk to them now. All three of us."

"They'll have to wait." Lex handed Valkerie a stack of petri dishes, and Valkerie dealt them out onto the bench under the hood. "We've got what may have been a wet sample."

"Of course it's wet. Kennedy sprayed you down," Bob said.

"See the way the clay was pressed into the crease?" Lex said. "It was wet before the spray. And it's clay. Do you know what that means?"

Bob looked at the EVA suit on the bench, clearly skeptical. "It's been sitting in the lockers for more than a week. A few more minutes aren't going to make any difference."

"Bob is right." Valkerie lit a Bunsen burner and started sterilizing her equipment. "Lex, go with him and tell them Kennedy made a pass at me and got mad when I said no. Tell them it's no big deal."

"No big deal? Have you seen yourself in a mirror?"

Valkerie looked up from a glowing platinum loop. "What if this turns out positive? What if we really are infected by an indigenous bug? Do you want to stay here for the rest of your life?"

Lex stared at the wand in Valkerie's hand. "Maybe . . ." Her voice choked. "Maybe that would be the best thing. I mean, what if it made Kennedy crazy? Would you want that . . . for people on Earth?"

Valkerie swallowed back the brick in her throat and flamed down the petri dishes on the bench until the autoclave tape across their tops charred. A lot was riding on this sampling. The last thing she could afford was contamination.

"Speaking of crazy"—Lex shifted from one foot to another—"just how well did you tie Kennedy up? Most of our food supply is in there with him. The Hampster isn't exactly known for being a good loser."

Valkerie scooped a bit of clay and broke it into a sterile solution of media. "You don't think he'd actually do anything to the food? He has to eat too."

Lex shrugged. "To tell you the truth, I'd feel a lot better if he was somewhere we could keep an eye on him."

"No way." Bob sounded adamant. "You didn't see him. I'm not letting Kennedy come within two hundred yards of Valkerie. Or you."

"I don't know if I like the idea of him being there all alone." Valkerie dipped a sterile spreader in the solution and spread it across the agar in one of the petri dishes. "What if something happens to him?"

"Maybe if we rigged up some of our cameras so we could watch him?"

Bob gave Lex a slow nod. "Not a bad idea." He climbed up on a chair and started to unscrew a camera from the wall. "We could use a transmitter to send back the video."

"If he doesn't attack us while we're working." Valkerie raised a hand to her swollen face.

Lex shot an incredulous look at Bob.

"You didn't see him." Bob's expression turned grim. "He was an animal. Maybe we should give him a day to cool off. We can risk a visit tomorrow when he's not expecting us. Just Lex and me. Sorry, Valkerie. But I don't want you anywhere near him."

Wednesday, March 25, 2015, 7:30 p.m., CST

Nate

Nate sat perched on his chair, his eyes closed. This could not be happening. It just could not—

"She's lying."

Nate knew Cathe was right, but he didn't want to admit it.

But Cathe wasn't giving up. "First she was claiming Kennedy was trying to kill her. Then she said everything's just fine?"

Josh paced back and forth like a cougar on uppers.

Nate tried his most fatherly tone. "It's not your fault, Josh. We got here as soon as we could."

"Yeah? Well, it wasn't soon enough." Josh's mouth twisted. "I should have known. I should have come straight here when I first suspected."

"Listen"—Cathe stepped forward—"we still don't know that Kennedy did anything. Valkerie's sick. She could have been having another hallucination."

"Hunter, keep hailing the Ares 7," Nate said. "I want to know why nobody's answering the phone."

Dr. Frazier tugged at his goatee. "Or it could have been Kennedy that was having the hallucination. If Mr. Bennett is right and Commander Hampton is suffering from a delusional disorder—which is an unproven assumption—then his illness could have triggered an extreme episode. Either way it was unwise to allow Dr. Ohta and Dr. Kaganovski to leave them alone in that Hab."

"You agreed to it!" Nate turned to the shrinks, who were jabbering among themselves in low voices. "Abrams! I need an opinion here. Could a fever cause someone to become violent?"

"It isn't usually—"

"This isn't usual." Nate wanted to throw something. Maybe even a shrink. "The whole crew has been exhibiting erratic behavior for weeks. Valkerie and Kennedy have both been sick for days and almost died. Could that make them crazy?"

"Crazy is poor nomen—"

Nate swore at him, then stood up and pounded his fist on the table. "Just answer the question. Could a fever make them crazy?"

"That's not the real question." Josh said.

Exasperated, Nate him. "Fine. So what's the real question?"

"If Kennedy was already crazy, could everything else make him even worse?"

Abrams took off his glasses and stared up at the ceiling lights through the thick lenses. "Under normal circumstances, a person with a delusional disorder can function quite normally—unlike, for example, schizophrenics. Typically, they experience episodes that may last some weeks, but usually not violent episodes."

"What about someone scared out of their mind?" Cathe said. "Someone hallucinatory due to illness. And stressed out of their gourd. Could they go violent?"

Abrams put his glasses back on and studied Cathe. "All the conditions necessary for murder are met if you shut two men in a cabin and leave them together for two months."

"What?"

Abrams shook his head. "I read that a long time ago—I forget where."

"Houston, this is Ares 7, and I hope you copy. This is Bob calling from base camp."

Everyone turned to stare at the speakers. Jake Hunter cranked up the volume.

"Uh, Houston, this is Bob and Lex checking in. We went out on a field trip to the site of the biosample find, as you requested. Lex dug out the entrance to the cave and found strong signs of water. Looks like a thermal vent was feeding that area where Valkerie found the stromatolite. Lex spotted another specimen farther in but didn't take any samples. I'm handing off for her to report."

"Hey, guys, this is Lex. I'll keep this short and sweet. The cave is fed by at least two areothermal sources of steam. Until Valkerie and I unsealed it last week, it formed a relatively warm and moist microclimate. Our next foray will try to determine if there are any viable life-forms in the cave itself. Bob and I . . . came back a little early today. Here's Bob again."

Silence for a moment.

"It's only 3:30 p.m. on Mars." Cathe nodded to Nate. "They quit *way* early today."

"This is Bob again. Sorry for the mix-up there, I didn't realize Lex was going to hand off so quick." Another pause. "Uh . . . right. Valkerie is doing real good now. She's in the lab just . . . you know, working away. Biology-type stuff. We'd put her on right now, but she's kind of busy and doesn't want to bother. The . . . uh, the Hampster is over at the other Hab. I dropped him off in the rover and he'll be doing some testing. That's . . . uh, pretty much all. Josh, Valkerie asked me to just say once again that we . . . you know, we love you and all, and we're glad you're in charge down there, and she said to tell you—"

A burst of static cut off Bob's voice. Three-beats-per-second static.

Hunter turned down the volume and scrambled to adjust the controls.

Cathe stepped to his side. "I want a copy of this white noise as soon as you can get it to me."

Nate drummed his fingers on the table. "This static came at an awfully convenient time."

"They're hiding something." Abrams looked positively constipated.

Nate turned to stare at him. "No kidding. What was your first clue?" He ignored Abrams' scowl and turned to the others. "I want some ideas, people. What's going on up there?"

"Worst case, Kennedy and Valkerie are dead."

Nate stared at Cathe. How could she say that with so little emotion?

She met his stare. "Bob and Lex are trying to cover it up."

"Fine, and what's the best case?"

"The best case—" Josh leaned his elbows on the table, his face almost green. "The best case is that Valkerie and Kennedy are perfectly healthy, but Kennedy's cracking up because of a condition he's had and known about for years."

"I find that highly unlikely," Frazier said.

Abrams shook his head. "We don't have enough data."

"Can we get a video signal from those cameras in the Hab?" Nate said. "All we've got to do is watch that for a few hours and see if Valkerie and Kennedy are up and about. Anyone see a problem with that?"

"You mean other than the fact that the videocams are password-protected by the Hab's computers?" Cathe said.

"Who's the best Unix hacker?" Nate ground the question out.

"EECOM," said about six engineers simultaneously.

Nate pointed to EECOM. "Okay, then, get in there and grab us some signal!"

She nodded, grim-faced, and sat down at a terminal. Cathe and the Gold Team CATO huddled behind her, whispering suggestions.

Nate paced back and forth.

Josh was shooting daggers at him with his eyes. "I'm telling you, Nate. The Hampster's bonkers."

"Sure . . . so bonkers that he managed to fool every shrink in this place for years. Come on, Josh. Paranoids don't become fighter pilots. Be sensible."

Josh rewarded him with a look of shocked surprise.

Now for torpedo number two. "The way I see it, Kennedy was boning up on psychology just in case he needed to get rid of another crew member. Hmmm . . . Now, who do we know that's paranoid enough to be classified as delusional? Funny, but the name Bob Kaganovski comes to mind. Kennedy's chief competition at engineering."

# CHAPTER 18

Thursday, March 26, 2015, 1:00 p.m., Mars Local Time

Valkerie

"Ares 7, this is Houston with an important message for Dr. Jansen and Commander Hampton. Please come in. Repeat. We must speak to Valkerie Jansen and Kennedy Hampton. Please come in—"

Valkerie switched the radio back to local and eased down into her chair. The smell of Earl Grey filled the galley. She wrapped her hands around her teacup and brought it to her nose to breathe in the steam. Her head still felt like it had been trampled by a herd of water buffalo, but the smell of the tea made it better somehow. Like her father's kiss when she had scraped a knee. She set her cup on the table and reached for the microphone. Bob and Lex ought to be about finished setting up the cameras in Kennedy's Hab. "Bob, this is Valkerie. How are you and Lex doing over there?"

Silence.

"Bob, I'm serious. No playing around. Are you there?"

Static rippled through the airwaves like a breeze through autumn leaves.

Valkerie took a sip of tea and closed her eyes. What would it feel like to be back on Earth? Strolling through the woods with Bob on a fall day. The crush of fallen leaves. The smell of damp earth. She tried to imagine Bob running and laughing, free from the worries of day-to-day survival. Why couldn't she see it? Why couldn't she picture him having fun? The thought disturbed her. Could Bob imagine her having fun? They'd been under so much pressure for such a long time. When was the last time she'd allowed herself to relax? To be herself?

Valkerie took another sip of tea. Bob had been spending a lot more time with Lex lately. Working in the shop. Taking care of her and Kennedy. What if he was tired of her? What if he was losing interest? The way she'd been treating him, she wouldn't blame him. Ever since they'd landed, she'd been a very dull girl—professional, but dull.

Valkerie picked up the microphone. "Bob, this is Valkerie. Are you there?"

Nothing.

They had probably switched off comm when they got to the other Hab. Probably. Either that or they were still busy disabling the Ares 10 CommSat radio transmitter and couldn't respond. Or didn't feel like bothering. For all Bob's eager attentiveness and puppy-dog devotion, once he focused on a project, he tended to tune everything else out. Especially when he was working on electronics. You practically had to use a crowbar to get his attention. Either that or say something really . . . shocking.

Valkerie's heart started pounding in her chest.

What if she told him how she felt about him? It was like Russian roulette, except that she had no idea how many bullets were in the gun. She picked up the mike and rested a finger on the transmitter switch for a long minute. What had she been so worried about all these months anyway? She let her finger slide off the switch. Didn't she have the same right to pursue happiness as anyone else? What did it matter that she was on Mars? She'd already exceeded NASA's expectations. What she did off the clock was nobody's business but her own. Valkerie checked the transmitter to make sure it was still set to a local frequency.

"Bob, I . . . I really care . . . for . . . you. A lot." She held her breath and listened over the drumming that pounded in her head.

Nothing.

Every crackle of static hit her like a kick to the stomach. He wasn't answering. Had he heard her or not? What if he could hear but just wasn't answering? What if his transmitter was broken? What if Lex had taken comm?

"Lex, are you there? If you're listening, don't you dare breathe a word to Bob. Okay?"

Static. Normal static.

What was going on? They were supposed to stay in radio contact at all times. Had they turned their radios off? Surely they wouldn't have turned them off on purpose? A disturbing thought bubbled up from the back of Valkerie's mind. *No, Lex is married. Bob is in love with me, not Lex.* It was more likely that Kennedy . . . *No!* That couldn't be it. They were working, that's all.

"Bob, this is Valkerie." Her voice quivered. "Please answer me!" She adjusted the gain on the receiver and flipped through the channels.

Houston was still hailing on CommSat 1.

Back to local . . .

A faint groan sounded through the hiss of static.

"Bob? Is that you? Bob?" Valkerie was all but shouting into the mike.

The volume of the static seemed to drop. Like someone was transmitting—but not saying a word.

Valkerie took a deep breath. "Kennedy?"

The silence closed around her, mocking her helplessness.

"Kennedy, I know you're listening . . ."

A crash sounded below her. From the first floor. Valkerie spun around to the stairwell hatch. She stood, rigid, straining with all her senses. "Bob?" Her whisper sounded pitiful and weak, even in the blanket of silence. "Bob?" Valkerie called out louder, trying to control the tremors that shook her voice.

A faint groan sounded, then a loud clash of metal on metal. The groan seemed to be getting louder, as though someone was approaching the stairs.

"Lex, is that you?" Valkerie scanned the room, searching for a crowbar, a hammer—anything. Where had she put that pipe? She ran to her room and unhooked the knee brace from the wall. The eighteen-inch bar wasn't very heavy, but it was better than nothing.

She crept out of her room, holding the bar in front of her like a two-handed sword.

A dull thud—right below her. The sound of breaking glass.

Valkerie crept toward the stairs. It was Kennedy. It had to be. Bob and Lex wouldn't do this to her. They would have called out to her the minute they emerged from the airlock. She tiptoed down the stairs, pausing at each step. If the rover had docked with the Hab, she would have felt the jolt. And the airlock valves. Why hadn't she heard the airlock hatch open? It usually made enough noise to wake the dead.

But if it wasn't Kennedy or the others, then who . . . ?

Shivers ran a footrace up and down her spine as the implication hit her square in the gut. She held her breath and strained her ears. Nothing.

*Don't be ridiculous! There's nothing on this planet but the four of us.* No, what she was facing wasn't some kind of alien entity. It was human. And if it was Kennedy, she might as well get it over with. Better for her to surprise him than the other way around. She stepped off the last step and hesitated at the open hatchway. Maybe she should wait for Bob and Lex. Maybe if she hid upstairs? If she locked herself in the bathroom . . .

No. She had to face facts. If Kennedy was here, there was a good chance . . . Her throat tightened. Tears blurred her vision.

Valkerie tightened her grip on the knee brace and stepped out into the hallway.

Nothing.

She looked around, then raced into the suit room and grabbed up the steel pipe they had been using as a lock for the airlock hatch. Gripping the bar like a baseball bat, she swung it through the air. If Kennedy tried anything, she'd knock him to home and beyond. Even if it meant finishing out her stay on Mars alone.

"Kennedy!" Her scream echoed off the aluminum walls. She slammed her metal club into a wall panel. "Come out right now! Don't make me look for you." She strode out into the hallway and circled around the lower level, checking each room as she came to it. The supply bins, the EVA-suit lockers, the shop—she checked every possible place he could be hiding.

This was crazy. What did she think she was looking for? There were only three logical explanations for the noises. Either she was imagining things, or something had slipped and fallen, or it had been Kennedy. What else could it be? Mars was a barren, lifeless planet. Fossil or no fossil, the four of them were the only living beings on the planet. Valkerie stood up from the cable conduit she had been examining and stretched her back. Then, sweeping the room one more time for something she might have missed, she backed out of the shop and shut the door behind her.

The lab was next. She poked her head into the darkened room and turned the lights on.

Broken glass littered the floor in front of the sterile hood. A petri dish.

She hurried to the hood and stooped down to examine the broken dish.

A blop of amber agar medium stuck to the floor.

She examined the tape label on one of the shards of glass. It had held the sulfur-rich medium. Valkerie stood and checked the other petri dishes.

A gap in the middle of the line of dishes seemed to indicate where the sulfur-rich plate had been. All the plates were upside down, as they were supposed to be—well away from the edge of the bench.

She reached out her hand and flipped a plate over.

Plaques! The surface of the agar was covered with them. Tiny gray-white bacterial colonies—unlike anything she had ever seen.

*Life! Honest-to-goodness life!*

Valkerie staggered backward, crushing the shards of broken glass under her feet. She'd have to verify it. They'd have to go back to the tunnel and take a fresh clay sample, but she had no doubt of the outcome. She had found living bacteria on Mars.

And if Mars supported bacterial life, who could tell what other life-forms they might find?

Or might find them.

## Thursday, March 26, 2015, 2:00 p.m., Mars Local Time

### Bob

Bob ducked through the rover airlock and navigated the box of food through the narrow tube that connected the rover to the Ares 7. It was good to be back home.

Lex stood in front of him, balancing a box on her knee while she fumbled with the hatch into the Hab.

"Hurry up with that hatch. My head is killing me." Bob braced the box against the side of the tube and massaged his temples with his right hand. Kennedy had jumped them as soon as they'd entered the Hab. Bob had almost been knocked out by an EVA helmet to the side of his face. He probably would have been killed if Lex hadn't wrestled Kennedy to the ground. Even with the two of them, it was all they could do to subdue him. They'd left him taped to his cot while they disabled his CommSat radio, installed the cameras, and loaded some of the food stash into the rover.

Lex swung open the hatch, and Bob followed her into the airlock. Valkerie's face was peering through the window in the inner door. At her intense expression, Bob felt his pulse jump.

Had something gone wrong?

Lex pushed through the door. "Mission accomplished. Kennedy gave us a little trouble, but we—Val, are you all right?"

She was white as a bleached ghost, except for her eyes, which looked red and puffy. Bob stepped around Lex, put his box on a bench, and wrapped an arm around Valkerie's shoulders.

She leaned against him. "It's okay. I'm fine." She managed a less-than-convincing smile, which faded when she caught sight of his bruised face.

He reassured her with a squeeze. "I look a lot worse than I feel. Really."

Valkerie nodded. "I . . . I don't even know where to begin. I was so worried when you didn't answer." Her voice fell to a quivering whisper. "And then I heard something. Noises down here on this level. Strange groans and banging around. Whatever it was broke one of the petri dishes."

Bob searched her eyes. Whatever she had heard had really scared her, and Valkerie wasn't one to scare easily. He glanced at Lex. Apparently she was thinking the same thing.

"And that's not all."

Bob let Valkerie pull him through the corridor and into the lab.

Shards of broken glass covered the floor, surrounding a blob of goo. "Look at this!" She flipped over one of the petri dishes and held it up to the light. It was polka-dotted with tiny gray speckles.

"Oh . . . my . . ." Lex plopped her box of food out in the hall and collapsed onto a lab stool. "It's not . . ." Her stunned gaze met Valkerie's. "You're joking, right?"

Bob looked from one to the other. What on earth . . . ? No, make that what on *Mars* was going on?

Valkerie shook her head. "About all I can say is that it seems to be bacterial. I think. I've never seen anything quite like it. Whatever it is, it's alive."

"This is that . . . ?" A creeping numbness buzzed in Bob's brain. "You got this from the dirt on your EVA suit?"

Valkerie nodded.

"And you think this is what's making you and Kennedy sick?"

"I can't say for sure," Valkerie said. "But the evidence is certainly pointing in that direction."

"Great." Bob turned to get Lex's reaction. "Just great."

"Please tell me you didn't say anything to Houston." Lex's face was tense as she studied Valkerie.

Valkerie shook her head. "Not yet. I was too worried about searching the Hab. But this is huge. They're going to want to have a press conference right away. We'll have to—"

"No." Lex stood. "We can't tell Houston anything until we figure out what's going on. Josh gave us that warning for a reason. We can't risk them making a premature decision to keep us here."

"But we have to say something. At least we've got to tell them what happened with Kennedy. They haven't stopped hailing us since he—"

Lex shook her head. "No way. Not while they're in witch-hunt mode. If they knew about Kennedy, they'd blame it all on the Martian flu."

Valkerie cast a pleading look at Bob. "Don't you think we should tell them? I'm not going to lie."

He shrugged. On the one hand he didn't want to disappoint Valkerie, but . . ."Waiting just a little while won't hurt. We need a chance to figure it all out ourselves."

She looked down at the floor.

"Besides." He put a hand on her arm. "Don't you want to study those things first? Seems like we should have something to report on before we make the report."

Lex bent over and examined the wad of goo on the floor. "You're sure you didn't accidentally knock this off the bench without realizing it?"

"Positive. I was upstairs when I heard the glass break."

Bob started to bend over, but a sharp pain shot down his leg. He massaged the spot, gritting his teeth. "You're not suggesting that this bacteria got up and . . ."

Valkerie shook her head. "What I heard was big. Big enough to make a lot of noise. I have no idea what it was doing in here."

An ominous silence settled over the lab as the three of them stared down at the broken dish. Either Valkerie was imagining things or . . . No. There had to be a third alternative. She wasn't crazy and she wasn't lying, but that didn't mean he had to believe in little green men. It wasn't reasonable.

Or was it? Ten minutes ago he wouldn't have considered Martian life of any kind reasonable.

Valkerie looked from him to Lex.

Bob could tell something was bothering her—something that had nothing to do with the bacteria.

She glanced at the airlock hatch. "I know this sounds dumb, but I don't feel right about leaving Kennedy over there all alone. He *is* sick. And if something really is out there . . ."

"That's why we rigged up the cameras." Lex walked through the door and into the corridor. "You'll be able to keep an eye on the Hampster without having to worry about being shish-kabobbed during the night."

They followed Lex into the shop, where she pulled a video receiver out of a bin.

Bob helped her hook it up to a monitor. He switched on the monitor and started scanning through the remote cameras.

"If Kennedy goes ballistic, we'll know it before he can do too much damage to himself or—"

Valkerie gasped. The monitor showed the Ares 10 commons. Kennedy's still figure lay crumpled in a heap on the floor.

Surrounding him was a pool of what looked like blood.

# CHAPTER

Thursday, March 26, 2015, 2:30 p.m., Mars Local Time

Bob

"He's faking it." Bob stared at the monitor, searching for the slightest movement, anything to indicate that Kennedy wasn't really hurt.

"Bob, please . . ." Valkerie's pleading voice gnawed at his resolve.

"What could have happened?" Uncertainty filled Lex's voice. "He was fine when we left."

Valkerie spun and headed for the stairs. "I'm going over there."

*Oh no you're not!* Bob jumped up. "Valkerie, wait. You know Kennedy. It could be a trap. Lex and I will go. We know how to handle him."

Her gaze came to meet his.

Bob hesitated. She looked worried . . . and something else. Guilty? About what? Locking the creep up?

"But I'm the doctor."

Lex grabbed a radio handset. "Yeah, well, *I'm* the commander and I say you're not going anywhere near that weasel.

That's an order. Watch him on the monitor, and let us know if he moves."

Bob shot Lex a grateful glance, then followed her into the airlock.

"Be careful." Valkerie's eyes were wide.

Bob recognized the apprehension he saw there. He felt the same thing himself. He held up a big roll of duct tape. "Don't worry. I've got a little snack for Kennedy if he doesn't behave."

Bob hot-docked the rover to Kennedy's Hab and powered down. "Okay, expect an ambush. No way was the Hampster attacked by Valkerie's little green man." He grabbed his flashlight and a rubber hammer and followed Lex into the airlock.

"I'm ready for him." Lex stepped through the hot-dock ramp and pulled open the Ares 10 hatch, holding a heavy wrench at the ready.

Bob followed her in and secured the door behind him.

Darkness. Dead silence.

He keyed the Transmit switch on his local radio. "Valkerie, what do you see on the monitor?"

"He's still there on the floor of the commons." Her voice sounded staticky and thin. "You'd better hurry."

He spun the airlock hatch-wheel and pushed open the inner hatch. "Kennedy!" His voice seemed to bounce from wall to wall.

No response. The interior was completely dark. A fan whirred somewhere in the silence.

Bob reached around the corner and flicked on a row of LED lights.

Shadows sprang out to fill up the room. Nothing moved.

He peered around the corner, trying to remember how those guys on the SWAT teams in the movies moved. Of course, there was a major difference here. They had guns. He had a rubber hammer. Nice trade.

"I'm right behind you."

He nodded at Lex's whisper and stepped out, then spun a complete three-sixty, looking for movement. He cupped his hands to his mouth. "Hampster, come on down and be reasonable! We know you're faking!"

No answer.

He turned to the airlock controls on the wall and punched a button.

The pumps hissed as the airlock evacuated. Then he popped off a small panel next to the controls and unscrewed a wire. "Can't be too cautious. Know what I mean?" He fitted the panel back on. "Okay, wait here. I'll search downstairs, just in case."

Lex held up her wrench. "Got your hammer?"

Bob's pulse pounded in his neck. He grabbed the rubber mallet and flashlight. "Aye, aye, sir." Bob checked each room around the central circular staircase. Nothing in the med lab. Nothing in the workshop. Nothing in the bioreactor area. He already knew the suit room was empty.

Bob came back to the stairway hatch and shrugged at Lex. "It's secure. No booby traps. Now for upstairs."

"I haven't heard a thing. This is weird, Kaggo. Think he's really hurt?"

"Of course not. Kennedy's a cockroach—the ultimate survivor. It's a setup. He'll try to jump us when we get close to him."

Lex whispered into her comm, "Hey, Val, is our little friend still playing possum?"

"He hasn't moved a muscle."

"We're moving," Lex said.

Bob led the way to the stairwell. The metal hatch had a small rectangular hole cut out of it, and he shone the flashlight through. So far so good.

He tugged the stairway hatch open and flicked on the lights. "Kennedy!" His voice echoed in the narrow cylinder.

Silence.

They climbed the metal steps carefully and pushed open the hatch at the top of the stairs. Bob flicked on more LED lights and the Hab lit up. "Good grief, what a mess."

A dark pool of liquid stained the floor of the commons. Kennedy was gone.

Bob toggled his local transmit switch. "Valkerie, I thought you said he hadn't moved."

"He hasn't," Valkerie said. "I've got him on the monitor. He's lying right there in the middle of the commons. It's pretty dark, but I can see him."

"What the . . . ?" Bob looked around. "We're in the commons now with the lights on, and he isn't here."

"You're . . . Where are you, Bob?" The tension in Valkerie's voice ratcheted higher. "I don't see you on the monitor."

Lex swore and rushed to the videocam they'd installed earlier. A wire led down to a laptop. "He recorded a segment and set it to loop back over and over."

Bob's heart leaped into turbo mode. "Kennedy!"

Downstairs, the airlock pumps whooshed to life.

Bob spun and raced for the stairwell. He just beat Lex to the hatch. They yanked it open and rushed down the stairs and out to the airlock. Bob reached for the hatch-wheel, then froze.

The airlock pressure read empty. The outer door hung open—onto vacuum.

Lex peered through the window. "He's undocked the rover!"

Bob jerked his radio to his mouth. "Valkerie, Kennedy's escaped. Do you read? Kennedy's escaped. You've got to lock the door. Do you read? Lock the door now!"

### Thursday, March 26, 2015, 3:15 p.m., Mars Local Time

### Valkerie

Valkerie jumped to her feet, sending her lab stool skittering across the floor. She lunged toward the door, but her foot tangled in the stool, and she went down hard, smashing her right arm against the floor.

"Valkerie, do you hear me? Kennedy took the rover and is heading your way. You've got to brace the hatch."

Valkerie scrambled to her feet.

The Hab shook with a shuddering groan. The rover. Kennedy was trying to dock.

Valkerie dashed out of the lab and swung herself around the corner into the suit room. Careening off the lockers, she flung herself at the airlock hatch and pressed her face to the glass window.

Kennedy's face suddenly appeared, burning eyes narrowed into a malevolent glare. Mouth open, nostrils flared, his face was a mask of rage.

With a groan, the wheel of the hatch turned.

Valkerie threw herself against it, pulling at it with all her weight.

The wheel turned slowly—gradually opening the latches that held the door shut. She was too late. Kennedy was going to win.

Valkerie scooped the steel pipe off the floor and jammed it into the spokes of the wheel. She threw her shoulder into the pipe and heaved.

Slowly, the wheel began to turn back, locking down the hatch.

The wheel spun suddenly free.

Valkerie crashed to the floor. Climbing to her knees, she jammed the pipe again into the spokes of the turning wheel.

The wheel spun a quarter turn and slammed the pipe into the wall.

Valkerie pushed it back against the hatch, wedging it snugly in the corner between the floor and wall.

The hatch shook with a bone-crunching crash, but the battens held.

Valkerie leaned back against the wall, panting and holding the pipe in place with a trembling shoulder.

She pressed her face to the corner, not daring to look through the porthole.

Another crash shook the door. Another. Snarls and raging oaths carried through the metal barrier.

Cold sweat prickled Valkerie's skin. What had happened to Kennedy? He was crazy.

One final crash and then silence. Retreating footsteps.

Valkerie backed cautiously away from the hatch. Dark red stains smudged the window. Blood. He was hurt. Maybe he would give up and leave her alone.

A metal clang rattled through the airlock. Kennedy's shadow darkened the glass, then a resounding crash jarred the room. A spider web of cracks split the pane.

Valkerie turned and fled.

Another crash rang out behind her. The sound of broken glass hitting the floor.

Blind panic filled her senses like a piercing light. She ran, climbing stairs, crashing into walls, scrambling for a hiding place, blind to all else but the urge to get as far away from Kennedy as possible.

*Deep breaths. Slow, deep breaths.* She had to regain control. To think. She ducked into Bob's room and locked the door behind her. *Slow breaths. Think. Listen and think.* The Hab was too small. Bob's door wouldn't hold very long, and without the rover, without EVA suits, there was no way Bob and Lex could rescue her. She was on her own.

A squeal below deck, followed by the sound of the hatch at the bottom of the stairs being sealed.

Valkerie dropped and pressed her ear to the floor, straining to hear footsteps on the stairs.

A thunk right below her. The clash of a locker door slamming shut.

Kennedy was searching the suit room downstairs. But why? Probably he didn't know if she was upstairs or down. If he came up while she was hiding downstairs, she'd be able to escape in the rover. That must be how he sneaked past Bob and Lex.

She rose to her feet and flicked on the lights. An EVA suit lay on a sheet of plastic. The smell of bleach assaulted her. Bob had stayed up half the night cleaning her suit. She unlatched the door and tiptoed down the hallway.

The sound of Kennedy's search echoed up the stairs. He was still in the suit room. She had a little time, but time for what? Even if she bolted the hatch, he'd be able to cut through with a torch. All the tools were downstairs.

She pulled a fire extinguisher from the wall and hefted it in her hands. The spray wouldn't stop him, but the extinguisher was good and heavy. If she hit him in the head just as he opened the hatch . . .

She tiptoed to take up a position by the door, then took a practice swing. The metal cylinder swooshed through the air, throwing her off balance. A sickening feeling spread out from the back of her mind. She gripped the extinguisher tighter. Kennedy was evil. He was trying to kill her. Or worse. If she killed him, he'd be getting what he deserved. He was . . .

No, not evil—sick. Sick with a disease that *she* had given him.

Valkerie shut her eyes, trying to calm the fear that raged like a demon inside her. Trying to generate the tiniest spark of compassion. He was sick. He was their friend . . . If she hit him too hard she could . . .

No. There was a better way. Valkerie set the extinguisher on the floor and crept into Bob's room, shucking her clothes off as she went. Her Liquid Cooled Garment was downstairs, but if things went fast, maybe it wouldn't matter. She pulled on her EVA pants and lay back on the cot to struggle into the upper half of her suit. After wrestling with the stubborn suit for what seemed like hours, she finally climbed to her feet and clamped both halves together.

A squeak sounded in the stairwell. A clank. Kennedy was opening the downstairs hatch.

"Valkerie, it's me." His chilling, singsong voice echoed in the metal stairwell. "It's okay. I won't hurt you. Bob and Lex want to hurt you, just like they want to hurt me. I'm your friend."

She joggled to the commons and scooped up the fire extinguisher from the floor.

"That's right. I hear you. You don't have to hide. It's just me—Kennedy." A low laugh. "I escaped from Bob and Lex. They tried to kill me, but I was too smart for them." Footsteps sounded hollow on the metal stairs.

Valkerie backed away from the stairwell, holding the fire extinguisher between herself and that poison-laced voice. She stumbled back against the wall of the Hab.

The light from the porthole cast the shadow of her head on the floor.

Kennedy ducked through the hatch, peering cautiously from side to side as he entered the room.

"Stay back!" Valkerie kept her voice cool. "I'm warning you." She held the fire extinguisher up to the porthole glass. "One more step, and I'm blowing out the window."

Kennedy's face contorted into a sickening smile. "Not without a helmet you won't."

She swung the extinguisher up hard, smashing the edge into the glass with a sharp crack. "Not a step closer. Next time it's going all the way through."

He stared at the cracked porthole, eyes bulging, jaw sagging. His gaze came back to her, and he spoke softly, as though coaxing a frightened child from the dark. "Come on, Valkerie. It's me. Come away from the window. I'll be good to you. Now's our chance to—"

Valkerie swung the extinguisher at the porthole with all her might.

The glass shattered, and the room filled with an ear-splitting roar.

Thursday, March 26, 2015, 3:30 p.m., Mars Local Time

Bob

"Bob, come quick!"

At Lex's frantic yell, Bob dashed from the CommConsole to the porthole where she had her nose glued to the glass. "What—?"

"The porthole on the Ares 7 just exploded!" Lex turned to him, her eyes wild. "Explosive decompression! How long before they reach vacuum? Half a minute?"

It hit Bob like a hammer. There was no time to get an EVA suit on. "Maybe"—he could barely choke the word out—"they might have time to get downstairs to the rover." He stared at the rover, still hot-docked to the Ares 7, willing it to do something. A full minute passed in tense silence.

"Bob? Lex?" The radio crackled and hissed. A sob choked off Kennedy's voice. "I'm sorry. I begged her not to do it, but . . . she broke the window."

*Bob* grabbed the mike and began shrieking at Kennedy.

Lex wrestled it out of his hands. "Kennedy! Are you both in the rover?"

Hysterical crying flowed over the radio.

Bob couldn't breathe.

"Kennedy!" Lex shouted. "Where's Valkerie? Is she there with you?"

A long pause.

Finally Kennedy answered. "N-no." Another pause. "I . . . told her to come with me, but . . . she wouldn't. The Hab was decompressing so fast. I barely made it back myself. I'm sorry! She's still in the Hab."

*No!* Bob closed his eyes, his breath coming in short gasps. *No! How could you? She was so . . . good.* He grabbed the mike. "You killed her, Kennedy!" He slammed his fist on the table as pain knifed through him. He could feel his heart shredding within him. "You *killed* her!"

"It wasn't my fault!" Kennedy screamed. "She wouldn't listen to reason. I tried to talk to her, and she just broke the window. She killed herself."

"And I'm gonna kill you, Kennedy." The words came out low and cold. "I'm gonna kill you with—"

Lex snatched the mike from him. "Bob, get a grip!" She pushed him away from the table. "Cool off. We've got a maniac out there in the rover, and he'll be coming for us next. I need you thinking straight. Whatever you have to do to get there, *do* it!"

He stared at her fierce eyes, then turned and staggered across the room to the far wall. He closed his eyes, forcing back the ragged sobs building deep inside of him.

She was gone. Valkerie was gone. *God . . . why?* Bob pressed a fist into the wall. *Think straight. Cool off.*

*Peace . . .* The word whispered through him, echoing off the steel walls of his mind.

*Be still.*

He closed his eyes, letting his forehead fall against the cool plastic of the wall. *Valkerie . . . I know I should, but I can't . . . I can't.* In this business, you couldn't afford to rest, ever. Couldn't trust anything, because you never knew when a life-critical system might fail. Couldn't trust anyone but yourself, because when it got right down to it, you were responsible for your own survival. Not your buddy, not Houston, nobody. You packed your own chute, and if it didn't open, then it was your own neck.

Bob fought back the tears. On this mission, he was supposed to be the fix-it man. The guy who kept every system A-OK, protecting them from a hostile environment. And he'd been trying so desperately to protect Valkerie too, protect her from a hostile maniac, protect her from herself.

He'd failed. He couldn't be everywhere, know everything, fix every busted part. Sometimes horrible stuff happened to sweet, trusting people. Where was God in all that?

*Where is Valkerie?*

The question kicked him in the face. He didn't want to think about that. Valkerie was in the Hab with all the air sucked out of her.

Tears, finally. Bob put his face in his hands and wept. Valkerie was gone, gone back to her Maker. Safe at last. Safe at last.

But if she was safe now, dead at the hands of a murderer, then . . . hadn't she been just as safe before, alive? Dead or alive, God had her in the palm of His hand.

*And me too. Whatever Kennedy does to me, I'm safe.*

A presence bent over Bob. *Lex.* He could feel her just above him, her warmth comforting him, her hands caressing his head with a feathery touch. Now it was just the two of them against Kennedy. But they were not alone.

Bob straightened. Pushed back from the wall. Opened his eyes. “Thanks, Lex.” He turned to look.

“What?” Lex stood across the room at the porthole, looking out.

Bob’s heart did a little flip-turn. How’d she get all the way across the room? Half a second ago, she’d been . . .

“I . . .” He shrugged. “Nothing. I’m just . . . I’m okay.”

She turned from the porthole, and her narrowed gaze raked him. Finally she gave a curt nod. “I hope so, Bob. Because I need you.”

“What do we do now?” He wobbled over to the table, grabbed a chair, and slumped into it.

She sat down across from him and shook her head. “We’re stuck in this Hab. We’ve got no rover and no EVA suits. We have plenty of food and water, and all the electricity we want—until Kennedy decides to cut our wires or crash the rover through our walls. And we’ve got no comm with Houston. We disabled that pretty good yesterday.” Anguish twisted her face. “We’re on our own, Kaggo.”

Bob put his hand on hers and squeezed. “Maybe not.”

# CHAPTER 20

Thursday, March 26, 2015, 8:30 p.m., CST

Josh

"I'm sorry, Cathe, it's not you at all." Josh turned onto NASA Road One and stepped on the gas. "I'm just . . . I don't know. I'm just not very good company tonight. Maybe dinner isn't such a good idea."

Cathe shifted in her seat to face him. "You're fine. Don't worry about it. But it *is* late and you have to eat. Let's just pick up Chinese. We can eat it at my place."

*At her . . .* ? Josh turned to give her what he hoped was a casual glance.

"So we can talk." She returned his gaze with earnest frankness. "Something's been bothering you all day. I can tell. If you feel like talking about it, I'm here to listen. And if you don't, well, that's fine too. That'll just give me more time to bore you with the details of my CommSat investigation."

Josh considered the invitation. He probably shouldn't. It wasn't fair to inflict his foul mood on Cathe. They still hadn't heard from Valkerie and Kennedy, and they'd been hailing for twenty-four hours. He pulled into the right lane and flicked on his turn signal.

"Well?" Cathe flashed him a pixie smile.

"Is Hidden Wok all right?" Josh turned at the entrance to the restaurant and pulled into a parking space.

"It's perfect. Stay right here. I know just the thing." Cathe stepped out of the car and glided toward the entrance. Hopping onto the sidewalk, skipping aside to let an elderly Asian couple pass—Josh couldn't take his eyes off her. Every move was like a finely choreographed dance. Poetry springing to life before his eyes.

Josh looked around the parking lot to see if anyone else was watching. How had he been so blind for so many months? She'd been right under his nose all this time, and he'd never even noticed. He leaned back in his seat and pressed his palms to his eyes. Because he'd been trying to keep his friends alive. Because his criminal stupidity had almost killed them. *Would* have killed them if it weren't for Cathe and her computer simulations. And he had written her off as a cold-fish engineer.

The irony was overwhelming. He, the one with a soul as cold and black as coal, *he* had written *her* off. Thank God she hadn't given up on him. *Yet.* But he still had to make it through dinner. And how was he supposed to be suave and charming when he was exhausted and cold and empty—when his best friends in the universe were probably dead or dying because of something he had set in motion fifteen months ago?

The car door jolted open and Cathe slid into the passenger seat, holding up two enormous bags.

"Josh, what's wrong?" She shut the door and turned to him.

"Nothing. I just . . ." He faced forward and started the car. "I just don't think this is a good idea. I'm really tired and—"

Cathe placed a hand on his. "Please. Just say it. Tell me the truth. Don't worry about hurting me. I can handle it."

He turned suddenly.

Her eyes brimmed with tears—her lips were pressed together in fearful expectation.

"Cathe, no." He took her by both hands. "It's not you. It's . . . You've got to believe me. Valkerie and Kennedy. We haven't heard from either of them since this time yesterday. And Bob . . . I know something's wrong, but he can't say anything—because of my message. My warning. Cathe, don't you see?" He stared at her, his throat constricting around the next words even as he forced them out. "I killed them. As sure as if I were there and pulled the trigger."

Cathe's arms eased around him, pulling him close, urging him to rest his head on her shoulder.

He didn't resist.

"It's okay. Let it go. It's not your fault. It's okay."

He abandoned himself to the sweet softness of her voice. Gradually he relaxed, trusting more and more of his weight to her slender frame.

She swayed back and forth, stroking his back, running her fingers gently through his hair. "It's not your fault. You got them all the way to Mars. If it weren't for you they would have died on the flight. I've heard their transmissions. They love you. They owe you their lives and they know it."

Josh pulled back reluctantly and swiped a sleeve across his face. "But the explosion. What if it was the straw that finally broke Kennedy? He attacked Valkerie. You heard the transmission."

"Kennedy is sick with a terrible fever. A *Martian* fever. You can't blame yourself for that. And Bob says Valkerie's working in the lab. I think he's telling the truth. I think she's working right now to isolate the disease—a Martian disease—that didn't have anything to do with your little explosion. You've got to learn to forgive yourself. This guilt thing is driving you crazy. You've got to let it go."

"But I *am* guilty."

"Josh, we're all guilty"—she gave his hands a shake—"of *something*. The difference is, you care. You really, really care. That's the important thing. That's the reason I . . ."

Josh looked at her.

She lowered her eyes. Her grip tightened and she took a deep breath and held it. Finally, she looked up. Her eyes were liquid and bright, glowing with emotions more intense than he'd ever dreamed possible.

"I—" Her voice choked off. "Josh, I . . . I never was very good at talking about . . . feelings."

Josh forced the words out in a whisper. "I love you too." He wrapped Cathe in his arms and lowered his head to hers, letting their first kiss linger, savoring it.

When he pulled back, he cupped her face with trembling hands. He smiled down at her. "You don't need to say a thing. Your eyes say more than a billion words could ever express."

### Thursday, March 26, 2015, 4:00 p.m., Mars Local Time

### Valkerie

Valkerie looped a cord around the locking mechanism of the outer airlock door and ran it back to the inner door, tying it to the wheel lock with knot after knot. There. Kennedy thought she was dead, but she wasn't taking any chances. She sank down onto the airlock floor, leaning the backpack of her EVA suit against the wall.

Her throat tightened and a gurgling cough exploded inside her helmet. Her mouth and throat burned. Her lungs seemed to be filled with liquid fire. If Kennedy had hesitated for ten more seconds she would have been a goner. As it was, she'd barely had enough time to get downstairs and find her helmet and gloves. She cleared her throat and coughed again. It had been terribly risky, but her gamble had paid off. Kennedy was outside, and she was inside. That's all that mattered—for now. She checked the gauge on her DCM. Five more hours of life support. Five more hours to come up with a plan.

"Lex? I know you're listening." Kennedy's forlorn voice sounded in Valkerie's ears. "Bob is a killer. I had to take the rover. If I'd let him get his hands on me, first time your back was turned, he would have finished me off. Remember who set off the bomb. Think about it. That's all I'm asking. If Bob hadn't turned Valkerie against me, Valkerie never would have killed herself. He drove her to it. It's his fault. Right? Lex, are you there?"

Silence.

Lex wouldn't dignify Kennedy with a response, if she was even listening. More likely she was consoling Bob. Valkerie placed a gloved finger on her transmitter switch. No, she couldn't. As much as it hurt her to know that Lex and Bob were suffering, she couldn't break radio silence and let Kennedy know she was still alive. She tested the cords she'd strung from hatch to hatch, wondering if they'd even hold. She had to think of something. Before Kennedy came back.

But what could she do? Bob and Lex didn't have EVA suits in the Ares 10. They had gone over there in street clothes, hot-docking the rover at both ends. There was no way they could get to her—unless Kennedy offered them a ride. She could forget that option. That left her with only two choices: She could repair the Ares 7 porthole and repressurize the Hab from the reserves, or she could try to get to the Ares 10.

To repair the porthole was to risk discovery. Even if she was careful, Kennedy would notice eventually. Then she'd be left alone with him laying siege outside, battering at her door in the middle of the night. No. Better to join Bob and Lex. If she could get across with an extra EVA suit—then maybe they could return to the Ares 7.

Valkerie waited in the airlock, ticking down the time on her life-support gauge. Kennedy hadn't transmitted for a long time. Maybe he was in one of the bunks of the rover—lying down or doing whatever he did when he locked himself away in his room. Valkerie pushed herself to her feet and stretched her cramped muscles. She carefully untied each of the knots in the cord, opened the inner hatch, and started fastening Bob's EVA suit together.

She circled her arms around the bulky suit and tried to lift it. *Great.* The legs dangled on the floor, tripping her as she tried to move around. Her own suit was bad enough. No way could she run two hundred yards carrying Bob's suit too. Valkerie fastened Lex's suit together and hoisted it. It was just about as heavy, but at least the legs didn't drag. She carried the suit into the airlock and set it on the floor.

Swinging the outer door open, she cautiously peered outside, sweeping the terrain with darting eyes.

The rover stood facing the other direction, about thirty meters away from the Ares 10.

She swung the door open wide, waiting.

Nothing.

Either Kennedy didn't see her, or he was waiting for her to move away from the door. There was no way to tell which. She had to make a break for it.

*If Kennedy isn't paying attention, I have a chance.* She pulled Lex's suit out onto the stairs and shut the hatch. Then, folding the suit double and wrapping her arms around the PLSS backpack, she staggered down the steps. She turned left immediately and headed off at a right angle to the direction of the rover. If she could just get out of his line of sight and circle around to the Ares 10 . . . maybe she could make it without being seen.

*Step, step, check the rover. Step, step, check the rover.* Valkerie picked her way over the rocky plain in a wide semicircle toward the Ares 10.

Something caught her eye.

She fell on her knees and lay flat on the ground.

The rover rose on its suspension and started to move.

"Kennedy." Lex's voice blared inside Valkerie's helmet. "I, uh, was wondering if you could go back to the Ares 7 . . . to look for Valkerie. Uh . . . what if Valkerie managed to . . . get inside a rescue bubble? What if she's alive?" Lex's voice was tense. Nervous.

Lex had seen her. That was the only explanation. Lex had seen her and was trying to send Kennedy off on a wild-goose chase. Valkerie flattened herself on the ground, praying Kennedy didn't notice the strain in Lex's voice.

"She couldn't have made it." Kennedy's words sounded slurred. "I waited for her as long as I could. I barely made it out myself."

"Kennedy, you've got to try!" Lex sounded almost frantic. "I know it wasn't your fault, but you've got to try. If for no other reason than to prove your innocence."

"Prove myself? To who? Bob? He knows I'm telling the truth. Just can't admit it. Know why? Because it would just prove he's the saboteur. He's the one who's been trying to kill us all along." The rover looped in a big half circle and headed slowly for the Ares 7.

Valkerie held her breath.

"Wait a minute!" The sudden suspicion in Kennedy's voice made Valkerie's heart pound. "Where's Bob? Why isn't he talking?" The rover slowed to a stop.

"I'm right here with Lex, remember?" It was Bob. "Locked in the Ares 10."

"What's going on?" Kennedy was clearly getting agitated. "Bob, are you out there? What'd you do? Set another bomb?"

The rover swung slowly around until its nose pointed directly at Valkerie.

An explosion of oaths filled her helmet. The rover leaped forward.

Kennedy had seen her.

She bolted to her feet and ran for the Ares 10, staggering under the weight of Lex's suit.

"Nice try, Bob, but I see you. What were you going to do? Blow up the rover with me in it?"

Valkerie kept running. Only fifty meters to go. So close.

"Kennedy, that's not me. It's Valkerie!" Bob was yelling. "Valkerie, say something. Tell him it's you!"

She flipped the transmitter switch. "Kennedy, it's true." She gasped out the words. "It's me, Valkerie." She turned to look back.

The rover was still closing. She wasn't going to make it.

"Did you really think I'd fall for that one? Face it, Bob. I'm on to you."

"Kennedy, it's really me." She stumbled toward the Hab. "Ask me a question—anything."

"Nice try, Kaggo. I've got tapes too. But mine have—"

"Kennedy, this is Lex. You said you didn't kill Valkerie. Don't do this!"

"Valkerie, watch out!"

Valkerie dropped the suit and swung around to face the rover, gauging its speed. Twenty meters. Ten meters. Five. She jumped aside at the last second.

The rover went bumping past.

She took a step toward Lex's suit, but stopped. Despair grabbed her gut. The rover had run over the helmet. She ran for the Hab.

The rover executed a slow, wide turn.

Twenty more meters, and she was home free.

"Valkerie, he's right behind you." The hoarse cry from Lex spurred her on. "Twenty meters, ten . . ."

She feinted to her left and jumped to her right.

The rover nicked the back of her left foot and spun her around, throwing her to her hands and knees. Pain shot through her ankle.

She tried to stand, but her ankle wouldn't take the weight. Valkerie began crawling. Exhaustion surged through her like fire, melting her muscles to water. Too far. She couldn't do it. Couldn't make it up the steps.

"Valkerie, he's turning around!" Lex's voice jolted her. "He's coming back! Get into the airlock!"

Valkerie collapsed on her face, spent. It was no use. She didn't have anything left.

### Thursday, March 26, 2015, 4:45 p.m., Mars Local Time

### Bob

Bob burst into the airlock and slammed the hatch shut behind him. He took a deep breath. This was going to hurt. A lot. Without an EVA suit, the books said he had about eleven seconds. He just had to trust that he wouldn't need more than that.

Bob punched the button to depressurize and watched the needle swing down toward zero. *Just exhale all the way.*

His skin began prickling, as though a thousand red-hot needles were river dancing all over him. Lex began banging on the airlock door, shouting.

Then the air thinned, melting her shouts into silence.

Still exhaling, Bob unlatched the outer door and stepped out into the Martian near-vacuum. His skin was on fire. Three feet in front of him lay a hazy white blob.

Valkerie.

A much bigger blob was speeding toward him. Thirty meters away. Twenty-five.

Bob scooped Valkerie into his arms. Her suit burned deep into his skin, but he hugged her tighter.

The rover was still coming. He turned and lunged for the door, rolling Valkerie up the last step and shoving with all his might. He exhaled the last of his air, felt the vacuum clawing his skin. His mind began turning muzzy and the sunlight dimmed to haze.

Darkness began closing in on him. He fell through the hatch and pulled his legs in. *Whatever happens, I'm safe.*

He groped blindly behind him for the hatch, but the world turned black before his wooden fingers could find it.

### Thursday, March 26, 2015, 5:45 p.m., Mars Local Time

### Valkerie

"I don't care what the books say. That was crazy and you shouldn't have done it." Valkerie shook her head and swabbed more lotion on Bob's face.

Bob couldn't help smiling. Sure, she sounded angry, but if that wasn't appreciation glittering in her eyes, he was a Martian toadstool. And something else shone in those blue depths as well.

"Thanks for shutting the door."

"Shutting the door?" She glared at him. "You run out into a vacuum to save my life and thank *me* for shutting a door?" She dabbed another blob of lotion on his neck, using a bit more force than he thought necessary.

Bob winced. His hands and face stung like fire ants had been using him for a buffet. But her touch felt . . . nice.

Lex turned from the porthole. "Kennedy just hot-docked over at the Ares 7. What's he doing?"

"He can't go in there without a suit," Bob said. "And the rover only had two suits. One of mine and one of yours. Neither one is going to fit him."

"Mine would fit him, sort of." Lex peered outside again. "Not good! Looks like he did it. There's a light on in the hab now. Val, that suit you dropped out there—whose was it?"

"Yours." Valkerie shook her head. "I wanted to bring one for Bob, but it was too awkward to carry. I'm sorry, Lex. Kennedy ran over it."

"He hit the helmet," Lex said. "But the suit looks fine. What say you run out there and pick it up? Then if I need to go outside, I could borrow your helmet. That way, both of us will have some mobility."

"Let me finish with Bob."

He sat forward. "I'm fine. Really. I probably look a lot worse than I feel." Which was pretty bad, but he didn't want to say so. Lex was right. They needed that extra suit.

Valkerie gave him a doubtful look.

Bob tried to smile at her. The skin on his face screamed in protest. "Go get the suit, Valkerie. This may be our last chance. Who knows what Kennedy might do next? If he wrecks all the other suits in the Ares 7, that one out there might be all we have." Which meant that he wouldn't have a suit. How was he going to get off the planet?

Valkerie stood up. "Kennedy's going to pay for this."

Lex grabbed Valkerie's helmet and set it on her head. "Let's get you out there before Kennedy decides to go for another joyride."

Valkerie and Lex disappeared into the stairwell. A minute later, Bob heard the *whoosh* of the airlock pumps.

He lay back in his chair and closed his eyes. His skin felt flayed. And there was no telling what kind of damage the vacuum had done to his lungs. But his rescue had worked . . .

Bob felt his pulse pounding in his temples. If he'd failed . . . if Kennedy had gotten to Valkerie first . . . He choked back the thought. It was simple. If that had happened, he would have just stayed outside and let the Martian vacuum take him. For half an hour today, he had thought Valkerie was dead. The pain of that was worse than being exposed to the vacuum. He had wanted to die. Then, when Lex spotted Valkerie creeping out from the Hab, he'd been so thrilled he could hardly stand the tension.

It had been nearly unbearable, watching her flit across the naked Martian plain. His heart had almost stopped as they tried to divert Kennedy's attention.

The airlock pumps whined into action downstairs.

Good, Valkerie was back. Bob waited, holding his breath.

Lex hollered something.

He bolted upright, then tried to ease himself out of his chair.

Footsteps pounded up the metal staircase.

Lex burst into the commons waving aloft a battered helmet. "Look at this! Whoever designed this thing at AresCorp gets a medal. Bend, but don't break! Wooo-hooo!"

Bob stared at the helmet. The visor had a series of cracks down the front, but the helmet looked intact.

A minute later, Valkerie clomped up the stairs in her EVA suit. "It's a miracle!"

Bob grinned. "Actually, if you think about it, it does make sense. That's a six-ton rover on Earth, but in Martian gravity, it's not much over two tons. It's got eight wheels, so each one bears about five hundred pounds. I can believe—"

"Will you just shut up and enjoy the miracle?" Lex grabbed a roll of duct tape. "Now observe the Jedi Master wield the power of the Force. It has a light side and a dark side—and it binds the universe together."

Thirty minutes later, Lex had given the helmet a meticulous cleaning and a triple layer of duct tape. “Good as new”—she held it up to admire her handiwork—”and as opaque as one of Nate’s metaphors.” She handed it to Valkerie. “Let’s just test it, shall we?”

Valkerie set it gently on her head, latched it down tight, and flicked on her life-support system. “Comm check, Valkerie.”

Bob grabbed the mike from the CommConsole. “Loud and clear. Comm check, Bob.”

“Loud and clear.” Valkerie switched off her life support again, then detached the helmet and lifted it off. She shook her amber mane.

Bob felt a shiver deep in his gut. *She’s beautiful. And she’s alive.*

“Can’t see a thing inside it, though. It’s not going to be much use.”

Lex smiled at Valkerie. “We’ll figure out something.” She stepped to the porthole and gazed out. “Guys, we’re going to have to powwow. It’s gonna be dark in a couple hours. When the sun goes down, we need to go on the warpath.”

“What are you talking about?” Suddenly Bob felt exhausted.

“We’re going after him,” Lex said. “He’s got the rover, remember? We’ve only got two EVA suits and no comm with Houston. We have water and a big stash of food, but Kennedy could cut our power cable any time he feels like it. Staying here long-term is impossible.”

She turned to meet their gazes, determination gleaming in her eyes.

“Tonight we take back the Ares 7.”

• • •

After a truly tasteless supper of freeze-dried vegetables and some kind of mystery meat—Kennedy had always called it "reconstituted varmint"—Valkerie and Bob sat down at the conference table.

Lex went to the porthole. "Our first objective is to take the rover. And we need to do it soon. That dust storm is gonna be here in a few more days."

Bob studied her. "Why isn't the Ares 7 our objective?"

"Without the rover, we're dead," Lex said. "Anyway, we need it in order to take the Ares 7. It's docked to the Hab, which means we can't even get in until we undock it. Once we undock it, we own it unless Kennedy goes back in there, which I doubt. If he does, then we own the Hab and we fight for the rover."

Valkerie folded her arms across her chest. "I . . . don't want to fight him."

Lex's gaze hardened. "Sister, we fight him or we die. It's him or us now. All other things being equal, I'd rather it was us."

Bob reached out and took Valkerie's hand. "She's right."

"There's got to be another way," Valkerie said. "I don't want to hurt him—"

"He tried to kill you today." Lex turned back to the porthole and peered out. "He's not sane anymore. He isn't the friend I knew and trained with back in Houston. We are going to fight him and we are going to win. If we can win by disabling him, fine. If we have to kill him—" Lex froze.

Bob spun his head to look.

She pointed through the tiny window. "The light shining out of the Ares 7 porthole just went dark."

"He's probably welding a sheet of metal over the porthole I broke." Valkerie moved to stand beside Lex and peer outside.

"I can't believe he broke the glass in the inner airlock door," Lex said. "It's crazy. It makes the airlock totally unusable."

Bob shook his head. "Unusable without the rover."

"Which is why we need the rover." Lex turned to face them. "Without that, he can't even exit the Ares 7—unless he wants to vent the whole Hab every time he walks outside."

"Who knows what he wants," Bob said. "Anyway, if he's fixing the porthole on the top floor, he'll probably figure out a way to patch the airlock door too, then he won't need the rover to get outside."

"It doesn't matter. We're not going to let him dictate the battle. We need to strike fast. I would like to move out tonight, but we need to rest, and this will take some planning. Tomorrow we're taking the war to his turf."

"But how?" Bob leaned back in his chair. "I haven't got a suit. And we've only got one good helmet between the two of you."

Lex gave him a crafty smile. "Valkerie and I attack the rover at dawn. If he's in it, we overpower him. If he's in the Hab, we take the rover, come back for you, and then all of us go back and attack Kennedy while he's sleeping."

Valkerie turned troubled eyes on Bob.

He squeezed her hand. "We're not going to hurt him. The real problem is this: How are we going to get into that rover? It's only got one door, and right now that's docked to the Ares 7."

Lex went to the DVD library, selected a jewel case, and handed it to Bob. "You are going to study the manual. Your mission, whether you decide to accept it or not, is to figure out how to undock the rover using tools Valkerie and I can carry."

Bob popped the DVD into the computer. "And what are you two going to do while I look for a miracle?"

"Sleep." Lex rolled her shoulders. "Tomorrow's a big day." She turned and headed for her quarters.

Valkerie stood and followed her, but halfway across the room, she turned, came back, and planted a light kiss on Bob's forehead.

It burned like fire for the next hour, but somehow, Bob didn't mind at all.

Friday, March 27, 2015, 5:30 a.m., Mars Local Time

Valkerie

"Valkerie, wake up. Quick!"

Valkerie staggered out of bed. "What? Is it Kennedy?" She spun around, searching the shadows.

A dark figure stood in her doorway.

"Bob?" Valkerie backed into the wall and felt along the surface of her desk. The hammer. Where'd she leave the hammer?

"It's okay. Valkerie, it's okay." Bob's voice sounded soothing, gentle. "You're safe. Kennedy's not here. But something's happening. Lex wanted me to get you right away. The Hampster's transmitting on the radio."

Valkerie followed Bob to the CommConsole.

Lex was standing at the porthole, searching the dark glass with both hands cupped around her eyes. Kennedy's amplified voice broke through the static.

"I mean it. Get away from the Hab or I'll blow it up! Hear me? Hear me?"

"Who's he talking to?" Valkerie asked.

Bob looked to Lex. "Anything new?"

"As far as I can tell, he thinks he's talking to you, Bob." Lex didn't turn from the porthole. "Thinks you're outside, banging on the walls. Apparently, he's—"

A faint metallic clank sounded through the radio. "Bob, I'm warning you. I'll blow it up. If I go, you go too. Do you hear me? Answer me."

"Blow what up?" Valkerie stepped closer to the radio. She could barely make out footsteps, rustling noises—Kennedy moving around the room.

Lex stepped back from the porthole. "I don't know. At first I thought he was talking about the Hab, but now I'm not sure. I heard glass breaking a minute ago."

"Maybe he's talking about the bacteria cultures." Bob turned to Valkerie. "Is there anything in the lab he could make a bomb with? You know, chemicals he could mix together?"

Valkerie ran through the lab's inventory in her mind. "Sure, but I doubt he would need to with all the hydrogen left in the fuel-cell tanks."

"Maybe I should talk to him." Bob picked up the microphone.

A hollow-sounding boom crackled over the radio. A burst of angry shouting faded to static.

Bob stared at Valkerie. "What was that?"

"Sounds like he ran out of the room."

Bob poised a hand over the transmitter switch. "Do I call him or not?"

Lex raised her hand. "One more minute."

Something tickled at the back of Valkerie's mind. "That noise. It was kind of like the sound of the rover docking with the Hab."

Footsteps pounded over the radio. A sharp clack. "Bob, I'm warning you. Come back!" Kennedy's voice wavered hysterically. "Don't leave me here. Come back and face me like a man! Come back right now, or I'll . . . I'll . . ." More footsteps.

"I don't get it. First he's yelling for Bob to go away, then he wants him to come back." Lex looked at Valkerie with a shrug. She pressed her face to the porthole. "What the—"

"What? What's happening?" Valkerie crowded in close behind Lex and tried to peer around her head.

"See for yourself." Lex stepped aside. "I don't know what he's doing, but he's up to something."

Valkerie shaded her eyes and looked out into the dark night.

Twin beams of light moved slowly over the rocky terrain. She could just make out the shape of the rover in the back-reflected light.

"Bob, it's the rover. He's driving it toward the nuclear reactor."

"Bob, I'm serious." Kennedy whined. "Bring back the rover and I'll give you the Hab. You can't take it by force. I'll blow it up before you get halfway in."

"Cut the radio," Lex ordered.

Bob flipped a switch and the Hab went silent.

"You know what he's up to?" Bob asked.

Lex shook her head. "It doesn't matter. This may be our best chance to take back the Hab."

"But why the little radio drama? Why pretend the rover was stolen? It doesn't make sense." Valkerie moved away from the porthole and offered Bob a chance to look out.

Bob shook his head. "I think the Hampster, in his own demented way, is trying to convince us he's still guarding the Ares 7."

"What if it's a trap? What if he's driving the rover by remote control?" Valkerie asked.

"He can't," Bob said. "I changed all the computer passwords in the Hab yesterday. He can't access the rover-remote program. He's got to be in the rover to drive it, but it doesn't make any sense why he's trying to draw attention to himself like this. Why didn't he just drive off quietly?"

"It makes about as much sense as wasting time trying to understand the actions of a madman." Lex moved toward the stairwell and turned at the hatch. "Bob, you keep watch at the porthole. Call us on local the minute you see Kennedy coming back. Valkerie and I are going to take back the Ares 7 and get a suit for you."

Valkerie followed Lex down the stairs. They donned their EVA suits without a word, checking and rechecking Lex's suit for leaks.

Lex pulled her helmet off and led the way to the shop. "As soon as I put my helmet back on, I won't be able to see. You'll have to lead me by the hand." She grabbed a piece of pipe from the bench. One end of it had been hammered flat and sharpened into a wicked-looking blade. "If Kennedy jumps out while I still have my helmet on, use this. Bob made it overnight." Lex put the pipe dagger in Valkerie's hand and picked up a crowbar from the bench.

Valkerie tried to imagine herself using the knife. Even thinking about it made her sick. She set the knife back down on the bench. "I don't think I could. How about we trade helmets? You take my helmet—*and* the knife."

Lex nodded, grim-faced, and handed over her helmet, then stepped out of the shop and over to the stairwell hatch.

"Okay, Bob. Is the coast clear?" Lex called up the stairs. "Valkerie and I are ready to go."

"No sign of Kennedy. Be careful!"

"No communications unless it's an absolute emergency," Lex shouted back. "We'll be listening on local." She headed into the airlock.

Valkerie followed, desperately trying to think of something she could say. One parting message—just in case it would be her last.

"Yank on my arm if you have any problems. One time if you need me to slow down and twice if the helmet springs a leak." Lex put her own helmet on and nodded impatiently.

Valkerie swallowed hard as she placed the taped helmet over her head.

Darkness.

Step after weary step, Valkerie plodded across the uneven terrain. Stumbling over rocks, tripping and falling to her knees, she clung tight to Lex's hand. If they got separated, if something happened to Lex, there was no way she'd be able to find her way to either Hab. Her breath roared in her ears. It felt like she had been walking for miles. Was Lex lost? Had she missed the Ares 7 in the dark?

Lex pulled her hand away.

Teetering in the darkness, Valkerie groped forward with outstretched hands. She felt dizzy, like she was going to fall. Her hand brushed against something and she grabbed it. An upright post. She pulled herself forward. Stairs. They had made it.

Lex took her by the hand and guided her up the stairs with a reassuring pat.

Valkerie stepped forward until she came to a wall. She held her breath, waiting.

A low rush sounded all around her. A loud snap at her neck. Her helmet turned and lifted off her head. Lex's face appeared close, with a finger to her lips.

Valkerie examined the inner hatch.

The broken glass had been covered with a large metal plate, crudely welded to the steel hatch.

The locking mechanism squeaked as Lex twisted open the hatch wheel. Pushing the door wide, Lex stepped inside, leaning forward in a low crouch. Her long blade swept back and forth, feeling its way through the darkness.

Valkerie followed, gripping her crowbar tight in both hands. Through the suit room and into the corridor beyond.

Lex raised her hand.

Valkerie froze.

A throaty hiss echoed in the dark. A rumbling moan, low and guttural, like the growl of a large dog.

Valkerie put her hand on Lex's shoulder and pointed. The sound was coming from the lab.

## Friday, March 27, 2015, 11:00 a.m., CST

## Nate

Nate sipped at his steaming coffee cup and looked around the war room. "Things are looking pretty bad back in D.C. right now. I spent yesterday morning on the phone with the vice president and all afternoon trying to talk to the Senate Finance chairman. Guess who's screaming like a wounded banshee over the budget to run that resupply mission?"

"That doesn't make any sense," Cathe Willison said. "How do you wound a banshee?"

"More to the point, why do we need to pursue the resupply mission?" Josh said. "We're pretty sure we're out of the woods on the back-contamination thing."

"Pretty sure ain't a hundred percent sure," Nate said. "And anyway, it'll put a muzzle on that *Bactamination* woman. There's already a backlash against her in yesterday's *Washington Post.* But until we can nail down the source of the crew's infection, we *have* to proceed with plans for the resupply shot, even if we're 99.99 percent sure we won't need it. It's a long pipeline, schedule-wise, and if we break it now, we lose that option for good. Which brings us to the next question. What do we know and what do we not know about the good ship Ares 7?"

"It's been almost forty hours since Bob and Lex last called in," Jake Hunter said. "Since then, they haven't responded to our hailing. They're purposely ignoring us."

"You know for sure it's not a glitch in the Deep Space Network?" Nate asked.

Hunter nodded. "CommSat 1 and CommSat 2 both report fine on all diagnostics. We've got fresh photos showing that dust storm moving north. It'll reach the Hab tomorrow or the day after."

Nate clicked his ball-point pen several times. "What about that static problem? Any recurrences?"

"The usual," Hunter said. "Once or twice per eight-hour shift, usually for about fifteen minutes. But it's intermittent. We haven't found a pattern on the schedule yet."

"Well, find it!" Nate snapped.

Hunter's face hardened and he bit his lip.

Cathe Willison leaned forward. "I've installed an analysis program on both CommSats to try to dig some Doppler info out of the data rates in the static signal. The programs are running and collecting data, but no luck yet."

"Keep working the problem," Nate said. "And maybe you shouldn't be depending on luck. Now, what about those video cameras?"

"They've gone dark on us," Josh said. "EECOM worked all night and finally got into the computers about three hours ago."

"What do you mean, 'gone dark'?" Nate said. "They've all failed at once?"

"No, we can't access them remotely. They're not responding to commands."

"That's ridiculous. How could that happen?"

EECOM twisted a strand of her bright red hair. "There's only one way. The crew physically disconnected them."

"Why would they do that?" Nate asked. "Is there any maintenance scheduled on those?"

"No way," Josh said. "You don't do maintenance on a camera. You run it till its warranty expires. Then it fails and you throw it away and buy a new one."

"So they have some reason they don't want us to know what's going on up there," Nate said. "And we have no first-hand evidence that either Kennedy or Valkerie is alive."

"Just Bob and Lex's say-so Wednesday evening," said Jake Hunter. "Since then, we don't even have evidence that Bob and Lex are still alive. We haven't heard a peep out of any of them."

"What about life-support queries?" Nate said. "Hasn't it occurred to any of you to ask the Hab how it's doing? Find out if it's still supplying energy and producing oxygen?"

"It is," EECOM said. "I've been following all that very closely, and the life-support functions are normal in the Ares 7."

"Did you check the Ares 10?" Cathe asked.

Nate turned on her with a scowl. "What's the point of that? Nobody's living in the Ares 10. They couldn't move it close enough to connect to the Ares 7."

"Last time he reported, Bob said Kennedy was working over in the Ares 10," Cathe said. "Which doesn't make a lot of sense. There isn't any reason to go over there. The workshop in the Ares 7 is better equipped. The galley is better. Even the head is better. Why would they say that?"

"As an excuse," Hunter said. "They didn't want to admit Kennedy was missing in action."

"It's a lousy excuse," Cathe said. "They could have said he was sleeping—anything. Instead, they give us a half-baked excuse. If it's a lie, it's a stupid one, and Bob isn't stupid. What if it's true?"

"It would be extremely easy to check," said EECOM. "I could run some life-support queries on the Ares 10. The instantaneous oxygen production would tell me if and when somebody is visiting that Hab, and the integrated oxygen production would give me a lower bound on how many people are staying there continuously. In addition, I could activate the video cameras there remotely."

"Why haven't you done it already?" Nate said.

EECOM's face turned red. "I'll . . . pursue that right away."

Nate turned to the shrinks. "Any clues on the crew's mental state?"

Abrams pursed his lips. "Sir, anything we could say would be a guess. If you're unable to give us any data, there's no point in speculating—"

"Fine, I'll write that down as a no," Nate said. He glared around the war room. "So basically, what you're all trying to tell me is we don't know anything."

"We don't even know that they're on the planet," Cathe said.

Nate tapped his fingers on the table. "You want to explain why that isn't the most tomfool thing anyone's said all day? Where else—"

"Mr. Harrington, do you have a problem with me?" Cathe glared at him with eyes of cold steel.

*Yeah. You're too smart for your own good.* "Just answer the question," Nate said. "Last time I checked, gravity still works. If they aren't on Mars, where else would they be?"

Cathe stared at him as if he were a clueless moron. "They have a fully fueled Mars Ascent Vehicle. There is no reason they couldn't have already lifted off and gone into orbit."

Nate shook his head. "That's crazy. What are they gonna do in orbit? That MAV has life support for what, about seventy-two hours, max?"

"The Earth Return Vehicle has a two-year supply, and all they'd have to do is dock with it." She glared at him. "Sir, you give us that Dilbert-speak all the time about thinking outside the box. Then when somebody does it, you just come down on us. Make up your mind—do you want us to think or not?"

A low murmur ran around the table.

"She's right, Nate," Josh said. "In principle, the crew could have launched and docked with the ERV. They're autonomous for launch. They have to be."

"Okay, fine," Nate growled. "You're telling me they could be sitting up there in a nice little tin can in Mars orbit, enjoying the hazards of zero gravity, exposed to cosmic rays and solar flares, instead of sitting safe on the ground in a much healthier environment. Why in the world would they do that?"

"To prevent us from locking them out," Cathe said. "Isn't it obvious? Once they get into the ERV, there's nothing in the world we can do to prevent them from coming back home—anytime they want to."

"The next window for a Hohmann transfer isn't till next January," Nate said. "They're not going to sit in low Mars orbit for the next nine months. That's absurd."

"I would," Josh said slowly. "If I thought somebody was going to lock my escape hatch, I'd make sure I came back through as soon as possible. Come to think of it, they don't have to wait for the next Hohmann transit window. There are plenty of transits that would get them home. Who's to say they haven't left already?"

"Strictly speaking, they weren't going to make a Hohmann transfer anyway," Cathe said. "The plan is for them to leave in January because they have enough fuel to make a higher-energy transit. That way they'll only have to spend seven months in zero-g. But if they were in orbit right now, having to deal with zero-g, they'd probably leave in October. That would get them home on a Hohmann ellipse nine months later—a month earlier than if they leave in January. If I were them, that's what I'd do. It's the smart thing—minimize time in zero-g."

"We may be barking up the wrong tree," Josh said. "Can't we just query the ERV and see if it's providing life support?"

"EECOM, run that query on the Hab and report back to us ASAP. Check on the Ares 10 too. We need that data. Then query the ERV, just in case they've flown the coop, which I doubt. Hunter, keep hailing the Ares 7 and try the Ares 10 for good measure. Miss Willison, I want a complete report by yesterday on all possible transits, including inner-system trajectories using Venus for a velocity boost. I want it all and I want it now."

"That's a lot of work."

Nate stood up. "Then the sooner you get started—"

"Yeah, yeah, yeah." She stood up and stalked out of the room.

"Okay, get to it," Nate said.

The rest of the team stood and made for the exits.

Nate caught Josh before he left and waited until they were alone. "You need to talk to Miss Willison about her attitude."

Josh studied his hands. "Uh . . . Nate?"

"Yeah?" Nate waited. "Come on. Out with it. My bite is no worse than my bark."

Josh's gaze rose until he was almost but not quite looking Nate in the eye. "Your bark's no picnic, Nate. And you're the one with the attitude. Cathe's just trying to do her job. We all are. And you're taking swipes at us. Just thought you'd like to know . . . people are talking." Josh turned and hurried out of the room.

Nate slumped down in his chair and put his head in his hands.

*Great. My crew is sick, maybe dying. Maybe bringing a virus back to Mama Gaia—a gift that'll keep on giving longer than that stupid Energizer bunny. My team is puking out on me. Congress is throwing another hissy. And now my boy Josh is going soft.*

*I love this job.*

# CHAPTER 22

Friday, March 27, 2015, 6:30 a.m., Mars Local Time

Valkerie

Wheezing sighs filled the lab, deep and nasal—like the snores of a drunken asthmatic.

Valkerie tugged on Lex's arm, motioning her back to the airlock.

Lex shook her off and pulled a flashlight from her belt.

Valkerie snatched the flashlight away and pressed her face close to Lex's ear. "Are you crazy? Let's get out of here."

"Why?" Lex whispered back. "He's asleep."

*He?* Valkerie turned back to the lab, confused. A wave of realization washed over her. The sound—she'd heard it a thousand times. It was Kennedy. Her face prickled with heat as she handed the flashlight back to Lex.

"Stay here." Lex pressed the flashlight back into Valkerie's hands. "If he wakes up, whack him. I'm going to get some tape." Lex crept around the corridor and disappeared into the shop.

*Whack him? With a crowbar?* Valkerie stood awkwardly in the corridor, praying Kennedy wouldn't wake up. *Skritch! Skritch!* The sound of unrolling duct tape rattled up Valkerie's spine. What was Lex thinking? Why not just shout in Kennedy's ear? She tightened her grip on the crowbar. If Kennedy woke up she would use it. She had to. He was dangerous—a monster. It wasn't just the infection. He'd been like this ever since she'd known him. He couldn't blame it on her. She'd never meant to lead him on. He was lying. And she'd certainly never been attracted to him.

Lex crept back with long strips of tape flowing from her arms like a superhero's cape. She transferred the strips to Valkerie's backpack and motioned toward the lab.

Valkerie followed quietly, pausing in the doorway to let her eyes adjust to the dim emergency lighting inside. She could just make out Kennedy's form, sprawled on a pile of blankets on the floor. She stepped closer. He seemed to be holding something in his hand. A friction lighter? What was he doing with a—

Her foot caught on a gas line. Another line ran to a Bunsen burner near Kennedy's head. A third to an acetylene tank.

Valkerie's heart beat so loud she was afraid the noise would wake Kennedy. She pointed at the gas lines and lighter, but Lex was already crouching at Kennedy's side.

His left leg was bent, so Lex wound a long strip of tape around Kennedy's left foot and right knee, binding his legs together into a loose figure four.

Kennedy snorted and rolled onto his side, trying to kick with his left foot. He opened his eyes with a gasp.

For a second Valkerie froze, staring into Kennedy's wide eyes.

Kennedy's eyes narrowed to a crafty smile.

Valkerie dove for the hand that held the lighter.

Kennedy pulled away a split second before she smashed into the floor.

She struck out with flailing arms and rolled into him, slamming her backpack into his stomach. "Lex, he's got a lighter!"

Kennedy pushed her roughly aside.

She rolled onto her hands and knees.

"Drop the knife or I blow us all off the planet." Kennedy was kneeling with his back to the wall, pressing an inflated, man-sized plastic bag to his chest—a NASA rescue bubble.

"Stand back!" Kennedy held the friction lighter to the bag. "This is a stoichiometric mixture of acetylene and oxygen."

"Val?" Lex's uncertain voice sounded behind her.

Valkerie nodded. "It might not blow us off the planet, but it would kill us for sure."

Kennedy's eyes blazed. "You heard her. Drop the knife."

"Since when did you become a suicidal terrorist?" Lex asked. "Looks like it's a stalemate to me."

Valkerie turned to look at Lex.

She still held the knife, not out in front of her, but cocked back over her shoulder, like she was about to throw it.

Valkerie climbed to her feet and backed slowly away from Kennedy to stand next to Lex.

"Bob's the terrorist." Kennedy struggled to free his foot from the tape that bound it to his knee.

"Bob's not the one threatening to blow us all up." Valkerie tried to make her voice sound natural—conversational. If she could just get Kennedy talking. If she could make him see reason. "And Bob's not here right now. I know you and Bob don't get along, but this isn't about Bob. This is about you, me, and Lex, right? I thought we were friends."

"Where is Bob, anyway?" Kennedy's eyes narrowed. "What did he do with the rover?"

"I was just going to ask you the same question." Lex stepped forward. "Where's the rover, Kennedy? What did you do with it?"

"I didn't do anything. Bob's got it. He stole it." Kennedy's eyes darted around the room.

"Bob was with us." Lex turned to Valkerie for confirmation. "The three of us watched you drive off in it an hour ago."

Kennedy pressed the lighter to the bag. "That's a lie! Bob stole the rover and you two are in on it."

"Honest, Kennedy," Valkerie said. "Bob was with—"

"The Hampster knows good and well where the rover is." Lex put a hand on Valkerie's shoulder. "I don't know what you're up to, Hampster. But if you so much as dented a fender—"

"I see how things are." Kennedy's voice shook. "You three have been out to get me from the beginning. And Josh too." Kennedy glared at Valkerie. "Don't think I don't know all about your little affair. What'd you do, Valkerie? How many people did you have to sleep with to get that bomb on board?"

Valkerie flushed. "I—"

"Don't listen to him, Val. See how he keeps changing the subject? The question is, Hampster, what did you do with the rover?"

Kennedy sneered at Lex. "I already told you."

"What if he's telling the truth?" Valkerie asked. "What if Houston took the rover?"

"Not a chance." Lex scowled at her. "Bob changed the password on the computer, remember? Kennedy drove the rover off and abandoned it. Then he came back here on foot."

Kennedy shook his head. "It had to be Bob. I heard him bumping around outside right before the rover undocked."

"How did he get in, then? The rover was docked to the Hab, wasn't it?" Valkerie circled slowly around Kennedy to the wall.

Kennedy eyed her suspiciously. "All he had to do was cut a hole. If I hadn't fixed the airlock hatch, the Hab would have decompressed."

Valkerie leaned against the wall and faced Lex. There, that was better. Now instead of the body language dynamics of Kennedy against the world, it was Kennedy and Valkerie against Lex. She hoped the clinical psychology textbooks were right. Now if she could just get the conversation flowing in the same direction. "He's got a point, Lex. Bob could have torched his way into the rover in less than a minute."

"What are you talking about? Bob was with us. We watched the rover drive off."

"But I was asleep, remember? What was Bob doing before you sent him to wake me up?"

Confusion wrinkled Lex's forehead. "What do you mean, what was he doing? He was with me."

Kennedy looked back and forth between Lex and Valkerie, still on the alert.

Valkerie gave him a warm smile. "Kennedy, remember when we planted the pansies in the greenhouse? What was Bob working on then?" She watched the lighter out of the corner of her eye. Kennedy's hand was drooping.

"What's that got to do with anything?"

"Remember, we were talking about the seeds. About the fact that you could never tell what color a flower would be by looking at the seeds. You made that joke about the difference between Bob and a pansy seed . . ."

Lex leaped across the lab and tackled Kennedy's arm—the one that held the lighter. White sparks blazed, missing the rescue bubble by inches.

Valkerie spun along the wall and yanked the bag from Kennedy's hands. Racing to the door, she tossed it down the corridor. When she turned around, Lex was grappling with Kennedy on the floor.

Kennedy lay on his back, reaching for the knife that lay only inches from his outstretched fingertips.

Valkerie kicked the knife away and stomped hard on his hand. She dropped to the floor and pinned Kennedy's arm to the ground, rolling onto her side to press her pack into his face.

Kennedy pitched back and forth, venting his rage with ragged shouts and screams.

"I've got one arm," Valkerie shouted.

"And I've got the other. Hold on."

Valkerie held on for what seemed like hours. Finally, when Kennedy's swearing had faded to exhausted panting and when he was too spent to put up any resistance, they bound his hands together with duct tape and wrapped more tape between his foot and knee.

"Okay." Valkerie leaned against a wall and tried to catch her breath. "What do we do now? I don't want to stay here with Kennedy, and I don't think I could carry Bob's suit back by myself."

"We can't just leave him here. If he gets loose, we're back to square one." Lex crouched over Kennedy with the knife in her hand.

"Hampster, are you sure you don't know where the rover is?" Lex asked.

Kennedy glared back at her.

Valkerie knew it wasn't logical, but for some reason she almost believed his story.

"There's only one way to go." Lex leaned over Kennedy with the knife. "Kennedy, I'm going to cut your hands free, and you're going to start doing push-ups. Make it to five hundred, and I'll let you live. But stop once or try to get away . . . and I kill you."

Friday, March 27, 2015, 12:15 p.m., CST

Josh

Josh shoved open his office door. *99.99 percent.* That's how sure Nate was that the crew was sick with an Earth bug. One more hundredth of a lousy percent and the resupply mission would get nipped in the bud.

Josh sat down at his computer and pulled up his e-mail program. No, he couldn't go to Jane Seyler again. That would backfire.

His tired eyes scanned down the list of twenty unread messages. The last one caught his eye. An urgent message from *Cathe.Willison@nasa.gov.* Sent all of about twenty minutes ago. Josh double-clicked on the subject line.

> Josh:
>
> I know I should be working now, but I can't stop thinking about you. I tossed and turned all night. I wouldn't have slept at all but for the hope that you would fill my dreams like you've filled my every waking thought. Please, Josh, I desperately need to

**see you. Something urgent has come up. Can you meet me in the cafeteria right away? I love you so much,**
**C.**

Josh leaned back in his chair, stunned. Was this the Cathe he knew? Yow! The more he got to know her the more astonishing she became. How many hidden facets did she have? He password-locked his computer and swept out of his office, flinging the door shut behind him.

The cafeteria buzzed with the usual noon craziness. Josh swept his eyes across the room. Where was Cathe? He looked at his watch. She'd sent the e-mail twenty-five minutes ago. Had he missed her? He ambled among the tables, scanning. No Cathe.

He saw a long table of engineers—some of the hotshot engineers in the Mission Evaluation Room. The kids in MER did essential support for Flight Control, and most of them would probably be working in the FCR someday. Cathe had spent two years in MER and had to know most of them.

Josh moseyed over to their table to ask if they'd seen her.

And as he came within earshot, their table suddenly got quiet. Real quiet.

Like they'd been talking about him.

"Hey, guys. Any of you seen Cathe Willison?" Josh said.

They shook their heads, the whole line of them looking guilty as sin.

"Well, uh, thanks." Josh felt his face burning. Had Nate and Perez already spilled the beans about his confession? They had told Dr. Frazier, and probably Abrams, and who else? A secret like that, well, once it got out, wildfire wouldn't touch it. Another couple of days and everybody would know.

Josh felt like he'd swallowed a lead brick. He'd spent the last year trying not to face the music. Now he was about to get hit with the whole orchestra, like it or not. He whirled and hurried toward the nearest exit. Who was watching him now? Smirking behind their hands? Whispering to their tablemates?

*Heard the scut on Bennett? Bombed his own crew—can you believe it? What kind of a jerk would do that?*

Josh burst outside and rushed toward the solitude of the duck ponds. This was the beginning of the purgatory he'd created for himself. The purgatory he deserved. Josh sat down on a bench and closed his eyes. What if that's why Cathe had split early? People knew she and Josh were an item. What if she'd been caught in the rumor-mill grinder too? The averted eyes, the offhand questions. It was too much for a girl to take. He wouldn't blame her if she dumped him then and there. Minutes dragged by—how many, he couldn't tell. What was he going to do? He ought to resign. But he couldn't. Bob and Lex needed him. Valkerie and Kennedy too, if they were still alive. There was no way he could leave them hanging, even if it meant walking through fire.

But Cathe was a different story. Even if she still wanted him, did he have the right to drag her down with him? She had such a bright future ahead of her. The last thing she needed at this point in her career was to be pinned under the hot lens of NASA scrutiny. But he couldn't just let her go. Not after her last e-mail. Besides, she'd said she needed to talk to him. Maybe she'd been caught at her office.

Josh stood up and strode toward Building 30, checking his watch. Almost 1:00. He only had a few minutes till he was supposed to be on duty. Cathe wasn't working console this afternoon, so she'd probably be in her office by now—if she wasn't in the cafeteria waiting for him. What did she need to tell him that was so urgent anyway? He raced into 30A and ran up the stairs. At the third floor, he flew out of the stairwell and dashed down the hall to Cathe's office.

The door was locked.

He punched in the five-button combination and pushed open the door.

The room was empty.

Footsteps padding down the hallway behind him.

"Looking for somebody?"

Josh spun around. "Cathe! I . . . I looked for you in the cafeteria, but you weren't there. What did you want to talk to me about?"

"The cafeteria?" She gave him a half-puzzled, half-exasperated look. "I was there to meet someone, but it turned out to be a really weird mistake."

"I know. I'm sorry. I should have waited longer, but I thought . . ." Josh shrugged. "I thought you might not want to be seen with me."

"Wouldn't want to be seen with you?" Cathe's eyes blazed. "What gave you that idea?"

"Word's out that I bombed the Ares 10."

"So?"

"So . . ." Josh took a deep breath. Cathe didn't seem that bothered by the news. Of course she wasn't. Just because he was a shallow, self-centered toad, didn't mean everyone else was too. "So didn't you have something you wanted to talk about?"

Cathe looked at him like he was losing his mind. "Am I supposed to?"

"You said . . ."

"Oh yeah." Cathe disappeared into her office and came back with a manila folder. "This is the list of transits Nate asked for. I thought you'd want to see it first. Turns out they have just enough delta-V for an October transit."

Josh took the offered folder without looking at it. "That's what you—"

"Oops, gotta run." Cathe glanced at her watch and bolted out the door. "Catch you in the FCR. EECOM asked me to bring her some data."

Josh stared after her as she hurried down the hallway and disappeared around the corner.

What had just happened?

### Friday, March 27, 2015, 7:30 a.m., Mars Local Time

### Bob

Bob peered out through the porthole at the party of three, now a hundred meters from his Hab.

Kennedy staggered along in an overly large suit—they'd made him wear one of Bob's. He wore the duct-taped helmet. Valkerie led him by the hand. His ragged breath hissed over the radio channel.

"Keep walking," Lex said. "Val, keep him at arm's length. Don't let him get too close. One false move, buddy, and I put this spike right through your oxygen tank."

"Please . . ." Kennedy stopped.

"Move," Lex said. "You stop again and it'll be your last time."

Kennedy shuffled forward.

Valkerie hadn't said anything since they left the Ares 7. Bob wondered what she was thinking. Which was crazy, because he'd never had a clue what she was thinking. Not really. He was as different from her as she was from Kennedy.

"Kaggo, you watching us?" Lex waved her sharpened club up at the porthole.

"Roger dodger," Bob said into the mike. "Careful with that samurai sword of yours. I'd sure hate to meet you in a dark alley, RoboLex. Valkerie, are you okay?"

"I'm fine." Her voice sounded tight, controlled. The voice she used when she was scared and trying not to show it.

It took another five minutes to cover the ground to the Hab. Bob went downstairs and prepared the airlock. He grabbed a rubber mallet and hefted it. Just let Kennedy try any funny business and Bob would whack him into next Tuesday.

Valkerie led the way into the airlock, holding Kennedy's hand to guide him up the steps. Bob flinched. Lex followed them in, pressing the sharpened edge of her club against Kennedy's oxygen pack.

Bob pressed the button to shut the outer door, then pressurized the airlock. When the needle stopped moving, he spun the wheel and yanked open the door.

Valkerie stepped out, her helmet already off, tears standing in her eyes.

"Valkerie, are you okay?" Bob said.

She nodded vaguely and walked over to her locker. Kennedy just stood there, blind, unmoving.

"Move forward slowly," Lex said. She still wore her helmet.

Kennedy fumbled for his helmet. "I can't see."

"I'll get it." Bob stepped forward.

"Stay back and let him do it." Lex prodded him with her club. "Kennedy, I'm right behind you and Bob's in front of you with a hammer in his hand. So you move real slow and take the helmet off like it was made of eggshells. You try anything, and I take your head off."

"Bob, talk to her!" Kennedy's voice sounded pathetic, childish. He found the latch at his neck and nudged it free. He eased the helmet off his head and held it out to Bob, blinking rapidly. "Tell her to back off, Bob! I didn't do anything to her. She's the one who stole the rover. Talk some sense into her head."

Bob grabbed the helmet and put it in a locker. He stepped back and motioned to Kennedy to follow him. "Take off the suit."

"Bob, I'm really tired." Kennedy's breath was coming in short jags. He staggered into the room and plopped onto a bench. "Can you . . . give me a hand with this?"

Valkerie nodded. "Lex made him do push-ups till he dropped." Her face clouded over and she looked back down at the floor.

Lex stood in the doorway, her helmet off now, her face a mask of iron. "He can take it off himself." She hefted her club and handed Bob the spare helmet she'd brought. "Five minutes, Kennedy."

"Bob, somebody stole the rover," Valkerie said.

"I saw."

"It can't be far," Lex said. "Kennedy had to walk all the way back to the Hab."

Kennedy leaned forward and let gravity pull the upper half of his suit off. "I . . . didn't . . . take . . . the rover."

Bob wrinkled his nose. When was the last time Kennedy had taken a shower? He smelled pretty gamy. And that was Bob's suit he'd stunk up, the little creep.

"If you didn't, then who did?" Lex said. "All three of us stood up here and watched that rover drive off. And all the while, you were yakking on and on about Bob. What kind of game are you playing?"

Kennedy lay down on the floor and closed his eyes. "I didn't . . . not playing a game."

Lex smacked the wall. "Move!"

Kennedy squirmed forward out of the pants of the EVA suit.

Thankfully, he was wearing his own LCG. *If he'd worn one of mine, that would be just too disgusting for words.* "What did you do with the rover?" Bob said.

Kennedy glared up at him. "What did *you* do with the rover?"

"Time to tell the truth." Lex swung her club in a semicircle, letting the blunt middle of it thud into her left hand.

"Um . . . guys?" Valkerie said. "I know you don't want to hear this, but . . . I think he *is* telling the truth."

Bob turned to stare at her.

Lex sighed impatiently. "Which means exactly what?"

"Which means . . . I don't believe Kennedy drove the rover away." Valkerie bit her lip. "So either someone in Houston cracked Bob's password and decided to play games with us, or—"She blushed and searched Bob's eyes. "Or there really is a fifth man on Mars."

# 23

Friday, March 27, 2015, 1:30 p.m., CST

Nate

"Not responding?" Nate said. "How can it be not responding?"

EECOM hunched over her console, typing furiously. "It's not complicated, sir. I send commands—the Ares 10 does not respond."

"But why?"

She glared up at him. "I am not a mind reader. Perhaps the energy supply has failed. Or the radio system. Or the crew may have disabled the radio. All I can tell you is that the Ares 10 does not answer queries on its life-support functions—nor on anything else."

"Is there any evidence that someone is in there?"

"Mr. Hunter has been hailing both the Ares 10 and the Ares 7, with no answer from either one."

"Okay, so show me those numbers again on oxygen usage in the Ares 7."

EECOM punched some keys and then pulled out a pocket calculator. "Over the last forty-eight hours, the oxygen production is consistent with the usage required by . . ." She tapped in some numbers. "2.14 adults."

"That doesn't make any sense," Nate said. "You can't have .14 adults."

"Please." EECOM slapped the calculator on the console. "I am not making up numbers, I'm just reporting them. I have a number for integrated oxygen production. I have another for the nominal usage by a normal adult. I divide the two numbers and report the result. If they're exercising, they are using more than normal. If they're all in a coma, they're using less."

"So you're telling me there could be two active people in there or three slugs," Nate said.

She nodded. "I'm very sorry, sir, but it looks like there are fewer than four people occupying the Ares 7."

"And we've got no videocams active?"

"None plugged in on the Ares 7. The Hab is reporting zero video sources active. And as I said, the Ares 10 is not reporting at all. For all practical purposes, the Ares 10 does not exist."

Nate felt a knot forming in his gut. Who was dead? Kennedy? Valkerie? Both?

EECOM opened a window on her console. "Sir, I'm ready to send those queries to the ERV."

"Let's do it," Nate said. "I want to know for sure nobody's on that ship."

Jake Hunter screamed something from across the room.

Nate scowled and spun around to look. Hunter was fidgeting with some dials at the Capcom station.

"Houston, this is Alexis Ohta, Commander of the Ares 7, reporting."

Nate blinked twice. *Commander? What about Kennedy?*

Lex repeated her hailing one more time, then continued. "With me are Bob Kaganovski and Valkerie Jansen. Check off, guys."

"This is Bob."

"And this is Valkerie."

Nate strode toward the Capcom station. *Where was Kennedy?*

"Kennedy Hampton is undergoing psychological difficulties and we've been forced to isolate him in the Ares 10 Hab. We have relieved him of command."

A small circle had formed around the Capcom station. EECOM's eyes were wide. "How do we know Dr. Ohta is telling the truth?"

Josh held up his hand. "Just listen."

Lex continued. "We've been a little busy lately and we apologize for not calling in sooner. Kennedy is seriously maladjusted and he's been a handful to deal with. Right now we have a question about the rover for which we demand an immediate answer."

Eyebrows raised around the circle.

Nate couldn't believe it. She *demanded* an answer? Immediately?

"How do we know they aren't on the ERV and playing for time?" EECOM said.

"The rover was moved from its docking position at the Ares 7 this morning," Lex said. "Bob and Valkerie and I observed it driving away. Right, guys?"

"Right," Bob said.

"We thought Kennedy was on it." Valkerie sounded nervous.

"Kennedy denies it," Lex continued. "And we think it's possible he may be telling the truth. So we request that you inform us at once whether you've sent any motion commands to the rover. We await your response. Over."

"That's ridiculous," Cathe said. "Nobody's been driving the rover."

"They're wasting our time," Jake said. "They could be in Mars orbit in the ERV and locking us out of computer access this very minute, while we fiddle around looking for rover commands."

Josh turned to Nate. "What do we do?"

Nate pointed to EECOM. "Get those queries queued up for the ERV. While we wait for an answer, Cathe can pull up the log of all commands sent to the surface of Mars for the last twenty-four hours. The rest of you check everything! I want a list of every command that's gone out of here through the Deep Space Network."

The engineers fanned out to their consoles and began typing furiously.

Cathe was first to respond. "Sir, I've got the log for every command to base camp since yesterday. There are a number of videocam queries, and those life-support queries EECOM sent." She typed something in. "Okay, I'm making a printout now, but I can tell you already there are no rover commands. I'd recognize those if—"

CATO shouted a curse.

Nate was behind him in a second.

"Sir, there's some kind of burn command queued up for the ERV."

"Cancel it," Nate said.

"I don't know what kind it is," CATO said. "Could be just ordinary station-keeping."

"We should find out what it is first," EECOM said.

CATO just stared at the screen. "The burn is queued up for execution in about twenty-five minutes. Radio delay time is almost twenty minutes. We won't have time to—"

"Cancel it right now!" Nate pounded the table.

EECOM leaned over CATO's shoulder and typed in something on the screen. "It's cancelled."

Cathe peered past them. "It was a burn of . . . 2,200 meters per second."

"That doesn't make sense," Nate said. "That's enough to break them out of orbit, but it wouldn't get them to Earth. What kind of a transit were they trying for?"

"You're making two mistakes," CATO said. "The direction of the burn would have de-orbited the ERV." He stared at Nate, his eyes wild. "It would have crashed into Mars."

Nate scowled at him. "And what's the other mistake?"

"It's obvious," EECOM said. "That command went out through the DSN. Whoever put that command on the stack queued it up from planet Earth."

Nate shivered, his gut turning to molten lead. Somebody had tried to crash the ERV. Tried to strand his crew on Mars. But who? There wasn't supposed to be a saboteur anymore.

"Hunter!" Nate bellowed. "Get back to the crew and tell them we've checked the command logs. Nobody's been driving the rover from here."

"Do I tell them about the ERV?" Hunter asked.

"Not a word," Nate said. "Not till we know what's going on." He smacked the table with his open palm. "I want you engineers to team up in pairs. You're all suspects until we figure out who did this, so watch each other. Track down that command and give me an answer—who queued up that de-orbit burn to crash the ERV."

The circle of engineers stared at him as if he had ordered them all to eat broken glass. Which Nate might very well do—to whoever had tried to strand his crew.

• • •

Friday, March 27, 2015, 11:30 p.m., Mars Local Time

Bob

Bob sat in a hanging chair in the command center and tried to make sense of it all. The girls had gone to bed an hour ago, leaving him on guard duty for the first half of the night.

Guard duty! It was ridiculous. There was nothing to guard against. Except maybe that big dust storm. Which wouldn't get here for another day or two. Kennedy was stuck over at the Ares 10 without a suit. No way in the world could he just wander out in the frigid Martian night and cross two hundred meters of vacuum. And finally, the door downstairs was locked up tight. Bob had made sure of that.

The Ares 7 was about the safest place in the solar system right now. Ought to be, anyway.

Except for one tiny little question mark.

Nate had called back pretty quickly this morning with a response to Lex's question. The engineers in the FCR had checked the logs and double-checked them and triple-checked them. Nobody in Houston had sent any rover commands in the last week. Matter of fact, they'd checked every command that had gone through the Deep Space Network from any source, looking for any robotic commands at all.

Zippo.

So either the rover had grown brains and driven off under its own volition . . . or there was somebody else on the planet—Valkerie's fifth man.

Bob got out of his chair and began pacing. This did not compute. You could prove mathematically that the life support on the outbound journey could not keep another living soul alive. Nothing bigger than a chihuahua, anyway. There hadn't been any stowaways on the Ares 10. And of course none on the Ares 7, which made the transit without passengers and without an atmosphere.

And there weren't any other manned missions to Mars. Not even close. Not possible. The Russians, the Japanese, the Europeans—none of them had that kind of operational experience, that kind of technology, that kind of money. If they had, they'd have been in line to put one of their people on this mission.

Which left . . . what?

A Mars monkey?

Crazy. Mars was dead. Had been dead for a billion years, or three billion, or whatever. Tectonically dead, even—no geological carbon cycle to fuel life. An atmosphere way too thin to screen out cosmic rays and solar flares. No ozone to block UV light, no magnetic field to divert charged particles. Regolith full of sterilizing peroxides.

Mars was dead. It was a miracle to find the bacterium that Valkerie and Lex had dug up—and even that was only thanks to a perfect little underground microclimate driven warm and humid by a thermal vent.

It was not biologically possible to find even a Mars mouse, let alone a Mars monkey or a Mars man.

*Right. So who drove off with the rover?*

Bob clenched his fists, digging his fingernails into his hands. The rover hadn't just disappeared by itself. It drove away. Under the guidance of an intelligent agent. Kennedy hadn't done it.

The proof was that Bob couldn't locate the rover visually. He'd made a quick sweep outside this afternoon, and it was nowhere in sight. The rover had to be at least a kilometer away.

And there was no way Kennedy could have driven it that far off, hopped out, and come walking back to the Ares 7 in the time it took the girls to cross just two hundred meters of open plain with the airlock of the Ares 7 in clear view. They hadn't seen him go in. Ergo, he had been inside the whole time. Which meant he had not driven the rover himself.

Nor had he driven it out remotely. The command logs showed no activity. And anyway, Bob had changed the super-user password on the Ares 7 computers yesterday. So the Hampster wouldn't have been able to access the computers.

Lex had suggested that Kennedy must have reinstalled the operating system and set the password to his own choosing. That was a fine theory. The only problem with it was that the password was the same today as it was yesterday—crAmNi5ef00D. So if Lex was right, then Kennedy had randomly chosen a twelve-character alphanumeric password that just happened to be the same as Bob's. The odds against that were three billion trillion to one.

*Okay, Sherlock, who or what is left? When you've eliminated all the impossibilities, whatever's left is the answer—however improbable.*

But there wasn't anything left.

Nothing but Valkerie's fifth man, and of course, that was impossible too.

Something creaked in the exterior walls. Bob froze for a second.

The wind. It had to be. He wished he could look outside, but the porthole was covered over with a piece of sheet metal.

Valkerie was scared. Even RoboLex was acting a little nervous, but something had really been bothering Valkerie. She'd been quiet all evening. Hadn't let Bob out of her sight since supper. Something had softened up in her all of a sudden. She wasn't so—

"Bob! Is that you out there, Bob?"

Bob turned to glare at the radio. Kennedy again. The paranoia act was getting old fast. According to Josh, Houston had evidence that Kennedy had some kind of mental disorder—the kind you could conceal under normal circumstances. The kind that leaked under heavy pressure. That was a fine explanation, but it didn't help much in the way of solving the problem. *What were they going to do with a wild Hampster for the next fifteen months?*

"Bob, I hear you out there," Kennedy said, his voice hissing with static. "I'm warning you, I've got a crowbar here and I'm not afraid to use it! If you come in, I'm gonna bash you, boy. I'm gonna hit you so hard you'll be pickin' your teeth out of tomorrow. Face it, loser. No matter what you do, I'll still come out on top. Poor Bob, always loses the girl. Face it, guy—she's in love with me. You're out in the cold—"

Bob grabbed the mike, ready to . . . No. That's exactly what Kennedy wanted. He took a deep breath and set the mike back down.

"I'm waiting for you, yellowbelly," Kennedy said. "That's right, run back home before I smash you."

A long static-filled silence, then a muffled thumping noise.

"I said, get away!" Kennedy shouted. "I kept you on this mission, did you know that? They wanted to get rid of you. They said you were afraid to come, that you'd chicken out. I kept you on the team and pushed out Josh, and what—"

A loud thump sounded over the radio. Static. "Bob, please . . ." Kennedy's voice was a whimper. "Please, don't. I didn't mean it. Please . . ." A resounding crash. "Bob, I'm sorry. I was just kidding . . ."

Bob rested a finger on the Transmit button but shook his head. "Fool me twice, shame on me." He flicked off the radio and set down the mike.

Blessed silence filled the Hab.

Saturday, March 28, 2015, 8:00 a.m., Mars Local Time

Valkerie

Valkerie lay on her back, floating above the terrors of the last couple of days. The whisper of blowing sand caressed her senses as it blew against the outer hull. A warm drowsiness stole over her. The tinkle of sleet and snow blowing against the windows of her family's Upper Peninsula cabin. She and her dad had been snowed in for six days after her mother died. Reading aloud to each other, playing chess by firelight, drinking hot chocolate—those had been the best six days of her life. And the worst. She remembered the pain etched in her father's face. The tears. The deep, burning void. But the snow kept falling. Silently. Blowing mounds of fluffy softness over the jagged fences and fallen limbs. White and pure, it coated everything with a blanket of peace.

"Kind of nice, isn't it?" Bob's voice sounded at the doorway. Footsteps. The steamy smell of hot tea.

Valkerie opened her eyes. "You're up already? Weren't you on watch pretty late last night?"

Bob knelt by her cot, holding out a steaming cup. "Sorry if I woke you. I thought you were up when I started fixing tea."

"I wasn't asleep. Just thinking." Valkerie sat up on the cot and took the offered cup.

"Thinking about what?" Bob sat down beside her and took a sip of tea.

Valkerie couldn't help smiling. His hands were so big. The cup looked like it came from a child's tea-party set. He stared back at her for several seconds, then dropped his eyes and took another sip of tea.

"Did I ever tell you that you remind me of my father?"

"No . . ."

"He used to play tea party with me. Tea party, house, school . . . but he drew the line at dress-up."

Bob's eyes took on a faraway look. "You miss him, don't you?"

Valkerie nodded. "How about you? Who do you miss the most?"

"Josh . . ." Bob closed his eyes and took a long sip of tea. " . . . and Kennedy."

Valkerie's insides twisted into a familiar knot.

"The way he used to be. Remember how it was before the mission? Remember wilderness survival training? The sim on Devon Island?" Bob leaned back against the wall. "Those were the best days of my life."

"But I was horrible to you then."

"And you aren't now?" Bob laughed and looked at her with a faraway expression. "I'll never forget the first time I saw you. The treadmill almost swallowed me alive. I'd never in my life seen a more—" Bob stopped and stared down at his teacup.

"What?" Valkerie leaned forward and placed a hand on his shoulder. "What were you going to say?"

Emotions rippled across Bob's face like a fine mist. "I really . . . shouldn't." He closed his eyes and shook his head.

"It's okay." Valkerie reached out and took him by the hand. "Look at me. You can tell me anything."

Footsteps in the hallway. "Hey, Val? We've got a big—" Lex barged into the room, then skidded to a halt. "Whoa, um . . . never mind. It can wait."

Bob pulled his hand away. "Lex, wait. What's wrong?"

Lex looked to Valkerie, her eyes two big, dotted question marks.

Valkerie nodded. "It's okay. We were just talking."

"Well . . ." Lex shrugged. "Remember why we went over to the Ares 10 the other day?"

Valkerie sighed. What was Kennedy up to *now*?

"Remember?" Lex motioned to Bob. "We took the rover . . ."

"Oh no!" Bob jumped to his feet. "How much food do we have left?"

"A couple of boxes," Lex said. "And the dust storm's going to hit us full force any hour now. It's already pretty gusty."

"Hold on a second." Valkerie set her tea on her desk and stood up next to Bob. "I thought you guys brought back a full load of supplies."

"We did, about two months' worth, but remember?" Lex searched her eyes, waiting. "Remember when we got back you hit us with the big news—that something had broken into the lab?"

"Not to mention the small matter of life on Mars," Bob added. "We were so distracted we only unloaded—"

"Two lousy boxes." Lex shook her head. "We've got maybe four hours before the dust storm really starts blasting us. Once it hits, we may be socked in for weeks."

"We've got to talk to Kennedy." Valkerie stepped over the corner of her cot and squeezed past Lex. "We can't just barge in on him unannounced and expect him to greet us with hugs and kisses."

"That'll just give him time to plan his attack." Lex followed Valkerie to the transmitter and laid a restraining hand on the mike. "We've got to hit him fast and hard. Take him unawares and pin him to the wall."

"Bob . . ." Valkerie waited for Bob to shuffle over to the transmitter. "Kennedy doesn't need knives and duct tape, he needs someone to listen to him. If we're ever going to reclaim him, we've got to start now. It'll only get worse if he isolates."

Bob shifted uncomfortably.

"We can't keep him in jail forever. Remember, we all have to ride back on the same bus."

Bob spread his arms wide. "She's got a point."

Lex didn't look convinced.

"We should at least talk to him. See what kind of a mood he's in," Valkerie said. "Maybe his fever's broken, and he's back to normal."

"Normal's what worries me." Lex pushed the mike toward Valkerie. "But go ahead and talk if it makes you happy. Just don't let him con you."

Valkerie picked up the mike and keyed the Transmit button. "Hey, Kennedy? This is Valkerie. Are you awake?"

She waited a long minute for a response. "Kennedy, this is Valkerie calling from the Ares 7. Do you read?"

Nothing.

"Kennedy, please. We'd like to talk. Before we can bring you back over here we've got to find out what your issues are. You know, talk things out as friends."

Valkerie set down the mike and turned to Bob. "Think he's asleep?"

"Maybe. He was up pretty late last night."

"How do you know?"

"He called on the radio—you know, the usual. Things going bump in the night. Me outside his Hab trying to kill him."

"Why didn't you say anything?" Valkerie turned back to the transmitter. "What if there really was something out there?"

"Of course there's something. Something wrong in the Hampster's head." Bob made a circle at his temples.

"I heard it too. Do you think there's something wrong in my head?"

"That's different. You hear things and you investigate. Try to figure out what could have made the noise. Kennedy hears things and fills a rescue bubble with acetylene. That's a big difference—the difference between sane and insane."

Valkerie held the mike to her lips again. "Kennedy, this is Valkerie. Please acknowledge. We want to help you. I want to help you."

Bob stood up and began pacing.

Valkerie tried again. And again. Finally she set the mike down. "Let's check the video monitors."

They went down to the lab and flicked on the video receiver. The monitor lit up with snow.

"He's unplugged the videocams." Bob turned off the receiver. "Guess he just doesn't want to talk to us."

Lex picked up the sharpened pipe-knife. "He's going to talk to us whether he wants to or not. We need that food and we need it now."

Bob sighed. "Lex, how about you and I go over there with the MuleBot? If Kennedy cooperates, fine. If he makes a ruckus, we feed him some duct tape. Either way, we load up the mule with as much food as we can lug back."

Valkerie grabbed his arm. "Bob, I think I should go—instead of Lex."

He stared at her as if she had just said she wanted to go to a strip club.

"Bob, I'm serious. He won't hurt me. Not while you're around. Maybe I can talk to him. He needs someone to listen to him, and I'm not nearly as threatening as Lex." Valkerie looked to Lex, hoping she hadn't offended her.

Bob shook his head. "It's too dangerous. He tried to kill you Wednesday. He tried again Thursday. Yesterday he tried to kill you *and* himself."

"And Mama Lexie." Lex pointed to the monitor for the sat-pix. "Guys, that dust storm is looking pretty wicked. We don't have long before it gets gnarly in this neighborhood. Bob and I need to go over there now."

"I won't stay here alone." Valkerie folded her arms across her chest and stared her defiance at Lex.

Exasperation furrowed Lex's forehead. "Val, there is no way Kennedy is going to come back over here."

"That's what we thought on Thursday." Valkerie took Bob's hand and looked up into his eyes. "Please?"

Bob turned to Lex with a shrug. "Listen, Lex, how about we try this. Valkerie and I will go over and talk to the Hampster. I'll take the knife along and I'll watch him real close. He tries anything, we back out of there and call you over. Then you and I go in and . . . deal with him."

Lex gave a short, hard sigh to show her impatience. But it also meant she was going to agree.

Valkerie squeezed Bob's hand.

"All right, all *right*." Lex led Bob and Valkerie to the EVA-suit room. "If anybody can sweet-talk the Mad Hampster, it's Val." She turned and punched Bob in the arm. "She sure turned you into the Pillsbury Doughboy."

### Saturday, March 28, 2015, 9:30 a.m., Mars Local Time

### Bob

The sun was brilliant, burning off the mental fog that had dampened Bob's spirits all morning. It was good to get outside. He hadn't realized until now what a difference having a window made. He stepped down out of the airlock and turned to help Valkerie down the stairs. She took his arm and they descended the stairs together. Bob felt for all the world like a schoolboy at his first formal dance. He patted her hand with an awkward glove and started for the back of the Hab, where the MuleBot was parked.

A rusty cloud blew across his visor with the faint hiss of a million tiny particles. Two hundred meters away, the Ares 10 flashed in the sunlight.

Something was wrong.

Bob shielded his eyes against the glare. The right side of the Hab looked too dark, the roof line too uneven, like the upper-right corner was missing.

"Valkerie." Bob held a hand up to block the glinting sun. "Tell me I'm not seeing what I think I'm seeing."

The walls of the Hab had melted through, exposing its blackened interior.

"Kennedy," Valkerie gasped. "Our food. Our food till next January is in there."

"What's going on?" Lex's voice crackled over comm.

"The Hab. It looks like there's been some sort of fire." Leaving the MuleBot behind, Bob started running toward the burned-out Hab. Valkerie's labored breath sounded in his ears. He turned back and waited for her to catch up and then set out hand in hand with her at a fast walk.

"Talk to me, guys," came Lex's controlled voice. "Is it a full breach? Think we can salvage the food supplies?"

"We'll know in a second." Bob peered up at the blackened hull. Wisps of sand blew around his feet.

"Guys, our weather station twenty klicks south of here is showing gusts up to a hundred kilometers per hour," Lex said. "You need to hurry."

"This won't take long." Valkerie's voice sounded tight.

"I agree." Bob tugged at the outer hatch of the airlock. It swung open. He stepped cautiously inside. The inner hatch was jammed. Leaning his back against one wall and bracing his left foot against the other, he strained at the wheel. Valkerie grabbed it and threw her weight into it.

Slowly, the wheel came unfrozen. Bob spun it around. They pushed the door open and stepped into the blackened interior. "Watch your step," Valkerie said. "The floor panels could be unstable."

"Right," Bob said. "I just want to see if there's any chance he could have survived."

"Bob."

Bob looked at the charred remains of the EVA-suit room. Soot covered the lockers. Some kind of fluid had spilled onto the floor—from the bioreactor next door? The liquid would have evaporated soon after the hull lost integrity. That was hours ago. Now all that remained was a greenish-grayish oozy stain.

Somewhere in this Hab was their food supply. Had it burned? And what about Kennedy? Bob peered at the stairway, the sagging ceiling, the charred floor. "Maybe you should wait here."

"No way. I'm going with you."

"Okay. But stay right behind me. Step where I'm stepping." Bob prodded the floor with his pipe-knife, probing for weak spots. "Let's check on the food stores." He eased his way across the floor of the EVA-suit room, probing with his pipe, skittering the beam of his flashlight around the room. At the hallway, Bob shone his flashlight into the storeroom next door.

A charred and twisted mass of plastic and metal. The fuel cells in the next room must have ignited. That was the only explanation. Hydrogen burned really hot, explosively fast. But how had it happened? Fuel cells didn't just light off by themselves.

Kennedy. It had to be Kennedy. A terrible way to commit suicide. He must have been in despair to take the final exit so dramatically. *And I ignored his last cry for help.*

Bob turned to look at Valkerie. Wide eyes peered back at him through her gold-tinted visor. He checked his comm switch. "Lex, I'm looking at the storeroom and . . . it's all gone." His voice cracked. "Burned. There isn't enough food left for afternoon tea."

Long silence.

"How about the pantry upstairs?" Lex's voice trembled.

"The structure's too unstable." Valkerie clutched Bob's arm. "Going upstairs would be too risky."

"We're down to one week of food." Lex emphasized each word. "We don't have a choice."

"But—"

"Lex is right." Bob stepped carefully to the bottom of the stairwell, pulling Valkerie along behind him. "Valkerie, I need you outside. If the floor collapses I don't want you cushioning my fall."

Valkerie clung to his arm tighter. "Let me go. I'm lighter."

"Not this time." Bob tried to pull his arm away.

"Val, clear out of there," Lex said. "Bob can carry more. And if he doesn't find any food . . . he might have to carry Kennedy out."

*Carry Kennedy out?* Bob shuddered as the implication of Lex's words sank home.

"Okay." Valkerie gave his arm a reluctant squeeze and picked her way toward the airlock. "Be careful."

Right. *Careful* and *Mars* didn't even belong in the same sentence. Bob placed a tentative foot on the bottom stair tread and gradually shifted his weight onto it. So far so good. He took the next step. The next. Halfway up the stairs a metallic groan vibrated up through his body. The whole stairwell sagged to his right.

He dropped to his hands and knees and clung to the tread above him, fighting to keep his balance.

"Bob, are you all right?" Valkerie's voice filled his helmet.

"Sure. No problems." Bob tried to keep his voice steady as he stretched forward in an awkward crouch. His arms shook as he reached for the next stair. Every instinct told him to turn back, but he couldn't. Without food they were dead.

He crept up the stairs, keeping his center of balance as low as possible. He crawled through the hatch and out onto the uneven floor of the upper deck.

A dusty orange-tinted beam of light stabbed through the commons area, filtering in through a gaping hole in the roof of the Hab. Almost a quarter of the upper deck had been melted away. The section right above the hydrogen tanks.

Bob stared at the molten mass of metal and plastic. His senses reeled. The crew quarters. If Kennedy had been in his room . . . Bob turned away from the grisly spectacle and blinked his eyes as the deck dissolved into an orange haze.

No. There wasn't time for this. Bob shook his head. He had to focus on survival—food. If he didn't bring back something to eat, they were all going to die.

He turned toward the galley and crept across the buckled floor. The structure popped and groaned beneath him, but by some miracle it held. He pried off the sagging pantry door and riffled through the charred boxes. Foil packets littered the cabinet, but they were all empty. All but four tubes of Jell-O in the bottom of the last box.

"It's all gone." Bob forced the words through his constricting throat. "Only four Jell-Os left. The pantry wasn't burned, there just wasn't anything else here."

A long silence.

"All right. We'll figure something out . . ." Lex's voice trailed off. Another long silence. "You better get out of there. Looks like the wind speed is picking up. Are you sure there isn't more? Did you check the commons?"

"What about Kennedy's room?" Valkerie's voice was hollow. "You know how he likes to squirrel away food."

"Kennedy's room isn't even here anymore. It was right above the hydrogen tanks." Bob stashed the four packets in his stow bag and crawled back across the creaking floor.

"Careful, Bob."

*Like it matters now.* Bob eased down the stairs. A Martian dust storm could last for months. Winds up to hundreds of miles per hour. Trying to take off in the MAV would be out of the question. A knot tightened around his throat. He felt sick. Trapped. He jumped down the last three stairs and ran for the airlock.

"Bob!" Valkerie stood just outside the entrance, pointing to the south.

He turned in the indicated direction. A wall of swirling orange dust rose above the horizon. Already the tracks they'd made on the way over had disappeared. The storm was beginning.

### Saturday, March 28, 2015, 10:30 a.m., Mars Local Time

### Valkerie

"Houston, this is CDR Alexis Ohta, calling from the Ares 7." Lex closed her eyes and took a deep breath. "I regret to inform you that Kennedy Hampton died last night in a tragic accident. He was working alone in the Ares 10 when the Hab caught on fire and burned. We do not know for certain the cause of the accident, but it may have been the result of the psychological problems that he has been manifesting for the last several months. We are forced to consider suicide as a strong possibility." Lex looked to Valkerie with a grimace.

"Stored on board the Ares 10 were most of our nondurables—including most of our food and medical supplies. We currently have only enough food to last one week without rationing. Repeat . . ."

Valkerie crossed the room and fell into one of the hanging chairs. Bob sat on the floor slumped against the wall, staring out into space with vacant eyes.

"Bob, it's okay," Valkerie said. "We're going to make it. We'll think of something. Everything's going to be fine."

"Fine?" Bob's eyes blazed. "Kennedy's dead. How's that supposed to be fine?"

A guilty pang stabbed through Valkerie. "It isn't. I'm sorry. I was being selfish. It's just that . . ."

"I know." Bob's eyes softened. "I've been worried about the food situation too. As far as I can figure, we're just going to have to wait for a lull in the storm. If we could get into orbit—the ERV has plenty of supplies."

"Do you think we really could?" A fountain of hope welled up inside her. If only they could get off Mars. To go home early . . . It was almost too wonderful to hope for.

"We don't have a choice." Bob pulled his knees up in front of him and rested his forehead on his forearms.

Valkerie nodded. Who could fault them for quitting? They were out of food. What else could they do?

"I know you had your heart set on doing more research in that thermal vent, but we've got to be reasonable. We can't stretch a week of food to last nine more months."

"Why not?" Lex set the mike on the table and turned to face them. "We've got a greenhouse outside and another one inside with plenty of lights. Why can't we grow our own food?"

Valkerie turned to Lex. Surely she wasn't serious. "We don't have nearly enough. The vegetables were never intended to be anything but a supplement. And even if we had plenty, there's no way they'd grow fast enough. We only have food for a week."

"I don't know." Lex smoothed her hands down her hips. "I for one could stand a little dieting. How about you, Bob?"

Bob looked at her like she was crazy.

"Come on. We've got plenty of food." Lex strode to the center of the room. "We could easily stretch it to last a month. Maybe even a month and a half. That's plenty of time to get our crops going."

Valkerie shook her head. "It's not that simple. We don't have enough potting soil from Earth, and we still haven't figured out how to make plants grow in Martian soil. It's just not going to happen."

"You sound like you don't want it to happen." Lex fixed Valkerie with an accusing stare.

Valkerie felt herself flushing. "It's not that. I just don't think—"

"We've got to at least try. Maybe we can synthesize food. We've got plenty of carbon dioxide and hydrogen."

*Synthesize food?* What had gotten into Lex? Valkerie turned to Bob.

Bob shrugged. "Lex is right. We should start planting seeds—just in case the storm doesn't let up—but I don't see how we could synthesize food. Besides, most of our reagents were in the other Hab."

Valkerie looked from Bob to Lex. There was absolutely no way they could last nine months on the handful of seeds they had brought with them from Earth. They had gone through most of their greens in two weeks.

Bob stood up and lumbered toward the stairwell.

"Not yet, big guy," Lex called him back. "Formal blues first, then our overalls. Houston's going to want a memorial service right away, and I for one need to figure out what I'm going to say."

Valkerie slipped out of the hanging chair and followed Lex from the commons. Feeling her way through the darkness of her room, she sought out the comfort of pillow and cot. Kennedy was dead. She still couldn't wrap her mind around it. Had he really committed suicide? It didn't add up. He'd told Bob he was under attack. Something was wrong. Bad wrong. A floor-rattling *whump* sounded below.

"What was that?" Bob called out from his room.

"Val, was that you?" Lex's footsteps sounded outside Valkerie's door.

"No!" Icy fingers tightened around Valkerie's heart. She lay in her bed and listened as Bob and Lex clomped down the stairs. Footsteps. Closing doors. A bump on the floor.

"Nothing down here. Must have been our ghost," Bob called up the stairs. His laugh was tight, forced.

Valkerie started to get up, then collapsed back onto the bed. What did it matter? She lay in bed listening. Sand blasted against the wall with the relentless fury of a hostile planet. Hatred. Malice. She could feel it all around her. Like the planet was possessed by a dark spirit—Ares, god of war. They had intruded on his demesne, and he wouldn't rest until he'd killed them all. She buried her face in her pillow, trying to blot out the dark images that infected her mind. Twisted metal. Charred plastic. A gutted trophy, a monument to the planet's destructive force. *We never should have come. What have we done?*

The whole venture had been doomed from the start. One disaster after another. Storm after storm after storm. And now the beast had finally swallowed them. No food. No supplies. It was only a matter of time. Kennedy was dead and she couldn't even find the tears to mourn him. She was dead too—at her very core.

Soft footsteps sounded behind her. "Valkerie?" Bob's voice. "Are you okay?"

Valkerie didn't look up. "I . . . I can't help thinking. Kennedy would still be alive if we hadn't taken him to the Ares 10. It's my fault."

"No, it's not." The footsteps came closer, stopping by the side of her cot.

Valkerie rolled onto her side. "What if I had just let him kiss me? Would that have killed me? What if I had set him straight before he even tried? I should have seen the signs. He'd been crying out for help for months, but I was too caught up in my work to even listen. I should have—"

"Valkerie, listen to me." Bob leaned in close. "It's not your fault. You did the best you could with the information you had. We all did. Kennedy was dangerous. First he attacked you, then he threatened to blow up the Hab. According to Lex, he almost succeeded. Don't you get it? If we hadn't put Kennedy in the Ares 10, then we might all be dead right now. We couldn't have watched him around-the-clock. Eventually he would have found a way to kill us all—just like in the end he managed to kill himself."

"What if . . ." Valkerie searched Bob's face. Would he think she was crazy?

"What if?" Bob prompted.

Valkerie took a deep breath. "What if he didn't kill himself? What if it was . . . the ghost?"

Bob stared off into space. "I suppose we can't rule that out." He looked back at Valkerie. "But considering his mental state. Considering he'd already threatened to blow up the Ares 7—"

"Because he heard something outside."

"Because he *thought* he heard something outside."

"But what if he really did?"

Bob sighed and rose slowly to his feet. "Then I suppose it might have scared him enough to blow himself up." He shuffled for the door.

"Bob?"

He stopped at the door and turned. "Yes?"

"What if we're not supposed to be here? What if somebody doesn't want us here?"

"I can't answer that. We're here. All we can do now is try to get back home." He turned back to the door.

"Bob?" She listened as his footsteps paused at the door. "Thanks."

"No problem. Now get some rest. I've got to get the CamBot ready for the service."

*The memorial service.* The thought shivered through her. Why did it feel like she'd be giving her own eulogy?

# CHAPTER 25

Saturday, March 28, 2015, 7:30 p.m., CST

Josh

Josh stared up at the giant screen in Teague Auditorium, tears streaming down his face. The filled-to-capacity hall was silent. Valkerie had just finished her speech, and Josh couldn't shake the feeling that Valkerie had been saying good-bye to the world as well as to Kennedy. Bob stood next to Valkerie, working the CamBot controls. The camera swung to Lex and zoomed in on her face. She looked surprisingly good. Much better than the others.

"I met Kennedy back in the summer of 2005. We were ASCANs together. Co-workers. Friends. He even hit on me once when he'd had a few too many brews." She smiled into the camera. "Don't worry, Ronnie. He wasn't my type."

A short pause.

"In the past few months—actually, the past few weeks—we saw a dramatic change in Kennedy," Lex said. "We don't know what caused it. Some say he suffered from a mental disease, one that he carefully concealed during training. Others think he was done in by the constant stress of living so long in an extremely hostile world. We don't know the real reason, and we'll probably never know for sure."

Josh held his breath. *Mars Madness. She doesn't need to say it . . . but everyone is thinking it.*

"But the point is, he changed. Radically. He became a different person. He wasn't the man I knew for so many years, the man I respected, admired, loved." Lex took a breath. "Yes, I think we all loved that other Kennedy—the man who could drink any of us under the table, who could fly as well as any man alive—and even some women."

A pause for the viewer to smile, to reflect. Lex had obviously rehearsed all this.

"When we think of Kennedy over the months and years to come, let us . . . remember the man he was at his best, and forgive the errors he made at his worst, remembering that each one of us, but for the grace of God, could have been in his shoes. Kennedy, wherever you are, we will always remember you. Rest in peace."

The screen went dark. Slowly, the lights came up. Josh sat in his chair in the front row. Cathe gave his hand a squeeze and released her grip, fumbling for a tissue. She blew her nose and wiped her eyes.

Steven Perez walked slowly to the podium. "My friends, NASA today has lost a brave and . . . complex man. We may never understand the demons that drove Kennedy Hampton."

*Demons.* Josh felt his hackles rising. He had been so angry with Kennedy. Had hated him. Kennedy was a weasel and there was no varnishing that fact.

And yet.

And yet the guy had problems. Josh had been reading up on delusional disorders. You could hide your symptoms from other people if you worked at it, and the Hampster had obviously worked really hard. It looked like he had the paranoid subtype. Kennedy against the world, with the world winning. That was how Kennedy saw it, and of course it had an element of truth. In this world, it was dog-eat-chihuahua, and the coyotes got the leavings. Delusional people always fixed on some truth and exaggerated it way beyond reality. Kennedy had fixated on his fears of those around him—and it had killed him.

Kennedy knew he was sick. He could have gotten help, but it would have meant losing Mars. And that would have played right into his delusion. *The shrinks are out to get me by taking me off the mission.* Kennedy was sick and his sickness forced him to cover up, because admitting he was sick was the one thing his sickness wouldn't let him do.

*Catch-22, Hampster.*

The edges of Perez's face began blurring. Josh blinked twice, then gave up the battle. He reached into Cathe's purse and yanked out a tissue and let the tears roll. *Yeah, Hampster, I can forgive even a weasel like you. If I'd been you, I might have done the same.*

" . . . remember the heroic part Commander Hampton played in this mission, not forgetting his faults, but bearing in mind that all of us are human and all of us have fallen short. Kennedy Hampton, we salute you." Perez turned and began the slow trek to his chair.

And apparently that was it. Josh looked at the final line of his program. *Steven Perez: A Retrospective.* Yeah. All done.

A slow buzz built up in Teague Auditorium. People standing up, talking in whispers, their faces somber. It was a tough night for NASA when an astronaut died. Even a weasel.

Josh just sat quietly in his chair, trying to absorb it.

"You okay?" Cathe said.

"Yeah. Sort of. It's hard."

Nate pushed his way through the crowd. "Hey, Josh? Perez and I need to talk to you up in my office. Right now."

Josh turned to Cathe. "Wait for me in your office? I'll call you when I'm done."

She nodded. "See ya."

Josh stood up and nodded to Nate. "Shall we wait for Steven?"

"He'll catch up," Nate said.

Which was an odd thing to say, but you didn't argue with Nate. Josh walked outside with Nate and over to Building 1. CNN had a camera crew parked outside. Josh ignored their shouted questions. Inside, he and Nate walked past the security guard to the elevators. Nate wasn't talking and Josh had no heart for conversation tonight.

When they reached the office, Nate fished out his keys and unlocked the door. They walked in past the desk where Nate's secretary normally sat. A spine-busted copy of *Bactamination* lay facedown on her chair. Nate unlocked the inner door and they went in.

Josh sat down in a chair. Nate stood silently looking out the window. They waited.

Someone knocked at the outer door. Nate didn't move, so Josh went to get it. "Hi, Dr. Perez, and . . ." He knew the face of the other man but couldn't remember his name.

"This is Daniel Collins, Josh. Head of Security."

Collins nodded at him stiffly but didn't offer a handshake. Josh led them back into Nate's office. Perez and Josh sat. Collins shut the door and stood in front of it.

Nate turned around, his face dark, brooding. He sat down in his leather chair. Riffled through a sheaf of papers. Looked up at Josh. "Ever been to Star City, Josh?"

Josh stared at him, baffled. "Well, of course. I went there a couple years ago to check in on Jake Hunter before he did his tour on the ISS. Even got to visit Baikonur for the launch."

Nate nodded. "And you remember that sim machine they had for the Americans?"

"Well, it was in use most of the time, but yeah. I even played on it a couple of times. Sweet little cluster. Thirty-two CPUs."

"Ever do any sys-admin work on it?"

"Me?" Josh laughed. "I'm the wrong guy for that. I'm not exactly a Unix geek—the surgery always scared me."

Nate's eyes narrowed. "But you have an account on that machine."

"Had one. They must have deleted it when I left. I could even tell you the password. It's the same one I use on my machine here."

"Have you accessed it lately?"

Josh frowned. "Mind telling me what this is all about?"

"Just answer the question. Have you accessed that machine lately?"

Josh held up his hands. "Hey, I don't even know *how* to access that machine from here. Is it linked to the Internet?"

"Of course not. But there's a back-channel satellite linkup to MCC. Very fast. Very secure. And with a lot of event logging."

"And for some reason, you think I've been playing flight-sims in Russia?" Josh gave a short laugh. "I haven't got time for that."

"We've been in touch with the Russian Space Agency about some unexplained packets that originated on that computer. Somebody used it as a cutout to break into the computers at

Goldstone and place those unauthorized commands on the event queue for the ERV."

"Whoa, slow down," Josh said. "Cutout? What's a cutout?"

"It's a drone computer," Collins said. "A hacker breaks into it and works remotely from there to hack another machine. Then when the security people come looking, all they find are tracks leading back to the drone."

Josh looked at his watch. "It's getting late and I'm missing something here—like what does all this have to do with me?"

Collins sighed. "Your account, Mr. Bennett. Somebody used your account to hack the Goldstone computers."

A rush of fear. "Those idiots! Why'd they leave my account up on that box? That's some kind of security lapse."

"There's more," Nate said.

Josh looked up, suddenly aware of how loud your blood can sound when it's gushing through the arteries right next to your ears.

"The Russians had a lot of event logging on that box," Collins said. "So it wasn't hard to trace it back to the Ethernet address of the source machine."

Josh's mouth fell open. "You're probably going to tell me it was from my computer here at NASA."

"You're a good guesser, Josh." Nate leaned back in his chair, looking really old.

Josh just shook his head, wondering how lightning could fry him twice in one lifetime. "Nate. Look me in the eye, okay? I don't know who did this, but it wasn't me. All right? This isn't the first time somebody's hacked my computer. Obviously, Kennedy didn't do it this time. So let's figure out who did. I'll help you—"

"It's not that simple, Mr. Bennett." Collins frowned at him severely. "You've already admitted to doing something that grossly endangered the lives of the—"

"That's different!" Josh stood up. "I—"

Nate sighed. "The thing is, Josh, it's *obvious* you didn't do this. First off, you're computer-incompetent."

Josh opened his mouth to protest but thought better of it.

"Second, you're the guy least likely to try to strand our crew on Mars," Nate said. "You're the one most vocally in favor of bringing them home."

"Could be a cover," Collins said.

Nate shook his head. "Right, it *could* be a cover, but I know Josh. It isn't."

Collins' face hardened. "He deceived you, and me, and the rest of the world for almost a year, Mr. Harrington. Almost a year. I submit that he's capable of anything."

Nate tapped his fingers on his desk. "Josh, that's not true, is it? You're not capable of this, are you? Give me some evidence to back me up, okay?"

Josh hesitated. The problem was, he *could* have figured out a way to do the hack. It wouldn't have been easy. But if he didn't know where the bodies were buried, who did? If he'd wanted to plant those commands on the Deep Space Network, he could have. Probably.

Collins cleared his throat. "Mr. Bennett, where were you yesterday at 12:45 p.m.?"

"I was . . ." Josh tried to remember. He'd gone to the cafeteria but bailed when he couldn't find Cathe. That must have been about 12:30. Then he had wandered over to the duck ponds and sat by himself for half an hour.

"I was alone."

"In your office?" Collins said.

"No, just . . . outside. By the duck ponds."

"Anybody see you?"

Josh tried to remember. There must have been somebody who'd seen him. But he hadn't been paying attention.

"Simple question, Mr. Bennett. Anybody see you?"

"Maybe. Probably." Josh looked up at Collins. "I don't know. I was sitting down on a bench. Thinking."

"You do that very often?"

Josh saw where this was going, but there was nothing to do but tell the truth. "Just yesterday." Josh looked at Nate in time to see the last gleam of hope flicker out of his eyes.

Perez sighed. "Josh, you do understand this doesn't look good."

Josh leaned forward. "Sir—"

"There's an alternative to going to jail," Nate said.

"Jail?" All of a sudden Josh was sweating buckets.

"It might come to that in the end," Perez said, "but we'd like to forestall that possibility as long as possible. Fortunately, we have another option—a way we can protect you during the investigation."

"I guess you heard about the simulation we're running over in the Mars analog Hab in Building 29," Nate said.

"The rapid-growth edible plant experiments?" Josh nodded. "Yeah, but we should have started running those months ago."

"Late is better than never," Nate said. "We've got two women lined up to stay in there full time. We need a male volunteer. You know, to provide the . . . right balance for the soil."

That had to be the lamest excuse JSC had ever come up with. "So you want me to be the volunteer."

"We're *offering* you a chance to volunteer," Nate said. "We've got over four hundred applicants."

"And if I don't?"

"Look, Josh, it's just until we can find some evidence to get you off the hook," Nate said. "We've got the FBI monitoring all our computer systems. Whoever tried this is going to try again sooner or later. And we're going to catch them."

"What if I don't want to volunteer? My crew needs me."

Perez coughed. "Josh, it's for your protection."

"I don't *want* the protection."

"Mr. Bennett, whether you want the protection or not, you are going to receive it," Collins said. "You will be isolated from the rest of the world—no cell phone, no e-mail, and no unauthorized visitors. An armed guard will be posted outside with authority to arrest you should you attempt to leave."

Josh didn't say anything. Next time he wanted to buy a car, he was going to take these three campers to do the negotiating.

"The problem is . . ." Nate looked unhappy. "There's that little confession you made to me and Dr. Perez. It makes you a very plausible suspect right now, Josh. It's ridiculous, and I don't like it, but you can see the position I'm in."

Josh glared at him. "Do you believe there's any kind of remote possibility that I did it?"

Nate met his gaze for a few seconds, then turned to pick up the phone. He punched in a number. "Leroy, we'll be ready to start your sim in a few minutes. We've nailed down the last volunteer." A pause. "Okay, see you in five." He sighed and set the phone gently on the cradle. "I'm sorry, Josh. Let's hope they find the real hacker soon."

*Oh right, the real hacker.* Josh blinked hard, fighting back . . . whatever. Nate thought he was innocent.

As innocent as O.J.

## Friday, April 10, 2015, 2:00 p.m., CST

### Josh

Josh lay on the cot in his private quarters. The place was worse than prison. At times the two agonizing weeks he had spent in this place seemed more than he could bear. The two women assigned to work with him in this experiment were nice enough. But they had clearly heard the rumors about him, and believed them. Josh felt like a pariah.

Everybody thought he had done it! Unbelievable! Even Nate thought he was guilty. These idiots thought he'd somehow hacked in and queued up those commands that would have sentenced his crew to life on Mars. To death on Mars. They thought he'd do something to endanger his—

Josh clenched his fists. They were right. He already had done something to endanger his crew, as they knew full well. He had bombed his own crew. It was an accident, but he'd almost killed them. Was he ever going to get over that? Valkerie had forgiven him. And probably Bob. He hoped Lex had. Kennedy—that was a different story. Kennedy had been competing with him ever since they'd been named to the crew. Had tried to outdo him in everything—outpilot him, out-train him, outwomanize him. In the end, he had outcheated him—knocked him off the crew.

Josh covered his face with his hands. He'd blown it. The explosive should have been safe, should have never gone off until after aeroentry, should have . . .

Never mind. Should-haves didn't count. He had no right to do what he'd done. It was wrong. One big lie after another.

And it hadn't even been needed. His crew had found evidence of life without any help. Now somebody was out to get them. Somebody bad. Somebody willing to sentence them to life without parole on Mars.

Because he had gummed things up, he was out of the loop—powerless to help them when they needed him most. For that, he ought to be taken out and shot. Josh had never hated anyone like he hated himself right now. If they died because of him—

Voices in the stairwell.

Josh looked at his watch. 2:00 p.m. Too early for dinner. Maybe it was one of the soil scientists from—

"Josh!" Cathe Willison burst through the door.

A flood of emotions shot through Josh. Astonishment. Guilt. Relief. Fear.

Joy.

Josh catapulted himself off his cot and caught her up in his arms, spinning her around and around. "Cathe!" He set her down and looked into her eyes, feasting on her smile. "What are you doing here? How did you get in?"

"That's Dr. Willison to you." Cathe stepped back and he noticed that she was wearing a white lab coat. A stethoscope hung draped around her neck. "Complete with signed authorization from Nate Harrington." She held up a sheet of paper with Nate's handwriting scribbled across it.

"Nate sent you?"

"Read it."

Josh took the paper and struggled to make out the words. *Jake Hunter . . . Washington . . . Senate subcom . . .*

"It's hard to read. Either it's authorization for me to visit you—or it's an itinerary for a trip Jake Hunter is taking." Her face lit up with a wicked smile. "I found it on the floor next to Jake's desk. I'm sure he meant to give it to me."

Josh shook his head in amazement. He didn't deserve her. He leaned in close, brushing her lips with his. A fire, deep within him, roared to life. He pulled her in closer, cupping her upturned face in his hands.

Cathe pushed him away. "Josh, no," she said breathlessly. "I only have a few minutes. We've got to figure out how to clear your name so we can get you out of here."

Josh stepped toward her. He didn't care about that. Didn't care about anything but her.

"Josh, they're saying awful things about you in the FCR. Some people actually believe you did it—maybe even Jake Hunter."

"So?" He took Cathe by the hand and pressed it to his lips.

"He's been coordinating the investigation with the FBI." Cathe pulled her hand away. "He's practically in charge."

"How's the Mars crew?"

"Okay for the moment. They're saying there may be a lull in the storm in the next week or so. Nate's already announced that as soon as the storm dies down enough, they're getting off the planet."

"Will they have enough food to last that long?"

"If they get lucky, it might even happen in the next couple of days. And according to the crew, they've got food for several weeks."

Josh raised his eyebrows. "What does that mean—*according to the crew?*"

"There's some speculation they're making the whole thing up." Cathe looked up at Josh with worried eyes. "I'm hearing a lot of rumors."

"That's crazy."

"Well, we know they're not being straight about some things," Cathe said. "You and I know they don't have the Antarctica flu. It had to come from Mars."

"Maybe. But that's crazy too. Life on Mars couldn't infect humans."

"It could if it originally came from Earth on meteorite ejecta."

"That's such a long shot."

"Everything's a long shot. Josh, I think you should talk to Nate. Tell him what you know. It's always better to tell the truth. Always."

"You could tell him. If it's important, you should."

"Josh, I'd never do anything to hurt you. You should tell him yourself. It's the right thing to do."

"I'll tell him when they're off the planet."

Cathe's eyes glittered. "Josh, I can't make you do what's right, but . . . I wish you would."

"I need to do what's right for my crew." Josh slumped down on his cot. "And right now I can't do anything. I'm stuck here. Somebody set me up. Unless Jake Hunter figures out who framed me, I'm going to be here a long time."

Cathe didn't say anything, but her mouth tightened.

"Do you know something I don't know?"

Concern filled her eyes. "If you go to jail, I'm just wondering who might get promoted to Flight Director."

"Cathe, that is ridiculous. Jake wouldn't frame me."

"No, of course not. I'm just saying . . . what if he doesn't try too hard to find out who did?"

Josh closed his eyes. Would Jake do that? Of course not. Jake was a good guy. But Kennedy used to be a good guy too, and he had set up Josh for a big fall. "We've got to figure it out ourselves."

"Way ahead of you," Cathe said. "I brought some paper. We're going to brainstorm right now. I can be your eyes and ears on the outside. Now, think outside the box. Who hates you?"

Josh pointed to a chair. "Have a seat."

Cathe sat down next to him. Close enough that Josh's mind went blank. "I have a theory that it's the Russians."

Josh raised an eyebrow.

"Hey, we're brainstorming." She wrote *Russians* on her pad. "Just tossing out ideas. We'll criticize later. So who's the last person you'd expect to have done this?"

"EECOM."

Cathe giggled and wrote it down. "Who else?"

"Nate."

Cathe wrote that down too, a big smile on her face. "Okay, good. We're loosening up a little. Who else?"

"I don't know. Jake Hunter? Naw, scratch that. He couldn't have done it."

"Way outside the box." Cathe wrote down his name. "Jake couldn't hack his way out of a paper bag with a machete. Oooh! I've got an idea! How about Dr. Abrams?"

Josh snorted. "That's so far outside the box it's . . . in left field. What he knows about Unix you could put in a buckyball, with room left over."

"He pushed to get you off the Ares 10 crew."

Josh thought about that. "True. But he hasn't got any technical skills."

"So what? He's a shrink. All shrinks are crazy—that's why they study psych. What if he teamed up with EECOM?"

"Naw, I think she's got a crush on me."

Cathe frowned. "Really? Maybe she's seen us hanging out together and drew some conclusions."

"Cathe, she's a good ten years older than I am."

Cathe looked him boldly in the eye. "That's about how much older you are than me. Think I'm discouraged?"

"I don't believe it's EECOM."

"Okay, but we'll leave her on the list. For now. Who else?"

"What about CATO? Maybe he's jealous that you're walking on his turf?"

Cathe wrote it down. "I think we're running out of names."

Josh looked at the list. "They're all ridiculous. You might as well write down mine and yours too."

Cathe wrote down both their names, connecting them with a big, fancy ampersand. "Josh and Cathe, sittin' in a tree, H-A-C-K-I-N-G."

Josh laughed out loud. "Okay, seriously, tell me about the Russians. Why do you think they did it?"

"We already know they've been messing with our CommSats," Cathe said. "Plus, it was their flight sim machine that did the hack into Goldstone."

"They say it was from my account."

"Oh, good point! They say it, so . . . guess it must be true! Boy, if they hacked Goldstone, they'd be jumping up and down to point the finger at themselves, wouldn't they?"

"What's their motive?"

"Nationalism. Fear of back-contamination. Ego. Rage that you've stolen the hearts of all their women. I don't know. But it was their machine, Josh. They had the easiest access to it. Do you really believe they left your account open for two years after you left? That's so bogus."

"It couldn't have been the Russians," Josh said. "What's their motive? What does a whole country care about a few astronauts?"

"Maybe it was one person. Someone you knew while you were there. Someone who had access to your password."

"I was good friends with one of their security programmers." Josh stopped, feeling his ears heat up.

Cathe narrowed her eyes. "A woman programmer, I take it?"

"Yes." Josh refused to look down. If Cathe was going to get mad about every woman he'd ever dated, well . . . then she was going to be a pretty unhappy camper, wasn't she?

Cathe put her hand on his. "I like it that you don't try to lie about your ex-girlfriends."

Josh felt relief surge through his veins. "Did you tell Nate about this Russian woman? Maybe she's mad at you for jilting her."

Josh flushed.

Cathe studied him. "What's wrong? I'm not jealous. That was then. This is now. She's over there. I'm right here. I'd say that gives me a pretty good head start."

"It's just . . ." Josh tried to find the right words. "It's really hard when your past keeps coming back at you. Know what I mean?" He closed his eyes, wishing he had done things differently for the last few years. But you couldn't change the past, and wishing didn't do a thing except make your head hurt.

"Josh."

He didn't answer.

"Josh, you've got to learn to forgive yourself. Put the past behind you. Accept your mistakes and move on. It's bad enough when Nate and Mr. Collins and that Yamaguchi witch are on your case. Don't you jump on yourself too. Okay?"

*That's my problem. I hate myself.*

He felt Cathe's hands squeeze his. "Josh, listen to me. I don't care what you've done. What women you've gone out with. What mistakes you've made. I don't care about your past. I care about you now. Right here. I care for you the way you are. Do you understand?"

"I . . ." Josh couldn't go on, because a huge lump had jumped up into his throat and his heart was jackhammering. He wished Cathe wasn't looking, but somehow he was glad. He finally understood what it was to be loved.

Cathe's arms slipped around him, squeezing him tight. "Learn to care for yourself, Josh."

A dam broke somewhere, way inside his heart, and a river of peace—as big and broad and bodacious as the mighty Mississippi—came roaring through his soul.

Tuesday, April 21, 2015, 6:00 a.m., Mars Local Time

Valkerie

Valkerie rolled onto her side, pulling her blankets with her. The dust and sand pinging on the outer hull sounded just like frying chicken—her mother's homemade chicken with peppered crust and milk gravy. She sat up and took a gulp of water, but it wasn't what she wanted. She was hungry. Not the empty stomach kind of hunger she had experienced off and on all her life. That had long since faded. This was a deeper, emptier kind of hunger. The kind that cut right to the bone. The shaky-muscle kind of hunger. Light-headedness when she stood up. Fatigue that made her lie back down. Everything she was, everything she did, screamed out her need for more food. And the fried chicken sizzling on the outer hull wasn't helping.

A faint squeak sounded in the hallway. A bedroom door—but was it opening or closing? Valkerie stood up slowly and waited for the dizziness to pass. Then, wrapping herself in a blanket, she crept to her door and opened it just a crack. Nobody out in the hallway. She slipped outside and tiptoed to the commons, searching the dark room by the dim light that escaped around the stairwell hatch.

Nobody.

Searching the room one more time, she tiptoed into the galley, pulled open the middle bin, and started counting food packets. Forty. That couldn't be right. She counted the packets again. They had started out with exactly one week of rations plus the four Jell-O packets from the Ares 10 Hab. At a standard five packets per day per crew member, that was a total of 109 packets. For the last twenty-three days they'd been living on one packet per day—one-fifth the standard ration. Plus the extra Jell-O packets they got to eat at their Jell-O parties. And so far they'd eaten six. The numbers just didn't add up. Someone was cheating.

*Bob.* It had to be. Why hadn't she realized it earlier? She slid the bin back into the cabinet and snuck through the circular corridor. His door swung open at her knock.

"Bob?"

No answer.

"Bob?" She poked her head into his room and looked around.

He was gone.

Great. Valkerie pulled the blanket tighter around her shoulders and circled through the corridor to the stairs.

Footsteps sounded below. The weary thud of feet on metal treads.

She waited at the hatch, trying to control the fury that boiled up inside her.

"Hey, Valkerie! Good news. I was just monitoring . . ." Bob swayed on the top step, looking suddenly confused. "What's wrong? Is Lex okay?"

"I heard you get up." Valkerie let anger creep into her voice. "And I got up and counted the food packets. Want to guess how many there are?"

"I don't know." Bob shrugged impatiently. "Thirty-four?"

"Try forty." Valkerie's eyes filled with tears. "Bob, how could you? You promised—"

"It wasn't me. Promise." Bob held up three fingers. "But it doesn't matter. Houston just called with good news. The storm's definitely dying down. I just checked our weather stations. Wind speed's already down to eighty at station four."

A dark coal in Valkerie's soul blazed suddenly to life. The first ray of hope she'd felt in days. "What are you saying? Think we can launch?"

"We have to—if we can get the MAV ready today. It's our only chance. Even at fifth rations we don't even have enough food left for two weeks." Bob flicked on the light switch and ducked through the hatch.

Valkerie followed him through the corridor. He'd lost so much weight. She couldn't help but notice the way he sagged against the wall, using his right arm to maintain balance.

"Hey, Lex, wake up!" Bob pounded on Lex's door.

"What?"

Bob pushed open the door and flipped on the lights. Lex lay in bed blinking.

"The wind storm's dying down." Bob bustled into the room. "We've got to prepare for launch."

Lex's muscles trembled as she struggled to sit up. She looked terrible.

"Really?" Lex seemed almost disappointed. "What's the wind speed?"

"A hundred and twenty and falling, but—"

"Still too strong. We can't launch above eighty."

"Station four's at eighty. And Houston says the satellite photos show a definite lull. They're giving us a two-day window."

"Okay." Lex staggered to her feet with a sigh. "What are we waiting for? Let's suit up. Val, radio Houston. Bob and I have to run checkouts on the MAV."

"Not now. It's too cold." Valkerie stepped past Bob and put a hand on Lex's shoulder. "And I'm not even sure you can do an EVA. When's the last time you ate?"

Lex looked down at the floor.

"Come on, Lex. We're wasting time." Bob moved toward the door. "We've got to run an equipment check."

"Lex isn't going anywhere until she answers my question." Valkerie looked her in the eye. "I just counted forty food packets and there are supposed to be thirty-four. You've been cheating. And there's no way on Mars I'm letting you do an EVA if you haven't eaten in six days."

## Tuesday, April 21, 2015, 12:00 p.m., Mars Local Time

### Valkerie

"Lex, would you please hurry?" Valkerie's stomach tied itself into knots as she looked across the feast she and Bob had prepared. One last meal before leaving Mars. One last chance to build their strength.

"Houston is still go for tomorrow's launch." Lex trudged to the table and collapsed into her chair.

"Did you tell them about the bacteria?" Valkerie fixed apprehensive eyes on Lex. "What did they say?"

Lex turned to Bob with a shrug.

"I'm serious, guys." Valkerie got up from the table. "We've got to tell them. It wouldn't be right to just show up with it. Hi, Nate, we're home. And see? We've brought uninvited guests."

"Valkerie, wait." Bob grabbed her arm before she could get to the transmitter. "Please, now isn't the time. No matter what they say, we've still got to launch. We don't have a choice."

"Telling them now would only muddy the waters." Lex's voice was remote. Dead.

"We'll tell them as soon as we get to the ERV," Bob said. "Even if they didn't want us to come back, at least we'd still be able to eat. Speaking of which . . ." Bob motioned to the steaming dish at the center of the table.

Valkerie slumped back down into her chair and watched as Bob started serving the thick stew of peas, carrots, chicken soup, and meatloaf.

"Don't you think this is a bit much?" Lex stared down at her plate. "What if the wind picks up? This might be enough to last us another two weeks."

"Two days or two weeks. What does it matter?" Bob dipped Valkerie a huge serving. "If we don't launch tomorrow, we're dead either way."

Valkerie watched her glop of stew spread itself slowly across her plate. Maybe Bob was right. It would be silly to starve on Mars when two years of supplies was orbiting just above their heads. "I can't believe it's already time to leave." Valkerie looked at Bob with wondering eyes. "We have a lot to be thankful for."

Bob reached out and took her by the hand. She grabbed Lex's hand and held it tight.

"It's, uh . . . really a miracle that the storm's letting up." Bob looked up at Lex. "Don't you think?"

Valkerie's heart pounded as Bob crossed himself and closed his eyes. "Our Father, thank you so much for this food and for keeping us safe and for opening the door for us to go home tomorrow. And thank you for . . . thank you that we can share all this . . . together. Amen."

Valkerie gave Bob's and Lex's hands a squeeze. "Amen." She looked up at Bob and a smile lit his face. She felt so full. So satisfied. Like she'd already eaten a whole pot of stew.

Valkerie took a small bite and its rich, beefy flavor thrilled through her like a warm summer breeze. "What do you think?" She turned to Lex. "Was it worth the wait?"

Lex stared straight ahead. Her face hard and unreadable. "It's good." She scooped a large bite into her mouth.

"Just take it slow. Let your system get used to it."

Lex stared back.

Valkerie took another bite and looked down at her plate.

"So, Lex . . ." Bob spoke around a mouthful of stew. "What's the first thing you want to do when you get to the ERV?"

"Take a shower."

A long pause.

"Uh, what about you, Valkerie?"

Valkerie put down her fork and turned in her chair to face Lex. "Are you okay? You don't seem yourself at all."

Lex nodded. "I'm fine. Just a little tired."

"Look, I'm really sorry I got so mad about you not eating. I was just worried, that's all. What you did was very noble. Very unselfish."

Lex stared straight ahead.

"Is it something else? The food? We could eat just a little bit and freeze the rest. If you're worried . . ."

"We've got enough to last two more days at full rations," Bob said. "It really should be enough."

Lex pushed herself away from the table. "I'm just tired. Maybe I should go to bed."

"Lex, please." Valkerie hurried after her. "Talk to us. Something's bothering you. We're your friends. We want to help you."

"I'm fine, really. It's just that—" Lex's voice choked off and her eyes filled with tears.

Valkerie held out her arms and Lex collapsed into them. A chair scraped the floor behind her and she felt another set of arms wrap around both her and Lex.

Lex started shaking. "It's just that . . . I don't know if I want to go back. I know I should. I mean, what kind of a horrible wife wouldn't want to be with her husband?"

Valkerie held Lex tighter, trying to still the spasms that shook her trembling frame.

"It's not Ron. He's a . . . he's so perfect. I'm the problem. I don't deserve him. I'm just bad at relationships. I'm different with you guys. You're the best friends I've ever had. And I know when we go home . . . I'll never . . . It just won't be the same."

Valkerie felt herself being rocked back and forth by strong, encircling arms.

"It's okay," Bob crooned. "No matter where we go, we'll always be your friends. You're stuck with us."

"But Ronnie's always traveling. And you and Val will probably get—"

"I'll tell you what." Bob swayed a little too far and they had to shift their feet to keep upright. "We can buy a little round camper with three tiny rooms and a shower the size of a coffin. It'll be our Hab away from Hab."

"Can we cover everything with sand and grit?" Lex sniffled.

"The very finest." Bob pulled them in closer. "And we can board up the windows . . ."

"And filter our urine for drinking water," Valkerie said. "And flavor it with dirty socks."

She swayed too far and felt herself tipping over backward. She tried to back step, but her feet left the floor and they all fell over in a flailing tangle of arms and legs.

Shocked silence.

Then a soft hiccupping sound. Lex was shaking.

"Lex, are you all right?" Valkerie eased her weight off of Lex's back.

"I'm fine." The hiccupping crescendoed to Lex's hyena laughter. "But would you mind getting off me? My stew's getting cold."

Tuesday, April 21, 2015, 11:00 a.m., CST

Josh

"Josh, they're flying out tomorrow!" Cathe Willison burst through the airlock and stepped across a pallet of simulated Martian soil.

"What? Who?" Josh set down the pallet of soil he'd been mixing and wiped his hands on a towel.

"The crew." Cathe gave him a cursory hug and pulled away to pace the cluttered floor. "There's a lull in the storm, and they're flying out. Nate gave them the okay. He's still convinced they're starving to death."

"And you're still convinced they aren't?" Josh shook his head.

"All I'm saying is that it's awfully convenient that right after Kennedy gets sick, all their cameras just happen to go on the blink and Kennedy just happens to be by himself in the abandoned Hab when it just happens to burn down with all their food in it."

"I'd have put Kennedy in the other Hab even if he wasn't sick." Josh smiled. She had a good point, but he couldn't help baiting her.

"Come on. They knew about the dust storm for weeks. Would you leave all your food in the other Hab and not think about getting it until the day the dust storm was supposed to hit? They're probably feasting it up right now. Laughing at Nate for buying their little sob story."

Josh grinned. "I sure hope so. At any rate, it's really good news." He caught her arm as she passed within reach and spun her in a graceful turn to face him. "With the crew safe and sound on the ERV, Nate won't have an excuse to keep me locked up here. Not that I won't miss your house calls . . ." He pulled her close.

"Josh!" Cathe pushed him away. "This is serious. Nate could send you to jail. With the astronauts back on the ERV, he certainly won't let you back in the FCR. Not if he believes you sent that command script. We've got to clear your name."

Josh threw his hands in the air. "What can I do? I'm stuck here in Farmer Brown's cellar shoveling manure."

"What about the list of people in the FCR and their support people in the MER? Wasn't there someone on the list who could have framed you?" Cathe ducked under his open arms and stepped around a bank of LEDs into the corridor.

"I don't know." Josh followed her to the shop. "None of them seem very likely. I need more data. Did you get their computer records for me? What about their whereabouts when the Russians are saying the commands were sent?"

"I tried, but Jake Hunter wouldn't talk to me. Now that he's the big investigation coordinator, he doesn't even give his name to people who aren't wearing bad suits."

"He probably knows you're biased."

"Right, I know you didn't do it. Some bias."

"Send him to talk to me. I'll get the information out of him."

"How?" Cathe turned to look him in the eye. "I know I'm more biased than you, but I would hope that you're just a tiny bit biased."

"Let's just say I know a few things about his trip to Star City that his wife would be real interested to hear about."

Cathe's eyes gleamed. "Remind me never to get on the wrong side of you."

"Who says you aren't?" Josh caught her and pulled her in close for a kiss.

# CHAPTER 27

Tuesday, April 21, 2015, 1:30 p.m., Mars Local Time

Bob

Bob set his helmet on his head. "Comm check, Bob."

Valkerie adjusted the radio controls on the front of her suit. "Loud and clear. Comm check, Valkerie."

"Loud and clear on both of you," Lex said from upstairs at the CommConsole. "Okay, guys, I'm keeping my eyes glued on the weather data. If the winds go back up above a hundred klicks an hour, I'm calling you back."

"Give us a warning when it gets above eighty," Bob said. "But that doesn't mean we're coming back."

"It's now or never." Valkerie clomped into the airlock. "Let's go."

"Be careful, guys."

Bob followed Valkerie into the airlock and closed the door. After depressurization, they stepped out into the swirling dusty mist. Visibility was good—maybe a quarter mile. He could just make out the outline of the Ares 10 off to the northwest.

He breathed a huge sigh of relief. The storm really had died down. As much as he trusted the weather instruments, he'd been worried that, after eating most of their remaining rations, they'd get outside and find that the storm was still too strong for them to take off. Well, they were committed now . . . .

Valkerie turned right and headed toward the Mars Ascent Vehicle. Bob followed, checking the exterior of the Hab for damage. Not that it mattered. But he'd heard strange noises all night. Like something was bumping into the Hab. Probably just the storm.

"Wasn't that stew great?" He hurried to catch up with Valkerie. "Felt kinda like the Last Supper. You know. What with us preparing for our ascension into orbit."

"The Last Supper was right before the Crucifixion," Valkerie deadpanned.

"Which is what I'm going to do to you two if you don't hurry up and check out that MAV," Lex's voice burst through comm.

Bob reached out and took Valkerie by the hand. Today had been a real turning point. It was time to go home. Everything felt so right—as if Moses had parted the red storm especially for them, and they were going to fly out on still air. How could he ever have doubted—

Valkerie gasped and yanked on Bob's arm, pointing straight ahead.

Bob could just make out the MAV. He stopped and stared at it. Were his eyes playing tricks on him? He tilted his head to one side and then to the other. The MAV seemed to be tilted a few degrees from vertical. "Lex, it looks like there's a problem with the MAV." Bob took off at a quick, hopping run, pulling Valkerie behind him.

"Wind speed is about seventy-five," Lex said, "and rising."

Bob bounded toward the MAV. Two hundred yards to go. One hundred. When they reached it, Bob went around the right side. Valkerie circled to the left. Her ragged breathing hissed against the pounding in his ears.

Halfway around he spotted the problem. One of the support struts was bent. About waist high, a dozen fresh nicks shone in the thin afternoon light.

"Looks like somebody banged on it with a sledgehammer." Valkerie pressed up beside him.

Bob ran his gloved hand across the scarred surface. It didn't make sense. It just wasn't possible. "Um . . . Lex, we're looking at something funny here. Like one of the support struts was hit repeatedly with a sledgehammer."

"The wind definitely didn't do this." Valkerie sounded mystified.

"Anything lying around that could have done it?" Lex asked. "A loose cable? A panel banging in the wind?"

"We're talking really heavy," Valkerie said. "Nothing that could have been picked up by the wind."

Bob searched the ground around the strut. "Nothing here except rocks. I don't see any chipping on them."

"And it was hit more than once," Valkerie said. "There's more than one dent."

"Agreed." Bob counted the nicks. "Looks like at least ten to fifteen distinct marks." He stepped back and looked up at the MAV. "As far as I can see, there's no real damage to the structure."

"Eighty klicks," Lex said. "You guys need to think about—"

"Okay, we'll begin the check." Valkerie flipped open the checklist on her sleeve. "I'll take power and electrical and seals and pumps. You take fuel tanks and gauges."

Bob took one last look at the strut and walked around the base of the MAV, visually inspecting the tanks. If anything, the sandblasting had just served to polish them up a bit. So far so good. The bent strut was uncanny, but it wouldn't prevent them from taking off. He walked around to the side and wiped off the fuel gauges.

1.8 tonnes of methane.

That couldn't be right. The tanks had been filled with seven metric tonnes of methane before the crew ever got to Mars. They'd barely used two of that to fuel the rover. They should have a lot more than the gauge showed.

He checked the LOX tank. "16.1 tonnes of oxygen."

"What?" Valkerie came around to stand next to him. "You sound worried. Isn't that what it's supposed to be?"

"Yeah, but look at the methane."

Valkerie wiped at the smudged gauge with her glove. "1.8? This can't be right. Is the meter in dekatonnes?"

"No way. I've been monitoring it all along. Last month we had almost five."

"How much do we need to take off?"

Bob took a deep breath, then let it out slowly. "About 4.1."

"What's going on?" Lex demanded over comm. "Are you saying there isn't enough methane?"

"Not nearly enough." Bob checked the gauge again and then the hoses leading to the tanks of the MAV. The valve attaching the methane hose to the MAV was bent at a funny angle. The connection seemed to have been torn partway off. "Great! Just great!" Bob spat. "The valve's been damaged. The methane's been boiling away. We're short more than two tonnes."

"Can we take off?" Valkerie turned to Bob, fixing him with a wide-eyed gaze.

"We can take off all right," Bob said. "But we're gonna come right back down."

Tuesday, April 21, 2015, 1:00 p.m., CST

Nate

Nate walked toward his office, his body on autopilot, his brain metal-fatigued. Lex had just called in with the fabulous news that the fuel in the MAV was enough to get them about ten miles off the ground. Ten miles up. Ten miles down. Splat. And two days' supply of food left.

Nate yanked out a packet of antacids and shook out a handful. Every engineer in the FCR and the MER had been called in to brainstorm. He had a meeting with Perez in ten minutes, and he did not have a clue what he was going to tell him. *Sorry, sir, but it looks like failure is the only option.*

He reached his office.

His secretary, Carol, pointed across the room. "Miss Willison's been waiting to see you for twenty minutes."

"What are you doing here, Cathe? Get your carcass over to the FCR and start working the problem." He glared at her as he strode into his inner office and grabbed his briefcase—the bureaucrat's sword. Too bad he couldn't just fall on it and be done with it. He spun around and smacked into Cathe.

"Mr. Harrington, I really need—"

"I don't have time. Get over to the FCR." Nate pushed past her and out the door to the elevator. He punched the button three times, then swore at it.

Cathe grabbed his arm. "Mr. Harrington, please!"

He turned to look, shocked at the emotion in her voice. Big, fat tears stood out in those stainless-steel blue eyes of hers.

Then she was gabbling at him. Josh was innocent . . . couldn't have done it . . . Jake Hunter wouldn't talk to her . . . Josh had to talk to Jake so he could clear his name. Blah, blah, blah . . .

The elevator *ching*ed.

Nate yanked his arm free and stepped inside.

Cathe stuck her foot in the door, her eyes crackling with intensity. "Please, Mr. Harrington. Call Jake. Promise me you'll call Jake."

If there was anything that got to Nate, it was a hysterical female. He pulled out his cell phone. "Yeah, sure. I'll call him right now."

Cathe lit up with a five-hundred-kilowatt smile. She stepped back and pulled her foot away from the door. "Thank you! Thank you!" The chrome door slid shut, erasing her face.

Nate stared at the phone in his hand until his gut told him the elevator had found his floor. He stepped outside and selected a number.

One ring. "Hello, this is Jake Hunter."

"Yeah, Jake—Harrington here. I need you to do something and it's urgent."

"Everything's urgent. Name it."

"It's about Josh. I just talked to Cathe Willison."

"She's been bugging me about him all week. You know she and Josh are an item, don't you?"

"No kidding." Nate looked at his watch. He was late.

"So want me to talk to him?"

"Talk to the security guys watching him. I don't know how she's been communicating with him, but it's got to stop.

Under no circumstances are they to let Cathe Willison in to visit Josh."

"Gotcha."

Nate hung up, stuffed the phone in his pocket, and turned toward Perez's office.

He wasn't a genius about women, but he was pretty clear on one thing. A robo-chick like Cathe Willison didn't go all of a sudden blubbery on you unless she wanted something. Either that or she had something to hide.

Tuesday, April 21, 2015, 3:00 p.m., Mars Local Time

Valkerie

Valkerie trudged next to Bob, turning every couple of steps to look back at the MuleBot he pulled behind him. It had taken forever to fix the broken methane valve and she was exhausted. Her stomach locked up suddenly in another agonizing cramp. What would Bob think if she asked to ride back on the MuleBot? Probably that she was a wimp. He had done most of the work back at the MAV. If anyone deserved to ride back, he did. Valkerie kept walking.

"How are you doing?" Bob sounded dead.

"Fine." Valkerie's stomach stabbed her with another sharp pain. "Shouldn't have eaten so much for lunch, though."

Silence.

Valkerie reached out and took Bob's hand.

"You know we still have some hydrogen in the fuel cells," Bob suggested. "We could try to make more methane."

"It took the factory months to make the methane we have," Valkerie said. "Even if we had enough . . ."

"Which we don't."

"And we only have . . ." Valkerie couldn't say it. This morning, a big meal had seemed like such a great idea.

"I know."

Valkerie walked the rest of the way in silence, her thoughts lost in the red cloud that swirled around her. The final struggle to get up the steps. The hiss of the airlock. No need to wet-scrub the suits. Why bother? She stepped into the suit room and collapsed onto the bench, but the red storm kept swirling in her mind.

*Clack. Clack.* Valkerie's helmet lifted off her head.

"Are you okay?" Lex stared down at her with worry-lined eyes.

"Fine." Valkerie pulled off her gloves and dropped them on the floor.

Lex helped her out of her suit and collapsed on the bench with tired, vacant eyes. "Bob, what's the minimum amount of fuel we need to get into orbit?"

Bob leaned over and let the upper half of his suit fall onto the floor with a thunk. He pulled a phone from his locker and eased himself onto the floor. "I'd say fifteen tonnes of methane/LOX. Maybe a little less. That would get us off the planet, but we couldn't take any payload. And we couldn't quite reach our rendezvous orbit. The ERV would have to do a burn to catch down to us."

"So how much methane are we lacking?"

Bob checked an app on his phone. "You get the highest specific impulse by burning it at a mass ratio of 3.5 kilograms oxygen to one kilogram methane. Which means we need 3.4 tonnes methane total. We're short about 1,600 kilograms."

Lex nodded and slumped back against the lockers.

Valkerie turned and stared at Bob, letting his angular features defocus into a fuzzy haze.

"What if we hydrolyzed our water supply?" Valkerie suggested. "We could feed the hydrogen back into the fuel production unit and make more fuel."

Lex shook her head. "It took months to make the fuel we had. And that was at full power. We don't have enough food to last another week."

Valkerie nodded and went back to staring at Bob.

"Wait a minute!" Bob jumped up and stabbed the screen of his phone. "Making methane from straight hydrogen and atmospheric $CO_2$ is pretty fast. The problem is that you don't get enough oxygen that way, so you have to reduce $CO_2$ to $O_2$—and that costs a ton of energy. That's why our fuel factory took so long to make the fuel."

"Give me the punch line," Lex said.

"The punch line is that we have all the oxygen we need already. All we need is methane. Valkerie's right. Hydrolyzing water is very efficient, and we've got quite a bit in our tanks. Hang on, let me check." He typed a flurry of keystrokes into the device. "All right! Good news. We can spare about 2.6 tonnes of water from the Hab and 300 kilograms from the greenhouse outside. We're home free!"

Valkerie closed her eyes. "Um, Bob, remind me of one thing. How much methane do you get from a kilogram of water?"

He turned to her with a big grin. "Two kilograms of fuel for every kilogram of water. It's like getting something for nothing—the extra kilogram comes from the carbon dioxide in the atmosphere."

"But . . ." Valkerie tried to concentrate. "Part of that fuel is oxygen and part is methane. We don't need the oxygen—we already have plenty. How much methane do you get?"

Bob sat down and grabbed his phone. "Four hundred forty-four grams."

Lex leaned forward. "So our water is going to get us how much methane?"

Bob punched in the numbers, and his eyes lost their sparkle. "We're short. About five hundred kilograms of water short." He tossed the phone onto the bench. "We need a Plan B."

Valkerie shook her head. "We don't have a Plan B. This is our only option. We've got to go with it. Maybe we can strip down the MAV to lighten the load."

"I've already taken that into account," Bob said. "If we can't come up with more water somewhere, we're . . ."

The unspoken word hung in the room like the stench of death.

### Wednesday, April 22, 2015, 8:00 a.m., Mars Local Time

### Bob

Bob raised the plastic sheet, forming it into a tube that surrounded him. He heard the sound of duct tape being pulled and cut. Lex taped the seam on the plastic. The storm had kicked up again during the night. Even if they *could* make enough fuel, they'd still be in for a long, hungry wait. But first he and Valkerie had to bring back the water from the outside greenhouse. Hopefully there was more out there than he remembered.

"Okay, big guy. You're ready to go," Lex spoke into her mike and patted the top of his helmet. "The plastic should take the brunt of the sandblasting. Your other suits are a mess."

"Right," Bob said. Like it mattered. One way or another, they weren't going to be wearing their EVA suits much longer.

"Okay." Valkerie moved toward the airlock.

Bob shuffled after her, feeling for all the world like a giant toilet-paper tube.

Valkerie closed the airlock hatch behind them. "Depressurizing now."

A minute later, they were outside in the Martian dust storm, stumbling their way along the perimeter of the Hab. The sand blasted at their plastic shields, scouring them with corrosive, micron-sized particles. Bob shuffled to the MuleBot and pressed the ignition button. It started right up. AresCorp had designed it to really take a lickin'.

Valkerie joined him. She hadn't said much all morning. It was almost like she had given up. Resigned herself to their fate—starving to death on a hostile barren planet. The thought ate into his heart. If she had given up, what hope was left? He'd never in his life known anyone more determined. He opened his mouth to say something. Something encouraging. Something to give her hope. But what could he say? He squeezed her hand and pressed forward. They walked around the Hab. Ghostly pale in the swirling wind, the Ares 10 Hab stood like a gravestone in the hazy morning light. The greenhouse came into view—

"Oh no!" Valkerie stopped.

A long, horizontal slash ran along the polyethylene wall of the greenhouse. Bob stared at it, his heart pounding. The shredded plastic flapped in the Martian wind. The far side was ripped up just as badly. He stepped inside through what should have been the wall. A few sandblasted stems poked up through a rippled drift of sand. Bob dropped to his knees and started digging frantically. Where was all the equipment? The water tanks? Bob spun around to search the greenhouse shell.

Valkerie was walking around the edges, probing the drifts with her feet. "Bob?" The terror in her voice tingled up his spine.

Bob helped her search, digging like a dog in the sand.

"They were too big to just . . . blow away." Valkerie's whisper was barely audible above the ringing in his ears. "Somebody *took* the water barrels."

"Uh-huh." Fifty-five gallons each. Both of them three-quarters full. No way could the wind have done this. For an agonizing minute, he couldn't breathe. Finally he sucked some air into his lungs. Enough to hiss out a few words. "Bad news, Lex. Real bad."

# *Part IV: The Fifth Man*

"... it was related that the party of explorers, at the extremity of their strength, had the constant delusion that there was one more member than could actually be counted."

T. S. Eliot, comments on the Shackleton Antarctica Expedition

Tuesday, April 28, 2015, 3:00 a.m., Mars Local Time

Valkerie

Valkerie lay in her bed. The dust storm had blown over in the night. She stared up at the ceiling. Light from the corridor crisscrossed the ceiling with overlapping fans of gray and black. Her eyes traced the patterns, following them back to their sources. An alligator-shaped crack at the top of the doorway. Headlight pinpricks where the wall didn't quite meet the ceiling. A missile-shaped gap above the duct tape bandage that covered the knife wound at the heart of her plastic door.

She pushed herself up in bed, drinking in the dim outlines of her room and furnishings. The four walls, now solid and familiar even in darkness, were once cold and menacing, the steel bars of a dark and dreary prison. Now they were life. She knew she would be leaving them soon, but she was at peace with that. With acceptance had come freedom. Freedom and clarity.

A pang stabbed through her. Not hunger—that had long since faded. It hovered just out of reach like the half memory of a long-forgotten friend. This feeling was sharper, more invasive. The look of hurt in her father's eyes. The cry of a hurt child.

Valkerie hugged her knees to her chest. She was going to die. For the first time in her life she saw it for the inevitability it had always been. But it wasn't death that bothered her. It was life. Her life. All her hopes and dreams. Her ambitions. Her drive. She had worked so hard to make something of herself. She had wanted to be able to look back on her life without regret, knowing that she'd tried.

And tried and tried and tried. Deferring happiness for accomplishment. Peace for recognition. Working so hard to satisfy the demands of so many different people. Conflicting demands that could never all be satisfied. She saw it so clearly now. She had thought she'd been working for others, but it had all been for herself. For her security. For her glory. So that others would like *her*—not the other way around. If only her efforts had been better directed. If she'd focused on the One instead of the many. The One who didn't make demands—only sacrifices.

A clang sounded below. Bob working in the shop. Valkerie looked at her watch. 3:02 a.m. local time. Maybe there was still time to make things right. She should have said yes months ago. If only he'd give her another chance. Another clang downstairs. Valkerie wrapped a blanket around her shoulders and pushed her way through her bedroom door out into the glaring light of the circular corridor. Picking her way through the rows of pots that lined both walls, she made her way into the commons and across it to the stairwell.

She crept down the stairs, counting out three-Mississippi for each breath so she wouldn't hyperventilate. She'd have to readjust the scrubbers. Bob had set them to leave more $CO_2$ for the plants, but there was only so far they could go before it got dangerous. She tiptoed through the pallets of red regolith that circled the stairwell and poked her head into the shop. "Bob?"

The room was empty.

"Bob?" She circled the corridor and checked each room.

No Bob.

That's funny. Bob couldn't have gone upstairs. She would have heard him. Valkerie stepped over a large pallet and made her way to the lab. Probably a thermal ping. Uneven expansion of the wall panels. Either that or she was imagining things again.

She slid onto a lab stool and started checking the soil in a long, makeshift pallet. It was a new batch and still smelled slightly of human waste, but its pH was good and it seemed to have enough nitrogen. Still, no matter how she doctored it up, the germination rate in the porous Martian soil so far had been abysmal. If only they had brought more potting soil with them from Earth.

Valkerie stood up and walked over to the microscope. Kennedy's pansy had grown two more tiny little blossoms. Purple with delicate yellow beards, they stabbed her to the heart with their impossible beauty. Valkerie picked up the pot and carried it carefully over to the bench where she was working. Setting the pot under the light, she crossed to the seed cabinet and pulled out one last envelope. Zucchini seeds. She shook them out onto the bench. Only five of them. She dug five little holes in the freshly made soil and started to plant them. A healthy zucchini plant could feed them for weeks. One of them had to take. It just had to.

*Mmmmmm. Zucchini.* Valkerie broke into a giggle. If only her mother had lived to see this. Her daughter praying for zucchini. She'd come a long way since the summer of the zucchini wars. Every family in their church must have planted zucchini that year. Valkerie and her father were meticulous about locking the car doors, but even that was no protection. Often as not, they'd get back to the parking lot and find a bag of zucchini on their hood or in a basket sitting next to the driver's door. Her mom would make such a fuss—as if she'd been given something that was actually edible. She would bustle about trying to identify and thank their dubious benefactor—while Valkerie and her dad crept through the parking lot like commandos, seeking out pickups with open beds or cars with unlocked doors. Car bombs, they called them. Long green car bombs. It truly was more blessed to give than to receive.

Wiping her eyes with her sleeve, Valkerie reached out a trembling hand for Kennedy's pansy. Planted in good, Earth-origin earth. "Kennedy, I'm so sorry. I promise I'll never forget." She pulled up the pansy by its delicate roots, replanted it in the Martian soil, and planted the last zucchini seed in Kennedy's pot.

### Tuesday, April 28, 2015, 2:00 p.m., CST

### Josh

Josh lay on the cot in his room, wondering what had gone wrong with his life. In the past week, he'd had no news from the outside. And no visitors. No Nate. No Jake.

And no Cathe.

Why?

Nate, he could understand. Nate had made it clear he thought Josh was guilty. Nate didn't want to have anything to do with him.

And Jake . . . Cathe obviously hadn't gotten around to talking to him. Or maybe he did have a vested interest in staying away. He knew good and well Josh had dirt on him and would use it to make him cooperate with Cathe's investigation. Yeah, that was probably it. Jake would stay away as long as he could.

But Cathe. Josh hadn't seen her in a week and the obvious conclusion was that she'd decided to bail. She was on the way up, and he was on the way down. Smart girl. She deserved better—

A tap at the door.

Josh bolted upright on his cot. "Who is it?"

"Can I come in?" Jake Hunter's voice.

Josh flopped back down and covered his eyes.

The door creaked open. "Josh?"

"Yeah, I'm Josh."

"Can we talk?"

"We're doing it."

Footsteps. The sound of a chair sliding on the tiled floor. "You wanted to see me?"

Josh opened his eyes.

Jake tossed a small stuffed penguin at him. "EECOM sends her regards."

*And Cathe doesn't.* She had abandoned him. Which meant it would do no good to try to make Jake cooperate with her. "How's the investigation going?"

"Not good." Jake shook his head. "Josh, I just got back from D.C. Spent days going over the data with a guy from Star City and a couple of cream puffs from the FBI. And they think you did it. I don't like it, but what can I do? The FBI has had people sitting on our network for a month, and no joy. They're packing out of here Friday."

"Friday? But I didn't do it. That's just going to open it up for the real hacker to take another swing."

"We'll continue to monitor. I'm putting EECOM on it. She'll keep our crew safe—but they can't lift off from Mars until we can figure out how to make them a little more methane."

A bolt of adrenaline. Josh sat up. Leaned toward Jake. "What do you mean make more—"

Perfume. A woman's perfume.

Cathe's perfume.

Josh's ego felt a Schwarzenegger-sized kick in the face. Cathe's perfume was all over Jake.

"You okay, Josh?"

"You smell like Cathe Willison."

Jake gave a short laugh. "Oh yeah, that. Crazy thing. I was down in the FCR just now. When I walked out—I was on the way over here to see you—Cathe rushed me and gave this big, weepy hug. Said she's quitting as of this next Friday. And she was just slathered in that perfume of hers."

"She's . . . quitting?"

"Yeah. Said she's moving back home to New York. Bummer too—she's one of our best. I think she's still carrying the torch for you, Josh."

Josh felt his head spinning. This did not compute. "Not anymore."

"Oh yeah?" Hunter looked uncomfortable. "Well, probably just as well." An awkward silence.

Josh stared hard at Jake until he began to squirm. "What's that supposed to mean?"

"Well, I wasn't going to say anything, but since you're asking . . ." The corner of Jake's mouth turned up with the flicker of a smile. "Cathe's been flirting with me on and off for a while. Remember the day we caught that de-orbit burn on ERV? Well, Cathe sent me a note asking me out to lunch that day, practically threw herself at me. But when I showed up, well . . . you know how she is. Hot and cold. Hot and cold. She downplayed the whole thing. Acted like it was all my idea. Like all she wanted was to talk about the CommSats."

Josh's heartbeat hammered in his ears. "She asked you out to lunch? Where?"

"Well, not lunch, exactly. Wanted to meet me in the cafeteria. I—What?"

Josh jumped to his feet. "Jake, you've got to get me out of here. I've got to talk to Cathe."

"I wish I could, but I can't. Besides, Cathe's no good for you. She'll just yo-yo you more. Plus, she's moving to New York. Her dad found her a job."

Josh grabbed Jake by the shoulders and looked him in the eyes. "Jake, I'm serious. I need to see Cathe right away. Tell Nate. It's important. Life-or-death."

"Okay, calm down." Jake looked at his watch. "I'll try to talk to Nate, but no promises. He's a busy man, you know?" He started for the door.

Josh followed him out. "I think I may have a clue, but I need to talk to Cathe. In person."

"You know, I'm coordinating the investigation." Jake stepped into the airlock. "If you know anything that might help, I'm the one you should be talking to."

"I need to check with Cathe first. Please. Just tell Nate."

The hatch slammed shut.

He stared at the hatch, trying to figure things out. Cathe had asked Jake out? She'd asked him to meet her at the cafeteria? It had to mean something. It was too big a coincidence.

And the perfume . . . It was a message somehow.

Cathe Willison never slathered on her perfume. Never. She belonged to the less-is-more school. And she was a fighter, not a quitter. There was no way she'd leave NASA.

Besides all that, she couldn't move "back home to New York" because she was a Texas girl. A Texas girl whose father was dead.

It was a message, and all Josh had to do was figure out what it meant.

Tuesday, April 28, 2015, 9:00 p.m., Mars Local Time

Valkerie

Valkerie slumped in her chair and looked across the table at Bob.

He returned her smile with a bewildered shrug.

Lex just stared off into space. Her bony shoulders seemed to sag under the weight of her head. Glassy eyes stared unblinking from a gaunt, lined face.

They had to do something soon. Moping around and waiting for their food to run out wasn't accomplishing anything. "I think we should go back to the vent," Valkerie said. "It has to have water somewhere. Ice, probably. Didn't you say you spotted underground pockets, Lex?"

Lex blinked her eyes. "Yes, but—"

"Hold on." Bob raised a hand. "We don't have the rover anymore, remember? We can't carry eight hundred kilograms of ice in our pockets."

"But we've got the MuleBot to carry our stuff," Valkerie said. "Eight hundred kilograms of water feels like three hundred in Mars gravity. We could walk four kilometers out, load the ice on the mule, and walk back."

"Not in one day, we couldn't," Bob said. "And not on one bottle of oxygen."

Lex sat up straighter. "You can do amazing things when you've got to. How many of our oxygen bottles are still usable? Ten?"

"Nine," Bob said. "And eight battery packs. But you can't run a marathon in an hour, no matter how bad you have to. Eight kilometers of walking is at least eight hours, probably more since we haven't been eating. Plus, we'd have to dig out the ice and haul it up. There is no way to do that in one day. And staying outside for a Martian night is suicide, plain and simple."

"So we camp out overnight in that cave near the thermal vent," Valkerie said. "It's got a microclimate that's a lot warmer than the open plain. We could bring the inflatable decompression chamber to sleep in. It would be cramped, but it would help protect us from the cold. And we'll still have our suits to keep us warm."

Bob shook his head. "Do you really think we could find eight hundred kilos of ice? What kind of odds are we talking about?"

"Oh, the ice is there, all right," Lex said. "That's not the question. The problem is surviving a night outside on Mars. Our suits aren't made for that. That hyperbaric chamber isn't made for it. We opened up that cave quite a bit, so the microclimate's destroyed. Who knows how much energy that thermal vent is pumping out? Even if we seal it up, it might take weeks to warm up to the freezing point. It's a gamble. So you want odds, I'll give you odds—slim to none . . ." Lex looked back down at the table.

Valkerie started to object but gave it up. Even if they survived the night, how would they be able to get almost a ton of ice up the cliff and back to the Hab? The whole idea was crazy.

"But what other option do we have?" Lex finally broke the silence. "If we don't get off the planet soon, we starve to death. And that's a probability of one."

"At least we'd be doing something. What do you think?" Valkerie looked at Bob. "I don't know about you, but I'm sick to death of sitting around."

"If we can figure out how to camp out overnight, I vote go," Bob said. "Trying is better than not trying."

"Good, it's settled." Lex smacked her palms on the table. "We're all taking one last big trip. In the morning." The room hung with a heavy silence. Valkerie looked at Bob. He was thinking the same thing she was. She could see it in his eyes. Lex wasn't strong enough to go. But she was the commander. How could they make her stay?

Valkerie did a quick tally. They had nine oxygen tanks at eight hours each. If all three went, that would last them only twenty-four hours. If it took seven hours to get there and another seven to get back, that would only leave ten hours to find the ice, dig it out, and hoist it to the surface. Plus, they'd need to eat and rest. If only two went—

"I don't think we have enough oxygen tanks for all three of us," Bob said.

"Um, Val? Bob?" Lex's voice sounded apologetic. "Listen, if the tent idea doesn't work, whoever goes isn't coming back. You know that, right?"

"Sure, Lex." Bob's voice sounded tight.

"And furthermore, two of us *have* to go," Lex said. "It's a two-person operation."

Valkerie nodded. She could see where this was going.

"I . . ." Lex's voice cracked. "I think it should be you two. If anything goes wrong, we're all doomed anyway. And you two ought to be together at the end." She grabbed Valkerie's hand and moved it across the table. Into a large, calloused hand.

Bob squeezed. "Are you sure?"

Valkerie squeezed back. "Lex, it'll be harder on you if we don't make it. We'll freeze in a few hours. You'll starve slowly."

"Ever since I was eight years old, I wanted to come to Mars," Lex said. "I knew it was dangerous. Is dangerous. It's the last frontier. But I love Mars. I don't know how to say this, but there's just a bigness, a wildness, about this place. I love it here. I wish I could stay."

Lex took a deep breath. "But it's not the things you do that make life important. Not the missions you run. The medals you earn. It's the people you love. Every morning I wake up and I want to cry, because here I am in the one place in the universe I always wanted to be, and I don't have . . . Ronnie here with me. Sometimes I talk to him. Even though he can't hear me, I just have to tell him about all the bizarre and beautiful things I'm experiencing. They don't seem complete without him here to share them with me. The weeping fissures—uncanny. Stonehenge—unbelievable. And probably the most bizarre thing I've ever seen in my life—two crazy people who obviously love each other but would rather suffer alone than be happy together."

Lex's eyes were gleaming now. "If I had Ronnie here, there's no way I'd let him go off to die with someone else. You guys belong together. So you're going, Val. Bob, tell her she's going with you."

"Valkerie, you're going with me."

Valkerie smiled at Lex, and her heart felt full. "Thanks, Lex." She looked up at Bob.

His eyes shone with an intensity that pierced her to the marrow. He opened his mouth to speak and the room around him faded into silence. An expression of intense pain spread itself across his features. Indescribable sadness.

He shook his head slowly and stood up. "If we're going to leave in the morning, we better get some sleep."

Wednesday, April 29, 2015, 11:30 a.m., Mars Local Time

Bob

Bob finished cinching down the last of the oxygen bottles on the MuleBot. They were taking every tank they had, every battery pack. If they didn't come back, Lex would never get out of the Hab alive. But of course, if they didn't come back, she would never get off the planet, so the gamble seemed reasonable. He turned to Valkerie. "Okay, let's get going!"

Valkerie plodded to the side of the mule. "We've only got seven hours of sunlight left. Maybe we should stay in the Hab one more night and try again tomorrow."

Bob checked his watch. Repairing the Bot had cost them almost three hours. It would be getting pretty cold by the time they arrived at the canyon. But time was precious. "We'll just be hungrier and weaker tomorrow. We can't afford to lose another day."

Lex's voice came in loud and clear over comm. "You've got time to get there. Bring us back some water."

Valkerie nodded. "I . . . guess you're right. Let's go, Bob."

Bob punched the Drive button, and the MuleBot lumbered forward. "Okay, take care of yourself, Lex, and keep the door locked, all right? Want us to keep comm on the whole time so you'll know we're okay?"

"Roger that, and take care of yourselves, guys." Lex's voice didn't betray any fear, but she had to be scared. "But feel free to go silent whenever you want. Some things Lexie just doesn't need to hear."

Bob rolled his eyes. Good grief, this wasn't a trip to Club Med. Leave it to Lex to get things started off on an awkward note. He guided the MuleBot forward, wondering what Valkerie was thinking. Last night after Valkerie had gone to bed, he'd taken Lex aside and told her about his promise to stop pursuing Valkerie until they were back on Earth, but she'd blown it off. Like Valkerie didn't have the right to decide for herself.

The mule jostled along behind him, silently adjusting its speed as he manipulated its joystick controller.

"Are you okay, Valkerie? Let me know if I'm going too fast."

"I'm fine. You can go faster if you want."

Bob stepped up the pace. They'd be able to make good time on the first leg of the trip. During their first two months of exploration, they had cleared a trail all the way to Stonehenge. It was the leg beyond Stonehenge that worried him. Without a trail, they would have to pick their way through the rocks. The mule's suspension was good but not nearly as good as the rover's, and its small tires couldn't go over rocks bigger than basketballs. One bad turn, one impassible barrier, and they would end up freezing to death in the cold Martian night. They *had* to make it to that cave before dark. He'd spent three hours kneeling on the frozen ground fixing the Bot, and the cold had bored up deep into his legs. EVA suits weren't made for doing outdoor repairs. Maybe if he walked faster, it would help warm him up.

Bob turned to make sure Valkerie was still beside him and then picked up the pace. "Valkerie, I'm sorry about the mule. I must have busted the strut when we were working on the valve."

Valkerie double-stepped to keep up with him. "Either that or Kennedy broke it before the dust storm. We haven't got out much lately."

A hard lump formed in Bob's throat. He didn't want to talk about Kennedy. Kennedy would still be alive if . . . if Bob had just listened. He hadn't told the girls about his last contact with Kennedy. Oh, he'd told them a little. But not the fact that he'd shut off Kennedy's final plea for help. Couldn't tell them. If they knew what he'd done—that he'd intentionally shut off comm with a guy who was begging for help—what would they think?

They walked in cold silence for a couple hundred yards. The burned-out hulk of the Ares 10 loomed slowly on their right. Bob wouldn't look at it. Somewhere in there were the mortal remains of Kennedy. They ought to go get his body, give him a decent burial. They hadn't dared during the height of the storm. Before Kennedy died, there had been a couple of tons of water in the Ares 10—more than enough to make the rocket fuel they needed. Now it was all gone, evaporated when the water tanks leaked in the fire. If he'd listened to Kennedy, the guy wouldn't have killed himself, and they would still have that water and all the food they needed.

"Bob?"

"Yeah?" Bob turned to look at Valkerie. She was looking at him with a funny expression. "What's up?"

"Could we . . . um . . . switch to local for a bit? Sorry, Lex."

"Ooh! Guys, this is just too hot for me. You go right ahead, lovebirds."

Bob switched his channel to local. Valkerie did the same on her suit, but she didn't say anything.

*Way to set things up, Lex.* Bob counted off ten steps. "What'cha thinking about?"

"Kennedy."

*Oh great.* Bob hesitated. "What about Kennedy?"

Valkerie didn't say anything for a long time.

"It's okay," Bob said. "We can talk about something more pleasant—like death and dying, or the futility of life, or—"

"Please. Don't make a joke." Valkerie's voice was pleading.

"It wasn't a joke."

"Bob, I feel so horrible about the whole thing. All these weeks, I've been wondering . . . What if Lex hadn't made him do all those push-ups? What if you and he hadn't gotten into that fight? What if I . . ." Valkerie turned away. "Do you think I was . . . was flirting with him? Leading him on?"

"Absolutely not!" Bob stopped the MuleBot and took Valkerie by the hand. "Valkerie, look at me. It's not your fault. You were nice to him, that's all. Because you're a nice person. There's nothing wrong with that." He leaned forward to touch his faceplate to hers. Tears were streaming down her cheeks.

"But you said I was . . ."

"Because I was being a jerk. I had no right to say those things. I was just . . . You have to believe me—it wasn't true and I knew it." Bob shook Valkerie's hands, trying to get her to look him in the eye.

"Valkerie, please. It's my fault, not yours. I left you alone with him even though I knew . . ." Bob tried to blink Valkerie's face back into focus. "Valkerie, I'm so sorry. I was so jealous. I almost wanted him to do something. I wanted you to see him for what he really was. If anyone's to blame, it's me."

Valkerie shook her head. "It's not your fault. I was the one who made you—"

"It was my fault. Listen to me." Bob choked.

Valkerie studied him intently through the two faceplates that separated them.

Bob closed his eyes. "The last night . . . before Kennedy burned up, he called me on the radio. Kept telling me to go away, to stop bothering him. Said he heard me pounding on his Hab. If I had just believed him. If I had just believed you when you said you were hearing noises." Bob pulled away and brushed vainly at his visor with his hand.

Valkerie grabbed his arm and held it.

Bob turned his head. "I killed Kennedy by my negligence. I could have saved him and I didn't. How am I going to face his parents when we get back?" He tried to pull away.

Valkerie hugged his arm tighter. "Kennedy was sick. It wasn't your fault. You did everything you could, but we didn't know how to help him. We gave him every chance we knew how to give him, and it wasn't enough. We didn't come prepared for him to go crazy on us. Some things are just out of our hands."

"Like getting off the planet?" Bob started the MuleBot and started forward again. They walked for a long time in silence. When they reached Stonehenge, they left the cleared path and slowed their pace to skirt its northern edge. Cold crept back into Bob's muscles. A cramp tightened his empty stomach.

Valkerie's breathing was becoming increasingly ragged and her stumbles more frequent. How long would she be able to last like this? "Valkerie, do you want to ride on the mule for a while? It'll help save your energy."

"If you're walking, I want to walk too."

"You can walk later and I'll ride. We need to have something left in our muscles when we get there." Bob stopped the mule. "Here, I'll help you climb up. There's room in the very back to sit."

A minute later, she sat perched on the rear edge of the mule. "Thanks, Bob."

"Hey, guys?" Lex broke in on the emergency channel. "Bob? Valkerie? I called in to report to Houston a while ago and I just heard back from Nate. He's tickled pink about your little excursion. Have a listen."

A crackle of static and then . . .

"Ares 7, this is Nate Harrington. I've talked to the boys and girls here in the FCR about your proposed trip out to the canyon, and the unanimous opinion is that it's not going to work. We're especially concerned about the overnight part of your proposal. Guys, this is a loser idea. That hyperbaric chamber hasn't got the insulating power. The ground is gonna suck heat right out of you, and you'll die in your sleep. So forget it. That's an order. Please acknowledge."

"This is me again," Lex said. "I sent Nate an acknowledgment that we heard his message and are considering it. I consider that his advice stinks. We're going to starve if we don't get off the planet, and we can't do that without water."

Bob switched to the CommSat channel. "I agree. It's our decision, and we're sticking by it."

"We have to go," Valkerie said. "But, Lex, Nate's going to be really mad. What are you going to do when he finds out we've left?"

"Ask forgiveness. Because I sure don't need his permission."

By the time they got past Stonehenge, Bob's feet were clunky blocks of ice. Why weren't they warming up? "Are you doing okay, Valkerie?"

"Mmm . . . Fine." Valkerie mumbled something that sounded anything but fine.

Bob looked up at the sun. It was already well past zenith in the amber sky. His watch told him they had just over four hours to cover the remaining two kilometers and set up camp. If they didn't make it to the vent by nightfall, they were Tastee-Freez.

They trudged on, not speaking. Bob's legs went from cold to numb and then painfully numb. After another hour of walking, he couldn't feel anything below the knees. He felt like a pirate balancing on two wooden legs.

"Bob?" Valkerie's voice startled Bob out of his reverie. "What made you want to go to Mars?"

Bob tried to think back. It seemed like such a long time ago. "I don't know. I guess because they needed me. It was probably Josh more than anybody. He's the one who convinced me. How about you?"

"I think it was the adventure. The excitement. The glory of being selected. Pretty dumb, huh?"

"Yeah. I mean . . ." Bob felt like an idiot. "I mean, most people come here for the balmy weather and pristine beaches."

They shambled along for another half kilometer. They'd now been outside for over six hours. Maybe they should have stayed overnight in the Hab. But tomorrow there would have been another reason not to go, and the day after another. If you were going to play poker for survival, then you had to just deal the cards. And pray for five aces.

The sound of Valkerie's breathing interrupted Bob's thoughts. Her breath was coming in ragged pants and gasps. He turned to look back and saw that she had hopped off the mule and come up alongside him. "I needed some exercise," she said, step-step-stepping determinedly by his side, doing her best to keep up with his long strides. Valkerie. Never a complaint for herself. Never a word of reproach for anyone. She deserved so much better than this. If only she was safe and warm on Earth right now. Walking through sun-dappled forests. Running through waving fields of wild flowers. He tried to imagine her wearing normal clothes. Jeans. A nice cotton dress. But he just couldn't picture it. The image kept twisting into dirty NASA coveralls. A clunky EVA suit that hung on her like the unrelenting weight of death.

Valkerie stepped on a rock and lurched sideways, stumbling into Bob.

Bob put a supporting arm around her and slowed his pace.

She glanced at him with a smile that pierced his heart.

So beautiful. So wondrous, through and through. What had he been thinking? He didn't deserve her. Never in a million years. No wonder she'd said no.

Valkerie leaned in closer. "If we don't make it . . . I just want you to know I'm sorry. I should have—"

"We're going to make it," Bob said. Way too quickly.

"Bob."

"We have to," Bob picked up the pace. "I . . . won't let anything happen to you. Ever."

Long silence.

"I should have said yes." Valkerie gazed up at him with wide, wondering eyes.

Bob's heart lurched, staggered. Warmth surged through his body, spreading through his limbs like a tingling fire.

"Bob? Did you hear me?"

"I heard—"

The MuleBot jerked to a halt, yanking Bob backward.

Off-balance, he windmilled his arms, then toppled to the ground.

"Are you okay?"

Bob struggled to his feet and tugged at the MuleBot's joystick.

Nothing.

Fear kicked him hard in the gut.

"I'm fine," he said. "But the mule's broken down again." *And we're still a long way from the nearest Motel 6.*

## Wednesday, April 29, 2015, 5:30 p.m., Mars Local Time

### Valkerie

Valkerie paced back and forth, stamping her feet to shake some warmth into them. Bob lay on the ground, pulling wires through an access panel beneath the dead MuleBot. It was getting late. They still had at least a kilometer to go, and maybe an hour to do it in—if they left right now.

That would be an easy pace if they were fresh and decently fed. Bob's quivering breath sounded in Valkerie's ears.

"Bob, you're freezing. Let me do it. You have to get off the ground."

"Almost there . . ."

"Can't I do something?"

"Climb up on the MuleBot again. You'll stay warmer if you're off the ground."

Valkerie looked out at the sinking sun. "Maybe we should leave the mule and try to make it on foot. The mule's not going to do us any good if we're dead. Or maybe—"

"Valkerie, listen to me. I'm almost there. You have to trust me. I want you to climb up onto the mule."

"Not while you're on the ground freezing to death. If we leave now—"

"Please. I need you to trust me. Everything's going to be okay."

Valkerie took a deep breath and let it out slowly. "Okay." She climbed up on the MuleBot and took a seat atop the large bag that contained the hyperbaric chamber. Turning to face the sun, she hugged her knees to her chest and tried to rub some warmth into her legs through the bulky fabric of her suit.

The rocky plain blazed like burnished gold. Too bright. She turned to look back the way they'd come. A couple of kilometers away, the great Stonehenge formations stood tall and purple with cloaks of aureate flame. If only they held water. A drowsy calm settled over her. She'd done all she could do. The rest was up to God.

"Okay, try it now." Bob's voice shattered the calm.

Valkerie slid off the mule and eased forward on the joystick. The robot rolled slowly ahead. "Bob, you did it! We've got . . ."

Bob still lay stretched out on the ground.

"Bob?" She hobbled over and reached down to tug on his pack. "Bob, get up. We've got to go."

"I . . . can't. Can't move my legs."

Valkerie rolled Bob onto his back and pulled him into a sitting position. "Come on. You can do it." She tugged on his arms, trying to help him to his feet.

"Go on without me. I'm too cold."

"No!" Valkerie circled behind him and dead-lifted him to his feet. His body hung like a sack of cement. When she let go, his legs gave way beneath him.

Valkerie guided the mule back to him and waited while she caught her breath. She got behind him and lifted him to his knees.

Bob's hands latched on to the mule.

"Can you pull yourself up?"

"Maybe. My legs aren't . . . working."

Valkerie squatted down and grabbed his torso. "Pull!" She lifted his slack body—higher, higher—and felt the load lighten as Bob got leverage on top. Finally he was on the mule's back, draped over the top of the hyperbaric chamber like a sack of wheat on a camel. Valkerie let go and stepped back. "Will you be able to hold on?"

"I'm trying."

Valkerie dug in one of the packs, found a rope, and lashed Bob down. Then, tugging hard on the joystick, she set out for the canyon at a shuffling jog.

"Valkerie, in case we don't make it, I just wanted to say how sorry—"

"Bob, don't. Please. We're going to make it." Valkerie kicked the speed up another notch. "Don't you dare quit on me. We're too close to give up now."

Almost there. Valkerie staggered the last twenty yards, fighting for every step. Finally she cut power to the MuleBot and let it coast to a stop five feet back from the edge of the ravine. "Bob, can you still hear me? We're here." She reached back on the mule's heaping pack and gave Bob a gentle shake. Pins and needles shot through her numb fingers. It was getting colder. The sun would be down in fifteen minutes. "Bob?" She shook him harder.

"Can't move my legs. Can't feel them at all. How am I going to—"

"You'll be fine. Just try to move around. Get some circulation going." Valkerie untied the loops of cable that bound Bob to the back of the MuleBot and helped him slide to the ground.

His legs crumpled beneath him, flipping him backward onto his PLSS pack.

"Bob! Are you okay?"

"C-c-cold. So, so, so cold."

"I'll get you down to the cave in a second. If Lex is right about the thermal vent, it should be a bit warmer inside." Valkerie checked the power level of Bob's suit.

The battery pack was almost dead.

"Bob, I'm going to swap out your battery first. Can you roll over onto your hands and knees?"

"So, so, so cold . . ."

Valkerie unlashed the rest of the mule's load and dug under the oxygen tanks near the front for a battery. There. She lugged the unit back to Bob, who was thrashing around with his arms. She turned him onto his side and braced him with her knee. "That's it. Keep on moving." She pried off the battery cover and swapped out the battery. "Move your legs too. You've got to get the blood flowing."

"Trying."

Valkerie could hear the strain in Bob's voice, but his legs still weren't moving. "You're doing fine. Just keep on trying." Valkerie staggered to her feet and started digging through their load. She buckled the remote controller for the winch to her wrist. Where was the piton bag? "Bob . . ." She fought to control her voice. "I've got to anchor the mule. Where'd you pack the pulleys?"

No response.

"Bob? Where are the . . ." She dumped the bulky hyperbaric chamber on the ground and snatched up the orange nylon bag that had been hiding underneath. "Never mind."

She pulled two titanium pitons from the bag and pounded them deep into the rocky ground. "Talk to me, Bob. You've got to keep moving." Pulling out the cables attached to the back corners of the mule, she fastened them to the two stakes. Then, slowly letting out cable from the winch on the front of the mule, she walked her way back to Bob and clamped the line onto the anchor clip on his chest.

"Bob!" She shouted into her mike.

"Over here . . ." Bob's voice was heavy. He sounded tired, sleepy.

"Okay. Wake up." Valkerie pushed Bob roughly onto his back. "I need your help, big guy. I need you to stand. We've got to get you over the edge of the cliff." She reversed the motor on the winch unit and pulled Bob up to a sitting position. "Okay, ready? And stand." She started the winch and strained with all her might to pull Bob to his feet.

He flopped forward and started plowing face first through the dirt toward the winch.

"That's one way to do it." Valkerie dragged Bob by the arm until he was between the winch and the cliff. Then, half pushing and half rolling him, she shoved him over the edge.

The line snapped taut and the mule lurched forward, but stopped short as the anchor lines tightened and held.

Panting to catch her breath, Valkerie clamped a line onto the cable and crawled backward over the side of the cliff. Her hand slipped and she fell out into space for a heart-stopping second before the cable snapped tight and slammed her into the wall. She scrambled for a handhold on the smooth rock, waiting for the cable to slip. Waiting for the mule to come crashing over the edge. Bob's backpack pressed against hers. They hung motionless, waiting—like two fuzzy dice hanging from God's rearview mirror.

"Almost there. Keep on moving." Valkerie pushed Bob aside and fingered the control box on her wrist. For a second she couldn't tell if they were descending. The winch they'd attached to the MuleBot had only one speed—slug-on-a-frozen-flagpole slow. It had been built for lifting torque, not speed.

Pushing and crawling and kicking against the rocky wall, Valkerie fought her way down the face of the cliff. Finally she and Bob were even with the tunnel and the rocky ledge beneath. She swung onto the ledge and hammered a piton into a crack in the wall. Bob couldn't crawl into the cave by himself, so she was going to have to use a pulley to pull him inside. And to do that she needed some slack in the line.

She hooked a short safety line to the piton in the wall and attached the other end of the line to Bob. Flipping the controller switch for Bob's winch, she lowered Bob until he was supported only by his safety line. The winch continued lowering until the cable hung down in a big loop below Bob. Wriggling her way feet first into the dark tunnel, she pulled the loop of cable behind her until the tunnel finally widened out enough for her to turn around.

"Hold on, Bob, just a little bit longer." Valkerie pulled a pulley out of the piton bag and looped the primary line around it before fastening it to the wall of the tunnel with a piton.

"I'm coming to get you." She scrambled back to the entrance of the cave and switched on the winch. The cable slowly tightened, drawing Bob back into the tunnel. Valkerie turned off the winch and released him from his safety line.

"Okay, big guy. I hope Lex dug the opening out wide enough." Valkerie switched the winch back on and maneuvered Bob back into the tunnel, carefully guiding him as the winch dragged him deeper inside.

When he was finally far enough inside the tunnel for her to get around him, Valkerie turned off the winch and transferred the cable to her harness. "Wait here and keep moving. It should be a lot warmer in this cave. I'm going to get our supplies."

Thursday, April 30, 2015, 1:00 a.m., CST

Josh

Josh looked at his watch. 1:00 a.m. Perfect. He sat up in bed and swung his feet to the floor.

The FBI was pulling out Friday, and he had to talk to Cathe before they did. No way had she invited Jake to lunch the day the commands were sent to the ERV. That was the day she'd asked him out to lunch, and he still had the e-mail in his files to prove it. But what did it mean? It didn't make any sense. If Cathe hadn't sent that e-mail to Jake, who had? There was only one way to find out.

Josh laced on his shoes and tiptoed to the hatch. The guard out there was armed. Time for a little surprise. NASA had absolutely no legal reason to hold him. If Nate still wanted him in "protective custody," he could refuse the protection. What were they protecting, anyway? His reputation? That was already in shreds, at least within JSC. Everybody in the Mars Mission Directorate knew what he was accused of. And most of them believed it. What could be worse than that?

In any event, he had nothing left to lose. They had his back to the wall and they were holding the gun and all the bullets. Did they have the guts to fire?

Josh yanked open the hatch and jumped out.

The guard moved to block his way.

Josh dodged past him and ran.

"Stop or I'll—"

"Go ahead and shoot!" Josh shouted. "I'll sue your socks off."

Footsteps clattered behind him. But no gunshots. Josh skidded around the corner and sprinted for the door.

Behind him, the guard was bellowing something into his walkie-talkie.

Great. Any second now, the campus was going to be boiling with security goons.

There was nobody at the door. Amazing.

Josh raced through and out into the sweltering Houston night.

Already he heard a siren coming up the road from one of the security gates. Building 29 was on the edge of campus. They'd expect him to head toward one of the exits. Instead, he turned toward the heart of the campus, racing along in the shadows of Building 7, cutting across diagonally to the medical building, then around the dark side of the cafeteria. Finally, he turned left and headed to the last place anyone would look for a fugitive—Mission Control.

When he reached Building 30A, the door was unlocked. Security in this wing of the building was a joke. Josh simply walked in and ducked into a stairwell. At this hour of the night, there wouldn't be many engineers about, and most would take the elevator, not the stairs. Up two flights, then a quick peek out into the hallway.

Deserted, as he expected.

He slipped down the hallway, stopping at Cathe's office. It had one of those five-button combo locks on it. Josh had been here plenty of times. He punched in the combination with fumbling fingers and tried the door. *Oops! Try again. Slower, dummy.* He finally got it right on the third try and eased the door open.

The room was dark, lit only by screen glow at the far end.

Josh slipped inside and pushed the door shut. A filing cabinet stood just inside on the left. Josh leaned against it and tried to catch his breath while his eyes got used to the dark.

That had gone better than he expected. Now the first thing to do would be to call Cathe to see if she could smuggle him off campus somehow. He heard footsteps outside in the hallway. His heart hammering, Josh put his ear against the door and listened. The footsteps echoed on the tile floor, louder, louder.

Then passed. Josh heard the sound of EECOM humming to herself. He breathed a huge sigh, pushed himself away from the door and—

Two arms wrapped around him from behind. "Don't you dare move," a voice whispered in his ear.

Two heart attacks later, Josh found his voice. "Cathe, is that you?"

"Well, of course! Who else would be in my office after midnight? What are you doing here?"

"I broke out," Josh said. "I couldn't take it anymore and just decided that the worst they could do was shoot me."

She squeezed him tighter. "I don't hear any blood squirting."

"So I got lucky." Josh grabbed her arms. "Okay, you can ease up on the death grip. I'm fine. Why are you in here with your lights out? And what's the deal? Jake told me you were quitting."

Cathe let go of him and Josh flipped on the lights.

She looked red-eyed with fatigue. "You know I never quit. The guard wouldn't let me in to see you after I went to talk to Nate. When Jake got back from D.C. on Tuesday, I heard he was going to visit you, so I juiced myself up with perfume and flew a touch and go on him. It was the only way I could think of to tell you I . . ." Cathe buried her face in his chest. "Josh, I've been going crazy with worry."

"You need to get some sleep. What are you doing in so late?"

"Working. You haven't heard yet?"

"Heard what?"

Cathe's eyes glistened. "You better sit down."

"I can't sit down. I've been sitting for weeks."

"I'm tired. It's been a seventeen-hour day."

"Sit." Josh began pacing.

Cathe went back to sit in front of her computer. "All right, I'm just going to lock my workstation and . . . there, it's all tucked in for the night. Here's the scoop on the crew, and it's really bad. This afternoon, Valkerie and Bob went off to look for water. Without permission. Nate about blew his spleen when he found out."

"Water! They've got plenty of water."

"They need more. Somehow the valve broke on their methane tank. They're not sure when. Anyway, a lot of the methane boiled off."

Josh swore loudly. Finally he got control of himself. "How much did they lose?"

"About three tonnes, and they need to regenerate at least half of it." Cathe took a deep breath. "They want to convert their water to methane, but they don't have enough. If they converted every drop in the Hab to methane, they'd get off the ground, but they'd never reach the ERV."

"So they went looking for water?" Josh pounded his fist in his hand. "That's crazy! Where are they going to find water?"

"It's *really* crazy. When they suggested it, the FCR crew voted against it. Nate ordered the crew not to make the EVA. But they did it anyway."

"And . . . ?"

"We're waiting to hear back. I dropped by the FCR twenty minutes ago, and the latest news was that Lex says they arrived at the canyon where they found that halobacteria and are camping out for the night. There's nothing anybody can do now except wait."

"They'll make it. They're survivors." Josh paced back and forth.

"So are you going to tell me why you're here, or am I going to have to force it out of you?"

"Jake paid me a visit. He said the FBI is pulling out Friday and EECOM is going to coordinate the systems monitoring."

"And?"

"And I think I have a clue."

Cathe's eyes lit up. "Go on."

"Jake said you sent him an e-mail inviting him to lunch that day somebody hacked my computer. He—"

"He's lying." Cathe jumped to her feet. "*He* sent *me* the message. Said he wanted to meet in the cafeteria to talk about the CommSat calculations. But when I got there he tried to put a move on me. I—"

"Wait a second." Josh grabbed her by the shoulders and searched her face. "You went to the cafeteria to meet *him*? What about *me*?"

"I didn't stay." Cathe's eyes went wide. "You've got to believe me. I had no idea . . . I left as soon as I realized what he was up to. I didn't even sit down."

Josh's head spun. "Didn't you send an e-mail inviting *me* to lunch?"

"Josh, listen to me. I never sent him an e-mail. He sent the message to me."

"It's okay. I believe you." Josh took a deep breath and relaxed his grip on her shoulders. "But the day Jake sent you the e-mail. Didn't you send me an e-mail asking *me* to meet you in the cafeteria? You know, a real gooshy one?"

She stared at him. "Me? Gooshy? You know me better than that."

Josh just stared. He should have known. "I got an e-mail from you."

"I didn't send it. To you or Jake. What did it say?"

Josh told her.

She shook her head and pinned him with an incredulous look.

"I know . . . I'm an idiot. I should have known it wasn't you, but . . ." Josh started pacing again. "Somebody forged e-mails to me and you . . . and probably to Jake too."

"But why? How?" Cathe sank onto the edge of her desk. "Hacking mail protocols is really hard when there's good authentication at both ends."

"Almost like someone wanted the three of us together. Maybe they were trying to make me jealous. Maybe—"

A light outside the window caught his eye. Two flashlights sweeping the area near the duck ponds. "I've got to get out of here. Can you take me home with you?"

She grinned at him. "I thought you'd never ask."

"Believe me, I've been wanting to. Just got a little tied up at work." Josh walked over to the window. Two more flashlights crisscrossed the grounds.

Cathe came up alongside him and snuggled under his arm. "How are we going to get you off campus?"

Josh shrugged. "I forgot to bring my cloaking device, and I can't exactly drive my truck out through the gate."

Cathe leaned against him for a long time. She seemed to be thinking. "Where's your truck parked?"

Josh studied her face, trying to figure out what she was thinking. "I haven't driven it for four weeks. I left it in the lot across from Building 29."

"Give me the keys, then go sit in my chair over there and turn around."

Josh obeyed.

Rustling noises behind him.

"Okay, you can look now."

Josh turned around.

Cathe was wearing shorts and a tight-fitting tanktop. "See you in a few minutes." She glided toward the door. "I'm going running."

Josh settled back into her chair and closed his eyes, trying to hold on to the vision that filled his mind . . .

• • •

"Josh, wake up!"

Josh yawned. "I'm . . . awake." He looked at his watch. Cathe had been gone about twenty minutes.

She pointed in the general direction of the nearest parking lot. "Your truck is out there in the parking lot about fifty yards from my Mazda. In the corner by the cafeteria. Funny thing—it won't start."

"Then how did you drive it?"

Cathe tossed him a fuse. "That's for your ignition circuit. Do you have AAA?"

"Sure." Josh pulled out his wallet and sorted through it until he found his card.

"Here's what we're going to do." Cathe handed him her cell phone and spent the next three minutes explaining the plan.

Josh punched in the AAA 800 number.

Somebody answered on the tenth ring. "Hello."

"Good evening! Or maybe good morning, I'm not sure which. This is Jay Benet." Josh pronounced his last name so it sounded French. He gave the operator his membership ID and waited for her to type it into her computer.

"Yes, Mr. Benet. What can I do for you?"

"I need a tow truck."

"What's wrong with your car?"

"It just won't start," Josh said. "This has happened a couple of times, and I need to get it towed to my mechanic. Again. I'm gonna read him the riot act in the morning."

"And where are you located?"

"I'm at the Johnson Space Center in Clear Lake." Josh gave directions to his truck. "This is a secure facility, so tell the driver he has to tell the guard at the gate he's been authorized by a Mr. Harrington."

"But you're not Mr. Harrington."

"No, I'm *visiting* Mr. Harrington here at NASA, and he'll call Security to authorize your driver to come through the gate."

"I'll have a driver there for you in about fifty minutes."

"I'll need his license plate number to get him authorized." Josh heard the sound of computer keys clicking. The operator read off a license number.

"Thanks a million." Josh hung up and punched in the phone number for the gate on Saturn Lane.

"Security, Gate 1."

Josh tried to hoarsen up his voice a little. "This is Nate Harrington, Mars Mission Director. My pickup truck won't start, and I have requested a AAA driver to come through your gate to give me a tow. Here's his license plate number."

"No problem, Mr. Harrington."

"Any luck tracking down Josh Bennett?"

"Not yet, but we'll find him, sir."

"You'd better." Josh hung up and turned to face Cathe.

She grinned back and sauntered toward him.

"So." Josh held his arms wide. "What are we going to do now?"

Cathe snuggled up to him. "You know if this doesn't work, I'm not going to see you for a long time."

"It'll work. It has to." Josh looked down into her eyes and drew her closer.

Forty-five minutes passed a lot quicker than he could possibly have imagined.

"The tow truck's going to get here any minute!" Cathe said. "Take your stuff and run!"

Josh grabbed the cap Cathe had found for him and raced out of the door and down the hallway. If he met anyone now, it was all over. He reached the ground floor without seeing anyone and dashed toward the parking lot.

The AAA truck had already stopped in front of his pickup. The driver had left the engine running and was standing in the poorly lit lot looking around anxiously. He had dark hair and wore a T-shirt and trucker's cap.

Josh waved his arms and hurried to meet him. "Sorry," he said. "I'm Mr. Benet. Think I had a bad burrito for supper, and I've been having to hit the head every half hour."

"The head?"

"Bathroom."

"So what's wrong with your pickup?"

Josh shook his head in disgust. "I think the ignition switch is shot. The engine won't even turn over. It's the third time, and my mechanic swore up and down he had it fixed."

"Sign here and I'll get it hitched up."

Josh filled out the form and then walked all the way around the truck. By the time he came around behind the mechanic, his truck was hitched and the front end raised. Josh cleared his throat. "Hey, would you believe it, my right rear tire is way low on air."

The driver shrugged. "I can fill that up for you." He grabbed a canister of compressed air and walked around to the back of Josh's truck. "Which tire did you say?" he shouted. "They look fine to me."

Josh was already in the cab of the AAA truck. He slammed the door and looked at the dashboard. An automatic. Thank God even mechanics these days were wimps. And they *always* left the engine running. Josh shifted into drive, released the parking brake, and gunned the motor.

The truck lurched forward.

Josh looked in the side mirror.

The mechanic was running after him, shouting and waving his arms. It was a big parking lot. By the time Josh reached Second Street and turned left toward the main gate, he'd left the mechanic in the dust. He spotted Cathe Willison's lithe form jogging across the parking lot toward the mechanic.

In the three blocks it took to reach the gate, Josh yanked off his button-down shirt to reveal a T-shirt underneath and jammed the cap on his head, tipping it forward to shade his features. It wasn't the same color as the mechanic's, but who would notice? For sure, not the rocket scientists working the security night shift.

He drove past the parking lot to Rocket Park and slowed as he approached the gate. The security guard held up a hand for him to stop. Josh was sweating like a pig now. He raised his left hand in a friendly wave that also obscured his face.

The guard nodded and walked past him, his big flashlight sending out a yellow cone in the night air. Josh watched him in his mirror as he poked his light into the pickup truck cab, then inspected the bed. Cathe had been right. Security people were wired to ignore anything hidden in plain sight. Finally the guard nodded and waved Josh to go.

Josh began breathing again as he took his foot off the brake. *Easy. Don't go nuts now. Just drive normally.* Fifty yards past the gate, Josh punched the gas pedal. At NASA Road One, he turned right. Half a mile down the road, he turned left into the parking lot of the Holiday Inn. He cut the engine and leaped out. It took him a full minute to figure out how to get his truck detached. He popped the fuse-box cover and shoved in the ignition fuse, then turned the key. His engine started with a satisfying roar. He backed away from the tow truck, then pulled around past it.

As he turned left onto NASA Road One, he waved cheerily at a red Mazda sports car that was just pulling into the parking lot.

Cathe was sitting at the wheel ignoring the frantic gestures of the mechanic in the passenger seat next to her.

Josh jammed his foot to the floor and headed for freedom.

An hour later, Josh and Cathe arrived at her apartment, having ditched Josh's truck in a strip mall parking lot. Cathe unlocked her apartment door and they slipped inside.

"I can't stay with you." Josh took in the utilitarian furnishings with one glance. "Nate's going to send people here first thing in the morning. They may be on the way here already."

"Fine, he can search my apartment." Cathe dropped onto a worn brown sofa. "But he won't know to search Mrs. Truby's place."

"Who's Mrs. Truby?"

"My neighbor. She's about five hundred years old, and she's got the most amazing houseplants in her apartment. I hope you like green."

"I can't impose on your neighbor." Josh sat down beside her.

"She's been in Minnesota for the last month." Cathe held up some keys. "Guess who volunteered to water her plants while she was gone?"

"When's she coming back?"

"In a week." Cathe gave Josh a wicked smile. "But don't worry. That's enough time for us to figure out who set you up."

"I want to talk to EECOM."

"This is kind of late to be calling her. Even EECOM sleeps sometimes."

"No, I mean tomorrow. In person."

Cathe's eyebrows went up.

"I've been thinking. It's obvious someone wanted to lure me away from my computer. But why the cafeteria? Why involve you and Jake?"

"Yes . . . ?" Cathe leaned closer.

"Well, what if they wanted to give me an alibi? And what if they wanted me to see you and Jake together? You know—kill two birds."

"You think it was Jake?" Cathe frowned.

"Not a chance," Josh said. "The bogus e-mail to you lays a big, fat trail back to him. I say that makes him less a suspect, not more."

"So where are you going with this?"

"I think it was EECOM."

"Josh, be serious."

"That proves half my point. She's the last person anyone would suspect. As of tonight, she'll be in the perfect spot—monitoring the network. And while we were driving, it just hit me. Somebody wanted me out of my office, but they also wanted me to see you with Jake. Now, who would want to make me jealous?"

"You don't really think she's in love with you, do you?"

"Remind me," Josh said. "When we caught that burn command queued up on the ERV stack, who found it?"

"CATO."

"And then Nate ordered us to cancel it, right?" Josh closed his eyes, trying to picture the scene.

"Right . . ." Cathe dragged the word out.

"And somebody said we ought to wait. Wanted to study it first. Who said that?"

She shook her head. "That's just the way she is, Josh. She's hypercautious."

"Who said it?" Josh demanded.

Cathe clutched his arm. "You're jumping to a conclusion."

"It was EECOM, wasn't it? We could replay the tapes. Wasn't it her?"

"Yes," Cathe whispered. "Josh, she's been such a . . . help to me. Teaching me stuff. She loves that crew. She wouldn't do anything to hurt them."

"De-orbiting the ERV wouldn't hurt the crew—at least as far as anyone knew then. That was before Kennedy burned up himself and all the food. All she was trying to do was keep them on Mars. I believe hypercautious was your word."

Cathe stood up and went to the bathroom. Josh heard the sound of a nose blowing. He felt sick inside. He'd known EECOM for almost ten years. NASA was her life. She'd never been married, except to her job.

If anyone could hack into that Russian computer, it was her. EECOM was the acknowledged Unix wizard on a staff of supergeeks. And as of this evening, she would be in charge of monitoring the networks to protect the crew.

Cathe came back out, her nose red.

"What's the plan?"

Cathe grabbed a sleeping bag from her closet and some keys off the table. "The plan is for you to get into Mrs. Truby's apartment and get some shut-eye. You can sleep in tomorrow and meet EECOM anytime you want, but I need to be back at JSC at 8:00 a.m., so that gives me . . . almost five hours to sleep. Should be plenty. Let's move."

Josh followed her, wondering how one human body could hold so much energy.

Wednesday, April 29, 2015, 11:45 p.m., Mars Local Time

Bob

Bob's eyes flickered open. Total darkness. He tried to scratch his nose, but his right arm wouldn't move. There it was again. Something tickling his nose. Where was he? Why couldn't he move his arm? Frostbite?

Memories of his trip with Valkerie flooded over him. Fixing the MuleBot. Riding on its back. Winching down the sheer side of the canyon. Blocking up the exit to the cave. Making hot tea inside this tent using a spare battery pack and a NASA coffee maker.

He tried wiggling his toes and felt them pushing into the insulation of his thick EVA boots. They even felt warm. Next his legs. Then his left arm . . .

He brought his hand to his face and brushed away a damp curl. Valkerie. He traced the outline of her head. She was lying on her side, using his right arm for a pillow.

She sighed softly and snuggled closer, burrowing her head under his chin.

Bob's heart started pounding wildly. For a terrifying second he worried the noise would wake her, but he forced himself to relax. He was being ridiculous. He was still wearing his suit.

Slowly, in tiny, halting movements, he brought his hand to the back of her head and stroked her thick hair. She'd saved his life. Picked him up and tied him to the mule. His throat suddenly tightened. And she'd told him she should have said *yes*.

He turned his head slightly and brushed a kiss across her forehead. A tear traced across his cheek and dissolved into her curls.

### Thursday, April 30, 2015, 2:00 a.m., Mars Local Time

### Valkerie

Valkerie jerked awake. The scrubbers. She was supposed to have been monitoring the $CO_2$ level. She tried to sit up, but her bulky pack wouldn't let her get twisted around.

"Good morning." Bob's voice sounded close by her ear.

Valkerie's heart leapt. "Bob! How do you feel?" She groped in the darkness for the flashlight and switched it on.

"Happy." Bob grinned up at her, blocking the light with his hand. "Happy to be here. Happy to be alive. Happy to be with you."

Valkerie studied Bob's face. What was going on with him? He looked different—more relaxed. His eyes were lit with a strange glow. Like he knew something she didn't. "Um . . . how are your feet?"

"Warm and toasty. You picked the right spot for the tent. I think we're in a warm pocket near one of those thermal vents. It's probably just below freezing outside—practically the tropics in this neighborhood. And Kennedy's mattress is insulating us from the ground pretty well."

Again the strange look. Did he think something was funny? She brushed her hair out of her eyes with her fingertips and swept it back behind her shoulders. "I know I must look a mess . . ."

Bob shook his head wistfully. The corners of his mouth turned up in a slight smile.

Valkerie broke away from his gaze and checked the $CO_2$ levels. "We have another hour of oxygen left in here. We should go over our plan of attack."

"Valkerie?"

Valkerie drew in her breath. He sounded so serious. She turned slowly and searched his eyes through a sparkling haze.

"Valkerie, I made you a promise earlier. I meant it at the time, but I need you to release me from that promise. Do you know what I'm talking about?"

*His proposal.* Valkerie's heart sank. She nodded as her world dissolved into tears. He didn't want her anymore. Of course he didn't. Could she blame him?

"Please say you release me. Please."

The pleading tone in Bob's voice cut through her like a razor. She buried her face in her hands. "I . . . understand. You don't . . ." The words stuck in her throat. "You don't have to keep your promise."

Somewhere through her sobs she heard Bob moving inside the chamber. Probably trying to get away. She had lost him.

Valkerie wiped her face with the back of her hand and found herself looking up into Bob's downturned face. He was on his knees before her. "Valkerie, will you marry me?"

A gasp escaped her throat. "But you said . . . you wanted a release . . ."

"I'm sorry. I know I said I'd wait till we were back on Earth, but I . . . I just couldn't bear it. I love you so much. It's killing me."

"Bob." Valkerie flung her arms around Bob's neck. "Of course. Yes. The answer is yes."

Thursday, April 30, 2015, 2:15 a.m., Mars Local Time

Bob

They each ate a couple of food packets in haste, smiling. Bob's heart felt too big for words, too full, too . . . happy.

*Yes.*

There was no finer word in the English language.

*Yes.*

Bob put a fresh oxygen bottle on Valkerie's backpack. She put one on his. They swapped in fresh battery packs.

*Yes.*

If they didn't make it back to the Hab, or never got off Mars, or never reached the good green Earth again, it was okay. He had come to Mars to search for life—and he had found it.

*Yes.*

Valkerie pulled on her gloves and snapped the wrist connectors. "Ready to go out there and find us some water?"

Bob pulled on his gloves. Fastened them. Looked at her and grinned.

"Yes."

• • •

Half an hour later they found ice. They had followed the cave back into the side of the canyon for a few dozen yards. They moved slowly, wary of their footing, watchful for any crevices that might swallow them whole. And there it was, right where Lex had predicted.

"Pay dirt." Valkerie handed Bob a pick and kept a shovel for herself. "We've got two five-gallon buckets. How long is it going to take to haul out a ton of ice?"

Bob did a quick calculation. "If we could get eighty pounds per trip, that's twenty-five trips. But we're going to spill some and waste some of our volume, so thirty-five trips is probably safer." Bob raised his pick and slammed it into the ice. A small hunk broke off—maybe a pound. It was gonna be a long night.

It took five minutes to fill the first load. Bob handed Valkerie the pick. "Keep breaking it up. I'll carry this out." He hefted the two buckets and started walking. Thank God for Mars gravity, because hauling out the ice was going to be a papa bear.

They had taken down the hyperbaric chamber and left it just outside the entrance of the cave. Bob painfully pushed the buckets through the exit tunnel on his hands and knees, then dumped the ice into the makeshift tent. The pile looked pitifully small. One trip down, thirty-four to go.

When he got back to Valkerie, he was surprised to see how much ice she had already broken free. He scooped it into the buckets, picked them up, and started the trip back to the cache outside.

The night passed far too quickly. At first, Bob managed eight trips per hour, but soon he slowed to seven, then six. The last four loads took over an hour. It was almost 7:30 a.m. when they finished. The thin yellow sun had poked its head up into the peach-colored sky.

Bob flicked on his comm to call Lex again. He'd been calling in every couple hours to keep her posted on their progress. "Hail, Yoda. We've completed digging out the water and we've got it in a pile here on the ledge. This was almost too easy."

"Speak for yourself," Valkerie groaned. "My back is killing me and we've got a long walk ahead of us."

"Good going, guys," Lex said. "How you doing on oxygen supplies?"

"Two bottles apiece," Bob said. "Right, Valkerie?"

A long silence.

Bob turned to look for her. "Right, Valkerie?"

"Um, Bob, don't be mad, but I forgot to tell you something when you woke up last night," Valkerie said. "We . . . uh . . . we used a lot of oxygen in the tent while you were resting."

"How much do we have left?"

"Three bottles," Valkerie said. "Plus whatever's left in our tanks right now—maybe an hour's worth."

"Three bottles doesn't divide up evenly," Lex said. "Unless you two can figure out how to get into one suit."

"Splitting the oxygen isn't the problem," Bob said. "I'll use half of a bottle, then switch to a fresh one. When Valkerie finishes her first one, she uses the other half of my first. The real problem is that we're exerting ourselves awfully hard and we might run out."

"If you guys boogie, you can get here in six hours," Lex said.

"That's about all we're getting out of a bottle," Valkerie said. "Maybe six and a half. They're rated for eight, but that's for normal exertion."

"Okay, then you better scramble," Lex said. "It's gonna take a while to winch all that stuff to the top and load the MuleBot."

"Let's stay calm and stick to the plan," Bob said. "We have enough if all goes well. Valkerie, you go up first with some of the gear. I'll stay down here and load stuff up."

Valkerie strapped her belt to the winch line. "I'll leave you one bottle of oxygen and take the rest up now."

Bob loaded her up with gear. She pressed one foot against the wall and pushed the winch button until the line went taut on her. Then she just stretched out horizontally and hit the button again. The line reeled her in and she walked up the cliff.

Bob went to work frantically organizing the gear. The winch would be able to haul up several hundred pounds at a time, but he would have to ride up with it to keep the container intact. If it ripped on the face of the cliff, they were dead.

In fact, it took four trips up to get all the ice to the top, plus another trip for the rest of the gear.

"Doing okay, Valkerie?" Bob said.

"Sort of." Valkerie pointed at her left foot. "I got a blister yesterday, and it's slowing me down."

Bob checked his oxygen tank, then hers. "We've got time. Not much margin, but we've got time if nothing goes wrong."

He punched the starter button for the little methane/LOX engine on the MuleBot, and the green light came on. "Lex, we're underway and we've got a straight shot home."

"See you in a few hours," Lex said. "And I'm knocking on a wood-grain-textured synthetic surface."

### Thursday, April 30, 2015, 1:00 p.m., CST

### Josh

Josh watched from across the street as EECOM stepped out of her car and walked into the little pizza joint. Good, she was alone. He'd been almost sure she would be. Whether she was a bad guy or a good guy, she'd never turn in Josh. She had sounded so shocked and happy when he called that morning, he had decided to risk meeting her.

Josh checked traffic, then hurried across the road and into the pizzeria. "Hi, Margaret."

She turned around, her mouth a little O of surprise, and then she was hugging him. "Josh, it's so good to see you again." Up close, she looked exhausted.

"You look great," he said.

EECOM blushed. "Shall we find a table?"

"Better order first. What would you like?"

They got garden specials with all the veggies you could imagine on them and took a booth in the corner farthest from the door. Josh took the seat with a view of the entrance. He trusted EECOM, but still . . .

"So, is the crew getting used to zero-g yet?" Josh said.

"Oh dear, haven't you heard?"

"Heard?" Josh had, from Cathe, but he wasn't going to tell EECOM that.

"They weren't able to launch. They're in trouble again, and it's simply horrible. Bob and Valkerie went off on a mad search for water."

*Mad?* Josh raised an eyebrow. "Why water? I thought they already launched."

EECOM's face registered surprise. "So you haven't been in contact with . . . anyone?"

"Just you. I walked out last night and managed to get off campus and hide out, but I figured Nate would tap every phone in Houston. I didn't dare call anyone."

"Not even Miss Willison?"

Josh shook his head. "She stopped coming to see me more than a week ago. I have no idea why, but . . ." He let his voice trail off in a long sigh. Then he hardened his face. "When Jake came by on Tuesday, I smelled her perfume on him."

EECOM put her hand on his. "Oh, Josh, I'm so sorry." She even looked sorry. But she didn't take her hand away.

Josh didn't say anything.

"I've seen her talking to Mr. Hunter a lot lately. They're going to make him Flight Director, you know."

"Um, no . . . I hadn't heard."

"Josh, can I tell you something? For your own good?"

"Sure, Margaret."

"You'll think I'm silly, but . . . I don't think Miss Willison is doing right by you. I overheard her talking to Mr. Hunter this morning, and it sounds very much like they're more than just friends."

"Jake's married."

"That doesn't seem to have stopped his adventures before, if the rumors are true."

"I never listen to rumors."

"Of course not. I don't either." EECOM flushed and looked down at her Coke. "But I *must* tell you that I *have* seen them together socially. About a month ago. Eating together in the cafeteria."

Josh coughed to conceal his excitement. "You say they were eating? Both of them?"

"Josh, I'm so sorry. I know it must be terribly hard." She gave his hand another squeeze.

Interesting. Josh let her cling to his hand for a long second and then pulled away to take a sip from his drink. Eating together? Cathe said she hadn't even sat down. She couldn't have. He'd rushed straight to the cafeteria after reading her message.

*No, not Cathe's message . . .*

*EECOM's.*

Thursday, April 30, 2015, 11:30 a.m., Mars Local Time

Bob

"Bob, it's tipping!"

Bob spun around and instantly cut the speed on the MuleBot. They'd been climbing a small incline and he'd thought it was safe. Things fall slower in Mars gravity, but they still fall. Bob watched helplessly as the MuleBot tipped to the left and crashed onto its side, a ton of ice strapped to its back.

"What's going on, guys?" Lex sounded frantic.

"Take it easy," Bob said. "My mistake, but I've still got almost three hours of oxygen. We'll just reload the MuleBot and keep going."

"All right, Simon says you guys are behind where you should be." Lex's voice sounded tight with anxiety. "Remember, your main mission is to get home alive. Forget the water. Grab as many oxygen bottles and batteries as you can and come on back. Quickest way possible. We'll refill them when you get home, and we can all go back for the water tomorrow. That ice isn't going to walk away. I want you here in two hours, okay?"

Valkerie picked up two empty bottles and a battery pack. Bob grabbed three of each.

"Roger, Lex," Bob said. "We're on the way."

When they reached Stonehenge, they decided to cut through it. Without the MuleBot, they didn't have to worry about the terrain.

"We've only got about a klick and a half to go." Bob checked his oxygen. "I've still got over two hours' worth." He checked hers. "You've got three."

"We're gonna make it," she said. "We were right and Nate was wrong."

They crested the ridge and began picking a way down the shallow slope into the natural bowl. The beauty of the place awed Bob to silence. Mars was a hostile environment. Arid. Desolate. Otherworldly. And yet incredibly beautiful.

Valkerie grabbed Bob's arm.

He nearly dropped the oxygen bottles he was carrying.

She pointed off to the right, toward the place they called the Garden.

Bob squinted in the afternoon glare.

Through the forest of rocks and boulders in the center of the Garden, something glinted in the Martian sun. Something metallic. Something big.

The rover.

Valkerie flicked off her comm link, and Bob's, then put down her load of gear. Bob put his down too, and they pressed helmets together, creating sonic contact.

"What's with the cloak-and-dagger?" he said. "You don't seriously believe someone's in there, do you?"

"Just being cautious," Valkerie said. "I don't see how that rover could have just driven itself down there. Either somebody is in it, or they aren't. Either way, it won't hurt to keep radio silence."

"Okay," Bob said. "But maybe we should go back to the Hab first. Then we could come back with Lex."

"But what if it moves while we're gone?" Valkerie shook her head. "We may never see it again. And the last time we looked, that rover had enough food to feed us for months."

Bob thought about that. There couldn't be anybody in the rover. There wasn't a fifth man. Had never been a fifth man. It was not logically possible for a fifth man to exist. The rover had to be empty.

*So how did it get here?*

"Let's just go look," Valkerie said. "A rover in the hand is worth two in the bush. If you're right and it's empty, we can use it to go back and get our water. Bob, it's got *food*."

Bob sighed. He'd rather come back here with Lex. Just in case there was somebody in there. But if there was, that somebody might drive it away. Especially if they saw Bob and Valkerie. Or they might attack.

Here in Stonehenge, it would be easy to dodge the rover. But out in the open plain, there would be no way to run away from it.

On the other hand, if the rover were empty—and it *had* to be empty—he and Valkerie could drive back to get the water, drive home to Lex, *and* eat like kings tonight.

"Okay," Bob said. "I'm with you. Let's go have a look."

"I love you . . ."

Bob's chest constricted and his eyes misted over. He tried to say it back, but the words caught in his throat. Finally, he blinked the tears out of his eyes and nodded like an idiot.

*Smooth . . .*

Valkerie beamed at him and leaned over to pick up the batteries.

Bob grabbed the oxygen tanks and led the way across the valley, weaving in and out through the largest rocks, trying to keep out of sight of the rover. Just as a precaution.

At fifty yards, they cached their cargo behind a large rock. Bob led the way, scooting from rock to rock as they moved around toward the back of the rover.

Twenty yards. Bob looked at Valkerie. She nodded. Squeezed his hand. He grinned.

Crouching low, he scooted the last few steps.

No blazing machine guns. No lightning bolts. No phasers set on stun. The rover looked deserted.

Bob pulled open the outer door and climbed inside. He reached down and pulled Valkerie in after him. They closed the door and hit the button to pressurize the airlock. When it reached atmospheric pressure, he unlatched his helmet.

Beside him, Valkerie switched off her oxygen and unlatched her helmet too. She shook her damp curls. She looked awful—and better than anything he'd seen in his entire life.

Valkerie pointed to the inner door of the airlock behind Bob.

He reached for the door.

It swung in before he touched it.

As he turned to look, Valkerie screamed.

Something hit Bob in the side of the head.

• • •

Thursday, April 30, 2015, 4:00 p.m., CST

Josh

Cathe stopped her car fifty yards short of the security gate. Up ahead, Nate was standing alone at the gate. "You sure about this, Josh?"

Josh watched the lonely figure standing outside the security hut. He had finally tracked down Nate on the phone an hour ago and warned him of his concerns. Nate hadn't sounded all that impressed with the case against EECOM. It was mostly hunches, circumstantial stuff. But Nate had promised to give him a fair hearing if he came in.

*Do I trust him or not?* Josh gripped the door handle. Either Nate was going to lead him straight to the cops, or he was going to play square. Josh didn't get to decide which. All he got to decide was whether to play the game.

"We can always bail," Cathe said. "All we have to do is turn around and drive away. He's on foot."

"You sure you never had lunch with Jake?"

Cathe nodded.

Josh opened the car door. Climbed out. Closed the door. Took a step toward Nate.

Another.

Another.

Nate came toward him and there was nobody with him. A big, fat sloppy grin covered his face, and all of a sudden he was walking real fast toward Josh and there was something wet lighting up his eyes.

Josh kept walking.

Nate opened his arms and bulldozed into him, wrapping him up like a grizzly. His voice shook when he spoke. "Welcome home, Josh. I called all the people you asked me to bring in. They're ready up in MCC."

"Bruce! Good to see you, dude!" Josh shook hands with Bruce Dickey, the Unix system administrator. The console room hummed with a dozen Unix servers. The air was as cold and dry as the computers liked it. Josh shivered and sat down next to Crystal Yamaguchi. A couple of FBI suits hovered just behind her, looking completely out of place on high four-legged stools.

Cathe came and sat on a stool behind Josh. Nate grabbed the chair next to him.

"I've already started monitoring, sir." Bruce turned to face Josh. "But it would help if I had a better idea what I was looking for."

"Some sort of command to get queued up on the Deep Space Network," Nate said.

"No, probably not." Josh leaned forward. "If you're EECOM and you get superuser status at 4:00 p.m., you don't go abusing it at 4:01. Might as well wave a red flag and shout, 'Arrest me!' She'll probably set things up as if she was doing a real security scan. Right, Cathe?"

"She has to," Cathe said. "That's her cover. She'll follow through. My guess is she'll set up a cron job—"

"Whoa! Buzz word alert!" Nate said. "What's a cron job?"

"A shell script you set up to be launched at a preselected time," Bruce said. "Actually, they're usually daemons, but I know a way—"

"It's a way you can launch a program automatically when you aren't at your computer." Cathe nodded to Josh. "That way, you can be somewhere else with a cast-iron alibi when the job runs. It can even be set up to erase itself after it's done."

"Which means we need to be looking on her computer." Bruce's fingers flew over the keyboard. "Whoa! She's got a hot little Sparky."

Cathe stood up and leaned over Bruce's shoulder. "Um, Bruce, could you do me a favor before you go fiddling on EECOM's box? Could you change the superuser password on Josh's computer? I'd just as soon not have her putting that cron script on his machine. Come to think of it, maybe you should change my account too."

"Josh is on a PC, so it's a moot point, but I can set something up on your machine." Bruce pecked furiously at the keys. "Just rlogging in to your box . . . Changing superuser password . . . now. And we have . . . no users other than background processes and me. I'm just going to fire up an event logger. This will show every command executed on your machine." He typed in something, and a separate window launched on the console. "Next stop, EECOM's honeypot." He opened another window. "Logging in right . . ."

"Wait," Cathe said. "She's probably got her machine wired pretty tight. The second you log in, she'll see what you're up to."

Bruce leaned back and looked at her. "I thought that was the idea. Take a swim in the honey and watch the watcher. See how she responds."

"Not as superuser." Cathe shook her head. "I know! I have an account on her machine for running sims. Why not log in as me? That should spark some activity. She's real fond of me, isn't she, Josh?" Cathe turned to Josh with an impish grin.

"She'll be on Cathe like ugly on a gorilla."

"Score one for the little lady in blond." Bruce rolled back away from the keyboard. "Be my guest."

Cathe typed in her username and then her password, then stepped back and sat down by Josh.

"All right, then. I'll just monitor the processes," Bruce said. "And how about I start by grepping through her files? Something big and ugly to put a little strain on the system."

Bruce began typing. "Okay, there it goes."

Silence for fifteen seconds.

A command appeared on the event logger.

"Score a point for EECOM," Bruce said. "She's trying to log in as superuser on Cathe's machine. But oops! The punt is blocked, ladies and gentleman. The old superuser switcharoonie got her. Two-zero Cathe!"

Josh leaned forward. "What's EECOM doing?"

"She's trying to get into my machine," Cathe said. "She's suspicious and wants to know what I'm doing on hers."

Another line appeared on the command logger.

"Uh-oh, EECOM tries an end run," Bruce said. "She's trying to log in as Cathe Willison herself. Here comes the password attempt and it is . . . denied! EECOM is tackled for a loss. Sorry, babe! Random guesses aren't going to cut it."

Josh stared at the eight characters on the screen: *worfRat5*. His fingers clenched the edge of his chair and all of a sudden he couldn't breathe.

Bruce was on his feet. "And EECOM picks herself up and makes another login attempt as Cathe Willison. This time with . . . a different password, and she is . . . into the end zone! Touchdown, EECOM!"

"She knows my password!" Cathe shrieked. "That's my password she just typed in. Nate, did you see that?"

"What's it mean?" Nate said.

"It means she can log in as me," Cathe said. "Right, Bruce? She could send e-mail masquerading as me. That's how she got Josh out of his office that day. And how she sent Jake an e-mail."

"That's real interesting." Nate turned to Agent Yamaguchi. "But don't we kind of need more evidence than that?"

Josh sighed deeply, wishing he didn't have to say it. "You need more evidence? How about this? That first password she typed in? Did you all see that?"

"It failed," Bruce said. "She messed up."

"You might say she messed up," Josh said, "because she typed in my password."

A collective gasp ran around the room.

"She knows my password, Nate," Josh said. "She could have logged in to my computer and hacked the Russian machine. Nobody else knows my password except the Hampster, and his alibi is pretty tight."

Yamaguchi stood up. "Gentlemen. I think I've seen enough."

She walked to the door with the FBI suits at her heels. "It's time to go ask this EECOM woman a few questions."

# CHAPTER 34

Thursday, April 30, 2015, 12:00 p.m., Mars Local Time

Valkerie

A twisted figure crouched in the darkness. Heavy breathing. A low, gurgling growl.

"It's okay. We won't hurt you." Valkerie crouched slowly and reached out a hand to where Bob lay moaning on the floor of the rover.

Blood-red eyes glowed dully in a shaft of light. Rounded, heaving shoulders. A wild black beard. The man stepped forward, holding a thin metal bar in front of him like a two-handed ax. Angry red blisters covered his face. Blood and filth stained his tattered clothing.

"Kennedy?" Valkerie shrank back in horror.

"Leave me alone . . . kill you all!" he cried out in a rasping voice.

The bar flashed through the darkness.

"No!" Valkerie dove to cover Bob's face. Her arm exploded in white-hot pain.

*Whack. Whack.* Her backpack thudded. Bits of plastic skittered across the floor.

"No! Kennedy, he's—"

"Get off him. He's a traitor." A kick to the shoulder. Another.

"Kennedy, please . . ." Valkerie wrapped her arms around Bob and held on tight.

A boot pressed itself into her face. Strong arms. Grasping hands. Her arm was torn free. A knee wedged between her shoulder and Bob's neck. Foul-smelling breath hacked and gurgled around her. His lungs sounded like a rumbling ocean of phlegm.

"Bob never did anything to you. He's your friend."

"Never did anything?"

Valkerie's head was snapped back by two fists full of hair. A pus-smeared face pressed itself close. Bleeding and blistered skin. She caught her breath. His eyes—whites the color of blood. Unfocused pupils, black and impossibly large, darted back and forth.

"Never did anything? Look at me!" Kennedy shook her by the hair. "Look at me!"

Valkerie's stomach turned. The sickly sweet odor of infection clung to Kennedy like a death shroud. Her strength drained out of her, leaving her limp and trembling. "Kennedy, you're sick. I can—"

"Bob did this! Hear me?" Kennedy's shout dissolved into a gurgling cough. "Tried to kill me. Burn me alive!"

Her head jerked backward, and the room spun around her. Something slammed into the side of her face with a sickening thunk.

She heard the sound of flesh and bone meeting flesh and bone. *Smack. Smack.* The sound echoed in her ears, punctuated with grunts and muffled groans.

Valkerie crawled unsteadily to her feet.

Kennedy crouched over Bob, raining a shower of blows on his unprotected face.

"No!" She charged forward, driving her shoulder into Kennedy's chest. He toppled over backward and she landed on top of him, fighting to get her hands around his throat. She could feel him shaking beneath her.

His eyes opened wide with . . . fear.

Valkerie drew back in surprise.

She took a long, deep breath, forcing her clenched fists to open. Swallowing her revulsion, she brushed the hair out of his eyes with a trembling hand. "It's okay, Kennedy. You're sick. We'll take care of you. We won't let anybody hurt you." She smoothed back his hair, wondering at the tears that streamed from his eyes.

Kennedy's body began to shake as silent sobs wracked his body. Valkerie got off him and moved to his side. "It's okay. We're your friends. We won't let anything happen to you." Cradling his head in her arms, she held Kennedy close. "It's all right. Nothing's going to hurt you." She repeated the words over and over as Kennedy's sobs slowly faded with the dying light.

After what seemed hours, a gentle moan sounded behind her.

"Bob, are you okay?" Valkerie whispered in the same lilting tones she was using to comfort Kennedy. "It's Kennedy. He's alive."

Another moan. "Now I know what a baseball feels like. Did he hit a homer?"

"Shhhh . . ." Valkerie turned to see Bob picking himself off of the floor. "He didn't know what he was doing. He's sick. He thinks you're trying to kill him."

Bob knelt beside Valkerie. An angry welt stood out on his temple. His cheeks and eyes seemed a little puffy, but she could tell he'd be fine. Which was a lot more than she could say for Kennedy.

"Is he okay?" Bob mouthed the words.

Valkerie shrugged and shook her head slowly.

"Hang on, Hampster," Bob said. "We'll get you home and get some medicine in you. You'll be just fine."

Kennedy's body suddenly went rigid and his eyes opened wide.

"It's okay, Kennedy. We won't let anything hurt you," Valkerie soothed.

Kennedy jerked to a sitting position, watching Bob with wide, fearful eyes.

Bob backed slowly away, with palms held outward and fingers spread wide.

"He thinks you burned down the Ares 10," Valkerie whispered.

"Kennedy, that's ridiculous. Why would I do a thing like that?"

"Kennedy, you've got to believe him." Valkerie put her hands on Kennedy's shoulders to hold him back. "Bob was in the Ares 7 with me and Lex. He couldn't have started the fire."

"But I heard him outside . . ." Kennedy looked back and forth between Valkerie and Bob, his face a mask of confusion.

"You've got to trust us." Valkerie loosened her grip on Kennedy's shoulders. "If we had wanted to hurt you, we would have done it already."

Kennedy's eyes narrowed to points. "Maybe he's afraid to do it in person. That's why he sent the rover. Maybe he doesn't want to do it in front of you."

"Maybe I don't want to do it at all." Bob's voice was soothing. "Why would I? You're my friend."

"Maybe—" Kennedy cleared his throat and doubled over coughing.

Valkerie put a comforting arm around him and eased him to the floor. After several minutes, he looked up warily at Bob.

"One thing I don't understand is how you were able to control the rover," Bob spoke in low tones.

Kennedy turned to Valkerie. He seemed disoriented. Confused.

"How did you escape the Ares 10?" she asked.

"Hid in the airlock till it got too hot. Then I ran outside and . . . there it was. Just sitting there." Kennedy's head drooped onto his chest.

"There *what* was?" Bob asked.

"The rover," Kennedy whispered. "Thought you were in it."

Bob glanced at Valkerie with raised eyebrows. "And it was you who banged up the MAV? You're the one who let all the fuel leak out?"

"No leak. Just needed fuel. Fuel and supplies."

"So it was you I heard outside," Valkerie said. "It was you all along."

Kennedy started to rise. "I had to have fuel and oxygen. You couldn't expect me to live without that. And water." Kennedy cringed and shrank back. "Sorry about . . . the greenhouse. Didn't mean to, but I was so thirsty. I had to have water."

"It's okay, Kennedy." Valkerie eased him back to the floor. "Nobody's blaming you. We're glad you survived. We're just curious, that's all. You've helped us solve a big mystery."

"Oh no!" Bob gasped.

"What's wrong?"

"Lex! She's probably freaking out right now." Bob climbed forward to the radio controls.

Kennedy went suddenly tense and looked frantically around the rover with wide, darting eyes.

"It's okay, Kennedy. He's just calling Lex to let her know we're okay. Everything's going to be just fine."

Kennedy relaxed back into her arms.

"We'll all drive home and get you some medicine that will help you feel better—just as soon as we pick up a few bags of ice."

## Thursday, April 30, 2015, 4:45 p.m., CST

### Nate

Nate followed Crystal down the hallway to EECOM's office. EECOM! Losing her would be as bad as losing Josh. Maybe worse, because Josh was already lost. Once he stood trial for that bomb shenanigan, he was never going to work for NASA again.

And now EECOM too. A security guy and the Fibbies followed along behind Nate. After them, the rest of the troupe. Nate slowed as he approached EECOM's door. Crystal turned with a finger on her lips. No sense giving EECOM any advance warning.

The security guy stepped silently to the door, consulted a little book, and punched in the combination, 3-5-3-5-3. He twisted the lock, pushed the door inward, and stepped back. The two Fibbies pushed through. "Freeze! FBI!"

EECOM squealed.

Nate sighed. From here on, he was running without a playbook. He followed Crystal through the door.

EECOM stood backed up against the wall, her eyes wide, her hands shaking. "Mr. Harrington! What's . . . going on?" Her eyes flicked down to a slip of paper on her desk. One of the FBI boys scooted around the desk to peer at the paper. "Two passwords. The ones we saw upstairs."

Josh and Cathe and Bruce peered into the office, then stepped back, looking embarrassed, like they had walked in on EECOM naked.

"Her!" EECOM pointed at Cathe. "I . . . I heard her talking to her boyfriend this morning. That's how I got the passwords."

Josh eyed her coldly. "Me? I never told her my password."

"Not you! Jake Hunter!" she snapped, her eyes wide, furious. "Call him, Mr. Harrington! Call him right now and ask him! He'll tell you!"

Nate pulled out his phone and called Jake.

Two rings. "Hello, this is Jake."

"Harrington here." Nate took a deep breath. "Jake, I need to ask you about a conversation you had with Cathe Willison today."

"Cathe Willison? Haven't even seen her. I'm off duty. Hey, what's the deal with her, anyway? She told me on Tuesday she was resigning. Then I heard this morning that she's not."

"You didn't call her and she didn't call you?"

"Right, that's what I said. Is there some problem?"

"You'd have to ask her." Nate hung up and shook his head. "Jake never talked to Cathe today. Not in person. Not by phone."

"He's lying!" EECOM said. "You can't trust him. He's been cheating on his wife for years!"

Yamaguchi stepped in. "Give her Miranda and take her out. Quietly, if you can."

The two FBI men each took an arm and guided EECOM toward the door. As she went by Nate, she hissed, "That little bimbo doesn't love Josh! She—"

"Quietly, ma'am, if you would," said one of the Fibbies. "It's just easier that way." They all three kept walking out the door and down the hall. "You have the right to remain silent. Anything you say can be used against you in a court of law. You have the right to have an attorney present . . ."

Crystal pulled on some latex gloves, stepped to EECOM's desk, and started pulling out drawers. "You three." She motioned to Josh, Cathe, and Bruce. "Come in and shut the door. Tell me what I should be looking for."

Josh pulled on the door until it clicked and looked at Cathe. She shrugged.

"Actually, ma'am." Bruce shuffled forward, clasping his hands to his chest. "If I were going to hack Goldstone and I were in a big hurry, I'd put it on a flash drive."

"Put what on a flash drive?"

"The script to do the hack. A flash drive is easy to hide, and it wouldn't be accessible from the network."

Crystal opened the file cabinet and started riffling through it. Nate leaned in to look over her shoulder. Dozens of perfect files waved their tiny hands. Crystal went through each file, front to back. "Nothing here." She shut the drawer and moved on to the next one.

She finally finished the last drawer and stood up slowly. "She might have destroyed it." Crystal turned to search the trash can.

"Not if she was planning on using it again." Nate went to the desk and opened each drawer. The desk was one of those metal ones, three drawers on the right, one on the left with a file drawer underneath. Every paper clip was in place. Nate pulled open the middle drawer. A few pens. A ruler. Three Post-it pads. He slid it shut.

"Pull it back open," Crystal said. "All the way."

Nate moved the chair back and eased the drawer all the way out. In the far-right corner, something glinted. A DVD jewel case.

"Don't touch it," Crystal said.

Nate reached in with his comb and guided the case out. Crystal carefully flipped it open. Inside was a DVD marked "Halloween, 2012."

Nate sat down in front of EECOM's computer. "If this is what I think it is . . ."

"I can't believe she'd keep it around," Josh said.

"Give me some room." Yamaguchi popped the DVD out of the jewel case. A CD lay underneath it. She tapped open the drive and inserted the DVD.

A picture came on the screen. A bunch of kids in costume at a party. Nate ran it fast-forward for a few minutes. The screen went dark. Then it switched to Josh sitting at his desk without a shirt on. His body obscured the computer on his desk.

"I can see why she kept it." Cathe whistled. "I wouldn't mind a copy of that myself."

On the screen, Josh reached across his desk to pick up his phone. His computer came into view.

"That's how she got my password." Josh crowded forward to stand behind Bruce.

Crystal popped out the DVD and put in the CD. "Okay, now what, Mr. Dickey?"

Bruce grabbed the mouse and did something Nate didn't quite follow. An icon appeared. Bruce double-clicked on it. A window popped up. Bruce did some navigation and another window appeared with a lot of unreadable gobbledygook. Bruce whistled. "Nice little Perl script here. It's complicated."

"Would it get her into the Goldstone computer?" Nate asked.

Bruce shrugged. "I'd have to work through her code, but it shouldn't be that hard. Meticulous as all get-out. Beautiful comments. You see that?"

Nate didn't see it, but he got the point. Meticulous. Yeah, that was EECOM.

"I'll need to log these as evidence," Crystal said. "And once again, no fingerprints on it."

Bruce popped open the DVD drive. "Help yourself, ma'am." He stood up and turned to Nate. "Mystery solved, Mr. Harrington?"

Nate felt acid in his gut. "Yeah," he said. It wasn't a happy ending, but it was an ending. "Mystery solved."

# CHAPTER 35

Thursday, April 30, 2015, 1:45 p.m., Mars Local Time

Bob

Bob leaned back in the hanging chair, waiting. He checked his watch. Houston should have responded by now. Lex had radioed back with the good news forty-two minutes ago, and he couldn't wait to hear their reaction.

"Ares 7, this better not be a joke!" Josh's voice was almost drowned out by the background noise of the FCR.

Cheers, shouts, thunderous applause. Josh was finally back and it sounded like he was transmitting from the monkey cage at the zoo. "Let me get this straight. You've got food, water, the rover, *and* Kennedy is alive?"

"And ice . . . ask them about the ice." Nate's shouts were barely audible above the roar.

"Nate wants to know if you've had a chance to analyze the ice." Josh's voice. A shout sounded in the background and the din started to subside. "And make sure you observe sterile protocol. The last thing we need is to reopen the back-contamination can of worms."

Bob glanced at Valkerie. She looked miserable. Raising his eyebrows in silent question, he stood up and walked to the microphone. Valkerie nodded grimly and crossed the room to join him.

Josh continued. “I’m afraid our news isn’t so good.” A long pause. “Several weeks ago, a person here in Houston attempted to post a command sequence onto the ERV’s command queue. This sequence would have initiated a de-orbit burn.”

Bob clutched at Valkerie’s hand. *What?* Why hadn’t the crew been informed of that?

“We caught the attempt before it was executed,” Josh said. “For the last few weeks, we’ve been trying feverishly to track down the culprit. The reason you haven’t heard from me lately is that I was the prime suspect—for reasons you can easily guess. I am thrilled to be able to report to you that we have found the real perpetrator. I’m very sorry to say this, but it was someone we all knew and trusted implicitly—EECOM. We arrested her just about an hour ago. I can give you more details later, but I have a whole control room full of engineers clamoring for a more detailed report of your little adventure. This is Houston, standing by.”

Bob sank to the floor. He couldn’t believe it. EECOM had tried to strand them? She was his friend. He’d just been talking to her a few days ago about the terrible odor in the water supply.

Valkerie knelt beside him, holding on to his arm, her breath coming in short little jags.

Bob was sweating like a pig. He turned to Lex, who was sitting in the other hanging chair.

“That’s . . . unbelievable.” Lex shook her head. “EECOM! If we can’t trust her, who’s left?”

“Maybe Kennedy wasn’t so crazy after all.” Valkerie glanced in the direction of the crew quarters where Kennedy was sleeping under sedation. “Maybe *she* burned down the Hab.”

Bob shrugged. "I don't see how. Didn't they say they checked the command logs?"

Valkerie nodded and took a deep breath. Bob could tell she wasn't thinking about the command logs.

"We're going to have to tell them." Bob blinked his eyes to clear his head. "About the Mars bacteria. It's the right thing to do. They have to know what to prepare for."

"I know." Valkerie looked at the floor. "I just wish we had told them already. We should have told them weeks ago. But if we had . . . You remember what they were thinking about doing."

"Now that we have enough food . . ." Lex let the suggestion hang.

Bob's throat and mouth felt suddenly dry. "I feel sick."

"I do too," Valkerie said.

"No, you don't understand." Bob put a hand to his burning forehead. "I feel sick. *Really* sick."

## Friday, May 1, 2015, 11:15 a.m., Mars Local Time

### Bob

Bob checked his watch. "Five minutes till your report to Houston." He drummed his fingers on his kneecaps.

"Would you relax?" Lex came back from the galley with another tube of pudding. She hadn't stopped eating since they'd returned in the rover. "Come on. Cheer up! You two look like you're getting ready for your own funerals."

"Mmphhh!" A noise from down the hall. Kennedy's room.

"Not again." Lex didn't hide her disgust. "I'll see what the big baby wants this time." She turned and disappeared into the corridor.

Bob laughed. "Looks like Lex is getting back to normal."

"Looks like."

Bob was struck by the hollowness in Valkerie's voice. She sounded so tired, so distant. He twisted around in his hanging chair to face her. "Don't worry. They'll let us come home. Once you tell them how well I'm responding to the ceftriaxone, they won't give it a second thought."

Valkerie reached across the gap that separated them and felt his forehead for what must have been the twentieth time that morning. "I still can't believe how fast it brought your fever down."

"I've got a good doctor." Bob tipped his head back so that her hand slid down over his eyes.

"We caught it early." Tingling fingertips traced down the side of his face, sending an avalanche of chills down his spine. When he opened his eyes she was staring into space.

"We'll be fine. Just tell them about the antibiotics."

Valkerie's face clouded. "That's not what I'm worried about. Okay, maybe a little. I admit I feel terrible about not telling the truth earlier, but have you thought about the effect our announcement is going to have on people?"

Bob grinned. Life on Mars. Not some petrified Mars snot from a billion years ago. Living cells right now—on a planet supposedly dead. It was the biggest discovery of the twenty-first century. The consequences were staggering. Valkerie would get the Nobel Prize.

"Bob, this is serious. Some people are going to be really hurt by this. Remember those protesters back at JSC?" Her eyes gleamed. "They've been telling people for years that there can't be life on Mars. They've bet their faith on it."

"What's the big deal?" Bob shrugged. "They weren't bothered when you found thermophilic bacteria in volcanoes and hot springs. They don't seem to mind desiccation-resistant bugs in Antarctic ice."

"But this is Mars. It's a whole different planet—in case you haven't noticed."

"So?"

"So, I don't want to be monkey-trialed. Ostracized. I don't want to be—"

"Valkerie, nobody's going to ostracize you. Most people get it. They'll say hallelujah, look what God created on Mars. They know life is robust. Just like faith. It's hardy. It's diverse. It flourishes in strange places. That's its nature. People know that. And you're a role model for that kind of attitude. People know where you stand. They know you're not out to destroy anyone's faith. You're not going to hurt anyone. These are one-celled bacteria you've found, not the missing link. Does the Bible say there's no life on Mars?"

Valkerie shook her head.

"Just like it doesn't say Earth is flat or pi is exactly 3," Bob said. "Some people see what they want to see in the Bible, even if it's a stretch, even if it's not actually there, and they'll argue themselves silly. They'll paint themselves down the hallway and through the kitchen and right into a corner. But then when the facts turn out otherwise, hey—most people go with the facts and readjust their interpretations. Truth is robust too."

He patted Valkerie's hand. "You're not going to destroy anybody's faith. People trust you to tell the truth."

Valkerie looked down at the floor. "Like I told Houston the instant we found the bug?"

"Like you're going to tell them right now."

"Time to rock and roll." Lex swept into the room and grabbed the mike off the transmitter. "Houston, this is CDR from the Ares 7. Stand by for a very important announcement." Lex held the mike out to Valkerie.

Valkerie took the mike and swallowed hard. "Houston, this is Valkerie Jansen reporting from the Ares 7. Several weeks ago, we discovered evidence for a halobacteria that once lived here on Mars. Shortly after that discovery, we found a piece of dried clay pressed into one of the joints of my EVA suit. That clay housed an extraordinary guest . . ."

Bob listened to Valkerie's broadcast with a huge grin splitting his cheeks. She was perfect, of course. Just the facts. Mars harbored at least one species of real, living bacteria. It appeared to be genetically related to life on Earth. The bacteria was close enough to Earth's Tree of Life to cause infections in humans—a major scientific surprise that strongly suggested a common origin. The transmission vector for the disease appeared to be in water droplets—probably inhaled by the crew members when they sprayed off their suits. Just like Legionnaires' disease.

Bob's mind drifted as Valkerie started to get more technical. It wouldn't be long now. He slipped out of his chair and began pacing the floor. His palms were already sweaty and his throat was dry. If Josh didn't follow through on the instructions, Bob was going to make a red-giant-sized fool of himself.

" . . . should give us many valuable clues into the history of life in our solar system. Standing by for your response. Over."

Bob took the microphone from Valkerie and hit the Transmit button. "Just a second. Josh, this is Bob. Could you transfer me to that private line now?"

Valkerie and Lex exchanged questioning glances.

"Uh . . . this is kind of private," Bob nodded to Lex. "Mind waiting downstairs for a few minutes?"

A broad smile split Lex's face. "No problem, Sir Bob de Gallante."

"What?" Valkerie fixed a puzzled look on Bob.

"Come on, Val." Lex dragged her to the stairwell. "This could take a while. Sir Bob hasn't quite figured out what century we're in."

Bob waited until the hatch shut behind them, then keyed the microphone. Josh had had plenty of time to set up the transfer. A lot was riding on this. He hoped he hadn't made a mistake. "Hello, Mr. Jansen. This is Bob Kaganovski. I know we haven't really met yet, but I've heard a lot about you." *I sound like an idiot. Get to the point.* "Anyway, uh, Valkerie and I have been spending a lot of time together and we're . . ."

Bob felt panic rising in his throat.

"Uh . . . we're in . . . love, and . . . and I'd like to ask your permission for your daughter's hand in marriage."

Bob took a deep breath and let it out slowly. "I know how much you're wanting to walk Valkerie down the aisle . . . I mean, I sure would if I had a daughter. But . . . well, I . . . we are hoping to, if you agree, get married here on Mars. It's such a long flight back to Earth and, well . . . and I guess that's all. I hope you'll say yes, but if you don't, I'll respect your wishes."

Bob set the microphone down on the transmitter and sank back into a chair. The radio transit time was almost twenty minutes. Each way. Which meant he'd be sweating bricks for the next forty minutes. And either he or Mr. Jansen was going to be one very disappointed puppy.

Saturday, May 2, 2015, 12:00 p.m., Mars Local Time

Valkerie

"Kennedy?" Valkerie knocked on the open door to Kennedy's room. "Time for your medicine."

A raspy wheeze issued from the room. The sound of a dragon asleep in his lair.

Valkerie backed away from the door. She could come back later. Maybe when Lex was awake.

The breathing stopped. "Valkerie, is that you?"

Great, he'd heard her. She turned a desperate glance toward Lex's door.

"Valkerie?" The brittle tone in Kennedy's voice brought her up short. He sounded frightened.

"It's okay, Kennedy. It's just me."

No response.

"Are you okay?" Valkerie took a deep breath and moved cautiously to his door. "I just came to give you some medicine. There's nothing to be afraid of." She poked her head in the room and found Kennedy lying in bed, clasping his covers to his chin.

"Afraid?" A mask of easy confidence dropped onto his face. He smoothed the blankets down on his bed. "Who said anything about being afraid?"

"Kennedy, the time for pretending is over. We know all about your . . . problem." Valkerie handed him a tablet and a glass of water. "You have a delusional disorder, don't you? Paranoid subtype?"

Kennedy eyed her suspiciously.

"Kennedy, you can trust us. We aren't going to hurt you."

"Maybe *you* won't, but Lex—"

"Lex won't either," Valkerie said. "Think about all we've been through together. Remember who took care of you while you were sick? Remember who repaired the Hab? Who took care of you when you were in a coma? Don't you think if we were going to hurt you, we would have done it by now?"

"But . . ." Kennedy's eyes clamped shut. His face contorted in an agony of conflicting emotions.

"Kennedy, we aren't going to hurt you." Valkerie placed a hesitant hand on his shoulder. "We . . . love you."

Kennedy's shoulders started jerking up and down. "I never meant to . . ."

"It's okay. Let it out. You can trust us."

Silent tears ran down his face. "It's just that . . . that . . . everything's so mixed up. I don't know what to believe anymore."

"Yes, you do. Just remember your condition."

"But . . ." He buried his face in his hands.

"Kennedy, you have a delusional disorder. You can live with that. Knowing it and accepting it is half the battle."

"But the noises . . . the fire . . ." Kennedy looked up at her with wild, beseeching eyes. "If Bob and Lex didn't attack me in the Ares 10, who did?"

Valkerie hesitated. Should she tell him? Or would it only make things worse to have his fears confirmed? No, she had to tell him the truth. Like she'd finally done with Houston. "Kennedy, we heard from Houston yesterday. Someone on the ground, the Gold Team EECOM, tried to de-orbit the ERV, but they caught her before she succeeded. Apparently she was worried about us bringing back the disease. We think she used the rover to attack you in the Ares 10."

A broad smile lit Kennedy's tearstained face. "I knew I wasn't crazy."

"Maybe not." Valkerie couldn't help laughing. "Bob and I think EECOM figured out how to control our robots without using the DSN—either that or there's an awfully big Martian out there with six chips on his shoulders. Anyway, I checked the height of the CamBot against the bruises on my legs. It was a perfect match. EECOM was probably just trying to uncover what we were hiding from them. Anyway, that explains the broken Petri dish and . . . lots of things. We think she drove the MuleBot over to the MAV during the dust storm and took some whacks at it. A strut got bent on it, and we saw some scratches on the MAV. And she must have been the one who stole the rover."

Kennedy wiped his eyes with a blanket. "I knew it. I could feel it in my gut."

"This time your gut was right." Valkerie looked him in the eye. "Next time it might not be. Just promise me one thing. Next time you start worrying, check it out with one of us first. You *have* to go with the facts. And listen to people who care about you. Because your gut is the one thing you can't trust."

"I know, I know. I've read the books." Kennedy sighed. "But I couldn't tell anybody before, don't you see? If the flight docs found out about it, I'd have been off the mission. Call me paranoid, but they really were out to get me."

"Out to protect you. Out to protect all of us." Valkerie shook her head. "If you really thought they were after you, why'd you stay in the astronaut corps? Why not go into a safer profession?"

"I'm not afraid of danger. I just don't trust people. I was the best fighter jock in my wing. The other jocks thought I was crazy. I flew stunts even the instructors wouldn't try. But I learned to watch my back, that's all. Checked up on the mechanics' sloppy work. Never flew a plane without having the design checked and rechecked by other engineers. You'd be amazed what engineering students can find if you give them a spec and tell them there's a mistake hidden in it."

Valkerie nodded. The leak of the Ares 10 schematics Bob and Josh had been so worried about. This explained a lot. Kennedy didn't trust NASA engineers, so he found some young-and-hungries to check their work.

"That's why I'm such a good mechanic." Kennedy smiled. "Self-taught, mostly."

"Good mechanic?" Bob poked his head into the room. "You drive a Honda. What kind of mechanic drives a Honda?"

"Aren't you supposed to be resting?" Valkerie scolded. "Now shoo!"

"I'm feeling fine." Bob stepped into the room and let Valkerie feel his forehead. "See? No fever." He put an arm around her shoulders and kissed her gently on the top of the head.

Out of the corner of her eye, she noticed Kennedy's eyes narrowing. "Um . . . Kennedy." Valkerie pulled Bob around to face Kennedy. "Bob and I have a big favor to ask."

Kennedy went suddenly tense. He studied Bob through tiny slits.

"Oh yeah. That's right." Bob looked at the ground and shuffled his feet. "Uh . . . Valkerie and I are getting married.

And I want you to be the best man. Here on Mars, that is. And Valkerie wants you to give the bride away."

"I'd be—" Kennedy's grin melted into a frown.

"It's okay." Valkerie moved to the side of his bed. "Lex will be the matron of honor, and Josh will be the best man on Earth. You'll do fine."

"Valkerie . . . know how you said to tell you if I ever got worried?" Kennedy studied his bleeding fingernails. "Well, I'm worried now."

"Why?" Valkerie knelt beside him and put a hand on his arm.

"As best man it's my responsibility to throw the bachelor party, and . . . how am I supposed to do that without chips and beer?"

### Wednesday, May 6, 2015, 1:00 p.m., CST

### Nate

"Thanks for the good word, Crystal. Talk to you later. Josh and I are going flying this afternoon in a *real* plane." Nate put his phone away and grinned at Josh. "That'll put the fear of God in her. She hates ultralights."

"What's going on with Margaret?"

"Who?"

"EECOM." Josh smiled.

"The word is that, thanks to your outstanding help in bringing in EECOM, there isn't a lot of pressure from the justice system to nail your sorry hide to the wall. You *are* gonna face charges, but you're looking at a couple years in minimum security, worst case. As for EECOM, she denies everything—even the crush on you. Insists she never saw that DVD or CD, says she's innocent, blah, blah, blah. Any more righteousness and they'd elect her president. She even refuses to get a lawyer. But Crystal's team got a warrant and opened her apartment up. Place is immaculate, and she's got about three full scrapbooks with guess who's picture on every page."

Josh's face turned red. "I had no idea she was so . . ."

"You did too, and you enjoyed it." Nate shook his head. "You're good at being a celebrity, Josh. Nothing to be ashamed of. You'll be an old coot like me soon enough."

"You're not a coot."

"What am I?"

"A . . . codger. A curmudgeon." Josh gave him a fifty-carat smile. "Cathe says you're nothing but a big old teddy bear."

"You serious about her?"

Josh shrugged. "I like her. A lot. After my legal thing gets settled, if she's still around, we'll see what happens."

"Don't be in any rush to give her a ring," Nate said. "George Carlin used to say that the shortest sentence in the English language is 'I am.' Whereas the longest sentence is 'I do.'"

Josh snorted. "The voice of experience?"

Nate looked out the window of the JSC cafeteria. He'd been married for fifteen years once, but it turned out his real love was space. His wife gave him a choice one day, and it was no choice at all. Which wasn't the answer she was expecting, but life was full of surprises, wasn't it?

"Hey. Sorry."

"Skip it." Nate drained his bottle of Snapple. "Speaking of the chains that bind, I hear you're going to be an accomplice for Bob and Valkerie when they commit matrimony."

"I don't deserve it." Josh picked up the little paper tube that his straw had come in and knotted it around his forefinger.

"Don't give me that," Nate said. "You made a mistake. I made a bunch. So did they. Every one of us meant well, and it all worked out in the wash. We squeaked through, and we're gonna finish this mission. You know what they say. All's well that ends without a pox on your house."

Josh just looked at him. "I bet you have to work pretty hard to mix up your Shakespeare that bad."

"Shakespeare?" Nate shook his head. "Never read him. I tried once, but the guy used clichés like they were going out of business."

Josh stood up. "Let's go check in on the kids in the FCR and then get over to this rinky-dink little airport of yours."

Nate grabbed his tray and headed for the trash can. "Who's holding the fort today?"

"Cathe's on the EECOM console and Jake Hunter's Flight Director for the afternoon. The rest is the usual cast of suspects."

Outside, Nate blinked against the May sun. It had been an awful spring. Worse than awful. But now he had his crew back together. Lex, firmly in command. Kennedy, back from the dead and behaving himself about as well as most dead people. Bob and Valkerie doing the matrimony thing this coming Saturday—and the TV rights for that were gonna pay a lot of bills. The crew now had enough food to last them for weeks, and their fuel supplies were getting replenished.

The Martian bacteria was a big surprise—a real sock in the gut. Nate ought to be mad at Josh and the crew for lying about that Antarctica archaebacteria for a month, but what was he supposed to do? Take them to court for lying? Oh right. Like he'd never told a fib himself. Anyway, according to Valkerie, they had a handle on it. Antibiotics nailed it pretty quick. As long as Valkerie was being honest—and she sounded truthful—it shouldn't be a big problem.

So despite the Mars-bug thing, NASA had decided to bring the crew home. They had an obligation to their astronauts, and they were going to honor that. He was going to announce it to everyone Friday morning at the All-Hands Meeting in the FCR.

And best of all, Josh was off the hook over the de-orbit burn with the ERV. Free and clear. Just like Nate had known all along.

So the two of them were going flying this afternoon. They had earned a break, and they were gonna take it, because you never knew when the next storm was gonna hit.

It was a great day to be alive.

# CHAPTER 36

Saturday, May 9, 2015, 12:30 a.m., Mars Local Time

Valkerie

Valkerie flung herself onto the lab stool and spun around in a tight circle. She was getting married tomorrow—no, today. Was it really going to happen? How could she be so impossibly happy? It was all so perfect—like an early morning dream. She swallowed back an uneasy feeling—like the dream would grow shimmery and insubstantial and then dissolve into the ragged shadow world of hollow reality. She could already feel the longing, the sense of deep loss as the phantoms faded into another day of hard work. Unreasonable expectations. Senseless tasks. And no end in sight.

But this wasn't a dream. Valkerie slid a pallet of soil out from under a grow lamp. Only eleven more hours and she'd be Mrs. Valkerie Kaganovski. "Valkerie Kaganovski." She couldn't help laughing as she said the name aloud. It was the worst name she'd ever heard. Maybe she should go back to being just Valerie—or maybe even Val. Val Kaganovski? Great. It sounded like a medical procedure—for removing plaque from collapsed arteries.

Valkerie grabbed a water bottle and squeezed a few drops on a scrawny pansy—the only plant from that particular pallet that had managed to survive the harsh Martian soil. A small, curling bud peeked its head above the sickly green foliage.

"It's okay. Don't be shy. Come out and say hi to Mrs. K." Valkerie wrinkled her nose and stroked the tiny bud. If only it would open for the wedding. She already had two blossoms from the pansy she had transplanted, but three would make the bouquet so much more . . . well, bouquet-like.

"Come on. You've worked so hard to get this far. I'm sure you'll be the most beautiful of them all."

A burst of laughter floated down the stairwell.

"Don't listen to them. They just don't understand you." Valkerie slipped off the stool and started toward the stairs, but stopped at the door of the lab.

*No. Let him enjoy himself.* Splitting a can of grape Nehi with Lex and Kennedy wasn't much of a bachelor party. But when you were two hundred million miles away from Earth, you had to find normalcy wherever you could. And brides did not belong at bachelor parties, just like guests did not belong on honeymoons—even on Mars.

Valkerie tiptoed through the corridor to the airlock and spun open the inner hatch. Crossing through the airlock chamber and ducking through the outer hatch, she stepped into the rover. "Just Married" and "HoneyMars Bound" had been clumsily painted on the insides of the rover's windows with bright white paint—her mother's paint. Lex had used more than Valkerie expected, but she had a feeling her mother would have approved.

She stepped farther inside and wrinkled her nose. The rover reeked of cleaner fumes and air freshener. Bob had spent the last three nights cleaning it out. After a month of Kennedy treating it like a latrine, Valkerie had been hesitant about using it for a honeymoon trip, but Bob had insisted on privacy and cleaned the rover so thoroughly that every surface sparkled—even the plastic surfaces that were supposed to have a stippled grain.

Valkerie stepped carefully around the makeshift bed that Bob had set up on the floor. Two NASA mattresses wide and two mattresses high, the pallet was only half the size of a normal bed, but after a year and a half of sleeping on a six-by-two-foot cot, it looked huge. She crouched uneasily by the bed and reached out a hand to touch the clean white blanket that covered it. Lex's blanket, fresh from the bag. She'd been saving it for months. It was a wonderfully self-sacrificing wedding present, but somehow it made her uneasy. Nervous.

Valkerie didn't know the first thing about being married. They hadn't been to marriage counseling, nor had they read any books. They hadn't even dated. Not really. At least no dates that didn't end in disaster. What was she doing? Had she really thought things through?

The pine-fresh air pressed in on Valkerie from all sides. She felt sick, dizzy. Stumbling back through the airlock, she shut the hatch behind her and spun it tight. How well did she really know Bob? He certainly couldn't know her—not the real her. All he knew was the work Valkerie. The emergency-mode Valkerie working under life-and-death pressure. First it had been an accelerated ASCAN training program. Then a crisis-filled trip to Mars. Then the race to find life on a hostile planet. None of that was normal life. She couldn't even picture Bob in a normal situation. What would he do if he didn't have a life-critical subsystem to fix? What would they talk about? Would they even know how to talk?

Sure, he was attracted to her now—when she was the only available female within a hundred million miles, but what would it be like back on Earth when he was a hero? When thousands of beautiful women were throwing themselves at him? If not in real life, at least on television commercials. How was she supposed to compete with that?

Valkerie wandered over to the base of the stairs and poked her head through the hatch.

The radio blared out the raucous cheers of the flight control team in Houston. Lex's laughter tinkled down the stairs like a bamboo wind chime.

Lex had always been one of the guys. She was close to Bob in a way Valkerie would never be. What if Lex hadn't turned out to be married? Would Bob have preferred Lex? There was no way to be sure. How could she be sure about anything? It was all in the future, happening to people who didn't even exist yet.

Valkerie climbed up two steps and stopped. The most important decision of her life, and she didn't have any data to base it on. Sure, she had some data points that she could extrapolate from—feelings, instinct, shared experience. But nothing solid. Why was it that the most important decisions in life had to be based on faith? What was it about relationships in particular that made trust so critical?

Footsteps upstairs. Parting words.

Valkerie looked at her watch. Almost 1:00 a.m. The party was finally breaking up. She turned quietly and crept back to the lab, picking her way through the zucchini plants that crisscrossed the hallway. She'd have to wait until Bob and the others were asleep. Technically it was her wedding day. And even though they were all living in a tuna can, she was not going to let Bob see her before the ceremony. It was bad enough that she was going to have to wear a pink dress . . .

*Skeeeeerunch!*

The deck lurched beneath Valkerie's feet with the piercing shriek of tearing metal.

Valkerie tumbled to the floor and covered her face with her arms.

Pallets of dirt rained down on her. Footsteps sounded upstairs, shouting voices.

Valkerie tried to climb to her feet.

The Hab shook with a loud crash. The curved exterior wall of the Hab bent inward with the scream of buckling metal.

Valkerie hit the floor hard and rolled under the lab bench.

A metal shelving unit crashed down next to her.

"We're being attacked!" Valkerie's scream exploded in her head. "Get to the rover!" She crawled out from under the bench and tottered into the hallway, tripping over the planters that littered the floor.

"Don't just stand there! Help me pick her up!" Bob's voice rang out from the stairwell.

*Lex!* Valkerie ran for the stairwell. Bob and Kennedy came barreling through, carrying Lex between them.

"She fell down the stairs and hit her head." Bob backed through the suit room and waited as Kennedy spun the wheel of the airlock.

A red light flashed out a warning.

"The outer hatch is open!" Bob pulled Kennedy away from the airlock. "What happened to the rover?"

Kennedy let loose with an eruption of oaths. "Something's out there. Same thing as attacked me before." He pushed his way past Valkerie and threw open the door of his EVA-suit locker.

Bob shook his head. "That's impossible. Nothing's out there. It was probably just a—"

Another crash shook the Hab. This time the whole base seemed to twist under them.

"Kennedy's right." Valkerie crawled to the lockers and pulled her EVA suit down on top of her. "Something's definitely out there. It put a big dent in the wall of the lab."

Kennedy cast a look of triumph at Bob and muttered to himself as he pulled his LCG up around his shoulders. "Told y'all I wasn't crazy."

Bob looked dazed. Like his whole world was crashing down around him.

"Come on, Bob, you've got to get dressed so you can help—"

*Eeerrrkkkkk!* A grating sound vibrated through the Hab, like an armored dragon brushing past the outer hull.

Valkerie fumbled frantically with her suit. Whatever it was, it was enormous. She glanced at Bob.

He was ghostly white, but he seemed to be managing with his suit. He stared back at her with haunted eyes.

Focus. She had to focus. Valkerie pulled on her LCG with shaking hands. Something was outside. Something was trying to get in. She stuffed her legs into the lower half of the suit.

Ragged breathing filled the room. A high-pitched whine. It was Kennedy, panting like an injured dog. "It's lookin' for the hydrogen tanks. That's what it's after. The tanks."

"It's okay. It's going to be okay." Valkerie climbed into the upper half of her suit. "Maybe it's gone."

"Not now that it knows we're here," Kennedy muttered to himself. "It'll come back. And when it does it'll go straight for the tanks."

"What'll be back?" Bob demanded. "What are we even talking—"

A steel gray claw slashed through the outer wall. Rushing air whipped around them, roaring like a tornado. Valkerie clamped down her helmet and searched frantically through the flying debris. Her gloves were gone. Sucked out into the near vacuum of Mars.

She threw open Lex's locker and twisted one glove at a time into place. "Bob?" She searched the room. "Bob?"

An explosion threw her to the floor.

She lay on her side, grasping at a white-suited leg. "Bob?" Valkerie worked her way up his outstretched body.

Good. He already had his helmet on. She checked his hands. What was he doing with . . . Lex. Valkerie scrambled forward and helped Bob stuff Lex into the clear plastic rescue bubble. She stretched the plastic out while Bob zipped it shut and activated the seal.

"The tank. Where's the tank?" She looked down at her control panel and switched her comm on.

"—to get her into the airlock." Bob's voice sounded over the rush of frantic breathing.

"My hand. Help me. My hand." Kennedy's voice rose to a hysterical pitch.

"We've got to inflate the bubble," Valkerie shouted over Kennedy's cries. She searched the sides of the clear plastic bag, trying to find the switch that activated the oxygen tank.

The bubble suddenly inflated. She looked back at Bob. He had found the switch.

"Help me! Help me!"

A jolt passed through Valkerie's body, rocking the Hab beneath her knees. She swiveled around, searching for Kennedy.

He sat with his back against the lockers, pressing a gloved hand over the metal connector ring of his left wrist.

"Kennedy! Where's your glove?" Valkerie shouted.

"Help me. My hand!"

Valkerie stood and pulled a drawer from the spare suit bin. An old glove lay right on top. It had been patched several times. Had they patched it after the last leak? She dug frantically through the drawer, but there weren't any more. It would have to do. A leaky glove was better than nothing at all.

"I've got a glove!" Valkerie turned and held it out to Kennedy.

"My hand!"

The floor tilted beneath Valkerie's feet, throwing her to the floor. The lockers against the wall twisted and buckled as the wall behind them was slashed open.

"We've got to get out of here!" Bob shouted. "If the Hab collapses, the hydrogen and oxygen tanks could ignite."

"Kennedy, I've got a glove." Valkerie knocked on Kennedy's faceplate with the metal ring of the glove. She pulled Kennedy's arm away from his wrist-connector and pushed the sleeve back over his hand. Working his fingers into the fingers of the glove, she locked the connection down. "Come on!" She tugged on Kennedy's arm, trying to pull him to his feet.

"It's too late. It knows we're here."

The Hab shook. A pool of boiling water rushed into the room, filling the Hab with steam.

Bob grabbed Kennedy by the arm and hoisted him up. "Come on. Help me with Lex. We've got to get to the rover."

Bob picked up one side of the rescue bubble, but Kennedy just stood there. His breath wheezed through Valkerie's earphones.

She picked up the other side of the bag and followed Bob to the airlock. "Kennedy, get the hatch. Kennedy?" Valkerie searched the room.

Kennedy was nowhere in sight.

Holding the rescue bubble under one arm, Bob spun the hatch open with the other. The docking port was buckled and torn, like the rover had been ripped away from the Hab.

"Do you see anything?" Valkerie shouted over the static.

Bob set Lex down and leaned out of the hatch. "The steps are mangled. I don't see the rover anywhere."

"It's not safe. Maybe we should stay inside—"

A sudden jolt knocked Valkerie off her feet.

She rolled onto her hands and knees. "Bob? Bob!" She pulled Lex back into the airlock and cautiously peered through the hatch. It was too dark to be sure, but she thought she could see something moving on the ground below. "Bob!"

"I'm okay." Bob sounded anything but okay. "Here." His upper torso appeared at the hatch. "Get Kennedy to help you hand down Lex. We've got to get away from the Hab."

Valkerie looked back inside. The emergency lights must have gone out. The interior was completely black. "Kennedy, get out here. We're in the airlock."

No answer—only hoarse breathing. The sound of metal on glass.

"Kennedy!"

Something brushed Valkerie's leg. Lex was coming to. Valkerie felt along the plastic bag and pressed her face mask firmly against Lex's forehead. "Lex, can you hear me?"

"She can't hear you. She doesn't have a radio." Bob's voice crackled over comm.

"Lex, nod your head if you can hear me."

Lex's head rocked beneath Valkerie's face mask.

"The whole Hab's been ripped apart. The rover's gone. We had to put you in a rescue bubble."

A strange vibration rattled through the floor. A flash of light.

Valkerie turned back toward the suit room. A dull orange glow reflected off the metal walls. Had the emergency lights come back on?

"Kennedy!"

A dark blob pounded through the suit room. Kennedy carrying a large box.

"Get out!" Kennedy slammed into the airlock wall, tossed the box out the hatch, and vaulted through the opening.

"Valkerie, get out of there! Get out of there!" Bob and Kennedy's voices screamed in her ears.

Valkerie froze.

The light was getting brighter. Lex's face, etched in bewildered terror, showed plainly through the plastic that encased her.

"Move! Get out of there. Now!"

Valkerie tried to pick Lex up, but a pair of gloved hands grabbed her and dragged her through the hatch. She saw herself reflected briefly in a curved mirror of flaming orange. The next thing she knew she was lying on her side in a dune of dust and grit. A clear plastic bag, dancing with orange highlights, was lowered to the ground next to her.

"What happened?" Valkerie crawled onto her knees and was hoisted up by two sets of hands.

"It got the tanks." Kennedy's voice. "We've got to get out of here."

Valkerie turned to face the bewildering light. The backside of the Hab was lit up like a Bunsen burner. "What happened?"

One of the suited figures shoved an armload of oxygen bottles at her and knelt to pick up one end of Lex's bag. The other picked up the other end.

"Where can we go? What are we going to do?" Valkerie spun around, searching for some sign of the rover.

"Shhh. Don't talk unless you have to." Kennedy's voice had an air of command to it. "It might be able to home in on our radios."

Valkerie turned back around. Bob and Kennedy had already hauled Lex several paces. She hurried to catch up with them. "What's going on? Where are you going?"

"The MAV." Bob's voice was barely audible against Kennedy's breathing.

"We've got to get off this planet while we still can," Kennedy muttered.

"But . . ." Valkerie's mind raced. It didn't make sense. They couldn't just leave. They weren't done regenerating their rocket fuel. They still had another two hundred kilos of water to go. They needed supplies. The bacteria. She didn't even have a biosample. She looked back at the Hab. "Guys, the fire will die down soon. We've got to go back for a sample."

"Valkerie, don't you get it?" Bob sounded angry. "Something's trying to kill us."

"The rover and Hab were the first two courses," Kennedy mumbled. "If we don't hurry, the MAV could be dessert."

"Assuming it hasn't visited the MAV already," Bob said.

"Guys, listen to yourselves. There has to be a logical explanation for what's happening that doesn't involve—"

"Involve what?" Bob asked. "You already found one creature on Mars."

"Sure. Bacteria." Valkerie cast a cautious glance behind them. "The fire's already out. I could be back in three—"

"Let's move!" Kennedy hissed. He and Bob broke into a jog.

Valkerie fell in place behind them, reaching in to help support Lex's weight. Eerie shadows moved all around them, but she kept her head down and plodded on. It didn't make sense, but something was out there. They trudged on and on. Valkerie's arms started to burn. Her head felt like it would explode. Something was trying to kill them.

Finally, a dark shadow loomed in front of them. She stumbled backward, dropping her load of oxygen tanks. Bob and Kennedy set Lex down and stepped forward.

"Bob?"

"Shhh. It's okay," Bob said. "We'll just top off the MAV and be on our way."

Valkerie blinked her eyes.

Bob was standing at the base of the fuel-factory unit. To his left she could just make out the MAV silhouetted against the star-emblazoned sky.

Bob flipped a switch and a green light stabbed through the darkness. Valkerie could feel the pumps vibrating reassuringly under her feet.

"It should only take—"

The vibrations stopped and the light went dead. Bob flipped open a panel and threw another switch.

"No power," he said in a dull voice. "Whatever attacked the Hab may have just taken out the nuke."

Saturday, May 9, 2015, 2:00 a.m., Mars Local Time

Bob

"We can't leave Lex on the ground! She'll freeze to death." Bob stabbed Kennedy with the beam of his flashlight. "Valkerie, help Kennedy carry Lex up into the MAV. Try to get some heat up there so she doesn't freeze."

Bob turned back to the MAV's fuel gauge. They had made almost two tonnes of methane that week, in three batches. The last batch was still sitting in the fuel factory. Almost two hundred gallons of liquid methane, which they must have to get into orbit. But without electricity, there was no way to pump it from the factory into the MAV's tanks.

"We'll need to fire up the heaters soon or Lex isn't going to make it." Valkerie's voice sounded tense. She was trying to hide it, but Bob could tell she was scared.

"Do it." Bob looked up at the MAV. Good. They were already in. "Bring the cabin up to pressure and power on the heaters. The fuel cells have juice for seventy-two hours of life support." *And more than enough for the fuel pumps.* Bob pried open a service panel on the MAV and started searching for a cable—any cable long enough to run from the MAV to the fuel factory pumps.

"Stay inside with Lex." Kennedy's voice came over comm. "That *monster* is out there somewhere. Bob's going to need some help."

"Wait. Help me get her turned around." Valkerie's voice.

Bob turned back to the fuel factory and started ripping out every wire he could find. He twisted them end-to-end, fashioning them into a long cable. Not nearly long enough. *Think, Kaggo. There's got to be more wire.* He turned to the MAV. Was there a subsystem he could cannibalize without affecting launch?

Wait! The power cable. With the nuke dead, they didn't need the cable anymore. Bob started pulling the heavy cable out of the ground. But how could he cut it? He went to the tool shed behind the fuel factory and grabbed a pickax. Twenty yards should be enough cable. He paced it off and raised the ax.

A man-sized shadow moved across the darkness.

"Kennedy?" Bob set the pickax down and started toward the shadowy form. What was Kennedy doing back behind the MAV? "Kennedy, help me—"

The figure vanished.

Bob stood silent, blinking in the darkness. "Kennedy, is that you?"

"What?" Kennedy's voice grated through Bob's helmet. "Of course it's me."

"Would you stop playing games? I need help with this cable!"

"I'm coming, already," Kennedy grumbled. "You okay, Valkerie?"

"I've got her."

Bob lumbered back and grabbed the pickax. A movement caught his eye. Was that Valkerie climbing down the steps of the MAV?

"Valkerie, what are you doing? Stay in the MAV with Lex."

"I am. What are you talking about?"

What was going on?

The white-suited figure jumped down and shuffled toward Bob.

An icy chill percolated up through Bob's spine. "Kennedy?" He shined his flashlight at the figure.

Kennedy scowled back at him through the visor. "Yeah?"

"I thought I saw you back there." Bob pointed back behind the MAV.

"Oh yeah?" Kennedy mumbled something under his breath and then took off running in the opposite direction from where Bob was pointing.

"Kennedy, wait!" Bob searched the darkness behind the MAV. Had he seen something? "Kennedy, stop. I need help with this cable!"

Labored breathing sounded over comm.

"Kennedy, it's okay. It was probably just a shadow!" *Great!* Bob tossed the pickax aside and shouted up at the MAV. "Valkerie, start going through checkout. I've got to bring Kennedy back."

"Bring him back? What's wrong?"

"I wish I knew." Bob loped after Kennedy. "Hampster! Nothing's out there. It was just my imagination."

Static.

"Kennedy, this is Lex. Come back right now. That's an order!"

The static was getting louder. Louder.

"Be ready at the pumps, Bob. I'm almost there," Kennedy wheezed.

"Almost where?" Bob slowed to a stop. "Kennedy, no!"

A hailstorm of curses battered through the static. "It got the nuke. Beat it up pretty good."

"Get out of there, Kennedy!" Bob started back for the MAV. "If the nuke's lost its shielding . . ." His pulse hammered in his temples. Oh great, Kennedy was going off his rocket again. Beautiful timing.

"Bob, go find him," Lex said.

"No, I countermand that," Kennedy said. "Kaggo, stay at the fuel pump and be ready to move some fuel."

"Bob, I said go get him! He's nuts."

"You're not a shrink, Lex," Kennedy said, and he laughed, a thin, screechy kind of laugh that dragged fingernails down the blackboard of Bob's spine. "Those shrinks thought they were so smart. Well, I outsmarted them, didn't I? I outplayed them at their own game."

"Kennedy, let's be reasonable," Bob said. "Come back and let's talk."

"Kaggo, get to the fuel pumps!" Kennedy said. "I'm almost done."

"With *what*?" But Bob already knew the answer.

"One of the lines is ripped out, but I'm gonna fix it. The end's not broken, it's just hanging loose here."

"Kennedy, watch your rad monitors!"

No answer.

Bob went to the fuel pumps and waited. A bead of sweat dropped into his eye. He shook his head, powerless to stop the stinging.

Over the comm link came the sound of tuneless humming. Then Kennedy's voice, ragged, brittle. Singing. "Hush, little baby, don't say a word. Papa's gonna fix your power cord. And if that power cord holds tight, Papa's gonna give you electric light. And if those 'lectric lights don't turn, Papa's gonna get you some fuel to burn. And if—"

A green LED lit up on the pump panel.

"Hit it, Kaggo," Kennedy's voice rasped out in an anguished whisper.

Bob punched the switch and watched the fuel gauge begin to move. "Kennedy? You okay?"

"Bob, go check on him," Lex said.

Bob started walking toward the nuke.

"No!" Kennedy's voice again, faint. "The monster . . . ripped the shielding . . . off the nuke."

"Get away from there!" Bob ran toward the reactor.

"I'm . . . holding the wires . . . in place."

"Forget it!" Bob shouted. "There's too much radiation."

"I see the monster!" Kennedy shouted a string of curses. "I see it, but it don't see me. Get in the MAV, Kaggo, and be ready to roll. I'm gonna break that baby's head if it's the last thing I do."

"Bob, get back here now!" Lex shouted. "That's an order."

"We need you," Valkerie pleaded.

Bob stopped and turned back to the MAV. As he reached the fuel factory, the lights on the console went dark. The gauge read empty.

"We got it!" Lex shouted. "Kennedy, run for it!"

A gurgling sound filled the comm channel. Then Kennedy's labored voice. "Negative. Took too many rems. Get out of . . . Dodge, cowboys. This is my fight . . . not yours."

"What's it look like?" Bob stared into the darkness.

An anguished scream answered him. Then silence. The sound of Kennedy's breathing was . . . just gone.

"Bob, get in the MAV now!" Lex said.

"On my way. Get back in the rescue bubble, Lex." Bob ran to the steps and began climbing. He reached the top and waited.

"She's in," Valkerie said. "I'm pumping down to vacuum."

A minute later the hatch swung inward. Bob climbed inside, then took one last look at Mars. From out of the gloom, he saw a dark shadow heading toward the MAV. He pulled back inside and slammed the hatch shut. "I saw something!" he shouted. "It's headed this way! Get us out of here, Valkerie."

Valkerie dropped into the pilot's seat. "We're good to go."

Bob flicked some switches. "I'm pressurizing the cabin. Get us off the ground!"

Valkerie's hands flew over the console, setting switches, pressing buttons. "Igniting engines . . . now."

Something clanged down in the superstructure at the base of the MAV. The ship reverberated.

"It's attacking us!" Bob shouted. "Have we got enough thrust yet?"

"Another few seconds," Valkerie said. "I'll tell you when to release."

Another metallic clang. The MAV shook. Bob realized he wasn't even buckled into his seat yet.

"On my mark," Valkerie said. "Three . . . two . . ."

Another clang. The MAV shook, then began tipping.

"Mark!"

Bob threw the switch. Somewhere down below, six explosive charges fired, severing their connection to the base platform.

The MAV leapt off the base.

### Saturday, May 9, 2015, 2:30 a.m., Mars Local Time

### Valkerie

Valkerie unbuckled her harness and let herself float free above her seat in the tiny MAV capsule. She shut her eyes and relaxed into the zombie float of zero-g. She had forgotten how good it felt to be weightless—free from the burden of an overwhelming and terrifying planet. No more research. No more bogeymen. No more . . . Kennedy.

The realization came crashing down on her like the weight of an entire world. Dark images crisscrossed her mind, running helter-skelter through her emotions. She gripped the arm of her seat and held on tight. Kennedy was gone. He'd given his life for them. Her throat tightened. Her chest squeezed. For an agonizing second, her whole body locked up, refusing to respond to her desperate attempts at control. Then a long, painful sob convulsed her body as a flood of pain, tears, and emotion all tried to escape at once. She cried for what seemed like hours. Until the well of her tears was dry—until she was a trembling empty shell floating like a baby in Bob's arms.

Bob looked down at her with puffy, tear-streaked eyes.

She wiped her face with her hands and turned to face Lex, who floated nearby watching her with an expression of deep concern. "I'm okay. It's just that . . ."

Lex nodded and managed a tight smile. "I know," she whispered.

They floated silently in the cramped compartment, looking from one to another.

Silence. Calm. Valkerie was loath to break the peace, but she felt she had to say something. She couldn't hold it in forever. "I can't believe he's gone. That he gave his life for us."

Bob reached for the radio. "He wouldn't have wanted for it to be in vain. We've got to concentrate on rendezvousing with the ERV."

"No!" Lex grabbed at his arm. "Wait."

"Why?" Bob drew back his hand.

"I . . ." Lex stared into space. "I'm not sure it's safe."

"What do you mean *not safe*?" Bob asked. "You're not worried EECOM might break out of jail, are you?"

"No, but the *thing* that attacked us. You don't honestly think Valkerie's fifth man is some kind of a Mars monster?"

Bob considered for a long while and finally shook his head.

"So . . ." Lex looked from Bob to Valkerie. "It had to be the rover. That's the only thing that makes sense. I suppose it's *possible* Kennedy could have programmed it to attack, but . . ."

"No way," Bob said. "Impossible. I locked Kennedy out of every computer subsystem but his e-mail. He couldn't even use the head without my help. And besides, I don't believe he could do it. Psychologically, I mean. He was different after he came back. All busted-up inside."

"I agree," Valkerie said. "He's changed. And he died to save us. If that doesn't prove he's innocent, nothing will."

"I'm gonna miss him," Bob said.

"Me too." Lex brushed at something in the corner of her eye. She sighed deeply. "Crazy as that sounds, I'll miss him. But we still have to figure out who was driving that thing. And can they do anything to the ERV?"

"This might sound crazy," Valkerie said, "but what if that Russian orbiter was controlling the rover?"

"The Russians?" Bob looked skeptical. "What do they have against us?"

"Just listen," Valkerie said. "We never figured out how EECOM was controlling our robots. Houston checked the logs, and no commands ever went out through the Deep Space Network. But the Russians don't need the DSN. They've got their own radio antennas. So if EECOM was in cahoots with the Russians . . . it all fits."

"That's not such a crazy idea," Bob said. "It explains why nothing ever got logged on our network. That's the last piece of the puzzle."

Lex shook her head. "It's an interesting theory, Valkerie. It explains *how*. But it doesn't explain *why*."

Nobody said anything for a while.

"Maybe the Martian flu?" Bob said. "None of this weird stuff happened until Valkerie got sick. After that, everything hit the fan at once. The Russians have a strong paranoid streak, and they really got hit hard by AIDS. They're terrified of back-contamination."

"But what about the de-orbit burn on the ERV?" Valkerie said. "How did the Russians do that?"

"That's already explained," Bob said. "EECOM did it. She couldn't use the Russian network to access the ERV. Otherwise, she would have never risked going through the DSN. And we know for sure she did that hack. Nate and Josh found her script, and our guys checked every line—it's a perfect match. She had all the passwords to get into the Goldstone network, and she used the Russian machine as a cutout—probably with their cooperation. Then the Russians pointed the finger at Josh. That's it! They had to be working together on everything. EECOM provided the command sequences for the robots. The Russians provided the back-door network to transmit the signals."

Valkerie ran over and over the scenario in her mind. The more she thought about it, the more it seemed to fit.

"So what do we do?" Lex nodded to the transmitter. "They arrested EECOM, but the Russians are still out there. Think they'll go after the ERV again?"

"They can't." Bob smiled. "If they could touch the ERV through their back door, EECOM wouldn't have gone through Goldstone, and she would never have gotten caught. Anyway, Houston changed all the DSN access codes right after they caught EECOM. The ERV is safe."

Valkerie nodded her agreement.

Lex reached for the mike. "Houston, this is Commander Ohta calling from the Ares 6. Please come in. The Ares 7 has been attacked. Kennedy Hampton is dead. Bob, Valkerie, and I barely escaped to the MAV. We took off and we're in a low orbit around Mars. We don't have much fuel, so we need you to bring the ERV down to us for a rendezvous. Sending telemetry now."

• • •

Valkerie looked down at the monitor and caught her breath. The image of the ERV loomed closer, shining like a sterling-silver cross against a stippled velvet field.

"Relax, Valkerie." Lex touched the attitude controls. "I'm on it."

Bob patted Lex on the back. "Lexie here could do this maneuver with one eye closed and all her fingers taped together."

Lex laughed. "And after three beers. Right, Kaggo?"

The smile faded from Bob's face. "Valkerie, are you okay?"

Valkerie nodded. "Just nervous, I guess."

Lex nodded. "Fifteen meters. We're coming in at ten centimeters per second. A few more minutes and it's home sweet ERV."

Two minutes ticked by. Three meters left to go.

Valkerie glanced shyly at Bob, but he didn't seem to notice. He didn't look nervous at all, just sat there with the shadow of a smile on his lips.

"One meter." Lex tapped the controls. "Firing microjets."

Valkerie leaned toward the monitor, trying to catch Bob's eye. "Do you realize what day it is?"

Bob glanced at his watch. "May 9—that means more than a year before we get back to Earth. It could be worse."

Valkerie bit her lip. Surely he hadn't forgotten?

"Fifty centimeters." Lex's eyes were glued to the monitor.

Valkerie snuck a peek at Bob's face. What was he thinking? Did he want to wait?

"Thirty centimeters."

"Ten."

"Five."

The clang of metal locking to metal reverberated throughout the ship.

"Lockdown!" Lex picked up the mike. "Houston, this is Lex. We have a bull's-eye on the Ares 5. Preparing to egress the MAV." She unlatched her seat belt.

Bob did the same.

Valkerie fumbled with hers. This was it. She pulled herself behind Lex and waited with pounding heart for Bob to test the atmosphere in the ERV.

"Okay, atmosphere looks good." Bob floated back from the hatch. "After you, ladies."

Lex threw open the hatch and disappeared inside with a shout. "You guys won't believe how good it smells!"

Valkerie went in next.

Bob followed on her heels. "And clean! No grit, no dust, no more sewer water to drink!"

"Hey, Valkerie, champagne!" Lex called back.

"And Twinkies!" Bob grabbed a packet and started tearing into the wrapper.

"No!" Valkerie lunged for the Twinkies. "Don't touch it. Any of it!"

Bob and Lex turned on Valkerie with wide questioning eyes.

"What's wrong?" Bob asked.

"You're not thinking Houston would try to poison us?" Lex looked at Valkerie in disbelief.

"Of course not," Valkerie said. "I just thought that . . . seeing what day it is . . ."

"Oh!" Bob started laughing.

"What?" Lex threw her hands in the air. "Would somebody please tell me what's going on?"

Bob grinned and held up a package of Twinkies. "Wedding cake."

Saturday, May 9, 2015, 7:00 p.m., CST

Josh

Josh tugged at his overstarched collar, trying to restore circulation to his brain.

A burst of laughter echoed from the back of the Flight Control Room. At the front, six engineers stood in an uneasy cluster, stiff and unnatural in their ties and ill-fitting suits. The monitor overhead showed the bustle of activity in Teague Auditorium—florists setting out flower arrangements, technicians positioning lights. Facility managers were everywhere, attaching white bows to anything that didn't move.

"Birdseed, Mr. Bennett?" Nate's administrative assistant, Carol, held out a white basket filled with dainty gauze-and-lace birdseed packets.

"Thanks." Josh took a packet and stuffed it in his tux pocket.

"See ya over in Teague, Josh," the daytime MMACS called from across the aisle. "I've got to go home and change. I've been here since the bachelor party."

"Better hurry. You've only got an hour." Josh waved him out and shuffled down the aisle to the CATO station. Cathe was sitting next to the Gold Team CATO, typing away at a keyboard.

"Hey, how's the best man's best woman?" Josh leaned down and kissed Cathe on the cheek.

She swatted him playfully. "Don't you have work to do? Honestly. Dress these boys up and you can't take them anywhere."

"You think it's bad now." Josh grinned. "You should have been here for the bachelor party."

"I'm glad I missed it." Cathe gathered a stack of papers and rose to leave.

"Where are you going?"

"To finish my work." Cathe blew him a kiss and sidled toward the aisle. "There's only an hour till the big show starts, and I don't want to miss it. I hear the best man is gorgeous."

Josh watched her push past a glowing semicircle of managers. Somehow a cameraman had gotten in and was taping an interview. Josh couldn't believe it. Had Nate given CNN permission to come into the FCR? No way. What had happened to security? If he were a terrorist, this was exactly the time he'd choose to—

Josh froze.

*Wait a minute . . .* How had EECOM known to set up her attack on the Hab exactly during the bachelor party? It was the perfect time—when the whole FCR was distracted, when a ton of comm packets were flying back and forth to Mars. When a rover script could easily slip through undetected.

But the wedding hadn't been announced until last Saturday night. *Two days after EECOM was arrested.* Josh strode out of the FCR and down the hall to the nearest exit. For that matter, why had EECOM bothered with such a long delay time for her sleeper process? Why not send the commands with a short delay? The only thing a long delay did was increase the chance of detection.

He pushed through the doors, whipped out his phone, and punched in a number.

It answered on the second ring. "Harrington."

"This is Josh. We may have another emergency on our hands. Where are you?"

"I'm in Teague Auditorium with Crystal."

"I'm at MCC. I need you both as quick as you can get here. I'll meet you halfway. And if Ms. Yamaguchi's got any other agents, bring 'em."

"Josh, what is going—"

"Now!" Josh hung up and called another number. The geeks in IS just might get a chance to be heroes.

Josh paced back and forth in front of Building 16 staring at the seven crape myrtle trees, now in full bloom, planted almost three decades earlier in honor of the seven *Challenger* astronauts.

He spotted Nate in a tux. Running like a madman. Yamaguchi was behind him, looking rather put out, tap-tap-tapping at a very undignified pace. Josh strode to meet them.

"Josh, what's going on?"

"Have you got more agents?"

"On the way. This had better be good." Nate yanked out a piece of tissue and wiped his face.

Josh pulled out his phone and called again. He couldn't wait any longer. "Hello, Bruce?"

"Just got it started, sir." The sys-admin's eager voice blasted through the earpiece. "I got the whole list entered. So far, so good. No logins outside of the FCR."

"Good. Don't take your eyes off your computer for a second. Hear me? Let me know the instant anyone on that list logs in."

"You can count on me, sir."

Nate looked ready to wrestle a bear. "Josh, are you planning to tell me what's going on?"

Josh lowered the phone. "I think somebody's going to make another try for the ERV. During the wedding."

Nate scowled. "And I'm assuming you have some kind of evidence to back this up?"

Agent Yamaguchi arrived. "Mr. Bennett, I hope you intend to explain—"

Josh held up his hand and began striding back toward Mission Control. "There's not much time. Just listen. I got to thinking what an unlucky coincidence it was that the rover was programmed to attack the Hab during the bachelor party. When our guard was down. When we were sending a ton of packets back and forth. And then I asked myself how Margaret would have known the perfect time to set one of those cron job things to go off. We arrested her before anybody knew there was going to be a bachelor party last night. Before we even knew there was going to be a *wedding*."

"Go on . . ." Nate looked grim.

"That's when I realized what's been bothering me all this time. The DVD in Margaret's office. Where did she get that? From Kennedy's apartment? No way. From the evidence room? She doesn't have access. So the only possibility is if she set up the video camera in my office and then planted a whole bunch of DVDs in Kennedy's apartment. Why would she do that? And how would she know three years ago that she'd need my password? What's her motive? Fear of back-contamination? It doesn't make sense. She didn't put that camera in my office. You and I both know Kennedy did it. He's the one who got me kicked off the mission—the psych journals are proof."

"So you think EECOM's innocent?" Nate's face had gone white.

Josh nodded. "Somebody set her up."

"And the real hacker is going to strike again during the wedding?"

"Wouldn't you?"

"He's got a point," Yamaguchi said. "There'll never be a better time to attack than right now."

Nate nodded.

Josh raised his phone. "Bruce, how you doing there? Any nibbles?"

"Nothing yet, but . . . wait, somebody just logged on. Sid Reid. He appears to be on console on *Shroeder-xt*."

"Sid Reid? The night-shift CATO? Great job! Any idea how to find out where *Shroeder-xt* is?"

"In his office. Building 30A, second floor. Room 218."

Josh began walking faster, repeating the information for Nate and Yamaguchi.

"What's happening, Bruce? Keep talking. I want info."

"Just logged on to Yahoo!" Bruce said. "Checking his stock. Ouch. Looks like he has Microsoft. No wonder he's turning to a life of crime."

Josh ran up the stairs three at a time and led the way out into the hallway at a brisk walk.

"Uh-oh. This could get interesting. Logging on to ChatConnection.com. Looks like your Sid Reid is too hot to trot."

"Say again?" Josh whispered into the phone with his hand cupped around it.

"It's his handle. One word. 2-H-o-t-2-T-r-o-t. Here we go. Looks like he's makin' a move on Starla Bright. No. ASL . . . crashed and burned. Asked her stats too early. Rookie mistake."

"ASL?"

"Age-Sex-Location. Way overeager."

Josh stopped and motioned to Nate and Yamaguchi to gather around.

"Now he's changing rooms. Tango room—fifteen people. This is one not-intimidated dude."

"Sorry, guys." Josh gave the others an apologetic shrug. "He's in some kind of a chat room. Doesn't look like he's our man."

Yamaguchi straightened her pearl necklace. "What about—"

"Got another one!" Bruce hissed.

Josh silenced Yamaguchi with a raised hand. "Talk to me, Bruce."

"Roger Abrams just logged on to *Godiva-j2s*."

Josh switched his phone to speaker mode so the others could hear.

"That's Building 1, fourth floor, in case you're wondering."

Nate and Yamaguchi looked at each other.

"Incoming!" Bruce said. "Got another one. Hadley on *Tennyson-14s*. Hold on! Frye on *Melville-14s* and Weinberg on

*Kanga-j2s*. Can I stop recording 2Hot2Trot now? He's blowing it big time. Wait a minute! Got another one!"

"This isn't working," Yamaguchi said. "We should be getting reinforcements in about fifteen minutes. I called the office and asked them to send out a team."

"Mr. Bennett! Mr. Bennett?"

"Sorry." Josh turned off speaker mode and raised the phone to his ear. "Go ahead, Bruce."

"Sir, may I ask where you are right now?"

"What?"

Nate and Yamaguchi turned to listen.

"Where are you? What's your location?"

"I'm on the second floor of Building 30A. Why?"

"Well, I just noticed a login. It . . . um . . . wasn't on the list you gave me, but I thought you might like to know about it anyway. You know, just in case it was—"

"Bruce, just give me the login."

"It's you, sir. JoshBennett."

"Where?"

"You mean, where's the computer?" Bruce said.

All of a sudden, Nate and Yamaguchi were talking very loud.

Josh put a hand to his ear to block them out. "Bruce, where's the computer? What's its name?"

"Building 30A, third floor, room 353. *Banyo-j2s*."

Josh repeated it out loud as he dashed for the stairwell.

"That's EECOM's old office!" Nate said.

Josh raced up the stairs. "Bruce, I want to hear you talking!"

"Sir, you're connecting to a computer called *Berkelium*, somewhere in Australia, I think."

*On the Deep Space Network.* Josh reached the third floor and rammed through the door into the hallway.

"Sending a short, encrypted message. Only 128 k. Too long for a password."

"Take a . . . recording. Keep . . . a . . . record!" Josh hissed as he padded down the hall as silently as he could in his hard leather shoes."

321 . . . 339 . . . 353! He stopped ten feet from the door. What was the combination?

"More traffic, sir," Bruce said. "Sending another encrypted message. This one's a lot longer."

"Bruce, block those packets on the DSN. Then get hold of the Gold Team CATO down in the FCR and tell him what's going on. Have him call the ERV and tell them to shut down incoming data."

Nate and Yamaguchi still hadn't reached the floor. Josh tiptoed to the door and punched in the combination, 3-5-3-5-3. He took a deep breath, shoved open the door, and charged inside.

And stopped.

A blond head spun to look at him. Cathe Willison's perfect face. Ice-blue glaciers melting into cold streams of tears.

Josh staggered back against the wall. "No!"

"Josh, I can explain . . ."

An arctic blast stormed through his senses, numbing his soul to the core. No! It couldn't be happening. Please, God, no! It wasn't true. Couldn't be . . .

"Josh, please . . . talk to me." Cool hands pressed against his face, forcing him to focus. Large liquid eyes. "Josh, I did it for you. For everybody, don't you see?"

"No . . ." Josh shook Cathe off and stepped toward the computer. It was a mistake. Had to be.

She grabbed his arm and spun him around. "Josh, please. I can explain."

"Explain?" A sudden rage welled up inside him. He stepped toward her with tight jaw and clenched fists, spitting his words. "Go ahead. Explain."

"I did it for you. For us." She looked up at him with tremulous eyes. "The crew's sick with a Martian fever. Millions could die if we let them come back. Billions. I had to do something. Don't you understand? Valkerie had a fever of 104. Hallucinations. She was seeing things, hearing things. It turned Kennedy into a monster. He tried to kill Valkerie—twice. And Lex was losing her grip too. I heard her talking to her husband in an empty room."

"You *heard* her?" Josh grabbed Cathe's shoulders and shook her. "How could you have heard her?"

"Not just heard. I saw them too . . . with the CamBot. I used it to search the Hab—and I found a bunch of bacteria cultures in the lab. Martian bacteria. I knew weeks ago that they were lying to us."

A dull ache settled over Josh's heart. "You could control the CamBot? And the rover too? How? There weren't any robot commands sent from here."

"I'm sorry, Josh. I wanted to tell you, but I didn't know you then like I do now." Cathe's eyes pooled with tears. "Remember all that stuff about getting Doppler info out of the comm data rates? CATO was right—it would never have worked. I needed the CommSats to get access to the robots."

Josh closed his eyes, feeling a knife go right through his soul. She'd lied to him, used him—just like EECOM had said. "But . . . we checked the logs for rover commands. There weren't any."

"It's called *steganography*. I encrypted the rover scripts and hid them in the phony data streams I was exchanging with the CommSats. A program on the satellites decrypted them and piped them down to the robots on Mars."

"So it was you all along? You were creating the static."

"No, I think that was really the Russians piggybacking on our comm, but I was never sure."

"And you didn't care, did you? As long as—"

"Josh, don't you understand? I had to—"

"Had to?" Fury cut through him. "You *had* to?"

"Somebody had to. They were lying to you—lying to all of us. They were infected, and they knew it, and they weren't telling us, and . . . I couldn't let them be my father's dentist. And they're lying right now. They're still infected and they're going to contaminate us all when they get back to Earth. It's three people versus seven billion. Do the calculus of suffering, Josh, and then tell me what's the moral thing to do."

"And you burned up the Hab with Kennedy in it, didn't you? Was that moral too?"

Cathe's voice sounded cold as steel. "I had to. He was an animal by then. He tried to kill them all. Mars Madness is real, and they've been lying about it the whole way."

"Right, so you just elected yourself judge and jury? If you knew they were lying, you should have told somebody. Should have told Nate."

"I couldn't!" Cathe screamed. "You still don't get it, do you? You lied too! You told Nate they were sick with that Antarctica bug when you knew it was harmless. You forced my hand. If I told Nate the truth about that, I'd get you in trouble. Nate was ready to throw you in jail. I couldn't let them." She threw her arms around him. "Josh, I love you. I love you so—"

"You loved me so much you used my computer to hack that Russian computer. You set me up!"

"No!" She leaned back and looked up at him, and there were real tears in her eyes. "Josh, I needed that Russian machine for a cutout, and you had the password. I gave you an alibi—sent you that e-mail so you'd go to the cafeteria where a thousand people could vouch for you. Why didn't you just stay there? I gave you the perfect alibi and you blew it."

"You were using me." *Just like you're using me now. You're confessing all this just to stall for time. Only you don't know your script is blocked, you reptile.*

Josh tried to push her away, but she pulled him to her heart. "Josh, we're in this together. We're both in up to our necks. Either we both sink or we both walk on water."

Movement at the doorway caught his eye. Agent Yamaguchi stood just outside with a finger to her lips. Nate reeled his hand in the air. *Haul her in.*

Josh's heart pounded in his throat, but he forced his voice to be calm. "And EECOM pays the bill, is that it? Cathe, you and I sent an innocent woman to jail. That's . . . wrong!"

Cathe shrank back from him. "Josh, please don't be mad. I did it for you. I couldn't let you go to jail. I didn't want to bring her into it, but it was your idea. You were so convinced, and it was just . . . so easy. It was the only way."

"Easy? You made her look as guilty as sin. How? Why?"

"She suspected me, so I let her eavesdrop on me. She thought I was two-timing with Jake, so I pretended to be talking to him on my cell phone, telling him my passwords. Except one of them was yours. Then when you met her at the restaurant, I just slipped into her office and left the jewel case. I hate that she's in jail, but at least you're free. Don't you see? I had to do it. I did it for us." Her voice trembled and broke. She stumbled toward him and threw her arms around him. "We're finally free to be together. There's no way they can trace this back to us. I used the superuser password I got watching Bruce Dickey type."

*And you created a user account in my name on EECOM's machine. You set me up. Again.* Josh felt dirty. Repulsed. He pushed her away. "It's not us. Not anymore. You've used me for the last time."

Footsteps scraped at the door. Yamaguchi and two agents entered the room.

Cathe whirled around. "Josh?" She looked back at him with wide, disbelieving eyes.

"I'm going to have to ask you to come with me, Miss Willison." Yamaguchi pulled a pair of handcuffs out of her purse.

"Josh, please. Look at me. I love you."

Josh nodded to Yamaguchi and turned away.

"Come along, ma'am." A stranger's voice. "I'm gonna need to explain something to you."

"I love you, Josh! You have to believe me . . ." Cathe's voice receded down the hallway.

Saturday, May 9, 2015, 7:50 p.m. CST

Nate

Nate watched Yamaguchi lead Cathe away, sandwiched between two Fibbies. He grabbed his phone and called his secretary. "Carol? Nate here. Josh and I are gonna be a little late. Something's come up, but we'll be there shortly. Stall for time." He hung up and turned to Josh. "You okay?"

Josh shook his head. "I'm dead." His voice sounded thick with grief, anger, exhaustion.

"I'm not doing so good myself," Nate said. This was beyond horrible. This was a catastrophe.

Josh staggered to a chair and slumped into it. "I can't . . . go to that wedding."

"You can and you will," Nate growled at him. "I bought us a few minutes."

Josh put his face in his hands. "She's . . . right, you know."

"Right?" Nate's heart did one of those *pop-pop* things that his doctor said were no big deal, but they were still scary. "What do you mean she's right?"

"About the lying. The crew lied to us. Bob. Lex. Valkerie. And we lied to them. I lied to you."

Nate walked over to the desk and sat on the edge, pondering that. Because the truth was, he *had* lied. All of them had. They'd meant well, but . . . it had gone wrong somehow. Had led to more trouble. Had enabled that little . . . weasel to do what she did. Gave her the excuse she needed. She knew she was killing people, but she bent things around so she was saving billions of lives. Little Miss Morality.

"Nate?"

"Yeah?"

"I'm sorry. About everything. I fouled up bad."

"Me too, Josh."

"But you don't deserve to go to jail. I do."

Nate nodded. Josh would probably do time. Not a lot, maybe. He would plead guilty. Would show remorse. Had already demonstrated it by his actions. That was big with juries—remorse.

And maybe that was the difference between Cathe and Josh. The remorse thing. A willingness to stop, to backtrack. To admit that you'd made a muck of things. To choose to do better. Like those AA people.

*My name is Nate, and I'm a creep. Just for today, I won't be a creep.*

They sat in silence for a long time. Josh pulled a tissue out of the box on EECOM's desk and blew his nose.

Nate knelt down and put an arm around Josh's shoulders. "You gonna be all right?"

Josh sniffed and looked at him through bleary eyes. "Yeah." His voice came out in a croak.

"You loved her, didn't you?"

Josh shrugged. "I guess I was in love with . . . the person I thought she was."

"Maybe that person is out there somewhere. Somebody who's the same on the inside as on the outside." *And I wish to God I was like that.*

Hope lit up Josh's face. "You think so?"

"Yeah, sure." *Maybe.* Nate stood up. Maybe it was time for a clean start. *Just for today I won't lie.* Yeah, that was the ticket. Starting right now. "Ready to get on over to that wedding, Josh?"

Josh wiped his eyes and stood up. He straightened his collar. Finger-combed his hair. Brushed something off his left shoulder. "How do I look?"

Nate studied him carefully. Josh's eyes were red and puffy. A little line of grime ran down one cheek. He looked like he'd just ruined a perfectly good air bag and walked away.

Nate grabbed the door and held it open for Josh. "You look fabulous."

## Saturday, May 9, 2015, 9:30 p.m., CST

### Valkerie

Valkerie clung to a ceiling strap, nervous and tense in the fresh white jumper she'd found in the supply bin.

Bob hovered above the radio transmitter, gripping the mounting bracket with bone-white knuckles. His face was tense. Large beads of sweat dotted his skin. "It's broken. It's got to be. We've already waited twice the time delay."

"Take a deep breath. Relax." Lex floated nearby. "We've still got five minutes."

"Something's wrong." Bob started to move toward Valkerie.

"I'm warning you. Stay away from me." Valkerie pushed Bob back with her free hand.

Bob sighed and looked down at the transmitter. "Are you sure it was the rover? I know what reason is telling me, but what good is reason if you're dealing with something outside your experience?"

"Of course it was the rover. What else could it have been?" Valkerie's voice trembled. If radio waves traveled as fast as her heart was beating, they would have been finished hours ago.

Bob shook his head. "All I know is that if I hadn't been distracted by that . . . whatever it was back behind the MAV, I would have cut the cable before Kennedy restored power.

Whatever it was saved our lives. And it was definitely too small to be the rover—or the MuleBot."

Valkerie shook her head. "I don't know. We may never know. All the answers are still back on Mars."

"With our halobacterium fossil and bacteria cultures." Lex sighed.

A long, uneasy silence filled the commons.

"Come on!" Bob slapped the CommConsole. "Something's gotta be wrong. We're being jammed!"

Valkerie looked at her watch. Maybe Bob was right. They'd been waiting forever. She reached up for a handhold. Something moved at the corner of her vision. She turned to look. Lex was reaching for the videocam she had laid aside.

Bob swallowed hard. He looked ready to faint.

The radio crackled to life. The hiss of ambient noise. "Ares 5, this is Houston." The voice of Valkerie's pastor, two hundred million miles away.

Valkerie's breath caught in her throat. She leaned in to hear the next words.

"Bob, you may now . . . kiss the bride."

# AUTHORS' NOTE

One of the biggest questions astronauts will try to answer on any mission to Mars will be the Life Question—has there ever been life on Mars? Nobody expects to find much there now. Mars is a cold, sterile planet with a thin atmosphere that provides little protection from cosmic rays and the bombardment of meteorites and comets. We will not find monkeys there, nor mosquitos, nor marigolds.

The big scientific question is whether simple life-forms—bacteria, fungi, or something new—might once have lived there, and whether some still survive. Nobody knows, but the answer will throw light on some of today's most profound questions in both science and theology. It's going to be an interesting century.

# Glossary

**Archaebacteria**: A kingdom of primitive bacteria, many of which live in harsh environments

**ASCAN**: Astronaut Candidate

**Back-contamination**: Contamination of Earth by Martian organisms

**CamBot**: Robot with an attached video camera for remote viewing

**Capcom**: Capsule Communicator—the one person in Mission Control (other than the Flight Surgeon) allowed to talk to the astronauts

**CATO**: Communications and Tracking Officer

**CDR**: Commander

**Comm**: Communications

**CommSat**: Communications satellite

**Cron job**: A Unix term for a task that can be set up to execute at some specified time

**DCM unit**: Display and Control Module—the unit on the chest of an astronaut's suit containing all controls, displays, and interfaces to external gas, liquid, and electrical systems

**DEADHEAD**: Name of a fictitious encryption system

**Delta-V**: Change in velocity created by firing the rocket engines

**Doppler effect**: A change in frequency of light or sound due to the relative motion of the source and detector. Used by police to catch speeders and by astronomers to measure the speed of distant stars

**DSN**: Deep Space Network—an international network of antenna that support interplanetary missions and radio astronomy observations. The DSN has three very large radio antennae—at Goldstone (in California), Madrid (in Spain), and Canberra (in Australia). At any given time, at least one of these antenna can link with the communications satellites orbiting Mars

**EECOM**: Electrical and Environmental Command officer

**ELC**: Earth Landing Capsule—the capsule to be used by the astronauts for landing on Earth in the final leg of the journey home

**Energia**: A class of Russian rockets used for launch of heavy payloads

**ERV**: Earth Return Vehicle—a ship placed into an orbit around Mars in advance of the mission, used by the astronauts to return from Mars to Earth

**EVA suit**: Extra-Vehicular Activity suit—NASA's term for a space suit

**Extremophile**: A general term for an organism able to live and thrive under extreme conditions, such as high or low temperatures

**FCR**: Flight Control Room (pronounced "ficker")

**Hab**: Habitation Module

**Halobacteria**: Salt-loving archaebacteria

**ISRU**: In-situ Resource Utilization—a scheme for creating rocket fuel on the surface of Mars using hydrogen and native Martian carbon dioxide to synthesize methane and oxygen. Lots of electrical energy is required, which will be provided by an on-site nuclear reactor

**ISS**: International Space Station

**JSC**: Johnson Space Center

**Klick**: Slang: a kilometer—sometimes used for kilometers per hour

**Lagrange point**: One of the positions near Mars where the gravitational forces of the sun and Mars cancel out. A satellite placed at one of the Lagrange points will not orbit either the sun or Mars, but will appear to stay fixed relative to the two bodies. Communications satellites, placed at two of the Lagrange points, can provide nearly complete coverage of the entire planet

**LCG**: Liquid Cooled Garment—the spandex water-cooled undergarment worn inside an EVA suit to regulate the astronaut's temperature

**LOX**: Liquid Oxygen

**Mars Orbital Insertion**: An operation in which an interplanetary vehicle captures into a Martian orbit

**MAG**: Maximum Absorbing Garment—a diaper for astronauts

**MATLAB**: A mathematics computer program

**MAV**: Mars Ascent Vehicle—a small rocket, placed on Mars before the astronauts arrive and fueled by the ISRU. The rocket is designed to lift the astronauts into Martian orbit when they are ready to leave the planet. The MAV will rendezvous with the much larger ERV, which carries enough supplies to take the astronauts to Earth

**MCC**: Mission Control Center, located in Building 30 of the Johnson Space Center

**MER**: Mission Evaluation Room, which houses a support team for the Flight Control Room

**MMACS**: Mechanical, Maintenance, Arm and Crew Systems officer

**MoleBot**: A robot designed for digging and taking soil samples

**MuleBot**: A robot designed for carrying cargo on the surface of Mars. The MuleBot, or "mule," has no life support for astronauts and is designed for extreme durability and moderate carrying capacity

**MS**: Mission Specialist

**NSA**: National Security Agency

**Olympus Mons**: The largest volcano in the solar system, located on Mars

**ORU**: Orbital Replaceable Unit—stowage bins for living quarters in space

**Panspermia**: A theory that simple life-forms may have been widely seeded through the universe on comets or meteorites, either by accident or design

**Philogenetic tree**: A "family tree" of life-forms on Earth, constructed by comparing the DNA of different organisms. Also known as the "Tree of Life"

**Photomicrograph**: A photograph of a microscope image

**PLSS**: Primary Life Support System—the backpack on EVA suits containing water, oxygen, power, and everything else needed for life support

**PLT**: Pilot

**Regolith**: Martian soil, which has no organic material.

**Rem**: The standard unit of radiation dosage. A prompt dose of more than about 500 rems is fatal

**RSA**: Russian Space Agency

**Silver Snoopy**: A highly prized award, which must be voted on by the astronauts, given to recognize extraordinary efforts by persons on the ground for the success of a mission

**Sol**: The Martian day, about twenty-four hours and forty minutes of Earth time

**Stromatolite**: Laminated sedimentary structures formed by bacteria (usually cyanobacteria)

**TELMU**: Telemetry, Electrical, EVA Mobility Unit officer

**Tonne**: One metric ton—a thousand kilograms. About 2,200 English pounds

**Unix**: A commonly used computer operating system

**To Amy and Eunice**

# About the Authors

JOHN B. OLSON received his Ph.D. in biochemistry at the University of Wisconsin, Madison, in 1995, and did postdoctoral work in computational biochemistry at the University of California, San Francisco.

RANDY INGERMANSON earned his Ph.D. in theoretical physics at the University of California at Berkeley in 1986, and did postdoctoral research in superstring theory at The Ohio State University.

*The Fifth Man* is the sequel to the award-winning novel, *Oxygen*. If you'd like to know more about John and Randy and the calculations they did for this book, you're probably a bit unbalanced. Nevertheless, they invite you to visit their Web sites:

www.litany.com (John's site)
www.ingermanson.com (Randy's site)
www.AdvancedFictionWriting.com (Randy's site for novelists)

Follow John on Twitter: @JohnBOlson
Follow Randy on Twitter: @RIngermanson

# *Acknowledgments*

We thank Holly Briscoe for taking an extraordinary interest in this project and introducing us to several engineers and astronauts at NASA who gave us the insider view we so desperately needed. Holly, without your help, we wouldn't have been able to write this book. We already awarded you a Silver Snoopy Award for your efforts on *Oxygen*, so it seems a bit anticlimactic to give you another one. We'll settle for a simple, "Thank you, Holly."

# *Bonus Appendix A: Developing the Big Idea*

**By John Olson**
**March 2012**

## The Day We Realized We Are Idiots

After our first novel *Oxygen* was released, Randy and I were invited by our publisher to attend a big trade conference in Atlanta. *Oxygen* had been out for only a couple of months, and sales were already doing better than anyone had expected. The book was getting a lot of buzz, and we had a great book signing at the trade show.

Newbie writers that we were, we assumed that this was normal and that, if we played our cards right, they might ask us to write another book in a year or so, after *Oxygen* had had a chance to prove itself in the market.

Yes, we were totally clueless. I remember our publisher giving us blue and green Bethany House polo shirts. You would have thought they had just proposed. They fed us lunch at their booth, and we were jumping up and down and fluttering our hands like a freshman talking to her friends after being asked to her first dance.

The V.P. of Sales told us about his experience reading *Oxygen* aloud with a member of his sales team on a long road trip. They were all going out of their way to tell us how much they liked the book. Surely that was a good sign. We couldn't wait for the end of the year. Surely they would ask us for another book?

Right after our book signing, we were flying especially high. When we ran into our editor, Steve Laube, we were so full of ourselves it was a wonder both of us could fit in the convention hall. Steve was probably on his way to an important meeting, but he took pity on us and dallied to chat for a few minutes. Just as he was about to run off, he mentioned what a shame it was that we couldn't write a sequel to *Oxygen*.

What?

They didn't want us to write another book? Why not? Had sales suddenly tanked? Were the bookstores returning them by the truckload? Did we look that bad in our matching blue and green Bethany House polos?

Apparently he noticed our dismay, because he started backpedalling almost immediately. "What? You have a sequel? I assumed you would have mentioned that little fact to your editor if you had an idea."

I explained that we were hoping, in our newbie author little minds, that maybe . . . if *Oxygen* sold really well and won a few awards, then maybe, after they had a year to see how everything went, they might possibly ask us to write another book.

When Steve finally stopped laughing, he picked himself up off the floor and told us that that's not how the publishing industry works. If an author has an idea for a sequel, he usually submits a proposal right away so that they can get the sequel out six months to a year after the first book comes out. If it takes longer than that, then the readers will have moved on by then. We should have given him a proposal months ago—and even then it would have been an iffy proposition.

Right . . . Months ago . . .

I shot Randy a look. This was clearly his responsibility. He was the physicist. Surely he didn't expect the biochemist to invent the time machine.

I tapped my foot while Randy squirmed. Apparently he was as skilled at time machine inventing as he was at sequel planning. If he was any good at physics at all, he would have invented that time machine in the future and already come back to the present to tell us we had submitted the proposal in the past.

Steve seemed to sense Randy's distress. "Do the math, guys. It would take you at least a year to write a sequel, even if you had a contract today, which you don't because you never gave me a proposal for one."

"Okay . . ." Still no word from future Randy. Apparently he already is going to give up on the time machine in the future. I was on my own. "What if we gave you a proposal right now?"

"You have a story? What's your idea?"

Oh . . .

The idea thing . . .

Wasn't it obvious? We had four astronauts who had to survive on Mars for over a year. Wasn't that enough?

Steve stared back at me. Waiting.

Apparently throwing characters into a hostile environment wasn't going to be enough.

"What if we sent you a proposal in a week?"

"You'd still have to write the manuscript in three months. And it would have to be a really good idea . . ."

There he goes with the idea thing again. What is it with editors and ideas? I've read tons of books by authors who obviously didn't have an idea before they started writing. Not having an idea never stopped Danielle Steele.

Not that I've ever read her, mind you.

Much.

Okay . . . I don't remember what we told Steve. Probably something about our future selves having so many future ideas that we didn't know which one to choose, but I do remember walking out of that convention with only one thing on my mind. We needed a really good idea for a sequel, and we needed it really fast.

If you know me at all, you're probably scratching your head at this. You see, ideas aren't usually a problem for me. Normally I can't write a paragraph of dialog without coming up with at least a dozen new story ideas that are all better than the idea I'm working on—no matter how bad they are. I'm the story Easter bunny. I'm constantly giving them to all my friends. In fact I have friends who have published more of my story ideas than I have.

Randy sez: Hey, this is Randy cutting in for just a minute. John isn't exaggerating here. He really does have lots of ideas, and I've often seen him brainstorm books for other writers at writing conferences. I remember one year, on the last night of a major conference, while I was having fun with a bunch of other writers and editors in the lounge, John was at a table in the corner with a friend cooking up a story idea from scratch. At 1:30 AM, the writer came over to one of the editors and pitched the idea. A year or two later, that book came out. John is now going to give you some song and dance about how the shoemaker's children have no shoes. Don't believe him. He is just too humble sometimes. OK, back to you, John.

John sez: So where were all those ideas now that I really needed them?

I went through the rest of the convention in a daze, generating and rejecting one idea after another. The bar was really high this time. None of the ideas were good enough. The most obvious idea would have been for our intrepid crew of astronauts to fight for survival on a hostile planet, but who would have wanted to read that? That's what *Oxygen* was about—four astronauts fighting for survival after losing most of their oxygen. Our sequel needed to be driven by totally new story drivers or it would feel like the same story heated up in the microwave and served with a different garnish.

## Story Drivers

But I'm getting ahead of myself. First I need to explain what I mean by *story drivers*. As far as I know, I made this term up about a dozen years ago when I first started to teach writing. A *story driver*, as I define it, is the reason a reader keeps turning the page at any given point in the story. It shouldn't be confused with what a reader likes as she's reading a page; it's what she is looking forward to reading next.

There are dozens of story drivers, but I teach my writing students to focus on what I call the *Big Five*—a list of story drivers I derived from an analysis of the main genres of fiction.

Literary genres are important because they represent drivers that readers are universally hungry for. Some readers might be hungry for literature about dinosaurs—indeed I met such a reader in my library yesterday (Jimmy was ten years old)—but the desire to learn about dinosaurs isn't universal enough to anchor its own genre. Romance, on the other hand, is a huge genre because it feeds the universal desire to love and be loved. Likewise, suspense and thrillers feed the universal desire for survival and self-preservation. Adventures feed the desire for danger and excitement. Mysteries feed the desire for discovery and making the unknown known. And fantasies (and to a lesser extent historicals and even horror) feed the universal desire for transcendence—the desire to experience more than what we see around us in our materialistic, mechanistic world.

### The Big Five Story Drivers:

- Romance—the desire to love and be loved
- Mystery—the desire for discovery and making the unknown known
- Suspense—the desire for survival and self-preservation
- Adventure—the desire for danger and excitement
- Fantasy—the desire for transcendence

Every good book, no matter what the genre, is driven by all of these story drivers (and a host of others), but the genre of the book is determined by which driver is at the heart of the story. For example, *Oxygen* was full of romance, mystery, adventure, and fantasy (science fiction), but suspense was the main driver. Would Valkerie and Bob live or would they die? That was the big question. That was the question that gave the whole story its shape and structure. That's why Randy and I consider *Oxygen* to be a thriller—even though many readers consider it to be science fiction or even romance.

If we had used the same "will they live or will they die" story driver for *The Fifth Man*, we wouldn't have given our readers any reason to read the sequel. If the back cover said "Will Valkerie and Bob survive on the hostile red planet?" our readers would have put the book back on the shelf thinking "been there and read that."

That was my dilemma. The situation seemed to call for use of the suspense driver, but the very reason that the situation called for it made it obvious and boring. Sure we would make use of the suspense story driver, but it wasn't going to capture anybody's imagination. We needed surprise, originality—something to make the reader ask herself "how can this be?"

If reading the back cover copy of a book fills a reader's head with a dozen obvious scenarios, then she isn't going to be interested. Even if she's wrong, and the author doesn't make use of any of the obvious solutions, the reader will never find out how clever the author was, because she'll never read the book.

The back cover copy needs to ask questions the reader can't answer without reading the book. Either that or the answers have to be so thought-provoking that the reader wants to read the book just to find out what the author is going to do with it.

So if the suspense driver wasn't going to work for the sequel, what driver was I going to use? This was the question I was asking myself when I got on the plane with Randy to fly back home from the convention.

The romance driver wasn't very attractive. *Oxygen* ended with Bob proposing to Valkerie. In most readers' minds the objective of the romance story arc had already been met. Mission already accomplished. *And they lived happily ever after,* as pleasant as it is to live through in real life, doesn't a page-turner make.

Even though adventure is a decent way to spice up a book, I don't think it makes a very good primary story driver—especially not in this day and age when we've all been there and read that. The promise of adventure and excitement is implicit in almost every novel published today. It's not likely to be the reason the reader decides to read your book instead of all the other books she could choose. And it's not going to be the reason the publication board gives your book the green light. "What? You think we should publish your book because you say it's going to be exciting? What a novel idea! Here's a three book contract and an advance for two hundred thousand dollars. An exciting book . . . Imagine that!"

The science fiction/fantasy story driver seemed at first to be very promising. Bob and Valkerie were going to be living on a completely new world. Imagine the possibilities! No, seriously . . . Imagine them and tell me when you come up with something good. Me, I've still got nothing.

We wouldn't have had any problems if Bob and Valkerie had landed on Edgar Rice Burroughs's or C.S. Lewis's Mars, but we'd already established our story world in *Oxygen*. We were writing about the real world using real science and real technology. We couldn't bring out a horde of green Barsoomian warriors to bail us out now.

The best Bob and Valkerie could hope for was to discover some sort of primitive single-celled life, but unless you're a microbiologist who doesn't get out a lot, this probably isn't going to whip you into a fervor of foaming-at-the-mouth, transcendent ecstasy.

Still . . . no matter what I tried, I kept coming back to the life question. Scientifically, it's the most significant question that could be answered on Mars, and like it or not, Randy and I were stuck with a realistic, scientifically accurate story world. But how could we make it interesting—not just to us, but to the sales managers on the pub board?

I was about fifteen minutes into the flight when the answer finally hit me. What if we turned the life question into a mystery? The initial idea for *Oxygen* came from me wanting to do *Robinson Crusoe* on Mars. What if our intrepid astronauts found a fifth set of footprints on Mars? No—not a literal set of footprints. That would be too easy to explain away. But what if they came across evidence that there was a "fifth man" on Mars—even though they knew the notion was scientifically impossible? And what if the *fifth man* was hostile?

Not only does this make good use of the mystery driver, but it gives us a decent scaffold to build an effective high concept around. And considering how late we were submitting the proposal, we were going to need a very good high concept if we were going to have a prayer of getting the pub board to contract our sequel.

Randy sez: This has to be the easiest story idea I ever came up with. For the simple reason that I outsourced it all to John. What I remember is that we had a fine time at the trade show, met a lot of people, and discovered that in the grand scheme of things, we are amazingly insignificant.

OK, that last part wasn't so grand. But it's true. When you wander around a huge hall with tens of thousands of books on display, you realize that if you vanished from the earth along with your one measly book, nobody would notice. That can crush your ego, if you let it. Getting published is a great way to demolish your delusions of adequacy.

So by the time the show ended, we were both pretty low. We dragged our sorry carcasses onto the plane and collapsed into our seats. I was glad we were flying together, because I really needed a good friend along to tell me, “Hey, you’re not really as insignificant as you look.”

Tragically, John had nothing to say about that. Shortly after we got into the air, he suddenly said, “I’ve got an idea.”

Then he whipped out a little notebook and starting writing things down.

After about half an hour of that, I think I said something like, “Care to share?”

John said, “I’ll tell you later.”

I couldn’t get a word of his idea out of him for the rest of the flight.

A week later, after we were back into our normal lives, John called me and said, “Want to hear my idea?”

I did.

Like I said, this was the easiest story idea I ever came up with, since John did all the work. But it was also the most frustrating. Because our careers were riding on coming up with something good, and I had absolutely nothing to work with. Talk about a no-pressure situation.

OK, back to you, John. How about if you explain about high concept, so we mere mortals can understand how you come up with these ideas?

John sez: If you hadn’t interrupted me, we’d already be in the next appendix where I explain exactly that.

# *Bonus Appendix B: Developing a Powerful High Concept*

**By John Olson**

**March, 2012**

## What is a High Concept Exactly?

The concept of the *high concept* originated in Hollywood during the late 1970s and was popularized by film executives such as Barry Diller and Michael Eisner. *Jaws* and *Star Wars* were some of the original examples of high concept films, so a lot of writing students have come to confuse high concept films with blockbuster films even though the distinction is simple. High concept films are movies that can be described by a succinct premise statement whereas blockbuster films are movies that are smash hits at the box office.

The reason for the confusion is rather unexpected. There appears to be something about high concept films that makes them much more likely to become blockbusters. I know what you're thinking. A film that can be described by a succinct premise statement? That's all it takes to make a blockbuster?

Not exactly . . . But given a certain minimum standard of quality, high concept films tend to be much more successful than er . . . shall we say low concept films. Obviously there's more to the concept of high concept than meets the eye.

*High concept* is a hard concept for most writers to get a handle on. In all my years teaching writing classes, students have had more trouble grasping high concept than any other technique I teach. Yet it's by far the most powerful technique writers can have in their arsenal—especially if they're unpublished writers trying to get published for the first time. If there's such a thing as a magic bullet for breaking into the publishing business, that magic bullet is high concept.

Part of the reason *high concept* is so confusing to people is that the term is used in so many different ways. As I've already said, the simplest, most straightforward definition of high concept is that it's an artistic work that can be described by a succinct premise statement. Yes, this is the basis for the infamous one-sentence elevator pitch you've doubtless heard so much about if you've ever wandered within a hundred miles of a writing class any time during the last decade.

However, according to the above definition, "A woman struggles with guilt after having an affair" is technically a high concept, but it's certainly not a magic bullet for getting published. And it's light years away from what most people mean when they talk about a high concept book or film.

Don't get me wrong. The exercise of reducing your story to a one-sentence elevator pitch can be very helpful. If an author is able and willing to face reality, the exercise can help him see that his baby isn't quite as compelling as he thinks it is. And one-sentence elevator pitches are extremely useful for editors, because they help them figure out whether or not they're interested in a story without having to listen to an author ramble on forever. But this alone isn't going to sell your story. It may even make your story harder to sell.

So what is a high concept if it isn't a one-sentence elevator pitch?

My definition of an effective high concept—the magic bullet kind of high concept—is very simple. An effective high concept is any premise statement, one-sentence or not, that makes the reader want to buy your book—whether you can write or not. Or more to the point, it's any premise statement that makes editors want to give you a contract—whether you have a track record or not.

Here's the reality of the publishing world . . . Book publishers are very, very conservative. They're looking for known quantities that are safe, measurable, and predictable. If you're an unpublished writer, then you're not any of those things. You don't have a sales history the publishers can use to predict future sales. You don't have a reputation of being easy to work with. You don't have a track record for doing a good job marketing your books. You're a huge, hairy, scary unknown, and you're competing with hundreds of published authors who are much safer bets than you are. Even if you're an extraordinarily gifted writer, at best you're an extraordinarily gifted unknown writer competing with extraordinarily gifted known writers.

## Why You Need a High Concept

So if it's so hard to get published, how do new writers ever break into the business? In my experience unpublished writers have two things going for them. 1) Every editor wants to discover the next J.K. Rowling. Even though they realize the odds of that happening are comparable to the odds of winning the lottery, they can't help but buy that lottery ticket every once in a while when they discover a new writer who has some talent. 2) Every once in a while, new writers come up with really effective high concepts, and the editors have no choice but to contract the book.

It's as simple as that. If you can come up with an idea that's so compelling that people will buy the book based on the idea alone, then you've taken all the risk out of the deal for the publisher. If the idea is really that good, then it doesn't matter whether you're a good marketer or a good writer or even a good person. You're going to sell books.

It's a no-brainer for sales and marking. An effective high concept means the marketing copy will write itself, and all they'll have to do to sell the books into a store is tell them the high concept. They can't lose. And if the project has a really good high concept, the editor will be much more willing to put extra effort into the editing process to make up for your lack of experience and craft.

Okay . . . I know what you're thinking. So far my whole argument is tautological. If I define an effective high concept as any premise statement that's so compelling that it makes readers want to buy the book whether it's well-written or not, then of course editors will want to buy the book. But can high concepts really be that effective? How often does a high concept sell a story in the real world of book publishing?

In my experience it happens all the time. In fact nowadays, if a book sells at all—especially if the writer is unpublished—then there's a very good chance that the sale was at least partially based on the high concept.

So how does it work? How do you go about crafting a story with an effective high concept? Here is a technique that makes coming up with an effective high concept much easier.

An effective high concept should *suggest* what the story is about without actually *telling* what the story is about. The trick is to present an unresolved situation that is so compelling that the readers can't rest without trying to figure out how to resolve it. The more you can get the readers to think, the more likely they'll start writing the story in their heads. And once that happens, you've got them. Your story becomes their story. And once they start to take ownership of the story, of course they'll think it's brilliant. It's their story after all. And of course the story they're going to write in their heads is going to be exactly the kind of story they like to read, because they're the ones who are writing it.

## The Psychology of High Concept

I've seen this happen countless times, and I'm always amazed at how effective it is. A good high concept sucks editors in so that they start writing the story in their heads. And then, even though the author's plot synopsis takes them step by step through a completely different story, the editors can't let go of their initial impression. They persist in their belief that the author is going to write the story they see in their mind's eye. The psychology at work here is so amazingly powerful that it can cause all kinds of disconnects between the author and the publisher.

I once wrote a proposal for a high concept scientific thriller that the editors fell completely in love with. Everything was perfect at first. The publishers contracted the book right away and paid me the highest advance I'd ever received. Everything was smooth sailing until I turned in the manuscript. Then, during the first editorial meeting, the disconnects started to surface.

Three editors were assigned to the book, one male and two females. The females were both pleased with the manuscript, but the male was outraged. Where did I get off turning the book into a romance? My book was supposed to be a straight thriller like his favorite author wrote—not an emotional romantic suspense.

The female editors and I couldn't believe it. What planet was this guy from? Hadn't he read the proposal? I stated clearly at the beginning of the proposal that the book was a "scientific thriller with strong romance elements." Furthermore, the plot synopsis was very clearly focused on the romantic story line. I hadn't pulled a fast one. I'd written exactly what I'd said I would write.

The more we talked, however, the more I began to see what had happened. My statement of the high concept had made him start writing the story in his head, and once his vision for the story had gotten a foothold in his brain, he couldn't shake it—even when it conflicted with what I actually said in the proposal. He was so enamored with his version of the story that they eventually had to take him off the project. He couldn't let it go.

Yes, this was tragic, and yes, my high concept was responsible for the confusion, but don't lose sight of the bigger picture. If it weren't for the power of high concept, that editor never would have contracted my book in the first place. (Actually he wasn't the acquiring editor, but you get the point.) Your first job as a writer is to get the contract. Everything else is secondary.

So is using the power of high concept in a proposal akin to lying? Is the whole point to mislead the editors?

Not at all. The same thing that makes high concept so effective at selling your proposal to editors will also make it effective at selling your books to retailers and readers. You're giving publishers a powerful tool for selling your books. It's not your fault it has the side-effect of selling your proposal to pub boards as well.

## Six Roads to a High Concept

Okay . . . Enough squawking. Understanding high concept isn't going to get you anywhere if you can't create good high concept stories on your own. Here are six of my best tricks for developing good high concepts.

**1. Dilemma**: Put your hero in a situation that creates a huge, story-world-changing dilemma for him. There should only be a few choices for the hero, and no matter what he chooses there needs to be bad consequences. In other words, put him in the proverbial "tight spot." The tighter the spot, the more powerful your high concept will be.

This particular high concept pattern is my favorite, because it was through this pattern that I first discovered the power of high concept. Here's how I started to figure things out.

I was interrogating editors at a writers conference when I started to notice a pattern in what got them excited. It all started when I asked an editor if she had read any proposals that had caught her eye. Up to this point in our conversation she had been cool, collected and professional, but all of a sudden her eyes lit up and her hands started fluttering like she was trying to take flight.

"Get this." She leaned toward me and fixed me with an expectant look. "A man is helping his wife fix dinner for their grown-up son and his fiancé whom they haven't met yet. The man's son walks into the house and introduces his fiancé, and the man discovers that she's the woman he had had an affair with the year before." She leaned forward even more, waiting for my reaction. "Isn't that awesome!" She was so excited I thought she might actually manage to take flight after all.

What had just happened? She never once mentioned the quality of the author's prose. She didn't discuss plot or marketing plans or even branding. Yet she was more excited than any editor I'd ever seen. And she expected me to share her excitement based on the high concept alone.

So why was she so excited? It took her two whole sentences to get the premise out, and the sentences she used were far from elegant.

The answer was written in her eyes as she waited for me to respond. I could practically hear the gears turning in her head. She was working through the dilemma in her own mind while I was working through it in mine. What was the man going to do? Would he warn his son and spill the beans about his affair, or would he stay silent and protect his dark secret? In my mind the man attempted to warn his son without giving his actual reasons, which of course got him into more and more trouble as the story progressed. I absolutely loved where the story was going. The premise led inevitably to a huge comedic mess in which the man digs his own grave and then hangs himself with the shovel. I couldn't wait for the book to come out. I wanted to read it now.

But as I talked to her more, it became obvious to me that the story she had in her head wasn't nearly as good as mine. Her story was a dramatic tragedy full of devastation and heartache and soggy Kleenex. "Isn't it horrible?" she asked in a weepy voice.

"Yes!" I wanted to say. "How could you do that to my story?"

See how it works? All the author had to do was put her protagonist in a tight spot. No matter what the protagonist chose to do, he couldn't win. When we, as potential readers, hear this kind of dilemma, we can't help but put ourselves in the situation and try to solve the problem. Human beings are natural problem-solvers. We can't help it. It's what we do. But in this case there are no win-win solutions to the problem, so we keep working the problem and start writing the book in our heads. Which means that the author's story becomes our story, and we can't help but love it. Six points for the author!

**2. Implied Conflict**: Put your hero in a situation that's pregnant with implied conflict. It's very important that the conflict be implied and not explicit. If you make the conflict explicit, then the readers don't have to go that extra step of figuring out what the conflict is which leads them to the next step of trying to figure out how to resolve the conflict which leads them down the path of writing the story in their heads.

Here's an example of an "implied conflict" high concept: *An evil wizard rules a tiny kingdom with an iron fist. Nobody can stand against him. He's the only magic-wielder in the land. Until one day a peasant boy discovers that he has the power to make himself invisible . . .*

You'll notice that I never mentioned any conflict. I never said the boy was in any danger at all. I didn't even say what the boy was going to do with his new power. Maybe he'll only use his power for shower, er . . . meteor shower gazing. Maybe . . . But the smart reader knows he won't, because if he did then there wouldn't be a story and there wouldn't have been a reason to mention the evil wizard. We all know what's going to happen in this story, because we've already started writing it in our heads.

However, if I had made the conflict explicit, the readers wouldn't have needed to start writing the story themselves, so the statement of conflict wouldn't have been nearly as effective. Here's the same story with the conflict made more explicit: *A young boy discovers he has the power to turn himself invisible and sets out on a quest to overthrow the evil wizard who rules over his kingdom with an iron fist.*

See the difference? The first statement of high concept is incomplete, so it invites us to finish the story in our minds. The second statement, however, tells us exactly what happens, so our imaginations aren't engaged. There aren't any big unknowns for us to fill in, so we're much more likely to feel like we've "been there and read that."

**3. Paradox**: Our logical little brains have a love-hate relationship with paradox. When we hear a paradoxical statement, we can't rest until we've at least made an attempt to resolve the conflict implicit in the statement. The more we chew on the problem, the more different scenarios we walk through in our minds until, you guessed it, we start writing the story in our logical little heads.

Here's one of the high concept statements I used in my third book, *Adrenaline*: *Three grad students need feedback on the unbelievable results of an experiment, so they invent a fictitious scientist and publish a scientific paper under his name. The charade is a success. Everything is going according to plan until the fictitious scientist starts murdering people.*

See how this works? We know fictitious scientists don't commit murder, so we start trying to figure out what's happening. Is someone else committing the murders and blaming it on the fictitious scientist? Is it one of the three grad students? What happens when the police trace the scientist back to the three students?

Every time we ask one of these questions, our brains start to work through scenarios to answer the question . . . and before we realize it, we've already started writing the story in our heads.

**4. Darkest Hour**: Put your hero in a life or death situation that sounds like death is inevitable. If your readers can't figure out how the hero is going to get out of the situation, then they'll start writing the story in their heads. Technically this is a special case of an "implied conflict" high concept (as is the "dilemma" high concept if you want to get picky about it), but I like to treat the cases separately, because working through them helps me come up with more story ideas.

*Oxygen* is a classic example of a "darkest hour" high concept: *An explosion rocks America's first manned mission to Mars. Who will live and who will die when there's only enough oxygen left on the ship to support one of the four astronauts?*

**5. Twist**: Start your readers down one path and then pull the rug out from under them by taking them in a new unexpected direction. This technique isn't as effective as the others, but if you've already written your story and need to retrofit it with a more effective high concept statement, sometimes throwing in a twist or two can capture your readers' imaginations long enough to get them writing the story in their heads. Here's an example. In my fourth novel, *Fossil Hunter*, I had a very pedestrian story concept to work with. *While paleontologist Katie James is working in the deserts of Iraq, she discovers a fossil that seems to fly in the face of accepted scientific theory.* Try as I might, I couldn't distill the dilemma into something the readers might care about. I couldn't even come up with something I cared about, and I love this kind of stuff.

So I added a twist and used the revised statement as a pull-out in my book proposal: *When their findings don't fit Darwin's theory, only the fittest will survive . . .*

Was this a good high concept statement? Not in the least . . . But I wanted to mention it as an example of the kind of doctoring you can do if you need to add some spice to an existing proposal or manuscript. Anything you can do to engage your reader's imagination just a little bit more is going to help in the long run.

Here's another example of a twisty little statement I used as a pull-out in my *Powers* proposal: *Those who don't learn from the future are destined not to repeat it.*

See how the statement bounces right off the brain? Most people have to read it several times before they start to see the implications—which is exactly what "twist" statements are supposed to do. Your readers are supposed to say "Huh?" and then read the statement again. The goal is to get them chewing on the concept until next thing they know, they're starting to write the story in their heads.

**6. Implied Mystery**: Put your hero in a situation in which there is an implied mystery. Again, just as was the case with "implied conflict," making the mystery implied rather than explicit forces the reader to take that first problem-solving step in their minds which makes it easier to take second and third steps until they are writing the whole story in their heads.

You might recall that we wanted the sequel to *Oxygen* to be driven by the *mystery* driver to keep it from feeling too much like the first book which was driven by the *suspense* driver. So how could we use implied mystery to generate a high concept statement for our sequel? I'd like to be able to walk you step by step through my decision-making process on the airplane, but the truth of the matter is that the high concept statement and the mystery angle for the idea all came together in a flash.

If you work on high concept long enough, you start to develop an intuition for it so that the ideas spring to life in full high concept statement form. At least that's been my experience.

Here's the initial idea that flashed into my mind for the *Oxygen* sequel: *Four astronauts find a fifth set of footprints on Mars . . .*

That's it. Simple and sweet. The mystery is implied which gets the reader asking questions which leads them down the path of writing the book in their heads. It's not the most compelling high concept I've ever come up with, but it served as a good compass for writing the book—whether we ended up using it to sell the proposal or not.

If you started analyzing blockbuster books and movies, I'm sure you could come up with a lot more than the six high concept patterns that I've listed for you here, but hopefully the example patterns have helped you understand how high concept works and why it's so powerful.

In my experience, the more time I spend working on ideas, the better I get at coming up with good ones. I hope that will be your experience as well, but if it isn't, don't worry. I'm an extremely slow writer. I have hundreds of good ideas that I'll never have a chance to write. I'll be happy to sell you one for cheap.

# *Bonus Appendix C: Every Scene Is a Story*

**By Randy Ingermanson**

**March, 2012**

## The Basic Theory of Scenes

The basic unit of your novel is the scene. If you can write one really good scene, then you can write another, and another, and another and pretty soon you've got a novel.

If you can't write a scene, then you can't write a novel. Period.

It's important to remember that every scene is a miniature story, all on its own. The scene has a beginning, a middle, and an end. When you finish the scene, your characters will have changed in some essential way. If they haven't—if nothing has changed in your scene—then slit its throat and throw it off the ship, because the scene isn't pulling its weight.

It's also important to remember that a scene happens in real-time. It unfolds minute by minute, using these five tools: action, dialogue, interior monologue, interior emotion, and sensory description. Anything that doesn't use these five tools is not part of the scene. A scene happens at a particular place and time, with particular characters. Narrative summary is not a scene. Exposition is not a scene. Backstory explanation is not a scene.

Every scene must do some work—emotional work. In this appendix, we'll look at how that happens.

I like to divide up all possible scenes into two kinds:

Proactive scenes—in which the character is proactively trying to reach some goal (and usually fails).

Reactive scenes—in which the character is reacting to some previous setback and trying to find her way to a new direction.

The theory of each of these is pretty simple, but as we'll see, the author has plenty of room to bend the theory around to suit the story.

A proactive scene has a simple structure—a beginning, a middle, and an end. The beginning defines the goal of the lead character for this particular scene. The middle shows the lead character in conflict—a series of obstacles preventing her from reaching her goal. The end usually shows the lead character failing to reach her goal. Sometimes the end shows the lead character achieving her goal but then finding some unexpected problem.

We can summarize a proactive scene with just three words: goal, conflict, setback.

A reactive scene also has a simple structure—a beginning, a middle, and an end. The reactive scene is normally shown as the immediate followup to a proactive scene that ended in a setback. So the beginning of a reactive scene shows the lead character in emotional reaction to the setback of the previous scene. The middle shows the lead character working through a dilemma, trying to figure out the best option when there aren't any good options. In the end of the scene, the lead character chooses the least bad option and commits to it.

We can summarize a reactive scene with just three words—reaction, dilemma, decision.

Once the lead character reaches a decision on a new course of action, that decision serves as the goal for the next proactive scene. So proactive and reactive scenes naturally chain together to form a story.

## An Example Proactive Scene

In the first scene of *The Fifth Man*, we meet Valkerie Jansen walking on a barren, dusty plain. What does she desperately want?

Water!

Is she thirsty?

No, she's in a suit that contains enough water for her needs. Valkerie Jansen is a biologist on the first human mission to Mars, and one of her main mission goals is to search for signs of past life on Mars.

Valkerie is searching for signs of water because, without water, there can be no life as we know it. (There might be life as we don't know it, but we probably wouldn't recognize it.)

John sez: Pardon my interruption, but I believe the bigger question here is whether life as we don't know it would recognize us, and if it did, would it eat us for second breakfast?

Randy sez: Wow, John that was really deep. You go have a bagel while I finish talking to the class here.

Valkerie desperately wants to find signs of life on Mars. That's the point of this mission, which has gone so wrong in so many ways. If she can find something, then at least the scientific part of the mission won't have been a waste.

Valkerie's partner, Lex, rappels down a steep cliff to a small ledge, and there she finds some salt deposits. That's not water, but it's a sign that water has been there in the past.

Valkerie's depression lifts. This could be something. She rappels down to join Lex, but there's a conflict here. She and Lex have been out working all afternoon and their oxygen bottles are getting low. Is there enough time to do a thorough investigation right now, or should they come back tomorrow? Valkerie wants to try now. Lex would rather wait.

But Valkerie's a stubborn cuss, and she starts digging, collecting samples. She crawls into a cave. Sees something that scares her. Keeps moving. Keeps looking.

Time is running out. Lex wants her to quit. Now!

Valkerie spots what she's looking for in the ceiling of the narrow cave. Something she hasn't seen since they've come to Mars. A rock bearing the unmistakable signs of past life.

There's no stopping Val now. She reaches for it. Can't quite get it. Drives her pick into the ceiling of the cave to loosen things up a bit. This works too well.

Her pick brings down a shower of gravel that pins her to the ground.

Valkerie has found her precious rock, but she's trapped—and the clock is ticking on her oxygen supply.

It's a strong scene. What makes it work?

Three things:

1) Goal. Valkerie knows what she wants in this scene. She wants to find life on Mars. Wants it desperately, because if she doesn't find something, then the mission is a waste and she's burned three years of her life for

nothing. Finding life will give meaning to Valkerie's life.

2) Conflict. Nothing worth having comes easy. Most of the scene is filled with one obstacle after another. Valkerie is a proactive person. She doesn't roll over and play dead at the first sign of a problem. She pushes on. Because she has a powerful goal that is important to her.
3) Setback. Valkerie achieves her goal—she finds the rock bearing signs of life—but now she's trapped. If things go badly, she could be dead in the next few minutes.

These features are common to all proactive scenes. A clearly defined goal. Conflict in the form of numerous obstacles. A setback at the end, whether or not the character reaches her goal.

Readers love proactive scenes because readers love proactive characters. Characters like Scarlett O'Hara, who knows what she want and goes for it. Like Harry Potter, who never gives up, even in the face of overwhelming odds. Like Katniss Everdeen, who will do whatever it takes to survive.

Think of your five favorite characters from fiction. The odds are huge that all five of them are proactive. Characters who take risks, do exciting things, get knocked down but keep on keeping on.

Characters who sit around moping, never taking action to get what they want, are *boring*. Nobody wants to read about characters like that.

John sez: Sorry to jump in again, but I strongly object to this statement. I am *not* boring, and my mother loves reading about me.

Randy sez: That's not what she told me.

Now where was I? Oh yeah, I was trying to make the point that mopey, non-proactive characters who aren't named John are boring and nobody wants to read about them.

Why is that? After all, most readers aren't terribly proactive. Most readers are unhappy with their lives. They have things they want to change, but never get around to it. They hang on in treadmill jobs and lackluster relationships. They rarely take action.

But they *wish* they could take action. They wish they had the courage to do so. When they read fiction, they want to read about people who have the guts to make changes. Because it inspires them. Because after reading about a proactive character with the courage to pursue a dream, they believe that maybe they can pursue their own. And sometimes they do.

Stories change readers. Stories give them hope, courage, faith, perseverance, strength. That's why readers read. You write fiction to give them those things.

Every proactive character feeds your reader's dreams. That's what your reader pays you for.

Proactive characters have lots of proactive scenes. Scenes with a goal. Scenes with conflict that require perseverance. Scenes that usually end in a setback.

Setbacks hurt.

After a setback, it's natural to take some time to recover. That's what a reactive scene is for.

## An Example Reactive Scene

In the next scene that features Valkerie and Lex, fear is gnawing at Valkerie. She's trapped and realizes that she might die, right here, right now. The only part of her body she can move is her hands.

Can Lex dig out some of the gravel and then pull Valkerie out?

Nope, Lex tries and it doesn't work. They need a plan B.

Can Lex push her forward?

Nope again. She tries that and it doesn't work. They need a plan C.

Can Valkerie grab the MoleBot and pull herself forward while Lex pushes?

Nope, the MoleBot is out of reach. They need a plan D.

Can Lex use the remote to drive the MoleBot back just a couple of feet so Valkerie can grab hold of it?

Nope, Lex stepped on the remote and broke it while trying to dig Valkerie out. They need a plan E.

Can Lex call their team member, Bob, back at the base station and ask him to issue a remote command to drive the MoleBot back a couple of feet? It's not a great option, but it's the best one they've got. Time is ticking and Lex is willing to try anything.

They decide to go with plan E. This requires a commitment in time. If it fails, then there may not be time to try anything else. If it succeeds, then Valkerie has a chance to survive. But they've made a decision, and this technically brings the reactive scene to an end.

Please note that sometimes reactive scenes merge directly into proactive scenes with hardly a speed bump. That's what happens here. You may not have noticed it in the chapter. There's only a tiny indication that the reactive scene has ended—the simple sentence, "Minutes passed."

That's all, but that's the indicator that a reactive scene has ended, and a proactive scene is beginning.

What happened in this reactive scene? Three important things:

1) Reaction. Valkerie begins with an emotive reaction—desperation. There's no real need to dwell on this reaction here. The situation is desperate. She doesn't have time to wallow in emotions for very long. But it sets the stage for the rest of the scene. They don't have to solve the problem just yet. But they do need to decide how to solve the problem.
2) Dilemma. Valkerie is boxed in. She doesn't have any good options. If she had a good option, then she wouldn't be desperate. But she's trapped and if she can't figure out how to get untrapped soon, she's dead. She considers five different courses of action, from the most obvious to the least obvious. The first four aren't going to work. The last one might.
3) Decision. They could press ahead with any of the five plans of action. But choosing one means rejecting the others. Which should they take? Obviously, the one they think will work best. In practice, this often means taking the least bad option. They make their decision and now they have to live with it. Usually, in a reactive scene, we don't find out immediately whether it works or not. Usually, the scene ends, and only in the next scene will we learn whether the decision was a good one.

In fact, if you look closely, the reactive scene does end here. There's a time break—those pesky minutes pass. What happens during those passing minutes?

We never see that. But we can guess what happens. An entire proactive scene takes place offstage. Lex calls Bob on the radio. Bob fumbles around, contacts the MoleBot, issues a command, and moves the MoleBot. This is a small proactive scene. We don't need to see it, because it's not particularly exciting. It doesn't end in a setback. It ends with success. Success isn't nearly as interesting as failure. So we skip the entire proactive scene and merely summarize it in just a few words in the next scene, which begins immediately after the phrase "minutes passed."

You don't have to show every scene that your characters live through. You'll be fine just showing the most exciting scenes. Your reader is smart. She can figure out what happened off camera.

## Some Questions About Scenes

Whenever I teach on proactive and reactive scenes, I get a lot of questions. Here are answers to some of the most common.

Q: This sounds too complicated. I'd rather just write, instead of following a formula.

A: My experience is that most beginning writers actually *do* want a formula for their writing—some magic gizmo that will make their fiction zing without having to work hard. The patterns of proactive and reactive scenes are not that formula because they provide you far too much freedom. They tell you the general shape of effective scenes, but that's it. Goal, conflict, setback. Reaction, dilemma, decision. That's not complicated. That's simple. But it's not easy.

Q: Do I have to write a reactive scene after every proactive scene?

A: No. The trend in modern fiction is to eliminate as many reactive scenes as possible. Your reader is smart, and if you don't show a reactive scene, she can figure out what decision was made, because that decision forms the goal of the next proactive scene. The important thing is that you, the author, should know how your character reacts to each setback, even if you don't show that reaction to the reader. And you should know the character's reasoning process for deciding what to do next, even if you never show that to the reader either.

Q: Why would I ever show a reactive scene if my reader can figure out the decision that was made?

A: Because sometimes the decision process is interesting and exciting all on its own. Your goal is to show the most interesting and exciting parts of your story. When your lead character is backed into a corner with no possible way of escape, there's a puzzle to be solved. If you just show the final solution, your reader may accuse your characters of being stupid and missing a simpler, better, and more obvious option. So you may need to show your reader exactly why that option won't work. That is part of the dilemma phase of the reactive scene.

John sez: Showing a reactive scene also gives the writer a way to torture the reader a bit longer. I worked hard to put Valkerie in a tight spot. I wanted to keep her there as long as possible to make the reader squirm. If Valkerie had broken free right away, there wouldn't have been enough time for the tension to build. The readers would have gotten away without any emotional cuts and bruises. Where's the fun in that? Your job as an author is to hurt the readers. The longer you can make them squirm, the more they'll celebrate victory in the end.

Q: If I show a proactive scene and then immediately show the reactive scene that follows and then immediately show the proactive scene that follows that, I'll be stuck showing the storyline of one single character forever! Why can't I switch to another character?

A: You can. In fact, you should. In modern fiction, authors often show a proactive scene for one character (ending in a cliffhanger), and then switch to a new character's proactive scene (ending in a second cliffhanger), and then may switch to a third character's proactive scene (ending in yet another cliffhanger). When you do that, the tension builds nicely because you've got several characters hanging off cliffs. Eventually, you need to circle back and start getting them out of trouble, but you can juggle numerous storylines this way.

John sez: Did you guys know that when editors say to end your first scene with a cliffhanger, they don't actually mean your heroine needs to be hanging off a cliff? I wish I'd known that before.

Randy sez: Good thing I explained that after you wrote this scene, or things might have got Xtremely repetitive. There are only so many cliffs on Mars.

Q: You make it sound like every scene in my novel must have conflict. I don't want to do that. I want to have a whole scene where I just explain the character's backstory so the reader knows what's going on.

A: Yes, of course you want to do that. But your reader doesn't want to read a big, indigestible glop of backstory early in the book. Your reader doesn't care about your character's backstory until you've got her interested in the frontstory. So show the conflict first. Then work in a little backstory right when your reader needs it. It's important for you, the author, to know the backstory of every character. But it's less important for your reader to know it.

John sez: Another bad thing about backstory is that it kills the mystery driver. If your backstory explains away all the idiosyncracies of your protagonist, then the reader doesn't have any mysteries to solve. But if your protagonist reacts to her situation in unexpected ways, then all of a sudden your readers have something to look forward to. They'll keep turning the pages because they want to solve the mystery.

Randy sez: This can be overdone. I've read novels where there was so much mystery artificially injected by the author that I got tired of being yanked around and put the book down. Mystery is like perfume—a little goes a long way.

Q: Can't I just have a nice scene with no conflict where two characters are sitting there talking and I show the reader who they are? Can't I just develop my characters without conflict?

A: Of course you can do that. You are the god of your novel. You can do anything you want. And your reader can set the book down anytime your novel gets boring. You can't force your reader to keep reading. All you can do is to make the book so interesting that the reader doesn't want to quit. The normal way to do that is by using conflict. If you have a scene that has no conflict and yet is massively interesting, then go ahead and keep it. But remember that your readers are the ones who decide what's massively interesting and what's not.

Q: OK, so what makes a proactive scene "interesting?"

A: That's easy. Any character who desperately wants

something is automatically interesting. In *Gone With the Wind*, we see early on that Scarlett desperately wants Ashley. We haven't met Ashley and we have no idea whether he's a good catch or not. But we have met Scarlett, and the fact that she wants him so badly fascinates us. Will she or won't she get him? That is the story question of the novel. Every scene is a miniature story, and so it has its own miniature story question, which must be answered by the end of the scene. The story question is always the same. Will the lead character get her goal in this scene, or won't she?

Q: Fine, but what makes a reactive scene "interesting?"

A: That's also easy. A reactive scene is always the followup to a setback from a previous proactive scene. A reactive scene is also a miniature story, and its story question is always the same. What is the lead character going to do to get out of this mess?

Q: You gotta be kidding me! You're telling me that *every* scene in *every* published novel ever written is either a proactive scene or a reactive scene?

A: Nope. Didn't say that. You can find plenty of chunks in published novels that are done in narrative summary. You can also find big blocks in published novels that are pure exposition—nothing is actually happening at all. (Those are the parts you skim, aren't they?) You will occasionally find scenes in published novels that are poorly written. You will often find scenes in published novels where the author shows only pieces of proactive or reactive scenes. In every case, you can ask yourself whether the scene works. Could the author have done it better by using either a proactive scene or a reactive scene? Usually the answer is a clear "yes." Once in a while, the answer is "no." The scene structure of proactive and reactive scenes are guidelines to help you write better, not rules that you have to live by.

Q: But surely scene structure isn't all there is to writing fiction?

A: No, of course it isn't. There are six different levels of structure in the plot of any novel. The structure of scenes is just one of those six levels. Even if you get your scene structure right, you still have five other levels that you must also get right. Plus, you need to master character development, story world development, theme, and voice, which are entirely separate from plot. But let's remember one thing. The scene is the basic unit of fiction. If you *fail* to write emotively powerful scenes, then you are never going to be successful writing fiction.

Q: You make it sound like writing a scene is a "paint-by-numbers" kind of a thing.

A: No, actually I don't. Writing a scene is a bit like writing a limerick, which has a well-defined structure—five lines with a rhyme scheme of AABBA and a very precisely defined rhythm. But writing a limerick is definitely not paint-by-numbers. It takes great imagination and creativity to write within the structure required for a limerick. The payoff for keeping within that structure is that you produce something humorous. Likewise, it takes great imagination and creativity to write within the structure of a proactive or reactive scene. The payoff is that you produce something that moves your reader emotively.

Q: I can't plan my scene out in advance. I just write and the magic happens.

A: You don't have to plan your scene in advance. If you don't want to write without planning, you're in good company. Lots of writers do that. But then they have to edit after they write, because sometimes that pesky magic happens and sometimes it doesn't. After the scene is written, whether the magic happened or didn't, ask yourself if you can make the scene more magical by tweaking it into the structure of either a proactive scene or a reactive scene. If you can, then do so; you've gained something by applying the pattern. If the scene has no magic and if you can't pump some magic into it, then you need to kill the scene without remorse. Your novel is not a convalescent home for sick scenes. It's a stage where you show off only your best scenes.

## A Sequence of Scenes

Earlier, we looked in detail at examples of one proactive scene and one reactive scene from *The Fifth Man*. Two scenes are not a novel. Let's see now how the scenes in the novel work together to create continuing conflict that can carry on and on.

In what follows, we'll briefly analyze a long sequence of scenes. We'll decide if each scene is proactive or reactive, and we'll spell out the parts of each. We'll see what makes each scene work, and we'll see some places where we could have done better. (Tragically, every novel ever written has some scenes that could be done better. The author eventually has to quit fixing things and turn the beast in to the publisher. No novel is perfect, certainly not any of mine. Yes, this enrages me. No, I am not going to go on tweaking my novels forever.)

## Scene 1

Valkerie and Lex discover a cave that shows signs of water. When Valkerie digs into the cave, she spots a rock that appears to be a fossil of some ancient bacterial life form. While trying to dig it out, she triggers a fall of gravel, leaving her half buried and with little oxygen left in her bottle.

This is a proactive scene.

**Goal**: Search for signs of water, because that is a sign of ancient life on Mars.

**Conflict**: Valkerie's enthusiasm outweighs her good sense and she pushes into a cave without enough time to do the job well.

**Setback**: Valkerie half buries herself in gravel—and time is running out.

## Scene 2

Bob is inspecting the fuel factory that has created the fuel to be used to return to earth. He has a panic attack for no good reason, and then has a pointless argument with his coworker Kennedy. When an emergency call comes in from Lex, Bob races back to the home base, but he can't hear a thing because of static on the line.

This is a proactive scene.

**Goal**: Do a routine inspection.

**Conflict**: Bob is showing signs of paranoia—or maybe Kennedy is.

**Setback**: They have a right to be paranoid, because somebody is jamming their radio.

## Scene 3

Valkerie and Lex are trying to figure out how to get Valkerie unstuck. They try several options, but nothing is working and time is running down. Finally, Lex decides to radio Bob and ask him to teleoperate the MoleBot back a couple of feet so Valkerie can use it to help get free.

This is a reactive scene with some proactive elements.

**Reaction**: Fear. Valkerie knows she has limited time to get free.

**Dilemma**: Valkerie and Lex try and reject various approaches.

**Decision**: They finally decide to radio Bob for help, but it's a bit of a longshot.

Note the proactive elements in this scene, which might have tricked us into labeling this a proactive scene:

**Goal**: Get free and return to the rover before oxygen runs out.

**Conflict**: They try several things, but nothing is working.

There is no real setback in this scene, which is why it's not a proactive scene, even though it has proactive elements. Instead, the scene ends with a decision, which is why we believe this is a reactive scene. (Scenes aren't always easy to label. We feel horrible about this fact, but there you have it.)

Note that there is no scene break between this scene and the next. Instead, there's only a short sentence to say that minutes have passed.

## Scene 4

The Molebot suddenly begins working and moves backward right to Valkerie. She uses it to help pull herself free of the rubble. Lex digs out the tunnel and Valkerie refuses to leave until she's grabbed the sample and bagged it. By the time she's got her sample, Lex is screaming at her that they're down to fourteen minutes of reserve.

This is a proactive scene but the setback is rather buried.

**Goal**: Get free and get to safety.

**Conflict**: Valkerie wants to collect the sample too, which costs them precious time.

**Setback**: By the time she gets the sample, they're very close to being completely out of oxygen.

This scene isn't working as well as it could. The time pressure isn't being used well enough, and the setback at the end seems lost in the glow of discovering an actual sample of former life on Mars. A strong setback compels the reader to keep reading. A weak setback doesn't.

## Scene 5

Bob has been working remotely, trying to help Lex and Valkerie, but he has no idea if he's succeeded because of the radio static. Kennedy arrives and furiously accuses Bob of "pushing" him while they were outside, which is absurd. They argue for a bit, and Kennedy calls Bob a "loser." Bob finally decides to simply go out on foot to try to help the women.

This scene has elements of a reactive scene, but it's incomplete.

**Reaction**: Bob doesn't know if he succeeded or not in helping Valkerie and Lex, and he's terribly worried about them.

**Dilemma**: What should he do now?

**Decision**: He decides to go out on foot looking for them.

The scene lacks focus. It could be all about the crisis that Valkerie and Lex are having, but it doesn't stick to that problem. It could be a proactive scene about the friction between Bob and Kennedy, but the scene has only the conflict, with no clearly defined goal nor any resolution to the conflict.

## Scene 6

Valkerie and Lex return to the rover with very little oxygen left in their bottles. Lex is furious with Valkerie for violating every safety precaution they've ever been taught. They make the ascent at a wild pace and barely make it back in time. Valkerie realizes she's been an idiot.

This scene is a proactive scene.

**Goal**: Valkerie and Lex need to return to the rover before their oxygen runs out.

**Conflict**: They barely have enough time and Lex is so angry that she's making the ascent even more hazardous.

**Setback**: They reach the rover safely, but Valkerie realizes she's been an egocentric idiot and her relationship with Lex is now damaged.

## Scene 7

Valkerie and Lex both feel self-recrimination. They apologize to each other. The mysterious radio static stops, and now they can communicate with Bob back at base camp. They reassure him that all is well and then Valkerie reports on her find to Houston.

This is very roughly a reactive scene, which serves mainly to reduce tension and bring things back to normal.

**Reaction**: Self-recrimination and guilt.

**Dilemma**: There is no dilemma here. When you're wrong, you're wrong, so you apologize and move on.

**Decision**: They apologize to each other, talk to Bob, and then call Houston with the extraordinary news that they've found a fossilized sample of halobacteria—convincing proof that life once existed on Mars.

This is not a particularly emotive scene. Its main purpose is to restore things to normal after a life-threatening scene and make the transition to the main story of the book—what happens if we discover life on Mars?

## Scene 8

In Houston, Josh is ecstatic at the news that the team has discovered life on Mars. This is a fantastic discovery, and it means that the mission is a success. It also means there will be a next mission—and he may be on it. Right now, it's time to tell the world.

This is a reactive scene.

**Reaction**: Ecstasy and celebration. This is big, big news.

**Dilemma**: There is no dilemma here because there's no setback, from Josh's point of view. Everything is rosy.

**Decision**: Notify the networks and get ready to go to Congress and get back all the funding it's taken in the last few years, because NASA now has a reason to run another mission.

The reaction to a success is generally a lot simpler than the reaction to a setback, because there's no dilemma. This scene is short because there's no tension. That comes next.

## Scene 9

Bob is waiting back at the Hab to welcome Valkerie. He's excited at her big discovery and desperately wants to tell her how worried he was about her—to patch things up in their relationship. But Kennedy horns in on the welcome and Bob gets angry and makes a fool of himself. Valkerie is irritated that Bob is being a jerk again and she tells him she can't talk right now because she has more important things to do.

This is a proactive scene.

**Goal**: Bob wants to welcome Valkerie back, congratulate her, and finally find a way to express his feelings so he can patch things up with her.

**Conflict**: Kennedy horns in and Bob reacts badly, as if it were a turf war.

**Setback**: Valkerie is more disgusted than ever with Bob and she doesn't have time for him now because the halobacteria discovery is more important than her relationship with him.

## Scene 10

Nate presides over the late-night press conference at NASA announcing the discovery of life on Mars. The first questioner asks Nate about the religious implications of this discovery. The second is a reasonable science question. The third is by a left-wing ecology nut asking about the possible need to quarantine the astronauts in case the new life form turns out to be toxic. Nate brushes her off with a science-based answer, but she's clearly operating on fear, not logic. Nate realizes that his team may have won a great victory for science, but they may be in for a political battle.

This is a proactive scene.

**Goal**: Announce the discovery of life on Mars and set the stage for better funding for the Mars Mission Directorate.

**Conflict**: The religious right and the fear-mongering left aren't happy about this discovery.

**Setback**: A battle is brewing over the ridiculous question of whether the astronauts may need to be quarantined.

## Scene 11

Bob has asked Kennedy to give him a haircut so he can try some male bonding. It isn't working. Kennedy, who has only one good eye, is giving Bob the world's worst haircut. When Lex and Valkerie walk in, they're both appalled. Bob feels humiliated, and then Kennedy gives Valkerie a flower—the first one successfully grown on Mars.

This is a proactive scene.

**Goal**: Bob wants to repair the strains in his relationship with Kennedy.

**Conflict**: Kennedy is intentionally doing a terrible job.

**Setback**: Valkerie and Lex blame Bob for the horrible haircut, and Kennedy scores points by giving Valkerie a flower. Bob feels that his chances with Valkerie have never been worse.

## Scene 12

Josh calls from Houston and Bob takes the call in his room, encrypted for privacy. Bob is worried that both he and Kennedy are showing signs of psychological instability. Bob has been having repeated panic attacks. Kennedy has been behaving strangely. Bob worries that he might lose control and try to kill Kennedy. Josh tells Bob that he has learned that Kennedy manipulated the selection of the crew to get Josh bumped off the mission. Kennedy is not to be trusted, and it can't be a coincidence that the radio problems are happening right when Kennedy is getting weird. Josh decides to ask the FBI investigators to show him everything they learned about Kennedy, because there must be something more here.

This is a reactive scene.

**Reaction**: Both Bob and Josh are worried about the disintegrating relationships on Mars.

**Dilemma**: Who is going nuts? Bob? Or Kennedy?

**Decision**: Josh believes that Bob is fine and Kennedy has a screw loose. It's time to talk to the FBI and find out exactly what they have uncovered on Kennedy's psychological state.

## Scene 13

Back on Mars, Bob is listening to Josh when the radio static starts up again, breaking off most of Josh's message. This can't be an accident. This has to be man-made and Bob is going to find out who's doing it.

This is a very short reactive scene.

**Reaction**: Annoyance at the radio static problem, and increasing desperation. Without communication to earth, Bob is completely alone.

**Dilemma**: Is it atmospherics? A loose wire? An accident?

**Decision**: None of the above. This is a hostile attempt to break communication between earth and Mars, and Bob is going to track it down and solve it.

## Scene 14

Two days have passed and Valkerie feels run off her feet. She's got an enormous amount of work on her plate and it all needs to pass scientific scrutiny back home. Any mistake she makes will be jumped on. Valkerie is overly paranoid about the possible reaction by the religious right. Will they be furious at her for discovering life on Mars? Valkerie is a Christian herself, but she fears being called a wolf in sheep's clothing. Lex takes Valkerie out on a "field trip" in the rover, but the real purpose is to give them both a chance to take a nap and rest, safely away from Bob, Kennedy, and the people back on earth.

This is a reactive scene, in response to a series of setbacks that have not been shown. The scene begins by reviewing those setbacks in narrative summary.

**Reaction**: Exhaustion.

**Dilemma**: What to do about all the pressure to get the science exactly right? How to deal with the fundamentalists back home who might monkey-trial Valkerie?

**Decision**: Take a nap. You can only go so long without rest and then you snap. Lex forces Valkerie to take some down time to recover.

## Scene 15

Nate has returned from D.C. where he met with the president and various congress critters. They're not happy with him, but he's hopeful he can get more funding for future missions. Nate is surprised to learn that there is static on the Deep Space Network. After a short discussion with Josh and EECOM, he decides that the new Russian Mars orbiter satellite has probably lost its own communications capability and is piggybacking on the NASA network to boost its signal. The static could be nothing more than encrypted Russian signals. Nate has found the Russians uncooperative lately, so he thinks the simplest solution is to have EECOM try to decode their transmissions and find the smoking gun.

This is a reactive scene.

**Reaction**: Nate feels stressed by the response from the president, and now this latest crisis with radio static.

**Dilemma**: What could be causing the problems with comm?

**Decision**: Obviously it's got to be the Russian satellite, because there isn't any other possible cause. So EECOM should decrypt the Russian communications and find the smoking gun.

## Scene 16

Nate orders EECOM to decrypt the Russian signals. She's overworked and has no training in cryptanalysis, so she says she can't do it. Nate gets angry and berates her. EECOM responds by resigning and walking out.

This is a short proactive scene.

**Goal**: Assign EECOM the task of decrypting the Russian signals.

**Conflict**: She has no training in cryptanalysis and no time to learn. Nate thinks she should just work harder.

**Setback**: EECOM resigns and walks out.

## Scene 17

Nate is angry at EECOM for being a "crazy woman." Josh is upset with Nate for losing a brilliant engineer because of his hamhanded management tactics. Nate gives Josh the authority and responsibility to solve the communications problem—using whoever he needs for the job.

This is a reactive scene.

**Reaction**: Nate is angry at EECOM and Josh is angry at Nate.

**Dilemma**: Who is going to solve the communications problem?

**Decision**: Nate will hand it off to Josh with orders to solve it—somehow.

## Scene 18

Josh talks to EECOM and tells her he's been given the responsibility to decrypt the static, but he doesn't expect her to do it. He tells her how important she is to the mission and asks her to rejoin the team. She does and asks what Josh will do if Nate fires him. He tells her not to worry—he knows to whom he'll assign the decryption problem.

This is a reactive scene.

**Reaction**: EECOM is still upset and Josh mollifies her.

**Dilemma**: Who is going to decrypt the Russian signals?

**Decision**: Josh knows just the person.

Normally, when the lead character makes a decision, he should let the reader know. We chose to break the scene here, leaving this decision not fully explained. The reader has enough information to guess, and in the very next scene, we show that this guess is correct.

## Scene 19

Josh is waiting for young, sexy Cathe Willison to show up for a meeting. She's late and he spends his time worrying about the mission and speculating on the mysterious Cathe. When she arrives, he asks if she can help with the decryption of the Russian signals. She doesn't know anything about decryption, but she agrees to take the job because she's confident she can learn enough to ask for help from the right people. She's so eager for the task that she gets right to work, ending any hopes Josh had for dinner with her.

This is a proactive scene.

**Goal**: Get Cathe Willison to take on the decryption project—and maybe ask her to dinner.

**Conflict**: Not much. Cathe is eager to do the job.

**Setback**: Cathe accepts the assignment and then hurries off to start work on it, ending any hopes Josh had for dinner with her.

It's not that strong of a scene, but at least it's short, and it does hint at the romance that's going to bloom between Josh and Cathe.

## Scene 20

It's late at night and Bob talks to Valkerie and Lex to tell them his concerns about Kennedy's psychological state. He can't seem to find the right words. He doesn't have any real evidence, because Kennedy behaves differently around the women than he does around Bob. But Bob is certain something's wrong and Kennedy needs a psychological evaluation. The discussion goes badly. Lex and Valkerie think Bob is just jealous of Kennedy. Valkerie makes it clear that any hopes Bob ever had for a relationship with her have now evaporated.

This is a proactive scene.

**Goal**: Bob wants Valkerie and Lex to help figure out what's wrong with Kennedy.

**Conflict**: It sounds to the women like Bob is the one with the problem.

**Setback**: Bob is pretty sure from the look on Valkerie's face that he has lost her.

## Scene 21

Valkerie spends some time alone in her room feeling horrible. She really likes Bob, but now is not the time for a romance, and his constant outbursts of jealousy aren't helping. She's been putting off answering his marriage proposal for months now, and it's making things weird. She wants life to go back to normal. The best thing to do is just tell him no, she can't marry him.

This is a reactive scene.

**Reaction**: Valkerie feels angry and sad because Bob is making things weird.

**Dilemma**: But is it really him making things weird, or her? She should have answered him right away, instead of stringing him along for months.

**Decision**: She's just going to tell him no right now, and be done with it.

This reactive scene merges without a break with the proactive scene that follows.

## Scene 22

Valkerie goes to talk to Bob. He's in the common room, moping. Everyone else is asleep. Valkerie tries to explain that she just can't say yes, but she makes a hash of it. Her reasons sound ridiculous because they are. Bob isn't getting it, but he finally promises not to bring up the subject of marriage until they're back home on planet earth. For now, they can go back to being just friends. Valkerie gives him a hug—and then sees something large and alien and terrifying behind him, right outside the window of the Hab.

This is a proactive scene.

**Goal**: Valkerie wants to convince Bob to go back to being just friends.

**Conflict**: Bob can't make sense of what she's saying because it doesn't actually make sense.

**Setback**: Bob agrees to drop the subject of marriage until they return to earth, and then Valkerie thinks she sees an alien "something" outside the window and screams.

## Scene 23

Lex and Kennedy come running to see what's gone wrong. Valkerie tries to explain that she saw something outside. Lex and Kennedy are skeptical. Bob didn't see anything, but he defends Valkerie because he knows she doesn't make things up. They argue for a while and then decide to investigate in the morning when they have some light.

This is a reactive scene.

**Reaction**: Everybody is confused and wants to know what all the fuss is about. Did Bob try to hurt Valkerie?

**Dilemma**: Valkerie tries to explain, but what she saw seems so unbelievable that it's really hard to give it any credence. Was it something or was it nothing?

**Decision**: Bob wants to believe her, and he'll investigate in the morning as soon as it gets light.

## Scene 24

Josh goes to the evidence room to see what he can learn from the FBI investigation of Kennedy. He sees exactly how Kennedy manipulated the NASA psychologists into bumping him off the mission. But this is old news. What is Kennedy doing right now? Could he possibly be causing the radio interference? If so, why? Cathe Willison comes by and reports on her progress on decryption. She asks what Josh is doing in this evidence room and Josh tells her about his suspicions of Kennedy. Cathe volunteers to help and soon finds some hidden passwords that the FBI team missed.

This is a proactive scene.

**Goal**: Get inside Kennedy's head to see if he might possibly be causing the radio static instead of the Russians.

**Conflict**: Josh can't find anything new, but he finds plenty to make him hate Kennedy more than ever.

**Setback**: Cathe comes by and quickly finds a clue that nobody else has seen yet—some secret passwords hidden by Kennedy.

John sez: Okay . . . I've been following you until now, but how is finding a big clue a setback?

Randy sez: Uh-oh, I meant to explain that earlier. The ending of a proactive scene is *usually* a setback. Once in a while, you need to end a proactive scene in a victory. But if possible, find a way to snatch some sort of defeat from the jaws of victory. In this case, there's not any easy way to do that. But since the standard pattern of a proactive scene is Goal-Conflict-Setback, I often get lazy and call the ending a "setback" even when it really isn't.

## Scene 25

Valkerie has received orders from Houston to do a complete psychological evaluation of Kennedy. She doesn't know that this is Josh's idea, so she assumes Bob is pulling strings. She's furious because she thinks the whole thing is ridiculous. She confronts Bob, who denies it. Maybe Lex talked to NASA? But Lex denies it too. There's no choice but to do the exam, even if it's ridiculous.

This is a reactive scene which follows on a scene which is never shown but which we can easily guess—in which Houston orders Valkerie to do the exam on Kennedy.

**Reaction**: Anger. How could Bob do this?

**Dilemma**: It wasn't Bob who caused this. And it wasn't Lex. Then who?

**Decision**: It doesn't matter who caused it. Everybody denies it. Might as well just do the stupid exam and get it over with.

This reactive scene merges smoothly with the proactive scene that follows.

## Scene 26

Valkerie tells Kennedy that Houston has ordered a psychological exam. Kennedy takes this calmly. While Valkerie begins the exam, Kennedy steers the conversation to Bob and his weird suspicions lately. Is it possible that Bob is paranoid? That he might have some sort of delusional disorder? Bob overhears their discussion and barges in, looking ready to fight. Valkerie is disgusted and stops the exam. It's obvious that Kennedy isn't the one with the problem—it's Bob.

This is a proactive scene.

**Goal**: Give Kennedy a quick exam to make the shrinks in Houston happy.

**Conflict**: Not much conflict here. Kennedy appears to submit willingly, but he is manipulating the test. Valkerie is too bone-tired to notice, but the reader can't help seeing what he's doing. Eventually, Kennedy diverts the topic to Bob's strange behavior.

**Setback**: Bob barges in and makes a scene, and now it's clear to Valkerie that he's the one with the problem, not Kennedy.

## Scene 27

Lex offers to give Bob a fixit haircut to repair the damage Kennedy did. She spends the time quizzing Bob about his relationship with Valkerie, and she can't understand why Bob keeps changing the subject to Kennedy. Bob is sounding paranoid and Lex is angry at him, because she can see that Valkerie likes him. So why is he sabotaging the relationship? Can't Bob just play his own game and get off this weird problem he's having with Kennedy? Bob agrees to try that.

This is a reactive scene.

**Reaction**: Bob is frustrated and angry at Kennedy.

**Dilemma**: Lex wants to help him, but how is Bob going to get back on track with Valkerie when he keeps harping about Kennedy?

**Decision**: Bob is going to dial things back and just be friends with Valkerie.

This scene ends in an odd way. Bob has made a decision, but the scene continues on with him then overhearing Valkerie and Kennedy talking and laughing in the kitchen. This reignites Bob's jealousy and he has another attack of anger. He wonders what's going wrong with him. Are they all hypervigilant? It's hard to classify this segment because it's not a full-fledged scene in its own right—there's no real resolution to it.

It's clear that we didn't think carefully about the structure of this scene in advance. This highlights the problem with the "write it and let the magic happen" philosophy. Once you've invested a lot of time writing a scene, you may not want to spend even more time fixing it if it turns out to be a bit wonky. Changing one scene often means changing the scenes that come after it. You can't keep changing things forever, because every change has ripple effects downstream.

## Scene 28

Josh and Cathe go to Kennedy's old office on a fishing expedition. Can they find some incriminating evidence? Kennedy's office is a mess—very different from his apartment and every other aspect of his life. What's that about? They log on to Kennedy's computer and do some searching. They find a web site Kennedy has been using for e-mail and try the secret passwords. One of these works. They discover that Kennedy has some inexplicable friends in Japan, and there is evidence that he's given away top secret NASA satellite documents to one of them.

This is a proactive scene.

**Goal**: Find evidence that Kennedy has been doing something incriminating.

**Conflict**: Not much conflict, because Kennedy didn't cover his tracks well.

**Setback**: They find a smoking gun. Kennedy has given a satellite schematic to a student in Japan.

Note that this setback is in some sense a victory. Josh and Cathe were looking for dirt on Kennedy and now they've found it. But of course, this is also a setback, because Kennedy has betrayed some of NASA's most important secrets. This is exactly what Josh was afraid of, but now he knows it's true.

## Scene 28

Valkerie wakes up feverish and vomiting.

This is a very short proactive scene.

**Goal**: Valkerie wakes up hearing strange noises and goes to investigate.

**Conflict**: She has a high fever and is sweating and vomiting.

**Setback**: Valkerie passes out, but not before she realizes she is very sick.

## Scene 29

Josh and Cathe check out Kennedy's apartment with some help from FBI agent Yamaguchi, who is skeptical they'll find anything. The apartment is obsessively clean, unlike Kennedy's office. They discover a video showing how Kennedy got Josh's password long ago. Nate calls with the news that Valkerie is unconscious on Mars with some unknown sickness.

This is a proactive scene.

**Goal**: Look for more evidence against Kennedy.

**Conflict**: Not much conflict. Kennedy didn't cover his tracks well.

**Setback**: They find more evidence that Kennedy is a weasel—he has a secret video of Josh in his office logging into his computer. And Valkerie is sick with an unknown disease.

## Scene 30

Valkerie wakes up and learns that she's had a high fever for 36 hours, but nobody knows the cause of her infection. It's not any known earth bacteria. And it can't be anything else. Can it?

This feels like a reactive scene, but without a decision.

**Reaction**: Valkerie wakes up, bewildered. Why is Bob wearing a mask?

**Dilemma**: Nobody knows what Valkerie has, but she was extremely sick and could easily have died.

**Decision**: None.

It's hard to call a scene reactive when it lacks a decision. There is only a dilemma. The scene would not make sense standing alone, but it functions really as the first half of the scene that follows, in which the team in Houston works through the same dilemma in more detail and comes to a real decision.

## Scene 31

Nate presides over a secret meeting with all those within NASA who know that Valkerie is sick. A man from CDC has also come. The purpose of the meeting is to figure out what to do about Valkerie's infection. If the cause is not of earth origin, then they have a major disaster on their hands. They decide to form two tiger teams to study their two main options—a quarantine facility on earth, or a resupply mission to Mars so as to quarantine the astronauts there.

This scene is a reactive scene (because it ends in a decision) but it's also a proactive scene (because that decision is so disastrous).

**Reaction**: The entire group is extremely concerned at the news that Valkerie has a serious infection of unknown origin. This should not be possible.

**Dilemma**: What to do? Quarantine them when they return to earth? Or leave them permanently quarantined on Mars?

**Decision**: Both are horrible options. Two tiger teams will be formed to study them and return with recommendations as soon as possible.

**Goal**: Figure out whether this infection is a threat to earth or not.

**Conflict**: Nate produces new information—that on the outbound journey, a bacteria infested the ship after a spacewalk in which Kennedy put his gloved hand on a damage point caused by a micrometeorite. Valkerie might now be infected with this bacteria, which might be an alien life form.

**Disaster**: NASA is seriously considering leaving the four astronauts permanently stranded on Mars, or else quarantining them on earth in what would be a massively expensive facility, which would need to be built in a crash program. Either way, the crew faces the rest of their life locked away from their friends and family on earth.

This scene is a major turning point in the story. Until now, NASA has considered fears of "back-contamination" from

Mars to earth to be laughably silly. From this point on, NASA is reluctantly considering those fears to be at least possible. Of course, back-contamination makes no sense to them. But nothing makes sense to them at this point, because they are lacking critical information. So they have to consider all options, even options that seem ridiculous.

John and I should note here that we consider the danger of back-contamination to be infinitesimally low. As Nate and other characters point out, diseases evolve along with their hosts. A bacterium that had actually evolved on Mars would not be adapted to a human host, and would be supremely unlikely to infect humans. The only way out of this conundrum that we could think of is the one we actually chose.

## Final Thoughts

And so it goes for the rest of the book. Proactive scenes and reactive scenes. If you want a homework problem, you might try analyzing the rest of the book.

You'll find that most scenes in the book fit one of these two patterns. In some cases, we bent the pattern. In others, we broke it. We leave it to you to decide whether we did right to violate the patterns, but probably we were wrong. We've got no excuse except our own human fallibility.

The nice thing about working with a coauthor is that you can always blame the other guy. Or you can score some good-guy points by manfully taking the blame. We're not going to play either of those games. Instead, we'll just say, "mistakes were occasionally made" and leave it at that.

John sez: Speak for yourself. I love those games. Randy made all of the mistakes, but noble and magnanimous guy that I am, I forgive him.

Randy sez: I'm taking the high road here. Not going to play that game. I will manfully take the blame for missing a few of John's thousands of spelling errors. So if Bob occasionally tries to punch the buttons on a "wench," yes, it's my fault for not catching that. Apparently John prefers wenches to winches.

Oh, one more thing. You'll note that the president is sometimes referred to as "she." We wrote *Oxygen* in 1999/2000 and *The Fifth Man* in 2001, so we had no idea who the president would be during the years 2012 to 2015. At least one reviewer in 2001 thought we were trying for political correctness in making the president a woman. The truth is that we looked hard at the political landscape in 1999 and made a guess at who might be elected in 2008.

Our guess was Hillary Clinton.

We guessed close, but we guessed wrong.

We have resisted the urge to correct our error in this second edition. Life is about making decisions based on incomplete information. Life is also about living with those decisions. That's what we make our characters do. So that's what we've done too.

Restorer's Son
Sharon Hinck

FAILSTATE
JOHN W. OTTE

THE FIFTH MAN
JOHN B. OLSON
RANDY INGERMANSON

Daughter of Light

DAYSTAR

CPSIA information can be obtained at www.ICGtesting.com
Printed in the USA
LVOW111139130512

281506LV00001B/139/P